ROGUES IN CLOVER

Faithfully

Percival Wilde

ROGUES
IN
CLOVER

♣

percival wilde

introduction by evan lewis

STEEGER BOOKS

CONTENTS

INTRODUCTION

WHEN THE FIRST edition of *Rogues in Clover* was published in 1929, Percival Wilde sent a copy, with a note, to the Miami Herald:

> If you do not want to review my new book, published about two weeks ago, it will make an excellent missile to throw at some bothersome caller. The book 'Rogues in Clover' is a low-brow affair, but I am writing a high-brow novel now about which I do not wish to discuss any details.

That note is a fine introduction to Wilde himself, a man of rare humor, and one straddling the gap between low-brow and high-brow entertainment.

Rogues in Clover, as I'm sure you know, is a series of connected stories about a retired card sharp with a talent for exposing other crooked gamblers. Reviewers at the time made much of the gambling angle, recommending it to people who play cards or roulette. But the truth is that this collection has great appeal to everyone, gamblers or not. I have only the vaguest notions of poker and roulette, gleaned mostly from old episodes of *Maverick,* and whist is a complete to mystery to me. But I enjoyed the hell out of this book.

Wilde's focus here, as in all his writing, is on character, and the methods cheaters employ to beat the odds—interesting as they are—take a back seat to the fascinating people we meet along the way. Most of all, these stories are *fun.* Bill Parmalee, having mended his ways and retired from gambling, wants nothing more than to tend his Connecticut farm. But his friend Tony Claghorn, having discovered Bill's near-magical ability to ferret out cheaters, nags him into performing one amazing exposé after another.

In 1949, when *Ellery Queen's Mystery Magazine* reprinted one of these stories, the editor asked Wilde how he'd come up with the idea, and where he'd learned so much about crooked gambling. As Wilde told it, he'd once been in the habit of buying books so recklessly that they threatened to drive him out of house and home. One such purchase took place at a New York auction house, where he bid a whole dollar on a lot of seven books—and won. The lot consisted of Maskelyn's *Sharps and Flats,* a five-volume set of Robert-Houdin's *Confidences d'un Prestidigitateur* (Conjurer's Confession), and a battered copy of Hoyle. Years later, those books came to mind when the editor of Street & Smith's *The Popular Magazine* asked, "How about a series of stories for *Popular,* all around a central character?" Wilde replied, "How about the character of a reformed cheat who unmasks other cheats?" And Bill Parmalee was born.

The series began in January 1924, and finished a year later. During this period of its life, *The Popular Magazine* featured mainly men's adventure stories, with covers devoted to the Old West, the Northwest, and various sporting activities. Published twice a month, it cost a quarter, averaged about 200 pages, and offered a mix of novelettes, short stories, serials and occasional "complete novels." Regular contributors during Wilde's run included A.M. Chisholm, C.S. Montayne, James Francis Dwyer, Robert H. Rhode, Roy Norton and Kenneth Gilbert, with guest appearances by Francis Lynde, B.M. Bower, Dane Coolidge and William MacLeod Raine, among others.

The Bill Parmalee adventures are mystery stories, but markedly devoid of murders, detectives or police, and the only crimes committed (if any) involve cheating at cards or other forms of gambling. Parmalee takes the role of detective, with his friend Tony Claghorn as an eager but rarely helpful sidekick. Much of the humor comes from Tony's vastly overrated view of his own abilities, and Tony's pretty young wife, who is perfectly aware of his limitations, adds to the fun. The stories take place in private gambling clubs, where cheating is the greatest crime imaginable, and where scandal must be avoided at all costs.

Wilde's skill as a storyteller is immediately evident, and each of the ten tales in this book comes to a deliciously satisfying conclusion. The original edition of *Rogues in Clover* contained only eight stories, but this edition's editor has unearthed two more, "The Adventure of the Fallen Angels" and "The Fifty-Third Card," so what you hold in your hands is a new and much improved collection. As I said, I enjoyed the hell out of it, and predict you will too.

PERCIVAL WILDE'S GRANDFATHER, his father—and Wilde himself—were born and bred New Yorkers. Wilde made his first appearance there on March 1, 1887, and stayed for more than thirty years. As a boy, he had a love of mischief, and claimed it got him expelled from every school he attended. He left high school—by request—after his junior year, but still managed to graduate from Columbia University, at age nineteen, in 1906.

After college, Wilde went directly into the banking business, but soon drifted into writing, beginning with book reviews for the New York newspapers. His first short story, written in

1911, brought so many requests for dramatic rights that he quit the banking business and turned it into a one-act play. The play ran for four years on vaudeville.

Wilde wrote more plays for vaudeville, gaining a good understanding of audience psychology and a grounding in technique. But by 1914, he had tired of its limitations, and became interested in the newly emerging Little Theatre movement.

At the time, most big city theaters were controlled by a syndicate devoted to thwarting completion and increasing profits. This stifled dramatic experimentation and left productions mired in melodrama. Little Theatres, on the other hand, were community based, often non-profit, and open to new forms of storytelling. Wilde and other young playwrights flocked to this new movement as a way to spread their wings and defy commercialism. Wilde was particularly attracted to it, he explained, because it made it possible for the general public to enjoy drama—an opportunity they otherwise would not get.

WILDE'S BIG BREAK came in 1914, when Sir Arthur Conan Doyle was visiting New York. Wilde met him at the Princess Theatre, and made an agreement to write a play based on Doyle's short story "How it Happened." The play, titled "Dawn," was a great success, and a springboard to Wilde's career as a dramatist.

Because "Dawn" was so important to him—and because Doyle called it "the most startling situation" he had ever conceived," I believe it's worth revealing just what all the fuss was about. So here's a SPOILER ALERT. If you'd rather read the play for yourself, it's not hard to find online.

"Dawn" is set in a run-down shack in a mining town. A

young woman is inside crying when a doctor knocks on the door, demanding admittance. The woman, we learn, has been repeatedly beaten by her husband, sometimes with a hot poker. The brute inflicted the same abuse on their ten-year-old daughter Maggie, who died. To make matters worse, the doctor now has evidence that the husband and his cohorts have set off an explosion in the mine, killing many more people. At this point, the husband bursts in, spitting

fury. As the doctor accuses him of his crimes, the man picks up a bottle of nitroglycerin—much more, he says, than was necessary to blow the mine. A tussle ensues, the bottle breaks, and the house blows up. When the smoke clears, the house is a wreck. But the husband is still standing, as is the wife. Then we see the doctor, with a young girl at his side. "You—who are you?" the doctor asks. The girl smiles. "Why, I'm Maggie," she replies. "But you—you are dead!" the doctor protests. Still smiling, the girl says, "So are you." The curtain falls slowly.

Wilde's first book, published in 1915, was a collection featuring "Dawn" and four other one-act plays. Two others in that collection are also among his most famous. "The Noble Lord" is a comedy in which a conniving young woman gets her comeuppance, and "The Finger of God" hints at Divine intervention turning a criminal into an honest man.

Wilde quickly became the champion of the one-act play, a role he would relish for the rest of his life. He explained the difference between the "one-acter" and longer plays:

As a story is the miniature of a novel, so the one-acter has been considered a condensation of a longer work. Nothing could be more unjust. The one-acter is subject to limitations of which the writer of long plays knows nothing. It is not an abbreviated play; much less as a rule, it is the material out of which a longer play can be made.

The swiftness of exposition, the brevity, the homogeneity of effect which insists that every word contribute toward that effect, these are necessities unknown to the more leisurely three or four-acter. The entire first act of a long play may be given up to the narration of what has come before; the one-act play must accomplish this in a few minutes.

If in the course of the long play the interest flags, little is lost. Should this occur, even for an instant, the one-act play is ruined. The long play has dispensed with the Greek unities; the one-act play is their slave. The long play is punctuated by intermissions, during which the audience may reflect and digest; the one-act play is denied their help.

With the advent of the first World War, Wilde wrote a number of war plays, viewing the conflict from all angles, and published a collection of them. And he enlisted in the U.S. Navy.

He entered the service as chief machinist's mate, and was later promoted to ensign. He invented devices for airplane compasses that were still in use many years later. But he was eager to return to his writing. "Two years lost out of life those were," he wrote. "For in them were no women. No one can get writing material or happiness from an experience in which there are no women. What's an experience that has only men and engines in it?"

Wilde left the Navy after the Armistice was signed, and only then noticed trouble with his ears. "Most of my hearing went during the war," he said. "I should like to say that partial deafness was caused by the noise of guns, but, unfortunately, it is the result of a most unheroic cold." Though eligible for a Naval pension, he resolved not to apply for one.

By 1918, more of his plays were being produced in Little Theatres than those of any other American author. He wrote one-acters of all sorts. There were comedies and tragedies, romances and satires, and little slices of contemporary life. Some were designed to be performed by children or marionettes. Some were meant to be staged at Christmas. Some were fantasies set in mythical kingdoms. All were intended for small troupes working with limited budgets and varying degrees of acting ability. He insisted on adhering to the "probabilities" of life, reaching a happy ending only when it was the *logical* ending. A few of his plays would likely be unacceptable today, such as "The Dyspeptic Ogre," in which the title character keeps little girls captive in a dungeon until he's ready to eat them.

In 1920, Wilde married Nadie Rogers Marckres, and the couple had two sons, Roger and Daniel. By 1925, he had tired of the big city bustle and moved his family to the small town of Sharon, Connecticut. As he explained it, "I drove the first automobile in New York with boys yelling at me to get a horse. That was in 1902. In 1929, I was parked in New York and my car was banged by a telephone automobile going at top speed. The quiet places for me." He named his Connecticut home "Wildeacre."

For three years, he served on the local board of education, but became "a discredited politician" when he was defeated for reelection by the local druggist. The editor of the newspaper had supported him, Wilde claimed, until local politicians threatened to take him for a ride.

Wilde and his wife fell into the habit of spending their winters either on the Gulf Coast or in Miami Beach. He became a familiar figure on the Florida cultural scene, lecturing on drama at the University of Miami and writing music reviews for the *Miami Herald*. He helped found the Author's League of Florida, and served as its first vice president.

He also became an avid photographer. He wrote articles on the subject, waxing eloquent on the virtues of this or that type of camera or lens, and especially enjoyed doing portraits and shooting wildlife. And—somehow—he found time to become an authority on mycology, the science of mushrooms and other fungi.

With his hearing already diminished, he suffered damage to his eyesight in 1921, when a bottle of carbonated water exploded in his icebox. The cut eye required several operations, and he sued the beverage company for $50,000, claiming the bottle was overcharged. What came of the suit is unknown.

During this period, Wilde branched out, collaborating on several full-length plays, some of which were big successes on Broadway. And he began writing short stories. Along with *The Popular Magazine*, he wrote for magazines such as *Red Book*, *Blue Book*, *Collier's*, *Argosy All-Story* and *Pictorial Review*.

He also wrote scripts for two-reel silent films. One of his screen stories, "The Guttersnipe," (1922) involves an Irish working girl in New York, who compares her own life with the thrilling romances she reads in the pulp magazine *Sloppy Stories*. In "Moonlight Follies" (1921) a vamp meets a man who's immune to her feminine wiles. The colder he gets, the warmer it makes her, and they live happily ever after. Sadly, none of his Bill Parmalee stories made it to the screen.

BY THE LATE 1920s, Wilde's fling with magazine stories was pretty much over, and he returned to his true love—contemporary drama. He had amassed a collection of over a thousand volumes devoted to the subject, and put his knowledge to use writing *The Craftsmanship of the One-Act Play* (1926), a detailed guidebook for would-be playwrights. "For my sins," he told a reporter, "this ponderous volume of mine is used as a textbook." Wilde said this, the reporter noted, "as if he enjoyed sin."

Wilde became so popular that some of his plays were reprinted in newspapers around the country, and many were performed live on radio networks. He believed he was living in "the golden age of American drama," and for him, that was probably true. Still, he refused to let fame go to his head, telling one reviewer he believed his success was due to luck. The reviewer, as you would expect, disagreed.

In 1927, he published a book of twenty-one three-minute plays. Even more than his one-acters, these lent themselves to productions requiring practically no scenery or costuming, and a minimum of rehearsal. Wilde was ever more devoted to bringing drama to the masses, and making it easy for them to produce. In some cases, to facilitate productions, he chose to forego his royalties. To make his plays more accessible to audiences in England, he asked his British publishers to remove American expressions and replace them with British terms and idioms. His plays were translated into German, French and even Japanese.

WHEN THE FIRST edition of *Rogues of Clover* was published in 1929, Wilde received a letter from an inmate of a Louisiana prison:

> Dear Mr. Wilde: Just a line or two regarding a review I have just read of your book "Rogues in Clover." I am a convict—got the hook. Been here a long time as long times go in prisons, and have a long time still to remain.
>
> This review by McClure in the Times-Picayune has so interested me that I'm taking a cinch in the grub line and asking you cold turkey for a free copy of your book.
>
> Not that I'm worthy of even a Salvation preacher's handout—only that I was on the racket myself for years—not Belmont or Saratoga style but taking them when the taking was not too difficult and the John Laws too honest.
>
> If there was the remotest chance of scooping up enough butter to get one of your books I'd do it—and you may lay to it. But this rice and tule marsh country is hell—jack rabbits carry their own lunches 'round here— So I'm asking kindly and honestly if you can slip me a copy of your book, for which I'll remember you.

Wilde immediately sent the prisoner a copy of his book.

In his note to the would-be reviewer of *Rogues in Clover,* you may recall, which he called "a low-brow affair," Wilde said he was then at work on "a high-brow novel." He was in Miami for the winter, and added, "I am rejoicing now on my escape from snow and ice, and will finish my new novel while here, unless I succumb to an almost irresistible desire to spend all my waking hours in a bathing suit."

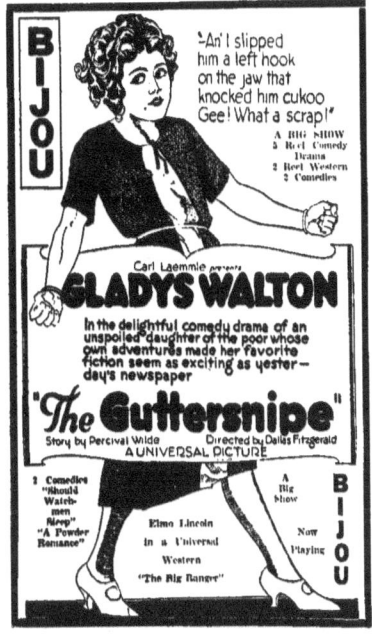

That novel, *The Devil's Booth*, was published in 1930. It's the sordid story of a fallen woman, beginning in 1889 and progressing through the decades to the present. One reviewer called it "a satire on American social customs, social leaders and their intelligence, and that of their followers," and compared it to Greek drama. Another reviewer was less impressed, opining, "A few of his characters manage to be sedately urbane in the naive canons of the nineties, but the bulk of his social satire is not more than a few inches above the level of horseplay burlesque." Still another feared the explicit subject matter must have shocked the author's New England neighbors.

Wilde went slightly less high-brow with his second novel, *There is a Tide*, in 1932. This one is set amid the Florida land boom (and subsequent crash) of the 1920s, and while the subject matter is serious, it at least employs Wilde's talent for humor. The main characters are a stupid but lucky business magnate and a charming but reckless adventurer, who demonstrate the thesis that people are to blame for their own misfortunes. A British critic called it "a portrayal of contrasts between small town life and plutocratic society." "It might sound dull," said an American reviewer, "but it isn't."

After those two books, Wilde returned to the world of drama, devoting the next six years to churning out plays for Little Theatres. By 1935, he was collecting $30,000 a year in royalties, despite not having a play on Broadway in fifteen years. The money came from amateur productions, which paid between ten and fifty dollars for each performance. One of his Christmas plays was produced by 261 organizations in a single month, and "The Finger of God" had been played 5,000 times.

When asked about his days as a struggling writer, Wilde replied, "I know only two kinds of authors: those who struggle— and those who have given up the struggle." His daily routine at that time involved rising at 11:30, playing tennis or swimming in the afternoon, and going out in the evening. He finally settled down to work at midnight, and often worked until sunrise.

WILDE'S NEXT NOVEL, the first of four mysteries, seems to have been written just to clear his head. He'd taken his wife to Florida for her health, he said, and did not feel like doing any serious writing. So he wrote *Mystery Week-End* instead.

Mystery Week-End (1938) sets the stage for the three mystery novels to follow. All four are set in New England, involve regular citizens rather than detectives or police, and break the mold of traditional mystery storytelling. In this one, guests at a ski resort find themselves trapped, during a snow storm, with a murderer. The story is narrated by four distinctly different characters, in succession, until the mystery is solved. Reviewers found it "innovative" and "refreshingly different," but it did not sell well.

In Wilde's next novel, *Inquest,* a famous New England romance novelist is murdered at a party in her home. The story is told in the form of a transcript of testimony at a coroner's inquest. Coroner Lee Slocum is one of Wilde's roguish characters. He hires his daughter to make the transcript, appoints his friends to the jury, and generally plays fast and loose with the law.

Wilde predicted the book would be "a grand flop." Instead, the *London Times* called it one of the best detective stories of the year, American critics loved it, and French, German and Italian editions quickly followed. "Wit and satire mingle with crime and mystery as witness after witness takes the stand, and the tension mounts," said one reviewer. Another called it "close to the perfect mystery." Pageant magazine rated Inquest one of the nine best mystery books of all time. Others in the nine included *The Maltese Falcon, The Big Sleep* and Richard Sale's *Lazarus #7,* which is mighty fine company.

In 1939, Wilde sold a short story to *Esquire,* "The Extreme Airiness of Duton Lang," which was later reprinted in *The Magazine of Fantasy and Science Fiction,* and even filmed as a cartoon.

Just before the outbreak of World War II, Wilde returned from a visit to England on the Queen Mary. The North Atlantic was then beset by prowling sea raiders, and he told reporters the ship took a zig-zag course, avoiding the regular steamship lanes. He and a group of other men slept in the ship's library, with everything blacked out. Among his fellow passengers was J.P. Morgan.

Wilde's third mystery novel, *Design for Murder* (1941), finds ten would-be sophisticates playing a murder game in a Connecticut farmhouse. As they ridicule mistakes made by classic mystery writers, one of them is killed. The survivors then attempt to solve the murder, penning theories in their own words, and each failing miserably. One reviewer called it, "a brilliant tour-de-force in its merciless exposure of a group of people through their own words."

His last novel, *Tinsley's Bones*, appeared in 1942, and featured the return of Lee Slocum, the coroner from *Inquest*. This time, Slocum looks into the charred remains of a pulp writer who turned out a short story nearly ever day and a novel nearly every week. Again, it's a literary experiment, with various characters telling the story in their own words. "Sometimes," wrote one critic, "the reader wonders if the author's purpose is to tell a mystery story or to analyze village New England life and character. Whatever his purpose, he has successfully done both."

THE END OF Wilde's career as a novelist marked a return to short stories, with a new series written especially for *Ellery Queen*. In an ad featuring many of their current writers, Wilde was quoted as saying, "Yours is the first and only mystery magazine in history which an educated man can be caught reading, without having to make explanation."

The series introduced Pete Moran, a chauffeur, taking a correspondence course to become a detective. According to Wilde, he had once taken such a course himself, under a phony name. Despite submitting lessons with outrageous misspellings and deliberate errors in judgment, he had received top grades. That inspired the adventures of Moran, who enrolls in the Acme International Detective Correspondence School. The stories are told in the form of letters between Pete and

his Instructor. No matter how simple the case, Moran always comes to the wrong conclusions, but somehow manages to get his man. He's a the ultimate bungler and the stories are played strictly for laughs.

When the series was collected in *P. Moran, Operative* in 1947, one reviewer called it "boff laughter, native American wit at its best. Either chain it to your shelves or buy a copy for all of your friends."

At the time of his death, on Sept. 19, 1953, at University Hospital in New York, Wilde had written more than 120 plays, appearing in nearly a hundred different anthologies, and was believed to have had more plays produced in American community theaters than any other writer. He was hailed as "the grandmaster of the one-act play," and ranked next to Eugene O'Neill as one of the foremost American dramatists of his day. He was 66. His son Roger followed in his footsteps, writing for radio and television.

Since its first publication over ninety years ago, *Rogues in*

Clover has become a forgotten book, and almost impossible to obtain. Now, thanks to Steeger Books, it's been reborn to entertain a new generation of readers. You're lucky enough to be one of them.

Read on!

A WILDE BIBLIOGRAPHY

PLAY COLLECTIONS

Dawn, and Other One Act Plays of Life Today, Henry Holt & Co. 1915

Confessional, and Other American Plays, Henry Holt & Co. 1916

The Unseen Host, and Other War Plays, Little, Brown & Co. 1917

A Question of Morality, and Other Plays, Little, Brown & Co. 1922

Eight Comedies for Little Theaters, Little, Brown and Co. 1922

The Inn of Discontent, and other Fantastic Plays, Little, Brown, and Co. 1924

Three-Minute Plays, Greenburg Inc. 1927

Ten Plays for Little Theatres, Little, Brown & Co. 1931

Comrades in Arms, and Other Plays for Little Theatres, Little, Brown & Co. 1935

Contemporary One-Act Plays from Nine Countries, Little, Brown & Co. 1936 (edited by Wilde, and including one of his own, "War Without End")

TEXTBOOK

The Craftsmanship of the One-Act Play, Little, Brown, and Co. 1926

NOVELS
The Devil's Booth, Harcourt Brace & Co. 1930
There is a Tide, Harcourt Brace & Co. 1932 (British title *June Harvest*)
Mystery Week-End, Harcourt, Brace & Co. 1938
Inquest, Random House. 1938
Design for Murder, Random House. 1941
Tinsley's Bones, Random House. 1942

SHORT STORY COLLECTIONS
Rogues in Clover, D. Appleton & Co. 1929
P. Moran, Operative, Random House. 1947

FILMS
The Woman in Room 13, (from a Broadway play) 1920
The Hunch, (from a short story) 1921
Moonlight Follies, (based on the short story "The Butterfly") 1921
The Guttersnipe, (story) 1922
The Woman in Room 13, (from a Broadway play) 1932
The Rise of Duton Lang, (cartoon, from a short story) 1955

TELEVISION
"The Finger of God," (play) Hour Glass, 1946
"To Thine Own Self," (story) Lux Video Theatre, 1950
"Confession," (play) Lux Video Theatre, 1951
"Confession," (play) Playbill, 1955
"The Way to Freedom," (from a short story) Schlitz Playhouse, 1955

1

THE SYMBOL

HE HAD BEGUN the week with a typical gambler's roll; ninety one-dollar bills neatly wrapped into a stout cylinder, and the outside adorned with a single yellow-backed twenty-dollar bill. It was a roll which spelled prosperity, for the persons for whose benefit it was displayed could not request the privilege of examination, and were obliged to accept it on faith. It was a roll fit to choke a horse, for horses choke quite as easily on ones as on twenties. It was a roll which brought comfort to the soul of Bill Parmelee, its possessor, for its bulk was so great that wherever disposed he could not help feeling its welcome pressure. If he stowed it in a breast pocket it interfered magnificently with his breathing; if secreted in a trousers pocket it reminded him of its existence at every step; if cached—as it usually was—in a capacious hip pocket, it called itself to his attention every time he sat down.

Like its many predecessors the roll had grown from nothing. Bill Parmelee was in hopes that it would grow still farther. Down nearly to his last cent he had fallen in with a traveling salesman who felt the need of excitement. Bill Parmelee had supplied the excitement in a two-handed poker game in which Bill's artless manipulation of the cards had converted the laws of chance into statutes which operated for his sole and exclusive benefit. The run of the cards had supplied him with a considerable number of satisfactory hands. The simple expedient of holding out an ace until it might be advantageously substituted for an indifferent card had helped to make bad hands less bad and had even made good hands better. Yet Bill knew enough to avoid resorting to his superior skill more often than was absolutely necessary. Three or four times in a session was sufficient—amply sufficient. Those times correctly chosen, there could be but one result. Hence the game had come to a grand climax in a deal in which Bill nursed two pairs against three of a kind; yet when Bill had been called and had unostentatiously laid down his hand the two pairs had miraculously become a full house.

That hand had seen the salesman's finish. "You're too many for me," he had admitted frankly. "I'll beat it while I've got my railroad ticket." He had done so and Bill had judiciously converted the miscellaneous notes which he had collected into ones, had decorated the outside with a lone twenty, and had begun to flash a roll.

There had followed a week which had been anything but satisfactory. The highly transient guests of the commercial hotel at which Bill made his headquarters had exhibited a pathetic lack of sporting spirit, declined Bill's friendly invitations and confined their gambling to bets placed upon rival flies crawling across a windowpane. For a monotonous afternoon Bill had participated in this innocent form of amusement and in three hours of hard work had won the munificent sum of twenty-five cents. He had quit in disgust. His overhead demanded a larger return. Twenty-five cents for three hours; his hotel bill was larger than that. And the game, by its very nature, was sharp proof; one could not hope to make an accomplice of a fly.

He had debated the advisability of moving to a more progressive town; had debated for several anxious days while the roll gradually grew slimmer, and had just about made up his mind to shift his base of operations when opportunity, in the form of an unexpected invitation, knocked at his door. It was a rainy Sunday afternoon; would Bill take part in a little poker game? Would he!

He allowed his objections to playing on the day of rest to be overcome and he retreated to a quiet room in company with four other enterprising spirits. He scanned their faces with more than passing interest as the play commenced; another of the inevitable traveling salesmen; a prosperous farmer, well along in years; a lean and acid individual who announced himself as an insurance adjuster, and a fourth, a chubby little man, who promoted the sale of patent churns. He surveyed his companions again, and stifled a smile. It was too easy. Bill might be the youngest of the five; his innocent face; his frank, blue eyes; his unwrinkled forehead proclaimed the fact that he had not arrived at his twenty-fifth year; but in experience he had an advantage which might be measured only by centuries. From his eighteenth year, when he had run away from a respectable home, filled with a desire to see the world, every day had contributed to his education along the lines to which his talent naturally ran. He had learned to play the great American game well—more than well—and then, by chance acquaintances, he had been introduced to the various devices with which misapplied ingenuity has endeavored to hamstring the legs of chance. He had tried—and discarded—the many varieties of sleeve and vest holdouts; he had experimented with the shading box; he had become an expert in the use of that little instrument known as the table reflector; but like all great artists he had succumbed to simplicity as embodied in the neat little device known as "the bug."

The bug, strangest of all insects, consists of three or four inches of watch spring, and a minute shoemaker's awl—nothing more. One end of the spring is sharpened to a fine point and is fitted into the head of the awl; and the remainder of the spring, flat against the under side of a table when the awl is pressed into the wood, is warranted to hold one or two cards in an inconspicuous manner.

Yet Bill was far too canny to make use of this apparatus until the arrival of the psychological instant. A profound knowledge of poker, supplemented upon certain occasions by a little sleight of hand, were sufficient to establish his superiority in nearly any game. The first half hour saw the prosperous farmer a loser to the extent of fifty dollars; the second saw his loss reach the limits of his available cash; the third saw him making hurried trips to the hotel clerk to cash a steady succession of checks. The joy of battle had seized upon the loser's soul—and Bill, quietly affixing his apparatus to the under side of the table, prepared for the killing. His capital had multiplied rapidly. Now—now or never—was the time to go over the top.

It was then that the catastrophe happened. Hardly had Bill finished dealing when the lean insurance adjuster laid a large-boned hand over what remained of the pack. "You've dealt out five hands, mister," he announced. "That's twenty-five cards. There should be twenty-seven left in the deck. That so?" Without waiting for an answer he spread the cards face down and proceeded calmly to count them. "There's twenty-six," he said quietly. "If you don't believe me, there they are; count 'em yourself."

Given the slightest of opportunities and Bill would have replaced the missing card as deftly as he had abstracted it. But the traveling salesman, the prosperous farmer, and the chubby vender of churns had risen, and watched his every move across the table.

He met the situation without embarrassment. "I dealt out the pack as it was given to me. If there's one short maybe there's only fifty-one cards in the deck."

"Maybe and maybe not," said the insurance adjuster with a scowl. "At any rate, we'll see what is missing."

Bill watched with a forced smile as his enemy quietly sorted the cards into suits, and established that the ace of hearts was absent and not accounted for.

Bill nodded sagely. "Now that I come to think of it, the ace of hearts has been missing all afternoon."

The traveling salesman drew a sudden breath. "Missing nothing!" he ejaculated, and his forefinger singled out the unhappy gambler. "Didn't you hold two pairs a couple of minutes ago? And weren't they queens and aces? And wasn't one of the aces the ace of hearts?"

Bill Parmelee rose to his feet warily. "You're not accusing me of cheating, are you?"

"And if I am?"

Bill's hand dove in the direction of his hip pocket. "Why, then—" he began.

His memory of the events which took place immediately was a trifle confused. He recalled that the traveling salesman, plunging suddenly, had seized his knees in a perfect football tackle, while the three other players had flown at him as a single mass. He had tried to draw his gun and had had it knocked from his hand. The cards had gone flying about the room, and the table, with the damning evidence still affixed to its under side, had turned a sudden and a most unexpected somersault. Upon that had followed several minutes of utter oblivion for Bill, and at their conclusion, he found himself marching along the street, being clammily wetted by a fine drizzle, with his right arm in the viselike clutch of the insurance adjuster.

For some minutes the men marched in silence. Bill inquired, "Where are you taking me?" and received no answer.

Then, as the arc lamps of the freight yards, lighted early in the afternoon, threw sickly beams through the mist, Bill's captor released him with a parting admonition. "Beat it," he advised.

Bill stood his ground. "Why aren't you taking me to the lockup?" he demanded.

The insurance adjuster smiled. "I will if I have to," he promised, "but I'd rather not. You see, brother, you and I are in the same line. You make a living out of the pasteboards—so do I. Now everything would have been lovely if you hadn't started fishing in my little pond. The world's big enough for both of us. You don't have to do it." He lowered his voice confidentially. "That old farmer's my meat. See? Higbie—the fellow who passes for a traveling salesman—he's my partner, and we've been trailing the old man around for a week. He's our private property: roped, hog-tied, and branded; and we've just been letting him take care of his money till we were ready to take it away from him. And when it comes to the killing we don't divvy up with anybody else—not on your life!" He turned mild brown orbs on his amazed captive and lowered his voice still more. "It's all going to work out nicely now. We've shown you up and the old man thinks the world of us for it. So we're going to start the game over again where it was before you came in, and we're going to make a present of your roll to the old man to sort of soothe his feeling? But something tells me that by the time the dinner bell rings, your roll—and his roll, too—will have wandered where they really belong—to Higbie and me." From some safe place of concealment the late insurance adjuster extracted a yellow-backed bill and pressed it into his victim's hand. "Brother," he counseled, "if I was you, I'd travel—and I'd start traveling right away—*muy pronto*. This here town's liable to be a bit unhealthy for you."

Bill Parmelee coincided in that opinion too.

WITH THE TWENTY-DOLLAR note—his own—which had just been handed him, and with the gold piece which—true gambler—he kept secreted in his shoe against a rainy day, he might have left the town in state, riding in a Pullman car. But upon his arrival he had made it his immediate business to familiarize himself with the timetable and his memory told him that no passenger train might be expected until six—more than two hours away. Debating the circumstances hurriedly Bill found many arguments in favor of a rapid departure, and none at all against. Were he to wait he might leave with dignity; but then again he might leave on a rail, warmly attired in tar and feathers.

The debate progressed no farther. From the distance came the roar of a laboring engine pulling a long string of freight cars up the grade. Bill watched his opportunity and swung himself into an invitingly open empty with an expertness born of many years on the road. He did not know where the train was going; but he did know that it was putting miles between his late companions and himself. That was enough.

He made himself comfortable in the freight car, lighted a cigarette, and then, because he was young and hopeful, he burst into a peal of laughter. The joke was on him—very much on him—but he was sufficiently broad-minded to see its point. He pictured the scene after his departure; the gratitude of the prosperous farmer, saved from one sharper to fall a victim to two others; and his thoughts flew to the inevitable hour to come, when the grateful farmer, lighter in purse and richer in experience, would go on his way convinced that he had played and lost in an honest game.

Well, such was life. One could not always win, and he, Bill Parmelee, was decidedly lucky that his adventure had not cost him his freedom. He jerked himself into a sitting position and through the open door peered at the rapid procession of mist-enfolded scenery. The up grade had become a down grade and the train was banging along at forty miles an hour. He wondered where he was and where the train might be taking him.

For six months, wandering about aimlessly, he had gradually been nearing his boyhood home. He had not the least desire to return to the little village which he had left so suddenly years ago, but he noted, with idle curiosity, how unconsciously he had been cutting down the distance which separated him from it. He had gone where money was to be had; where news of a game of satisfactory size had drawn him. He had traveled East and West: had set out, and had returned, and through it all, like some pawn being moved about on a gigantic chessboard, his progress had been slow, but in one direction. He noted it and wondered. Six months ago he had heard the beat of the surf on the Pacific coast. Now he was not very far from the thunder of the Atlantic. And the train, which clanked and lurched crazily around curves, might be carrying him to the seaboard itself.

The rain fell more heavily as he sat at the door, dreaming and gazing out into the mist. At the most he could not be a hundred miles from home. He wondered if the passing of the years had changed it beyond recognition. Distinctly he remembered his stern old father, saying a grace before every meal; the clock which had never been the same since the day that Bill, aged fifteen, had removed an apparently superfluous part; the clean-swept hearth in the big living room; the hickory switch over it—ah! here his thoughts impinged and would not let go.

A switch it was—not a stick—cut in the woods down by the creek. It might be two feet long—though it had looked like six to him in the days which were past beyond recall. He smiled at the recollection. Often—very often—it had been applied to the tenderest parts of his anatomy; and to-day he could take it up in the fingers of one hand and break it in half—that is, if it still existed; if, for all the wintry nights that had howled down the chimney it had never been fed to the flames which crackled so near it.

Bill smiled in tender reminiscence as his thoughts seized upon that tyrant of his childhood days. Often, of an afternoon, he had stood guiltily before it, awaiting the instant when his father's hand would remove it from its pegs and employ it upon his small person. More than once he had plotted to hide it; to burn it; to destroy it utterly. More than once he had seized it—and had lacked the courage to carry out his resolution. He chuckled at the remembrance. For him it had been the outward and visible sign of an ancient uprightness; rectitude; integrity. Often he had dreaded the switch; but there had been days when he had stood before it proudly, boldly, unfearingly, and had murmured to it, "Well, old fellow, you can't do a thing to me now!" Upon such rare occasions the switch had seemed positively friendly; had glistened in the slanting light—and Bill's childish hand had dared to caress its sleek, barkless surface.

Ah, well, those days were gone! For a fleeting, painful instant Bill Parmelee, straining his eyes into the mist, wondered what the switch might say to him, card sharp and cheat and gambler. It would not approve: that was clear. Yet Bill had not drifted into his profession through deliberate choice of his own. He had always played cards. Even his father, Puritan though he was, had relished a quiet game of cribbage or seven-up. Bill had been initiated into those mysteries at the early age of fourteen, and leaping recklessly into the turmoil of the world four years later had made the pleasant discovery that such abilities as he had cultivated brought their reward in the form of ready cash. Wandering from one poorly paid job to another Bill found this supplementary income useful—indispensable. He learned poker: learned to play it fairly and squarely, and then one day he made the amazing discovery that one of his boon companions did not hesitate to deal from a cold deck. Bill had protested, to be informed that wits, and not honesty, governed the game. Anything was fair if you got away with it.

To the young man fresh from the atmosphere of a puritanical home this was an eye opener; but he experienced little difficulty in adjusting himself to this new conception of morality. If cheating was the thing, he would cheat—and cheat more successfully than the next man. Within a month he had graduated from the ten-cent game in which he had learned to more expensive games where his undisputed talent was still better rewarded. From there to the game which invited the sucker to match his wits against those of men who made a living at it was but a short step. He made it grandly.

By this time he had subordinated all other occupations. Cards paid better: when they paid at all. But his life had never been one of easy luxury. Sometimes a roll grew—grew marvelously—but sooner or later it evaporated. Once or twice he had fallen in with sharpers cleverer than himself, to be relieved of his wealth in approved sucker style. On at least three occasions he had been separated from his capital at the point of a gun. Still oftener his love of gambling had led him to the roulette wheel, to lose in a night what had been months in the making.

Periods of high and low water had alternated. From the latter he had extricated himself by working for a stake. This achieved, a few cautious games had made more work unnecessary— until the next catastrophe. For nearly six years he had followed his profession, and had he taken an inventory he would have been forced to admit that he had little to show for it. A suit of clothes, expensive when new but now much the worse for wear; a pair of shoes which looked well from the outside but which allowed water to seep through; a shirt and a collar which had seen better days; a tie which was comparatively new, but which had never been worth twenty-five cents; battered cuff links, of no ascertainable value at all—these, plus a hat and a suit case which the hotel had already seized and the few dollars in ready cash which he had secreted upon his person constituted the sum total of his wealth. Bill Parmelee hoped for a game in which his slender capital might multiply itself. Lacking that he would have no choice but to go to work for another stake.

He glanced idly at the country through which the train was passing, and gasped. The mist had risen. The valley, mellow in the failing light and dotted over with low, round grass-covered hills, looked curiously familiar. Those hills: amazingly numerous and amazingly round! Through the long vista of remembrance came the voice of a school-teacher who had explained to a wondering lad that others like them were not to be found in miles and miles. Over these hills a glacier had passed æons ago and had left its sign manual written upon their backs. Like a cloudburst came a rush, a torrent of memories.

The train clanked past a little station. It needed hardly a glance for Bill Parmelee to identify it: only one building in the world could be so sublimely, so familiarly ugly. Before Bill realized what he was doing he had swung himself to the ground and set foot again upon the soil of his home town.

LEAVING HOME, HE had dreamed how he would one day return to these, the familiar haunts of his youth. He would go to the city, become rich, and come back to do honor to the village which had given him birth. Country boys who went to the city always returned rich: was it not thus written in the classics? "Mr. William Parmelee, our distinguished fellow citizen—" In anticipation he had murmured the mouth-filling phrase more than once. He would not be haughty; would carry his greatness as an unconsidered burden; would greet his old-time neighbors with a gentle democracy which would put them at their ease at once. In this modest program, visions of brass bands to welcome him, red fire and reception committees had played a prominent part.

Strangely, profoundly different was the reality; yet Bill Parmelee, squelching his way up the rain-sodden street, gave no time at all to vain regrets. His shoes leaked: but it was the water of home; his shapeless trousers clung clammily to his legs: but it was along the old familiar way that his legs were carrying him. With an odd thrill he recognized the homes of one-time playmates; wondered if after the lapse of years their inhabitants would recognize him. The scent of flowers lay heavy on the moisture-laden air; he inhaled it eagerly, gratefully.

He smiled as automatically he turned into the short cut across Riker's meadow. The lush grass clung to his ankles; wetted him to the skin; yet he squelched through happily. Thus, barefooted, had he done in the olden days; had thrilled at the cool ooze of the water between his toes. The man was but retracing the steps of his youth.

Abruptly—with dramatic suddenness, it seemed—the home of his childhood rose before him. It might have changed in its details—doubtless it had changed—but to the hungry eyes of the man who stood before it, drinking in its long-remembered outlines, it was what it always had been. There was the window of the room he had once occupied, the window at which he had sat and dreamed his dreams. There was the cellar door, with one broken hinge—curious how the sight stabbed him with poignant memories! There was the little porch, over-grown with woodbine; the familiar flower bed which he had so often weeded; the cherry tree which stood in the front yard and which he had so often climbed.

Over the freshly mowed grass he made his way to the door and stood hesitant with his hand upon it. His home-coming!

A merciful chance kept his eyes from the glass panel in which the reflection of his features mocked him. Instead he gazed at the worn mat and at the century-old knocker.

At another moment Bill Parmelee's mind might have over-flowed with thoughts. There were comparisons to be made between the lad who had quitted this place full of hope and courage and the man who returned to it sadly disillusioned upon life and upon life's rewards. Doubtless there were moral lessons to be drawn. But Bill Parmelee, cheat and sharper, was conscious most of all of a mysterious something that had seized him by the throat, of a lump that had risen inside of it, of an all-pervading ache that might have been weariness and was something very much different.

Then, because it was the natural thing to do, he pushed open the door—it was never locked—and stepped across the thresh-old. The big living room had changed little. The hearth, as always, was clean swept. The familiar chromos smirked—the picture of his long-dead mother smiled from the wall. The clock, with the obstinacy that had characterized it since Bill's improvements upon its mechanism, pointed serenely—and motionlessly—to an hour which had flown away many years ago. The carpet, with its impossible roses in impossible urns, was the same. And at the fireplace the never-forgotten switch, older, but uncompromising as ever, rested menacingly upon its pegs.

In the corner a talking machine—a recent acquisition, this—testified mutely to the intrusion of a blatant civilization. But nothing else had altered.

These things Bill took in at a glance—the hospitability, the unpretentious comfort of the room, always the same ever since he could remember—and then his eyes met the gaze of a thin, bowed man who had risen to face him. To Bill it seemed unbelievable that the passing of a few years could have aged his father so much. The accustomed lines in his face had worn deeper—and there were lines that had not been there before. His hair was grayer and there was less of it. He stooped; he had not stooped before. Yet something about his figure was stamped with the hall mark of prosperity. Time might have dealt harshly with the man's body but it had accorded his persistent efforts the material reward which was their due.

For it all, John Parmelee's expression was what it had been before. Sprung from Puritan ancestors, habituated to taking life seriously, the flesh might be weak but the spirit was as uncompromising as ever. The steady eyes bored through the young man, searched out his soul, peered into his innermost secrets. Under their relentless gaze Bill squirmed, shifted uneasily from one foot to another.

A maid of all work appeared at the door to announce that dinner was ready.

"Let it wait," commanded John Parmelee. He closed the door and returned to face his errant son. "Bill," he inquired mercilessly, "when will you be moving on?"

To the young man, thrilling at the sight of his familiar surroundings, suffused with a happy glow as each square inch of the commonplace room summoned up memories deep within him, the question came like a blow in the face. "Dad!" he gasped. "Oh, dad!"

The father repeated his inexorable demand. "When will you be going?"

"Dad! Dad! You haven't seen me in six years! Is that the only question you can ask me?"

John Parmelee gazed at his son. "It's the only question to which you can give a satisfactory answer. The others—you've answered already."

Bill refused to believe his ears. "I come here hungry, tired, soaked to the skin—"

The other would not let him finish. "Telling a story which I prayed never to hear from a son of mine! You don't have to say anything. I can see it all in your eyes. I don't want to know where you've been—what you've been. It would hurt me too much to know, and you've told me enough already."

"Dad! Dad!"

"I had no hard feelings against you when you ran away," pursued John Parmelee. "You were a boy and you didn't know any better. I wouldn't have cared if you'd come back to your home broke, starving, helpless. I could have fixed that and I would have fixed it because I'm your father. You wouldn't have been the first to find the world hard sledding. Bill, I wouldn't have cared about anything else if you'd come back clean; if you could have met my eyes and told me that my name had been safe in your keeping; but," and for the first time the older man's voice faltered, "Bill, that's just what you're not telling me."

A surge of indignation swept over the gambler. "How do you know I can't?" he challenged.

His father seized him pathetically by the shoulders. "Bill," he begged, "say I'm wrong! Say that when I looked into your eyes I saw things that weren't there! Say that you've been my son through thick and thin!"

"And if I say so?"

"Bill," faltered John Parmelee, "I'll believe you. God knows I want to believe you!"

For an instant the men faced each other. Then the gambler growled an unintelligible phrase and strode the length of the room.

"That's what I saw in your eyes—just that," said the father. He slumped suddenly into a chair at the fireplace. "I wonder," he soliloquized, "if you've thought much about me. Six years to you is nothing. It's a drop in the bucket—nothin' more. You're still a boy. But to me six years is a slice out of a lifetime. Did you ever think of that? I've been growing older. I've been growing richer. I've been growing lonelier. Bill, in that next room there's been a place set for you at every meal since you ran away. I've never sat down to my food without seeing that place opposite mine. I've been waiting for you to come and fill it." He smiled sardonically. "Well, you've come."

"I've come."

"But you're not the same Bill Parmelee who went away." He paused. "The best thing you can do now is to go away again."

"So that's what you think about it?" The gambler gazed about the comfortable room, pulled up a chair, and plumped himself down into it. "I'm here," he announced. "I'm here to stay."

"Yes?"

He gazed contemptuously at his father's slack frame. "If you don't like it, throw me out. But it would take just six of you to do that."

"Quite so," assented John Parmelee.

The tempting odor of cooked meats assailed Bill's nostrils. "Me, with a rich father, bumming around the country!" he grunted. "Not on your life! I'm here and I'm here for keeps! See?"

His father smiled ominously. "If you want to take the chance, Bill, go right ahead."

"What do you mean?"

His father smiled up at him. "You can't stay in this house five minutes longer than I want you to. I've got a dozen men working for me, Bill, and all I've got to do is say one word."

"And you'd say it?"

"I'd say it."

"Let the town know that you've got a no account, worthless son? That you had him thrown out of your house like a tramp?" The gambler rose from his chair.

"Why not?"

"What would people say?"

The corners of John Parmelee's mouth wrinkled into a wry smile. "Nothing they haven't said already."

The gambler gazed hard into his father's set countenance. Thus, many a time, he had appraised an opponent's hand across the poker table. "By George!" he ejaculated, "you mean it!"

"Of course I mean it!"

Something in Bill Parmelee's blood forced him to seat himself. "Dad," he announced, "I'll call your bluff!"

For a full minute the father stared into the clean-swept fireplace. "People have been talking," he ruminated aloud, "but they don't know. I think I'd rather not let them know." Suddenly he rose, crossed to a battered writing desk and extracted a dusty pack of cards. "Bill," he proposed, "let's settle this thing here and now. I'll leave it to chance. Will you?"

"Yes," assented Bill eagerly.

"We'll play cards. If you win you stay. If you lose you go. Agreed?"

"Yes."

John Parmelee made his way to the mantel and returned with a large box of matches. Gravely he divided a hundred between his son and himself. "These will have to do for chips," he announced. "I will cash each match for fifty dollars. You can quit when you like—now, if you want to."

Bill shook his head.

Parmelee, senior, took up the ancient pack of cards. "Bill," he inquired, "do you know how to play poker?"

BILL EXULTED AS he shuffled the pack with elaborate clumsiness. The ace of spades, he noted methodically, lacked a corner; the king of clubs had been broken squarely across the back, and might be identified in an opponent's hand at a distance of ten feet; half a dozen cards—and he hoped that his poker face concealed his amusement—had evidently been lost and had been innocently replaced with cards of a different color. With such cards he ran no risk at all of losing. Yet he dared not win too soon nor too easily.

"Limit?" he inquired.

"No limit," said John Parmelee easily.

Bill nodded, gathered up his cards and dissembled a smile as his father commenced the game by pushing a match toward the center of the table.

On the first few hands he lost—lost honestly—but it was as he had intended. It would hardly do to make his opponent suspicious. It was not until the fifth hand that he dared to spring the first of a series of pleasant surprises. To his father, he would deal three aces; to himself, a lonely pair of queens. His father, hoping for a full, would draw two cards, and have his hopes realized. He would thereupon bet in proportion. Bill, in turn, would draw three cards—to arrange his hand differently, and draw less might discourage betting—but of the three, two would be queens and the result would be four of a kind. It was a simple maneuver with which he had succeeded often in the past.

It was no trick at all to stack fifteen cards. Indeed it was made pathetically easy by the fact that the third and fourth queens were among the half dozen cards with red backs, the rest of the deck being blue.

Bill offered the pack for the cut, and smiled as with a lightninglike pass his well-trained hands restored the cards to their original arrangement. Artistic, he reflected; yet a game with fifty-dollar chips was worthy of such skill. Cautiously he glanced at his cards; verified the fact that his queens had arrived as scheduled, and met his father's opener with a raise. It was not until thirty matches—fifteen hundred dollars—had gathered in the pot that Bill took up the deck and inquired gently, "How many?" He spread the cards slightly. Three blues; then two reds, and the reds the queens which would give him a winning hand. "How many?" he asked again.

His father studied his hand intently, folded his cards together, and placed them, face down, upon the table. "I'll stand pat," he announced.

Bill could not suppress his astonishment. "What?" he gasped.

John Parmelee smiled. "I don't want any," he said. "I've got a pretty good hand."

The gambler thought quickly. The queens he wanted were the fourth and fifth cards from the top. He could deal seconds without being detected; upon occasion he had even succeeded in dealing thirds. In such a game as this, surely, he could deal cards still lower down in the deck. But to attempt such a thing when the cards he wanted were red, and the rest of the deck was blue, would be simply suicidal.

His father had stood pat. Bill wondered if by some mischance he had given him better than three of a kind, if, by some incomprehensible error, the full house had arrived ahead of time.

"How many are you going to take?" inquired John Parmelee.

"Three," grunted Bill. To his pair of queens he added the pair of nines which had been intended for his opponent.

The older man pushed five matches into the pot. "That's two hundred and fifty dollars," he announced.

Bill threw his hand down in disgust. "The pot's yours," he conceded.

Regardless of rules, John Parmelee faced his son's hand. "Two pairs," he murmured. From his own hand he plucked three aces. "Not as good as three of a kind."

"What are the other two cards?" demanded Bill eagerly.

With a cryptic smile the father shuffled them into the deck. "You didn't call," he reminded. "I don't have to tell you."

Bill's stack of matches had dwindled appreciably but his fighting blood surged hot within him. It would be easy—ridiculously easy—to turn the tables. He waited impatiently until a pair of threes against nothing at all gave him the deal and one match—the smallest pot of the evening. He would take no chances this time. He would start with three aces against three kings. The remainder of the deck would be topped with two pairs. Whether his opponent drew or not, Bill would hold a full house after the draw. Once again he set about stacking the cards. Half a dozen riffles and a pass—this combined with the proper placing of a neatly arranged discard—and he would be ready for battle.

It was then that Bill made the amazing discovery that his skill had deserted him. He shuffled and shuffled, to find the cards defying his uttermost will. He gazed about the room desperately for help. There was none forthcoming.

His father smiled gently. "If you shuffle much longer there'll be no spots left on the cards," he warned.

Bill offered the deck for the cut, noted that the cornerless ace of spades had been brought to the top, and made a pass to bring it back to the middle of the deck. Then—and to his overwhelming surprise—his hands refused to obey him and acted automatically. A second and a wholly involuntary pass brought the ace back to the top again.

He dealt in bewildered silence, bet wildly on a four-flush, did not succeed in filling it, and lost half his remaining capital to the pair of jacks which his father displayed on the call. Bill had called. Insanity. Madness. He had nothing at all and knew that his opponent held at least an ace. Yet his hand, seemingly uncontrollable, had pushed the matches which constituted a call into the pot.

He counted what remained of his capital—less than fifteen matches.

"Perhaps you'd better stop," murmured his father. "You don't seem to know much about poker."

"I'll go on!" flared Bill.

"As you will."

Despite his conservative betting, half a dozen honestly played and honestly lost hands reduced his capital to three matches. He had attempted every trick in his repertory, to find some unknown factor, deep down in his subconscious mind, checkmating him at every move. He had held out not one card but a whole hand—and then, against his concentrated will power, something had forced him to drop all five cards to the floor, pick them up, and declare a misdeal. When, holding four of the six red-backed cards in his own hand, he had discerned the two others in his father's, and had inevitably known them for a pair of queens, some force, absolutely incomprehensible to him, had compelled him to bet his hand as if he were ignorant of his opponent's holding. The result had been an inexcusable loss.

The sweat stood out on his forehead as, hazarding his last three matches, he won, and took up the deck in trembling hands. Even now it was not too late. Even now, by any one of a dozen devices of which he was a past master, he might recoup his lost capital. But his efforts to make use of them were in vain. Slowly, with maddening clumsiness, he shuffled the cards. Slowly he dealt them out, peering at them from suddenly dimmed eyes and aware that he could read no card either in his own hand or in his opponent's.

His cards seemed to weigh ten pounds as he lifted them, separated them, and gazed at them. His heart leaped with a sudden joy. His hand, honestly dealt and honestly acquired, consisted of four aces and a king. Perhaps luck had begun to turn; perhaps he would regain all that he had lost and more. With pounding pulse he pushed all of his remaining matches into the pot.

His father glanced at him keenly and met the raise. "All right, Bill," he said, "I'll take just one." He discarded one card, and laid the nine, ten, jack and queen of clubs face up on the table.

Bill Parmelee's thumb, resting lightly on the deck, felt the ridge which identified the broken-backed king of clubs. His father's eyes, he noticed, were gazing intently into his. It would be easy to deal a second—a third—or from the bottom; to deal any card but the one whose addition to those upon the table would mean a straight flush—the only hand which could beat the one he held.

His quivering fingers raised the deck; lost their hold upon it; allowed it to fall in utter confusion on the floor.

"Never mind, Bill," murmured his father, "give me one card at random."

Some suddenly resurrected thing in Bill made him shake his head resolutely as he pawed through the scattered cards. "No," he announced, "you get the card that was on top. I'll know it, because it has a broken back." He picked out the king of clubs and dropped it in its place on the table. "There you are," he said lightly, "you have a straight flush—and I'm broke."

Curious, reflected Bill, amazing, marvelous, incomprehensible, with what sudden cheerfulness he took a last glance about the familiar room and prepared to sally forth into the night. It was raining again—raining hard—he could hear the steady patter as he tightened up his belt upon his empty stomach. It would be muddy and there would be fearful miles between him and wherever destiny chose to take him next. But there was a surprisingly happy note in his voice as he turned to his father and extended his hand. "Dad," he said, "I guess I'll be going."

But the older man's arm fell like an accolade across the younger man's shoulders. "Bill," he exulted, "when I looked into your eyes across the card table I saw what I wanted to see. Bill, my son, I guess you'll be staying."

THAT NIGHT, STRETCHED out luxuriously in a clean white bed, gazing through the familiar window at the darkness outside, Bill asked himself a question. "Why?" he demanded. "Why was it? I wanted to cheat—I wanted to cheat—and I couldn't! I just couldn't!"

Then, like a blinding flash of lightning, came the memory of how all through the game he had sat facing the fireplace—the vision of the switch, the hickory switch resting on its pegs—and Bill knew.

2

THE RUN OF
THE CARDS

AS THIS STORY has to do with card cheat scene should be laid in the West. Literary tradition insists that every card game commenced on the other side of the Mississippi must culminate in a display of bowie knives and six-shooters, and must not end until one of the players—preferably the bad man—is made ready for the ministrations of the undertaker by a neatly drilled perforation, caliber .45, in the neighborhood of the heart.

But life, as so often, disagrees with literary tradition. A card game in Oregon, California—or even in Texas—may be a tame affair, conducted strictly according to Hoyle: while a similar game in Massachusetts, New York, or Connecticut may provide the sharper with an opportunity to profit by his cunning. And the Easterner takes such episodes with appropriate calm. If he has been victimized—and knows it, which is rare—he reflects that he has been unwise to play with persons whose ancestors did not come over with his in the *Mayflower*, and he resolves to commit no more such errors. To this praiseworthy resolution the average Easterner may stick for a month; the exceptional Easterner for a year; to break it only when some particularly impressive individual invites him into another and an even more disastrous game. Then more resolutions—and more broken resolutions.

When Bill Parmelee, professional gambler and card sharp,

after drifting about the country for six checkered years, drifted back to the home in the East from which he had begun his wanderings, he had immediately been given an opportunity to demonstrate his skill. His father, Puritan and card player—inconsistent, with the inconsistency of life—had invited him to hazard everything upon a game of poker, had boldly suggested that they settle, by the luck of the cards, the all-important question of whether Bill remained or whether he continued upon his wanderings. Bill had accepted the proposal gleefully, had, for a few brief minutes, gloated in the vision of how adroitly he would manipulate the cards, had rejoiced in the prospect of taking advantage of every trick in his remarkably complete assortment.

Then, to his utter astonishment, he had found himself quite unable to cheat. The sight of the hickory switch facing him at the fireplace had overpowered him with the memories of childhood. Looking at it, some force superior to himself had mastered him, had compelled him, for the first time in many years, to play a scrupulously honest game. Bill was only twenty-four—and childhood was not so far behind. The switch, ridiculously puny, ridiculously slight, had seemed to gaze at him warningly, had commanded, "Play fair!"—and Bill had obeyed.

He had played poker which would have been a disgrace to a beginner—an honest beginner—and had been wiped out in short order; and then his incomprehensible father, glowing with pride in the son whose background was such that he could not cheat against him, had opened his arms and had invited Bill to remain. That invitation had been accepted. With the same intense energy that had characterized his life as a gambler

Bill plunged into the myriad of details connected with the management of a farm. He had wasted six years in mastering every device known to the card sharp, but he was young, and, to his utter surprise, he found himself taking an amazing interest in Holsteins and Jerseys, in pure-bred Durocs, in Leghorns and Brahmas and Orpingtons. His acquaintances of the road, gentlemen who lived upon their wits, would have laughed at him. But Bill, settling down close to the soil for the first time, found himself curiously, incomprehensibly happy.

He was conscious, after a month, that he had not touched a card—and had not missed them. Rising with the sun, busy until dark, he found the diversions to which he had been accustomed oddly unattractive when evening came. It was so much more satisfactory to crank up the little roadster, to roll gently—as gently as it would allow him—through the clean-smelling country, to compare notes with neighboring farmers, to bow to old-time friends, occasionally to celebrate wildly by taking in the movies.

It had taken Bill Parmelee six years to find himself; but that he had done so there could be no possible doubt. He might never again have touched a card; never again have taken part in a game of chance, had it not been for Tony Claghorn, Tony's pretty wife, and a sleek individual who, for the time being, passed under the name of Sutliffe.

TONY CLAGHORN WAS an otherwise sane young man who believed implicitly in the laws of chance. If the run of the cards was bad to-day, it might be expected to be good to-morrow—odds two to one—and if, by some mischance, to-morrow brought disappointment, then the day after to-morrow was morally sure to make up for it—odds four to one. Mathematics, high, low, and middling, certified to the correctness of his theory, and Tony backed it unhesitatingly by doubling his bets on the second day and quadrupling them on the third day. To be strictly consistent he should have continued doubling them on each succeeding occasion: it was eight to one that he would win on the fourth day, and sixteen to one that he would win on the fifth day. But three consecutive sessions never failed to exhaust Tony's, available cash.

On the first of every month a fat check came tumbling into Tony's bank. It financed him until eleven p.m. on the evening of the third. At eleven-one Tony's mathematical investigations usually came to a temporary end.

For twenty-seven days thereafter he lived on his credit, which was excellent, and paid off the accumulated bills on the first of the following month. But the surplus, which was often considerable, had an expectation of life of something under seventy-two hours. At the end of that time, for Tony, it had ceased to exist.

Mrs. Tony Claghorn was a very charming person who might have been more useful to her husband had she not loved him so much. For her, Tony was right—even if he was wrong. Solemnly Tony would explain to her just why he could not lose; or why, in spite of his rosy predictions, he had lost after all. And Mrs. Claghorn, thrilling at the sight of her strong, handsome husband, rejoicing in the thought that he was hers—all hers—would murmur, "Yes, dear," at appropriate intervals, would nod her pretty head, and would decide that last year's dress, made over, might do for the present season.

"Pulled a bone last night," Tony would admit. "When he

stood pat I should have known he had a full house. I had no right to call him."

Thereupon Mrs. Claghorn, having understood only the first phrase, would wonder how her clever husband could do such a thing and would overflow with sympathy. "Never mind, Tony," she would assure him, "you'll make up for it to-night."

"You bet!" Tony would declare, and would wander in, stripped clean, around midnight, to explain that things had gone wrong once again.

Had Mrs. Claghorn loved her husband less she might have insisted that her occasional needs take precedence over the insatiable poker game. But the thought never entered her head. It would mean opposing Tony, and that was quite beyond her.

She reflected sometimes that in the days before Tony had met the clever Mr. Sutliffe the cards had not been so uniformly disastrous. He had played at the club, had won and had lost, but had usually finished the month with a small balance on the right side of the ledger. Poker had been a diversion: not an obsession. Then Mr. Sutliffe had come into the picture and almost at once everything had changed. Pursing her small mouth, wrinkling her innocent forehead, Mrs. Claghorn gazed blankly at the wall and wondered. Most of all she wondered why Mr. Sutliffe, who, by his own modest confession, was many times a millionaire, found it worth his while to play cards with Tony Claghorn.

Many times a millionaire: to be precise, eight times. Sutliffe, as he was never tired of recounting, had owned a small patch of land in Texas. "Just a little patch," he would explain; "three or four thousand acres—hardly knew I had it. And then—what do you think?—one day they started drilling on it, and zip!

the biggest well this side of kingdom come blew the derrick to smithereens and ruined all the grain for miles around. Yes siree sir! Since then," the millionaire would conclude modestly, "I've just been drawing royalties, and salting 'em away against a rainy day. How much? Oh, maybe eight millions—maybe nine." He would smile gently: "I can't tell you within half a million what I'm worth."

A successful man, Sutliffe, a singularly successful man. Six months ago he had been telling a very similar story to a group of acquaintances in Chicago. He had owned a little patch of land in Colorado—"just a little patch, coupla thousand acres. And then—what do you think?—one day a fellow sunk a shaft in it, and zip! if he didn't open up the biggest gold mine this side of kingdom come! Yes siree sir! Why, you could just walk into that mine and pick up nuggets with both hands. Since then," and again the modest smile would creep over his shrewd countenance, "I've just been drawing royalties, and salting 'em away against a rainy day. Eight millions—maybe nine."

Success had followed the remarkable man throughout his life. Out of the mail-order business he had made eight millions— maybe nine; and out of an invention which the government had bought from him with great secrecy; and out of a little flyer in the stock market, when he had cornered United States Steel; but it must have been his modesty which prevented him from recounting more than one story to a single group of listeners. Whatever he had touched had turned to money. What more natural that when he turned to cards the winning combinations came to him with almost monotonous regularity? What more logical that with remarkable judgment he should sense the presence of four aces in an opponent's hand and decline to bet on four kings?

Sometimes he mentioned that he had spent a winter down South. His address had been the Federal prison at Atlanta, though he did not allude to that detail. Sometimes he referred to his summer up North. Once again, he was vague concerning his whereabouts. He was a poor boy who had risen to the top of the ladder. Indeed, some months before falling in with Claghorn he had been reduced to the expedient of pawning his few valuables. By a remarkable coincidence they had reappeared on his person shortly after he and Tony had commenced their mathematical investigations.

The Claghorns had decided to spend the summer at a little hotel in the Berkshires. Rather than be separated from his newly found friends Mr. Sutliffe had volunteered to spend a few days each month—by preference, the first, second, and third—with them.

BILL PARMELEE, CLOTHED in overalls, leaned on the fence and gazed at the dusty road. It had not rained in some weeks; the sun was merciless overhead, and Bill, half closing his eyes, could see waves of heated air writhing upward in quivering layers. The fields were parched and dry. The earth was hot underfoot.

"If this keeps up," reflected Bill, "potatoes will be high next winter."

A heavy sedan whizzed around the turn of the road, climbed the hill with cut-out wide open, and vanished out of sight around another turn. A column of dust, twenty feet high and so dense that Bill could not see the other side of the road through it rose from the ground over which it had passed.

Bill inhaled, suffocated, and shook his fist at the departed car. "They ought to jail fellows like you!" he declared. Then, gazing into the cloud, he saw a smaller car, a roadster, wriggling valiantly through it. From side to side of the road it slued, as if suddenly blinded, and Bill, remembering the two-foot ditch, cried out a warning. Even as he called he knew he was too late. The car, careening dizzily, swung to the side of the road, two wheels went over with a thump, and the bumper fetched up with a crash against a telegraph pole.

Bill raced to the rescue. The car, perilously inclined, had not turned over, and in the driver's seat a young woman, pale, but with compressed lips, was already cranking the stalled engine and shifting the gears into reverse.

Bill flung open the door. "Get out!" he commanded the lone occupant.

"I'm going to."

"I mean, get out of the car!"

"Not till I get it back on the road." She let in the clutch with a jerk.

The car teetered dangerously for a second, a rear wheel spun convulsively, and the engine stalled a second time.

"That was a close squeak!" ejaculated Bill.

In silence the woman driver placed her foot on the starting pedal again.

"You'll kill yourself!" Bill warned.

"Not if I know it."

There are times when actions speak louder than words; when brute force is more effective than argument. Bill reached quietly into the car and shut off the ignition.

"How dare you?" demanded the young woman. Her protest ended in a shrill squeak as a powerful arm gripped her about the waist and lifted her bodily to the road. "How dare you?" she repeated. Then, suddenly, she became limp and collapsed into the strong arms which held her.

Bill smiled down into her face. "Nerve! Grit! Spunk! You've sure got plenty! But this here's a man-sized job!" He half lifted, half supported the quivering girl to the side of the road, made her comfortable against the fence, and noted that the color which had ebbed so swiftly in her cheeks was beginning to return.

Young Mrs. Claghorn attempted to stand. "I'm all right," she insisted. "I got into this mess and I'm going to get out of it."

"Sure you're all right," agreed Bill, "only you're going to watch the show from a ringside seat. Stay outside of the ropes."

He fetched planks and a shovel, enlisted the assistance of two or three farm hands, and cautiously backing the car inch by inch, brought it back to the road again. He opened the door with a flourish, and descended. "She's not hurt a bit. Your bumper saved you. Now, if you want to, you can drive on again."

Pretty Mrs. Claghorn did want to—did want to very much—but her nerves had been strained to the breaking point. She seated herself at the wheel, placed her hand upon the lever, and broke down altogether. "I—I just can't," she stammered. "Won't you—won't you do it?"

Bill Parmelee gravely occupied the seat as she slid into that adjoining. With equal gravity he let in the gears and piloted the car over the brow of the hill. The young woman, he had noticed, wore a wedding ring. That reassured him. Had her left hand been unadorned Bill might not have risen to the emergency with such self-possession. She was pretty; she was charming; she was attractive, and the courage which she had just displayed did not lessen her appeal. But she was married and Bill was safe. "Where to?" he inquired.

"Anywheres; oh, anywheres, till I pull myself together a little bit."

For over a mile they followed the winding road in silence, threading in and out between the gently rounded hills that encompassed them on all sides. Bill knew every inch of the country, and loved it. It was hot, but the heat was whisked away with the motion of the car. Suddenly he was conscious that his companion was speaking.

"I think we ought to introduce ourselves," she was saying. "I am Mrs. Claghorn—Mrs. Anthony Claghorn. My husband and I are stopping at the hotel."

Bill nodded. "My name is Parmelee—Bill Parmelee," he vouchsafed.

"I haven't thanked you yet," said the girl.

"It isn't necessary."

"But I do thank you," she insisted. "I don't know what would have happened if you hadn't been there, Mr. Parmelee. It was insane for me to try to back out, and it was wonderful for you not to let me."

"Now, now—" interrupted Bill.

"It's the first time—the very first time—that such a thing has happened to me. I've been driving for years and years, ever since I was a child, and never once, before to-day, have I been in real trouble."

Bill grinned. "Never is a long time," he asseverated. "Now I remember once, out West, sitting at a roulette table, and watching the ball drop into the red sixteen times in succession. But the black came on the seventeenth spin. It was bound to come sooner or later."

"Oh, have you played roulette?" inquired Mrs. Claghorn with sudden interest.

"A little," admitted the ex-gambler with a grin. "I remember a faro game," he went on reflectively, "where the bank won for half an hour without a break."

"So you've played faro also?"

"A little of everything," admitted Bill.

"Poker too?"

"Poker most of all."

Had the two met in orthodox fashion their conversation would certainly have consisted of small talk. To one of her own set young Mrs. Claghorn could not have unburdened herself as to this raw-boned, lanky farmer. But there was something in Bill's frank blue eyes, something in his quiet, attentive manner, that emboldened her to continue. She had met him by accident. In all probability she would never meet him again. She told him the whole unhappy story as frankly as if she had been talking to the grass-covered hills.

Only once did Bill interrupt her. "This man Sutliffe," he inquired, "what do you know about him?"

"He's a millionaire; many times a millionaire. He's worth eight millions—maybe nine."

The words sounded oddly familiar. "Eight millions—maybe nine," repeated Bill thoughtfully. Then the gates of memory opened. "I know now!" he ejaculated. "He made it out of gold—a gold mine in Colorado."

"No," corrected Mrs. Claghorn, "out of oil—an oil well in Texas."

"Oh!"

"He owned a few thousand acres—worthless, everybody

thought—and then they struck oil. Since then he's been living on his royalties."

Bill smiled. "I think I place him now," he said.

"Have you met him?"

"No. But I've heard a lot about him." He swung the roadster around a final curve and headed toward the hotel. "If I understand you correctly he'll be up to-morrow—the first of the month—for a little poker."

"Yes."

Bill gazed thoughtfully into the distance. "If your husband would take it kindly, I'd like to watch that game a little while."

"I think it could be arranged."

"I might learn something," soliloquized the man who had lived on his knowledge of the cards for six years, "with two such fine players. I could hardly fail to pick up some good tips."

"Don't play, though," warned Mrs. Claghorn, a little frightened at the eagerness with which the simple farmer had invited himself into the game; "the stakes are very high—and you might lose more than you can afford."

"It's very kind of you to tell me!" admitted Bill. "If I should play I'll try not to lose."

"That's what my husband always says," lamented Mrs. Claghorn.

Bill smiled brightly. "Maybe," he ventured, "maybe—if I do play—I'll have beginner's luck."

POKER, ACCORDING TO its definition, is a card game which may be played by a variable number of persons. It may be played by two or it may be played by half a dozen. But as Tony Claghorn and his parasite, Sutliffe, played the national game, it was two-handed, no matter how many were seated about the table. The others might have been described as among those present; they had little to say about the game.

Tony qualified as a liberal—a more than liberal player. If his hand were good he would support it as a good hand deserved. If it were middling he would support it even better, displaying unlimited confidence in the draw, and in his supposed ability to bluff his opponents. If his hand were poor he was not one to lay it down and wait for a new deal. His cheerful disposition required him to string along; to discard everything but a lone ace—for some deep, unfathomable reason aces seem to hypnotize certain players—and to draw four cards in the hope that they might contain pairs or even triplets.

Searing, and Mackenzie, and Trainor, who, along with Sutliffe, made up the game at the hotel, were not slow in learning Tony's weakness. They attempted to profit by it. Theoretically they should have called every bluff, and should have won in the long run. Practically their own hands did not always justify calling. As the size of the pots increased, so did their nervousness, and Tony, whatever his other shortcomings, was never visibly nervous. Searing and Mackenzie and Trainor observed the careless assurance with which he pushed his chips into the pot; observed, hesitated, and were lost.

A fine poker player is a dangerous antagonist. A bad player, well supplied with cash, and tempted to bet high by one other person in the game, is often even more dangerous. Tony fell into this latter category. Betting extravagantly, it was always expensive to call him; and just often enough to make it still more expensive his bluff turned out to be no bluff at all.

Upon such latter occasions, Sutliffe, invariably, was not

among those contributing. Smiling gently, he would decline to draw to his cards; would watch the play and would congratulate Tony upon its conclusion. But upon other occasions Sutliffe showed himself a player of boundless enterprise. Tony might feel inclined to bet high. Sutliffe would encourage him to do so. Then, after the other players had dropped, and when the battle had narrowed down into a combat between the two, Sutliffe's hand, on the call, proved just good enough to take the pot. If the oil millionaire, reflected Bill Parmelee, a close observer at the game, did not possess second sight he was endowed with something quite as satisfactory. It was camouflage poker, decided Bill; Tony, not Sutliffe, was the spectacular player. Tony, not Sutliffe, drew the fire of the opposition. Yet Sutliffe was the big winner and the only winner.

After an hour Tony had consumed his stack and was halfway through a second. Searing and Mackenzie and Trainor, losing slowly but steadily, changing their tactics, and changing back again, prayed for a change of luck—and prayed in vain.

With lofty condescension Sutliffe turned to Bill Parmelee, a lone spectator at the opposite side of the table. "Learning anything, Mr. Parmelee?" he inquired affably.

"Lots," admitted Bill. He nodded emphatically. "Lots," he repeated.

"For instance?" encouraged Sutliffe.

Bill smiled. He might have commented on the uncanny judgment which Sutliffe had displayed a few minutes earlier when he had declined to draw to three queens. But as Sutliffe had carefully shuffled his hand into the discard and as Bill was supposed to be unaware of its contents he felt it wise not to allude to that episode. He contented himself with a safer remark. "I'm learning that you're a very good player," he said.

The possessor of eight millions—maybe nine—bowed his gratification. "It's all in the run of the cards," he deprecated.

"Yes; I've noticed that they've been running nicely—for you."

Sutliffe shrugged his shoulders. "The game's still young. My luck may not hold." He waved a nicely manicured hand, adorned with a heavy gold ring. "How would you like to come in, Mr. Parmelee?"

Bill rose with obvious dismay. "Not tonight," he pleaded, "I've got to be up early to-morrow morning. I've got chores to do."

"We won't keep you long," urged Sutliffe. Despite the other's countrified clothes; despite his unpromising exterior, something whispered to the oil millionaire that money—real money—might be in the offing. Claghorn was the principal victim: but as many others as offered themselves were welcome. "We'll try to give you action," he promised.

"I've had enough action just sitting here and watching," declared Bill. "I never knew that the game had so many fine points." He glanced at his nickel-plated watch. "It's after nine. I guess I'll be going." He circled the table and shook hands with grave formality. When he came to Sutliffe he was particularly cordial. He enclosed the millionaire's hand in both of his own. "I'm immensely obliged to you; immensely!"

"Then perhaps you'll play to-morrow?"

"Oh, to-morrow's Sunday."

"Then Monday night?"

Bill's frank blue eyes gazed into Sutliffe's. "It's a date," he promised.

On the veranda he found Mrs. Claghorn gazing pensively

at the moon and patiently awaiting reports from the front. "Through already?" she inquired in surprise.

"Bedtime," explained Bill.

Mrs. Claghorn laughed. "Then you're not broke?"

"Not even bent. I didn't play. I was just getting the lay of the land."

"And what did you find out?"

Bill's level glance met hers. "All that I wanted to." Once more he offered his hand. "I think I'll be saying good night."

Had the light been brighter Mrs. Claghorn might have detected a minute, freshly made scratch across the ex-gambler's palm. As it was, she shook his hand cordially, and was surprised, some minutes later, to find a drop of blood adhering to her fingers.

IN A COUNTRY town—particularly in a New England country town—news travels swiftly. On Sunday morning, at ten o'clock, Sutliffe casually asked the hotel clerk if he knew one Bill Parmelee. At eleven o'clock the information that he had done so reached Bill. En route the news had passed from the clerk to a bell boy, to the postmaster, to his wife, to a farmhand and thus to its destination. It completed the circuit in fifty-eight minutes, elapsed time.

At three, the same afternoon, Sutliffe returned to the clerk with a fresh series of questions. "This Parmelee," he ventured, "how long have you known him?"

"Ever since we were boys together."

"What's he do?"

"What do you mean?"

"Is he a farm hand or does he own his own farm?"

"He works for his father, a mile down the road." Properly

encouraged, the clerk volunteered the information that Parmelee, senior, was affluent, even rich.

Sutliffe grunted "Um," and walked away.

This conversation, unexpurgated, was relayed to Bill in one hour and fourteen minutes. He smiled but made no comment.

On Monday, after an exceptionally successful session with Tony Claghorn the evening before, Sutliffe returned to the attack. "Look here," he asked the clerk, after preparing the ground by the gift of a cigar, "how big a check would you cash for Bill Parmelee?"

The clerk could not conceal his surprise. "Has he asked you to cash any?" he countered.

"No; no," explained the multimillionaire patiently, "I'm just asking."

The clerk scratched his head. "Well," he hazarded, "I'd cash his check for a hundred."

"Would you cash it for five hundred?"

"If I had that much money in the safe, yes."

"For a thousand?"

"Yes."

"For ten thousand?"

"What would he want with ten thousand?"

"I'm just supposing."

The clerk laughed. "I don't know what you're getting at, Mr. Sutliffe, but I'd cash Bill Parmelee's check for more money than I ever hope to own."

Sutliffe smiled. "That's exactly what I wanted to know," he admitted.

This conversation reached Bill in recordbreaking time, for the clerk, puzzled, immediately telephoned his friend and supplied him with full details. "Bill," he asked in bewilderment, "do you know what to make of it?"

"Yes," said Parmelee.

"Then for Heaven's sake let me into the secret!"

Bill laughed. "Did you ever sell a hog to the butcher?"

"No."

"If you had," said Bill cryptically, "you'd know that the first question the butcher asks is 'What does he weigh?'"

He chuckled as he cranked up the roadster, and made his way to the hotel in the evening. It was clear to him that Sutliffe, a true artist, did not propose to waste his skill on small game. With admirable foresight he had satisfied himself that Bill, his prospective victim, was good for enough to make a display of his talents worth while.

Bill threw back his head and laughed aloud. Then the laugh vanished as another thought flashed upon him. Sutliffe's elaborate preparations could mean only one thing: Claghorn had been cleaned out twenty-four hours ahead of schedule.

Mrs. Claghorn's greeting verified his suspicions. "As a special favor to me," she begged, "don't play to-night."

"Why not?"

"If Tony can't beat Mr. Sutliffe, you can't."

"But I thought that Tony—Mr. Claghorn—could beat him."

"Tony thought so too," assented Mrs. Claghorn sadly. "He changed his mind last night—around midnight. If he had changed it one minute earlier—but what's the use of talking? To-night Tony is going to be a spectator."

Bill gazed at Tony's pretty young wife and felt a sudden hatred for Sutliffe overmastering him. "Ma'am," he assured her, "don't worry about me. I can take care of myself."

"But if I ask you not to as a special favor—"

Bill took her little hand in both of his. "To-night," he promised, "I'm going to do you a bigger favor than you have any idea of."

THE GAME, WITH Tony sitting helpfully behind Bill's chair, began slowly. "I haven't played in some time," Bill confessed truthfully. "I'm going to take it easy." He did so.

It required only a few deals for Tony to decide that Bill was a novice. Like himself, Bill was willing to come in on a pair of fives. Like himself, Bill was hypnotized by a lone ace. But unlike himself, a single white chip seemed to satisfy the farmer's gambling propensities.

In a whisper, Tony protested.

Bill smiled. "You've got to remember," he whispered back, "there may be better hands out than mine."

"They may only be bluffing!" foamed Tony.

"Just wait. I'll try some bluffing too."

He was as good as his word. On the next deal he staked five whites on a four-flush and lost ignominiously. "You see?" he pointed out ruefully; "it doesn't always work."

"I didn't tell you to bet on a four-flush!" hissed Tony.

"No," admitted Bill, "but you didn't tell me what to bet on."

"I'll tell you next time," Tony promised. He prodded Bill vigorously when a deal brought him three kings, and when the subsequent draw made them part of a full house. To his horror, Bill promptly called the only other player who had not dropped, and raked in a small pot.

Tony foamed at the mouth. "I didn't tell you to call!" he whispered.

"What's the difference? I won."

"But you should have raised him first! You should have let him call you! You could have made the pot ten times as big!"

Bill scratched his head in perplexity. "I don't see it," he admitted.

"Don't see a full house with kings up?"

"The other fellow might have been aces up."

"But he wasn't!"

Bill turned innocent orbs upon his counselor. "Now, how under the sun was I to know that?" he demanded. He indicated his stack of chips, neither larger nor smaller than it had been an hour earlier. "I haven't lost anything—you can look for yourself. Honest, I don't see anything wrong with my game."

"There's not a thing wrong with it!" boomed Sutliffe from the other side of the table, "All you need is more confidence."

"You see?" challenged Bill.

Sutliffe leaned forward ingratiatingly. "Since you're winning," he ventured, "how about raising the limit a little? It'll give you a chance to win faster."

"Limit?" echoed Bill; "limit? I didn't know there was a limit."

Sutliffe laughed. "There isn't any from now on, if you say so." He gazed questioningly about the table. Searing and Mackenzie and Trainor, the hopeful trio, agreed cordially. Poker such as Bill was demonstrating had not come to their notice previously. They might profit by it. They need hardly fear a loss.

A second hour of the Parmelee brand of poker brought Tony to the verge of hysterics. Bill turned calmly to his mentor. "I'm not doing badly," he commented. "Look: I've got two more white chips than I started with." During the hour he had actually gathered in two pots.

"Not doing badly!" foamed Tony. "Not doing badly! Why, you should have won everything in sight! I've never seen such a run of cards in my life and you're just murdering them! That's what you're doing: you're murdering them! If I'd ever had such cards I'd have cleaned up! Nobody on earth could have stopped me! And what are you doing? In two hours you've won two white chips!"

"More confidence," adjured Sutliffe from the other side of the table, "more confidence, Mr. Parmelee!"

Searing and Mackenzie and Trainor, the hopeful trio, smiled. For the first session in three they were nearly even.

Bill hung his head like a whipped dog. "Sorry," he murmured, "real sorry. I'll try and do better." He dealt the cards slowly, inspected his hand, and for the first time a gleam of enthusiasm flickered in his eyes. Searing had opened. The rest of the trio had come in. Sutliffe had followed suit. Bill gravely pushed a whole stack of chips toward the center of the table.

Tony gazed at him aghast. "Do you know what you're doing?" he challenged.

"Yes."

"You're raising before the draw."

"Yes."

"You're advertising that you've got a good hand. Nobody will come in."

Indeed, the trio had already dropped. But Sutliffe smiled from across the table. "I'm coming in," he announced; "I'm even raising him back."

Bill turned triumphantly to his adviser. "You see?" he crowed; "it's my turn now and I'm going to raise him some more."

"Let me see your hand!" snapped Tony. The pot contained

over a thousand dollars, and the sweat stood out on his forehead.

Bill deliberately spread his cards face down on the table, and placed both hands over them. "I'd rather not," he pleaded.

"I insist!"

Bill's jaw stiffened. "That's not in the rules!" he retorted. "Anybody that sees this hand has got to pay good money to do it!"

"Good for you!" boomed Sutliffe. "And now, just to show you what I think of it, I'm going to do a little raising myself." With one hand he pushed his remaining chips into the pot and with the other he extracted a bulky wallet from an inside pocket. He picked out a thousand-dollar bill, and added it to the collection. "There you are, Mr. Parmelee," he challenged.

Bill gazed about helplessly. "I don't carry thousand-dollar bills in my clothes," he confessed, "but I'd like to make that pot a little bigger."

"How about a check?" suggested Sutliffe.

"Good idea!" assented Bill. He drew a neat check book from a hip pocket.

In desperation Tony seized him by the shoulder. "Parmelee!" he begged, "Parmelee, don't make a fool of yourself! Stop before it's too late! You haven't gone crazy, have you?"

"I'm afraid I have," smiled Bill.

What followed always impressed Tony as partaking of the character of a nightmare. Bill drew checks—while Sutliffe exhausted the wallet. It had contained but a single thousand-dollar bill; it disgorged bills of smaller denomination, and topped the heap with the checks which Tony had written on previous evenings.

Mackenzie felt moved to protest. "Look here, Sutliffe," he remonstrated, "this isn't right! Parmelee doesn't know the first thing about the game—"

"He's twenty-one, isn't he?" interrupted Sutliffe.

"I'm twenty-four!" corrected Bill.

"Exactly. He's of age and he knows what he's doing."

Bill flashed him a look of gratitude "You bet I know what I'm doing!" He gazed at the pile in the center of the table and poised his pen over a blank check. "Any more raising, Mr. Sutliffe?"

The millionaire shook the empty wallet. "I'm through," he declared, "I haven't got another cent on me."

Bill smiled at him brightly. "If that's so," he said, "I'll call."

Sutliffe laughed loudly. "You can't call! We haven't drawn yet!"

Bill nodded. "You're right," he admitted. He took up the pack gravely. "How many?"

"Just one." With appropriate solemnity he discarded a single card.

Slowly Bill passed the uppermost card to his opponent. "I'll stand pat," he announced.

"You must have a pretty good hand," taunted Sutliffe.

"I think so."

"But mine is going to be just the least little bit better!" Smilingly he took up the card which Bill had passed him. Smilingly he glanced at it. Then the smile vanished, his lips paled, a greenish hue crept into his cheeks, and his eyes protruded. He gazed at the card as if he could not believe his vision, gazed, gasped, seemed in an instant to shrink and become suddenly a smaller man.

"Well?" murmured Bill.

"What have you got?" gasped Sutliffe.

In silence Bill displayed his cards: three queens, a jack, and a deuce.

Sutliffe gazed at them, tore his own cards across, and stumbled from the room.

"Which means," said Bill, "I win."

IT WAS TONY who regained the use of his tongue first. "You mean to say," he sputtered, "you mean to say you bet like that on three queens?"

Bill smiled. "Look what he bet on."

From the floor they collected three jacks, a queen, and a ten-spot.

"What did he discard?" gasped Mackenzie.

"An ace." Bill turned the card face upward on the table.

Searing seized his head in both hands. "I've played poker, man and boy, for thirty years, but this gets me. Triplets! Nothing but triplets! And look at the pot they staked on it! Lunatics, both of 'em! Lunatics! I can understand how Parmelee did it—but Sutliffe!"

Bill raked in the pot and began to separate it into neat piles. "Suppose you call in Mrs. Claghorn," he suggested. "I'll explain."

But Tony's pretty wife did not need to be called. She burst excitedly in the door. "What's gone wrong?" she demanded, "I just saw Mr. Sutliffe running out of the hotel. He didn't wait for his hat or coat. He was headed for the station."

Bill laughed aloud. "Nothing's gone wrong," he assured her. "Sutliffe's gone broke—that's all."

"But he was worth eight millions!" This from Tony.

"Eight millions my eye! There's his eight millions on the table! Sutliffe's a card sharp—just as I used to be."

"What?"

" 'Eight millions—maybe nine'—that's how I knew the man. He's got more names than the Prince of Wales, and he changes his name every six months, but his story is always the same: in gold, in oil, in the mail-order business he's always made eight millions—maybe nine. But his real business is gambling. Why, he was working Kansas City when I was working St. Joe."

Trainor swallowed two or three times. "But I don't understand it yet," he admitted.

"It was easy," said Bill. "It took me only a few minutes to find out that he was using marked cards."

"But we always started with a fresh deck!"

"It didn't take him long to mark them." From his finger he drew a seal ring, armed with a minute needle point. "Look at this: he was wearing one like it. I made sure of that when I scratched my palm shaking hands with him two nights ago. All you do is prick the corner of the card and you can read the back as easily as you can read the face. He didn't bother with the suits, and he didn't mark anything smaller than a ten-spot, but look at the picture cards—just look! This is an ace. Do you see where he put the mark? This is a king. This is a queen. This is a ten. Get it?"

Mackenzie's deep voice boomed through the silence. "Damnable! Utterly damnable!"

"But how could you beat such a game?" demanded Trainor.

"I gave him a dose of his own medicine. I had to string him along for two hours till I was ready for the killing. I couldn't do it more than once: the second time he'd be on to it. So I waited for my chance and then I dealt him this hand."

"Dealt him?" echoed Searing; "dealt him?"

"Just a little legerdemain," admitted Bill. "I put up the cards while he was arguing with Claghorn. I dealt him three jacks, a queen, and an ace. I dealt myself three queens, a jack, and a deuce."

"But what in time made him bet on three jacks?"

"Well," drawled Bill, "when I spread my cards face down on the table he read the three queens all right. He knew I couldn't draw four, because he had the fourth in his own hand."

"But three queens are enough. Three queens beat three jacks!"

"They don't beat four jacks! The card on top of the deck—Sutliffe knew it was coming to him on the draw, and he looked at the back before he bet—was a ten-spot, only I gave it an extra prick and promoted it to be a jack. Sutliffe was expecting four jacks—nothing less."

Again Mackenzie's deep voice punctuated the silence. "The fourth jack was in your hand."

"Just to be safe."

"Why didn't he read that?"

Bill smiled. "You know," he admitted, "I had a sneaking suspicion he would, so I gave it two extra pricks and promoted it to be a king." He extracted his own checks from the gigantic pot and waved his hand toward the exceedingly substantial remains of it. "He collected this from you fellows. I don't want a cent of it. Take back what you lost. If there's any left over. I guess Mrs. Claghorn will know what to do with it."

SAID MRS. CLAGHORN: "I haven't understood a word you said, but I think you're just wonderful!"

Said Tony: "And to think that I tried to teach you to play!"

Said Searing: "Look here: suppose Sutliffe had discarded the ace and the queen?"

"It would have told everybody that he had bet sky high on nothing more than three of a kind. He didn't dare do that."

"But suppose," persisted Searing. "Suppose he had done what a straight player would have done: discarded and drawn two. He might have licked you! He might have drawn a full house!"

"He would have drawn a full house," corrected Bill. "I gave him his chance. Only a crook wouldn't take it." Gently he turned over the card which rested on what remained of the deck.

It was another ten-spot.

3

—

THE POKER DOG

Telegram

WILLIAM PARMELEE

    WEST WOODS

        CONNECTICUT

HAVE DISCOVERED ANOTHER CARD SHARP WHAT DO YOU
ADVISE

           ANTHONY P CLAGHORN

Telegram

ANTHONY P CLAGHORN

    HIMALAYA CLUB

        NEW YORK NY

ADVISE YOU NOT TO PLAY WITH HIM

        WILLIAM PARMELEE

Telegram

WILLIAM PARMELEE

    WEST WOODS

        CONNECTICUT

I HAVE PLAYED WITH HIM

      CLAGHORN

Telegram

ANTHONY P CLAGHORN

55

HIMALAYA CLUB

NEW YORK NY

THEN YOU DONT NEED ADVICE YOU NEED SYMPATHY

PARMELEE

Night Letter

WILLIAM PARMELEE

WEST WOODS

CONNECTICUT

MY DEAR FELLOW COMMA DONT YOU UNDERSTAND QUES-
TION MARK I THOUGHT HE WAS ALL RIGHT UNTIL I PLAYED
WITH HIM STOP THATS HOW I FOUND OUT HE WASNT STOP
NO HONEST PLAYER EVER HELD SO MANY GOOD HANDS STOP
YOUVE GOT TO COME DOWN AND HELP ME EXCLAMATION
POINT DONT FAIL ME STOP WIRE YOUR ANSWER MY EXPENSE
STOP

TONY

Telegram

ANTHONY P CLAGHORN

HIMALAYA CLUB

NEW YORK NY

YOU DONT HAVE TO PLAY CARDS FOR A LIVING STOP CUT IT
OUT AND TRY SOMETHING ELSE FOR A CHANGE STOP I AM NOT
COMING DOWN STOP I AM A FARMER NOT A BLOODHOUND TWO
EXCLAMATION POINTS AND ONE STOP COLLECT

BILL

Telegram

WILLIAM PARMELEE

                    WEST WOODS

                              CONNECTICUT

PLEASE COME

                              MRS ANTHONY P CLAGHORN

                         Telegram

MRS ANTHONY P CLAGHORN

                    CARE ANTHONY P CLAGHORN

                    HIMALAYA CLUB

                         NEW YORK NY

COMING

                              BILL PARMELEE

A NICE-LOOKING YOUNG man, dressed in clothes which whispered "country" to the initiate, descended from a train at Grand Central Station, and cast his eyes towards the roof. "What an elegant cow-shed this would make," he reflected, "large, well-ventilated, and room enough to store a million tons of fodder. I'd put the stalls there—right there—" and he nodded approvingly at the many gates through which travelers were streaming, "and I'd put up a silo in this corner. An indoor silo—never heard of such a thing in my life—but there's room for half a dozen of them. I wonder whether I'd keep Holsteins or Jerseys?"

Six months ago Bill would not have reacted thus; but the six months had witnessed a decisive change in his character. He pushed through the gate, and glanced along the long line of ticket offices. "Great," he mused, "wire gratings and everything: fine for hogs."

His ambitious dreams were cut short by the vociferous greeting of a citified couple.

"Bill!" shouted the man.

"Mr. Parmelee!" said the young woman.

"I knew you'd come," declared Claghorn happily "I knew you wouldn't leave me in the lurch."

"It's awfully good of you, Mr. Parmelee," supplemented Mrs. Claghorn. "We do appreciate it."

"I said to myself," Tony rambled on, "I said to myself, 'Old Bill will never go back on me. Not old Bill!' And he didn't!"

Bill favored him with a glassy stare. "If Mrs. Claghorn hadn't telegraphed, I wouldn't have lifted a finger. You got into trouble once, and I got you out of it. You ought to know better than get into trouble a second time."

"But it's not my trouble," protested Tony, "it's all on account of somebody else."

"What did you lose?" demanded Bill.

Tony grinned. "Everything but my clothes."

"And you don't call that trouble?"

Pretty Mrs. Claghorn led the way to a waiting automobile. "We'll tell you all about it."

In the privacy of their nicely furnished apartment, the Claghorns unbosomed themselves to their friend.

"To begin with," prefaced Tony, "it isn't my fault at all. I tried to help a relative of Millie's."

" 'Millie's'? And who's Millie?"

"That's my name, Mr. Parmelee," admitted Mrs. Claghorn.

"Oh, I see." Bill nodded his approval. The name Millie suited her admirably.

"It's all on account of a relative of Millie's—"

"My first cousin," supplemented Mrs. Claghorn.

"A young idiot named Ted Wayland—"

"Only he isn't a young idiot—"

"Nobody but an idiot would have gotten into such a scrape—"

"You got into it worse trying to get him out of it!"

"I sacrificed myself," protested Tony, "I acted like a hero—"

"Only something went wrong."

Tony straightened up with dignity. "That doesn't make me any the less a hero."

Bill broke into the conversation. "Suppose you tell me just what happened."

Tony nodded. "To begin with," he started a second time, "Ted Wayland's a nice fellow. I'll admit that even though he cost me a pretty penny."

"Ted Wayland," said Mrs. Claghorn, "is a junior in college. He does the hundred-yard dash in ten and one-fifth; he's number one man on the tennis team, and he played on the basketball five that won the intercollegiate championship. He's an all-around athlete."

"Including poker," said Tony.

"A boy must have some amusement," countered Ted Wayland's pretty cousin, "and it would have been all right if you hadn't taken him to the Himalaya Club."

"What's that?" demanded Bill. The Himalaya Club, well named, was famous for the size of the games which took place under its roof.

Tony hung his head. "I suppose I did make a mistake," he admitted, "but I didn't expect Ted to lose his head. They play for pretty big stakes at the Himalaya; but there's always a small game for the fellows who don't want to go too deep. I expected Ted to stick to that. At a ten-cent limit he wouldn't have lost enough to hurt—twenty or thirty dollars, maybe. Instead of which—" He broke off.

"Go on, Tony," encouraged his wife.

"Well, somehow Ted managed to get into the wrong game. He played with fellows I don't know, and a man named Schwartz stripped him clean."

"If Ted is a college boy," ruminated Bill, "he couldn't have had much money to lose."

"That's just the trouble," explained Mrs. Claghorn, "at any other time he would have been safe. But his father had just given him his year's allowance: tuition fees, spending money, everything, in advance. He lost every cent of it."

"He came to us," said Tony, "and threw himself on our mercy. He didn't dare tell his father what had happened: he would have been taken right out of college. It was up to us to help him."

Bill smiled. "Something whispers that that was when you started to get heroic."

"Quite so," said Tony with dignity. "I could have advanced him the amount he had lost. I wish I had done it, because it would have cost me less in the long run. But I couldn't forget how you slipped one over on that crook Sutliffe when we were up in the country, and I made up my mind to follow your example."

"What?" gasped Bill.

"I knew," pursued Tony, "that this man Schwartz wasn't honest. He held too many good hands to make it possible for me to be in doubt. I decided to do just what you had taught me. I invited him up here to this apartment; I invited in three or four fellows I could trust; and after Schwartz had been winning for an hour, I managed to substitute a prepared deck for the one we had been playing with."

"You mean you rang in a cold deck?"

"Exactly. I had stacked it beforehand, and I had fixed things with the man on my right so that his cut wouldn't disturb the arrangement."

"And how did you do that?"

Tony permitted himself the luxury of a smile. "After the deck was all stacked, I slipped the bottom card to the top. Then Billings—he was the man to make the cut—cut just one card, and brought the deck back to the original order. It was rather clever, if I say so myself."

"Very clever indeed," commented Bill; "so clever that it told any experienced gambler—Schwartz, for instance, or me—that something was in the air."

Tony's jaw dropped. "I never thought of that."

"Go on."

"I had fixed it," said Tony, with rather less assurance than before, "for Schwartz to hold a full house: three aces and two jacks. I dealt myself just a little better: a queen, and four little three spots."

"Which was nothing but robbery," interrupted Bill. "When I took a fall out of Sutliffe, I gave him a chance. If he had played honestly, and drawn, he would have beaten me. He didn't play honestly, and he licked himself. You didn't give Schwartz a look in."

"Wait till you hear the rest of the story. As I said, I gave him a full house, aces up. I gave myself four treys. Four of a kind beats a full house, you know."

"I have heard something to that effect. Go on."

"The deal came out exactly as I had planned it."

"How do you know?"

Once more Tony smiled. "I had marked the back of every card in the deck, barring only the five that were intended for Schwartz."

Bill laughed. "If you keep it up," he warned, "you'll land in jail!"

"Or in the poorhouse," interjected Mrs. Claghorn.

Tony felt it beneath his dignity to comment. "Straker opened, and we all came in. Schwartz and I stood pat. The rest drew. After a couple of raises everybody dropped, leaving Schwartz and me to fight it out. We raised back and forth ten dollars at a time. That was the limit, and we kept on raising as long as either of us had any chips in front of us. When we had used up our chips, we put in cash, and when that was gone, we put in IOUs.

"Finally Schwartz called. I laid down my hand: four three spots. I said, 'That wins, doesn't it?' Schwartz grinned and said, 'It doesn't,' and I'll be shot if he didn't lay down four aces!"

"What?"

"That's just what happened. I dealt him three aces and two jacks. He didn't draw, but when it came to the show-down, he held four aces and one jack."

"What happened to the other jack?"

"I don't know."

"Where did he get the other ace?"

"You've got me."

Bill laughed, laughed till the tears ran from his eyes. "If that's all you learnt from me, I'll say I'm not much of a teacher!"

IT WAS MRS. CLAGHORN who broke a protracted silence. "When Tony explained to me what had happened, I asked him to let me examine the pack of cards."

Bill nodded vigorously. "That's the first sensible thing I've heard in some minutes. What did you find?"

"Fifty-two cards."

"How many jacks?"

"Four."

"How many aces?"

"Four."

"One of each suit?"

"Yes."

Tony cleared his throat. "I see what you're driving at, but it doesn't lead anywhere. He couldn't have held out a card."

"Why not?"

"Where would he have concealed it? He took off his coat when he sat down to the table."

"How about his sleeve?"

"You could see clear up to his elbow."

"Did it ever occur to you that he might have slipped the card under the table?"

"His hands were never out of sight. Straker watched."

"Yet a jack somehow changed into an ace."

"Exactly."

"Unless you believe in miracles, there must be an explanation."

"I haven't found it."

Bill frowned. "Go on with your story."

"That's all there is. With that hand, the game broke up. Naturally it broke up."

"What happened next?"

"Schwartz went home. No—before he left, he took the cards and showed us some tricks."

"A-a-ah!" It was a long gurgle of satisfaction from Bill. "The tricks, I take it, were not particularly good."

"How did you know?" gasped Tony.

"And Schwartz impressed you as being a bit of a dub. You could have done the same tricks quite as well or better."

"How did you know?" gasped Tony again.

Bill smiled. "I was thinking what I would have done if I had been in Schwartz's place. Yes, I am almost sure that is what I would have done. And I think I would have said, when I was leaving, that I would be glad to give you your revenge some time."

"Schwartz did say that."

"We'll hold him to his word to-morrow night.

"I'll telephone him."

"But first," said Bill, "I'd like to see the cards you played with."

He examined them with care.

"I'll show you the marks I put on them," said Tony.

Bill shook his head. "You don't have to. I could see them ten feet away. So could Schwartz." Yet he produced a magnifying glass, and scrutinized half a dozen cards with extreme minuteness.

"I told you," said Tony, "that I had marked forty-seven out of the fifty-two cards. You will find that forty-seven are still marked."

"Correct."

"I will swear that not one of the five cards I dealt Schwartz bore my mark."

"Also correct."

"Then you haven't found out a thing that I don't know already."

Bill laughed and looked around the room. "You played in here?" he asked.

"No; in the dining room."

"A small room, I should say."

"As large as you will find in most New York apartments," said Mrs. Claghorn.

"Doubtless. That sideboard, I take it, occupied the same position as now?"

"Yes. But the mirror in it doesn't explain how a jack changed to an ace." Tony was becoming impatient.

"I didn't say it did. That serving table was in the same place?"

"Yes."

"And you used the table that is here now for your game?"

"No," said Mrs. Claghorn, "it wasn't big enough. We sent out for a larger table."

"With the result that there was not much room between the backs of the chairs and the furniture."

"There was no room at all. In fact, one of the chairs was badly scratched the next morning."

"I don't see what you're getting at," fumed Tony. "I've told you already that Schwartz's hands were never out of sight."

Bill laughed. "Nevertheless," he declared, "I think I've solved your problem. But I'll need help to go further with it."

"I'll give you any help you want."

"You mean it?"

"Of course I mean it."

"Then to-morrow—"

"Yes?"

"After you've telephoned Schwartz and a few of your friends to come up in the evening—"

"Yes?"

"Get out your car, take me down town, and help me pick out a dog."

TONY CLAGHORN WAS a man of many virtues, but the list of them did not include patience. When Bill first expressed his wish for a dog, Tony laughed, and tried to bring him back to the subject under discussion. But Bill was not to be denied.

"I've always wanted a dog," he said, "and it strikes me that this is just the time to get one."

"What are you going to do with a dog?" demanded Tony.

"I don't know, but I want one."

"What kind of dog do you want?"

"I don't know."

"A big dog or a small one?"

"I'm not sure."

"Long haired or short haired?"

"I'm not particular."

Tony gazed at him in utter bewilderment. "If you want a dog for your own pleasure, I'll be glad to buy you the best the market affords."

Bill shook his head solemnly. "I'm afraid a pleasure dog wouldn't do at all."

That night Tony gravely discussed the question of Bill's possible insanity with his wife. She laughed at him. "Mr. Parmelee knows exactly what he's doing," she assured him.

"How do you know?"

"Woman's intuition."

"Humph!" Then Tony's eyes brightened. "Perhaps he wants a bloodhound!"

"Perhaps."

The more Tony thought about it, the more right and logical it seemed. He was up bright and early in the morning, and with an air of having guessed Bill's secret, piloted his wife and their guest to a kennel on Long Island.

Bill glanced at the sad-looking canines, whistled at one or two, and shook his head decisively.

"Don't want one of them?" asked Tony in surprise.

"No."

"Why not?"

"Too mournful," said Bill. "Why, those dogs look as if they had lost their best friends. It would make me unhappy just to have one of them around."

Tony choked down his disappointment. "I take it you'd prefer a cheerful dog."

"I guess so," said Bill hesitantly.

Tony proceeded without hesitation to an establishment specializing in wire-haired fox terriers. "These are cheerful dogs," he announced.

The statement was almost superfluous. The terriers overflowed with the joy of living, filled the air with their clamor, and as Bill neared their pen, rushed to its side to leap wildly at him.

"Are they cheerful enough?" inquired Tony anxiously.

Bill nodded.

"Then we'll pick one out?" urged Tony.

Bill shook his head, and lowered his voice. "I'm afraid they're entirely too cheerful."

"But you said you wanted a cheerful dog."

"Yes; but only middling cheerful."

With the growing conviction that he was the victim of an ill-timed practical joke, Tony drove many miles to the domain of the Old English sheep dog, to the region of the Chinese chow, to the habitat of the Mexican hairless dog, the King Charles spaniel, and the Pekinese. Thence, stifling his growing impatience, he proceeded to the haunts of the collie, the abode of the Great Dane, the dwelling of the St. Bernards, and the home of the greyhounds. He even crossed the Hudson, and penetrated to the wilds of Jersey, the stronghold of the Belgian police dogs.

Bill followed him about patiently, observed, whistled, occasionally petted a head or two, but declined to choose any dog for his own.

Three o'clock in the afternoon found the party, a little weary, but thoroughly determined, at the store of a dealer in lower New York City. Tony, thoroughly disgusted, had resolved to carry on until Bill gave in. The joke, he had made up his mind, would not be on him. But Mrs. Claghorn, discerning traces of method in Bill's madness, was curiously silent.

Tony strode manfully into the store. "We want a dog," he proclaimed, "about so high, or a little higher—or lower. He must have hair, but he mustn't be too hairy. He mustn't be too mournful—and he mustn't be too cheerful; but we'd like him to have a touch of mournful cheerfulness or of cheerful mournfulness. Do you keep dogs like that?"

"No, sir," said the dealer decisively, "we drown 'em."

"By George!" ejaculated Bill, "that gives me an idea!"

Tony promptly found out that the idea involved a visit to the city pound, and wondering at the strangeness of Bill's humor, piloted the car thither. He wondered still more when Bill, in the short space of three minutes, selected a dog which he declared satisfied him in every particular.

"Look," said Bill. He whistled. The dog came bounding towards him. "Go away," said Bill. The dog moved off. "Sit down." The dog followed orders. Again Bill whistled. Like a thunderbolt, the animal leaped in his direction. "That's what I call a dog!" Bill declared.

Tony surveyed the curious beast with disapproval. The head was mostly collie, though adorned with most un-collie-like prick-ears; the coat—what there was of it, for the animal had suffered from mange—was reminiscent of the traditions of the Airedales; yet the shape of the body was that to be expected in the ancient and honorable order of Irish wolfhounds. "What is his breed?" he inquired suspiciously.

Bill inspected his choice gravely. "It's much easier to say what his breed isn't. A product of the great American melting pot; a true cosmopolitan. I'm going to invent a new variety, and call him a poker dog."

AT SEVEN THAT evening Bill went over his arrangements with the care which might have been expected of a stage director just prior to a first performance. The table—the same large table that had been used on the previous occasion—was in place, with the result that the little room was nearly filled by it. Indeed, Bill, easing himself into one of the chairs, found that a movement of less than an inch brought it into contact with the sideboard.

"I can get a smaller table," said Tony.

Bill demurred. "This one is just right."

"It's altogether too big for the room."

"It's not too big for my purpose."

Tony watched Bill, closely followed by his newly acquired pet, edging about the table. "Do I have to watch that mongrel all evening? He'll hoodoo my game."

Bill gazed affectionately at the maligned animal. "Mongrel? Mongrel?" he echoed. "Why, that dog has some of the best blood in the animal kingdom flowing through his veins!" He caressed the poker dog's muzzle. "Hard life, old boy, when even our friends don't understand us."

"Humph!" snorted Tony, "if you hadn't taken him out of the pound, he'd have made a little trip to the gas chamber by now, and he wouldn't have a worry on his soul this minute."

"Do you hear that, old boy?" inquired Bill, "there's gratitude for you! He's only a man, so he doesn't know he'll have you to thank if he and that Ted Wayland friend of his have no worries on their own souls to-morrow."

"Thank him?" scoffed Tony. "I hate the sight of him already."

It must have been in deference to that uncomplimentary opinion that Tony, upon returning from the near-by tobacconist's with supplies for the evening, found the poker dog nowhere in evidence. He was secretly relieved when the dog remained out of sight as Straker and Wayland and Chisholm and Billings and Schwartz trickled in. Such an animal, Tony felt strongly, would bring discredit upon his household.

He tried in vain to fathom Bill's plans as the poker game got under way, and progressed in the manner which Tony had come to regard as inevitable. Schwartz won slowly but steadily; Bill, playing cautiously, lost with the same regularity, and the remaining five, playing even more conservatively, barely managed to hold their ground. To Tony's horror, Bill showed himself an exceedingly bad loser. He swore vigorously when he failed to fill a four-flush, and revealed unsuspected heights of profanity when triplets, in Schwartz's hand, beat two pairs in his own.

At the end of an hour Bill was two or three hundred dollars in the hole, and had made every person present aware of it by calling repeated attention to the fact. He rose angrily, and raked his remaining chips together. "I'm going to quit; I've got no luck to-night, and it's foolish to play when your luck's bad."

The players protested, but Bill was obdurate. "This seat is hoodooed," he declared, and he indicated the chair in which he had been sitting, so close to the sideboard that its back actually touched it.

Schwartz, the lone winner, felt it incumbent upon him to be gracious. "If you think there's something wrong with the seat, I'll be glad to change with you."

"Umph," grunted Bill thanklessly, and accepted the offer. "I suppose now that I've left that chair, the hoodoo's left it with me."

His gloomy prediction must have been correct, for the remains of his stack vanished with unexampled rapidity. He bought a second stack, to see it follow the first, and swearing loudly, rose to make the announcement, "I'm through."

Schwartz laughed. "Stick to it, old man," he urged, "and your luck's bound to change."

"Next week, maybe."

"Perhaps in ten minutes."

"I've lost enough for one sitting," declared Bill.

Schwartz persisted. "You may win it all back on a single hand. Listen: I'll make you a proposition." He piled up a neat stack of chips. "Five hundred dollars' worth of chips, you see? I'll sell them to you for four hundred dollars." His left hand had arranged the chips; his right hand, palm up, hovered eloquently above the table.

And then an extraordinary thing happened.

From Bill's lips came a piercing whistle, and simultaneously from Schwartz's right sleeve shot three cards, two queens and an ace. They were visible for but a fraction of a second, for they flashed back into their hiding place with equal rapidity, but the men about the table had seen.

Schwartz stumbled to his feet, and his hand groped towards his hip pocket.

Bill held out a blue-barreled revolver. "Is this what you want?" he inquired politely. "I slipped it out of your pocket when we changed places." At his side the poker dog, barking furiously, pointed a menacing muzzle in Schwartz's direction.

FROM A LONG and solitary interview with Schwartz in the privacy of a bedroom, Bill returned to the excited group around the table. "Mr. Schwartz has asked me to announce that he was playing just for fun. He doesn't want your money, and I couldn't persuade him to keep it. He has handed me the amount he took from Ted Wayland the other night—here it is; and he has given me what he won from Tony Claghorn, and in addition to that, he has given me all of his remaining cash, and his promise to leave town. And, oh, I forgot, he's given me his shirt."

"His shirt?" echoed Tony. "What do we want with that?"

"It's worth looking at," declared Bill. "You've probably never seen a shirt like it." With a penknife, he slit the right sleeve from top to bottom. "Do you see? It's a double sleeve. When he wore it, you could look right up to his elbow and see nothing; but there was enough room between the inner sleeve and the outer sleeve for a little machine known as the Kepplinger hold-out." He dumped a complicated mass of elastics, pulleys, and strings to the table. "This is it."

Tony fingered the apparatus gingerly. "You may understand it, but it's all clear as mud to me."

Bill smiled. "I'll demonstrate." He indicated a metal shell, shaped like a flattened bottle without a bottom. "This fastens between the inner and outer sleeves. It's just big enough to hold a few cards. Now, when I pull on the string, a little clip shoots out into the palm of my hand, and gives me the cards I have previously fastened into it. When I let the string go, the clip shoots back out of sight again, and takes the cards I don't need with it. A very useful invention, the Kepplinger hold-out: it gives the man who wears it a chance to hold out five cards if he feels like it; it makes him absolutely unbeatable, and it's so simple that you can't detect it even when he isn't wearing his coat."

"You say that it's operated by pulling a string," said Straker. "We watched him as if our lives depended upon it. How could he have pulled a string without moving his hands?"

"By running it down inside of his clothes; by bringing it out through the seam at one knee, and by fastening the end of the string to the other knee. When he separated his knees, the hold-out shot out of his sleeve; when he brought them together, it disappeared again."

"It's all very wonderful," said Tony at length, "but I don't see yet how you tumbled to it. You had never seen him play."

"I didn't have to," laughed Bill, "you told me what happened.

Try to reconstruct the scene in your minds. A week ago he played with you. Tony dealt him three aces and two jacks, and when it came to the showdown, Schwartz held four aces and one jack. There's only one possible answer: he had an ace or two in the hold-out before the hand was dealt; he exchanged one for one of the jacks; and he must have used a hold-out because there's no other way in which he could have done it.

"That struck me the moment Tony told me his story, and it struck me too that the moment the hand was over Schwartz was in a rather dangerous position. He couldn't walk off and leave behind a deck containing three jacks and five aces, so he picked up the cards, and showed you a few simple little tricks. He did them badly, because he didn't want you to think he was a sleight-of-hand artist, but he did them well enough to slip the fourth jack out of his sleeve, and slip the fifth ace back into it. When he left, he said he'd be glad to give you your revenge some time. He said that because you had tried to cheat him, and he knew it, and because he knew, moreover, that you didn't have a chance in a million of putting anything over on him. At honest poker you might have won; but at dishonest poker you didn't have a chance, and he was willing to go just as far as you would.

"But Schwartz made one fatal mistake. For a few minutes the jack he didn't need had been hidden in the hold-out, and when I examined it, I found the mark of the clip on its edge. If Schwartz had been just the least little bit cleverer, he would have wound up his card tricks by tearing the pack in two, and I should never have been the wiser. But he didn't, and that told me what he had done as plainly as if he had written out a confession."

Through the buzz of voices, a few seconds later, came the sound of a rap at the door. "May we come in?" asked pretty Mrs. Claghorn. "The poker dog wants to go to his master."

Tony exploded into laughter. "The poker dog! The poker dog! After all the trouble we went to, the dog had nothing at all to do with the game!" He turned to his friends. "Bill insisted on getting a dog before to-night, so we drove over a hundred miles to find one to suit him, and we had to go to the pound to do it. And now that it's all over, the dog hasn't cut any figure at all. Bill was just having a little joke on me."

"Is that so?" Bill was strangely serious. "I told you you'd have that dog to thank before the night was over. You don't seem to realize what he's done for you." He indicated the chair which Schwartz had occupied. "I wanted our friend to sit in that chair. There were six other chairs, and the chances were seven to one against. I lost out on that, so I took the seat myself and got him to change with me after a while."

"But what has that to do with the dog?"

"Not much," confessed Bill, "only he was parked in the lower compartment of the sideboard, smack up against the chair, gnawing contentedly at a bone until I needed him. I waited till Schwartz's hand was palm up on the table at a time when I knew he had cards up his sleeve. Then I whistled, and that dog, that dependable poker dog, burst out of the sideboard, and made a dash for me by the shortest possible route—right between Schwartz's legs. Schwartz separated his knees, or the dog separated them for him, and you all saw what happened." He gazed invitingly around the table. "Are there any other questions?"

"No questions," said Ted Wayland, "but I want to tell you that you've earned my undying gratitude."

"And mine too," said Mrs. Claghorn.

"And mine too," said Tony.

Bill rose with proper solemnity. "There being no further business before the meeting," he announced, "we will all take comfortable seats and watch Mr. Anthony P. Claghorn get down on his knees and offer his humblest apologies to the poker dog."

4

—

RED AND BLACK

SOME MEN ARE born mean; others achieve meanness; still others have meanness thrust upon them. Whitney Burnside was all three.

If there was anything in heredity Whitney had inherited largely from his father, Jeffrey Burnside, who had gone to an unlamented grave leaving behind not a single person to call himself his friend. Jeffrey Burnside had begun life filled with the conviction that if he did not look out for himself, nobody else might be expected to do so, and he had looked out for himself so exceedingly well that long before his fortieth year he had been compelled to retain a firm of lawyers whose exclusive business was to extricate him from his troubles. Not that Jeffrey Burnside ever violated the statutes: far from it. Well posted, well advised, and utterly unscrupulous, Burnside had sailed very close indeed to the wind—and had never capsized.

After his notorious falling out with his partner, for instance, Burnside had been decisively blackballed at the Windsor Club; but Faulkner, his victim, had been compelled to admit that he had been ruined by strictly legal methods. Burnside had grimly seized a sheet of ledger paper, had entered in the credit column the amount of which he had despoiled his trustful partner, and had set opposite it, as a debit, the item "Blackballed—Windsor

Club." He had grinned. "At that rate," he had reflected, "I'd like to be blackballed at some more clubs."

He ended his life as stormily as he had lived it: dropped dead in an apoplectic seizure, and left his seventeen-year-old son an estate mounting far into the millions.

Whitney Burnside bade fair to carry on in his father's footsteps. Tall, powerfully built, heavily muscled, he had never succeeded in whipping an adversary even approaching him in size. Picked at sight for his college football squad, he had been ignominiously dismissed after two or three scrimmages had revealed the presence of a large, ineradicable streak of yellow. He had revenged himself by betting heavily against the team, a proceeding which had not added noticeably to his popularity, and the fact that he won regularly from less affluent classmates and thereupon bet upon a still larger scale made him disliked still more acutely.

His roommate had preached the subject of loyalty to him. Whitney had listened with a superior smile, to counter heavily with the question, "What do you expect me to do? Throw away my good money because we've got a rotten team?"

"Other fellows are doing it: fellows who can't afford it nearly so well as you."

"I know that." Whitney laughed and slapped his trousers pocket. "I've got some of their losings right here."

With an effort his roommate kept his temper. "I've got just one request to make of you: if you won't bet on the team, at any rate, don't bet against it."

"Why not?"

"Well, hang it all, man, it's our team, don't you see?"

Whitney did not see and most emphatically did not want to

see. "I bet to make money," he proclaimed. "I can make more money betting against the team than betting on it. That's what I'm going to keep right on doing."

There may have been no connection between the two events, but exactly twenty-four hours later a self-appointed committee escorted Whitney from his room to a secluded spot far away from the campus, laid him over a barrel, and paddled him until he howled for mercy.

After graduation Whitney ran true to form. It was not for him to settle down into the dreary rut of business: his father had left him so large a fortune that Whitney could never hope to spend it. It was far more congenial to the young man's temperament to become a gentleman of leisure, to spend his winters in Florida and his summers abroad, to extricate himself from one embarrassing episode only to become entangled in another.

There was Carlotta, for example, daughter of the good-natured Italian who ran a fruit stand around the corner of the street in which the Burnside mansion occupied its place in the sun. The newspapers never ascertained just what took place, but it was an undeniable fact that Whitney staggered home one night with both eyes blackened and his coat in tatters, while Joe, Carlotta's father, strutted up and down at his stand, proud as any fighting cock, and without a mark on him.

After that adventure Whitney invariably carried a cane, artfully made of a steel tube painted to resemble wood. It weighed several pounds and would undoubtedly crush any head unlucky enough to be struck with it. Whitney consoled himself with the reflection that it would be useful were he ever again cowardly attacked by a man half his size.

There had followed the usual adventures with susceptible members of the chorus—rather more than the usual number—and at the ripe age of thirty Whitney had decided to settle down. His choice had fallen upon a nice girl—a really nice girl—a girl so nice that after accepting him, because her family was poor, the thought of Whitney somehow cast the Burnside millions into the shade and caused her, most unexpectedly, to change her mind and reject him. Wealth had its advantages, she had reflected, but not ten times Whitney's wealth could make Whitney's wife happy. She allowed Whitney's engagement to drag along three months. At the end of that time she gave Whitney's self-esteem a sad jolt by eloping with another man. Whitney declared he would never forgive her, but in spite of that she lived happily ever after. For his part, Whitney reached the age of thirty-three with a short temper, a well-developed paunch, and a sluggish liver.

BACK IN THE eighteen-eighties a group of Westerners, well supplied with money, and in need of a gathering place where its researches into the great American game of poker might be pursued undisturbed, founded the Himalaya Club. To it the original founders elected their friends—and the friends of their friends—and the friends of their friends several times removed, the sole and sufficient membership qualification being the ability to pay one's losses. The natural result was that the club became a compound of new-rich and old-rich, of suddenly made millionaires to whom plunging was the breath of life and of men who, along with their wealth, had inherited a taste for gambling. Scions of the oldest and staidest families rubbed shoulders with men who had been unheard of a few months before, with men, in many cases, whom they would not have dreamed of introducing into their own homes.

In time many of the newly rich settled down and became staid. But more than once enterprising sharpers, seeing a golden opportunity, obtained membership in the Himalaya and lined their pockets richly before departing. In the Himalaya social distinctions simply did not exist. A plethoric bank roll was the best of all possible introductions. Further than that it was unnecessary to go.

"Once," Tony Claghorn liked to explain, "a man was black-balled because he had the Asiatic cholera. But that was long ago." Being one of the respectable minority which came to the club, in search of a thrill, Tony could afford to jest. But Whitney Burnside, who had joined promptly upon graduating from college, proudly spoke of the Himalaya as "my club." Subconsciously, perhaps, Whitney realized that there was not another club in the metropolis to which he could have been elected. Wisely he made the most of what he had.

Whitney's visiting cards bore the legend "Himalaya Club" in a lower corner; the Himalaya Club was Whitney's forwarding address; most of Whitney's evenings were spent in the club quarters. And when Whitney had a tale of woe to tell he could always buttonhole some fellow member of the Himalaya and pour the story into his ear. The response would generally be a series of sympathetic grunts. Whitney found them consoling.

"I've been robbed," he complained bitterly to Tony one evening. "I've been robbed just the same as if highwaymen had pushed me up against the wall, pointed a loaded gun at me and cleaned out my pockets."

Tony Claghorn smiled. One of Whitney's endearing traits

was a chronic inability to lose graciously. Tony had seen him play poker, at a ten-dollar limit, match coins, at twenty-five dollars and more a throw, and indulge in bridge at a dollar a point; had seen him lose at all three pastimes, and had yet to hear him attribute a loss to the superior skill of an antagonist. If Whitney won, and that could not help happening at intervals, he never tired of relating how his expertness had brought about that result; but if he lost, and that happened much more frequently, he had invariably been robbed—and did not hesitate to say so. "I seem to have heard those words before," Tony commented, stifling an impulse to throw a convenient ash tray at the fat, foolish face so near his own. "According to my recollection you are the most-robbed man I ever met. It's about time for you to put a new record on your phonograph."

"I'm serious, Claghorn. I've been robbed: shamelessly robbed."

"Again?"

"I may have been wrong in the past. But this time there's no doubt about it."

"Well, what do you take me for? A policeman?"

Whitney seized his arm. "Listen, old man," he pleaded, "I heard how you helped Ted Wayland out of a hole. Do as much for me."

"And how do you expect me to do that?"

"I wish I knew," confessed Whitney.

Tony leaped at the chance to end the interview. "If you don't know, I'm sure I don't. Good night."

Again Whitney seized his arm. "Just a minute," he begged. "They've gotten into me for more than a hundred thousand."

"What?" gasped Tony.

"More than a hundred thousand," repeated Whitney.

"Dollars?"

"Good American money."

Tony made a wry face. "If you had to lose that much, why didn't you invite me to sit in the game? I'm one of the few men who would have known just what to do with that amount of change."

"Be serious," Whitney urged. "I'm not talking about stage money."

"What were you playing? Poker?"

"No."

"Well, what was it?"

Shamefacedly Whitney hung his head. "The game was— ahem—it was roulette."

"The poker game at the Himalaya wasn't stiff enough for you? You had to go outside?"

"I thought I'd have better luck."

"Perhaps you did," Tony philosophized. "You've lost so much that now you'll lay off gambling for a while."

"But it wasn't gambling: it was just robbery."

"If you knew that, I don't see why you played."

Whitney swallowed hard. "I thought I could beat it," he confessed. "Of course there's nothing in playing the numbers: the odds are too heavily against you. But red and black, even money, ought to win in the long run if you keep on doubling your bets every time you lose."

"But you didn't win?"

Tony's informant shook his head. "You've got no idea how soon bets run into real money if you just double them half a dozen times. Do you realize that you can start betting as little as ten dollars, and that if you double every time you lose, you'll be putting up over five thousand dollars on the tenth spin? And then, if you win, you're ahead just ten dollars, and if you lose, you're out ten thousand."

"That's a good game to keep away from."

"Of course, it's a million-to-one shot that you won't lose ten times hand running."

"But I take it that that's just what happened."

"Even more so," Whitney confessed. "I was betting on the red: and the ball dropped into the black thirteen consecutive times."

Tony whistled. "I've always heard that thirteen was unlucky."

"It was for me. I stopped doubling after the tenth loss. They wouldn't let me bet any higher. I just strung along, playing the limit."

"And lost a hundred thousand at a sitting?"

"No," corrected Whitney, "it took three evenings."

"Even at that," commented Tony dryly, "you got action for your money. Nothing slow about roulette!"

Whitney Burnside brought his fist down on an ash tray with a crash. "Claghorn," he declared, "that game was crooked! Thirteen consecutive blacks prove that! I'll give anything to show it up!"

"And how does that affect me?"

"I want you to do for me what you did for Ted Wayland."

Tony smiled. Ted Wayland, his wife's relative, had fallen in with a sharper. Tony had tried to help him, with the result that Tony himself had been artistically shorn. Thereupon Bill Parmelee, a reformed gambler, had come to the rescue, and, as told in the tale of "The Poker Dog," had neatly turned the tables on the crook.

Nevertheless Tony was receiving credit which he hastened to disclaim. "I tried to help Wayland," he admitted, "and I made an awful mess of it."

"That's not what the boys say."

"But it's the truth nevertheless. I thought I was going to show how smart I could be," said Tony candidly. "I found out I wasn't nearly smart enough. Then a fellow named Bill Parmelee, a man I had met on my vacation, came down to New York and did the trick so easily that it was almost a joke."

Whitney Burnside nodded. "Then Parmelee's the man I want."

"What do you want of him?"

"He's got to prove that roulette game crooked! Nobody can fleece me and get away with it! He's got to show up that gang, and then I'll run them out of town!"

"And what makes you think that Parmelee would help you?"

"He's got his price, hasn't he?" With millions at his command Whitney found few things in life which could not be purchased. "Name his figure—I'll pay it."

Tony reflected. On two separate occasions Bill Parmelee had come to his aid. On the first, his recompense had been a few words of thanks. On the second, his fee had consisted of a mongrel dog with a market value of rather less than fifty cents. Tony had not even been allowed to defray the cost of Parmelee's railway tickets. But sober second thought told Tony that Whitney Burnside did not fall in the class of men for whom other men gladly did favors. About Whitney there was nothing lovable. His talent for making enemies was highly developed. It would take him barely five minutes, Tony foresaw, to antagonize Bill Parmelee, easy-going and good natured as the latter was. Tony himself, patient and long suffering, had been on bad terms with Whitney more than once; had, in fact, been secretly delighted when Whitney confided the huge total of his losses to him.

"Name his figure," rasped Whitney a second time. "What's his charge? Out with' it!"

"Five thousand dollars," said Tony decisively.

"What?"

"Five thousand dollars," Tony repeated.

"It's robbery!" declared the young millionaire. "I won't pay it!"

"Then that ends the matter." Tony heaved a sigh of relief and headed for the door.

"Wait a minute! Wait a minute! Perhaps he'll take less."

"I won't allow him to."

Whitney hesitated. "You think he'll show them up?"

"I don't know. But there won't be any charge if he doesn't."

Whitney's eyes narrowed. "All right, Claghorn," he said. "If Parmelee proves that roulette game crooked I'll pay him five thousand dollars. Is that satisfactory?"

Tony extracted a blank check from his pocket. "I believe you and I keep our balances with the same bank. You might write out a check for the amount to my order."

"What's the matter?" blustered Burnside. "Isn't my word good? Don't you trust me?"

"Who does?" countered Tony candidly. "Honest, Burnside, would you trust yourself?" He filled out the body of the check and passed the pen to Whitney. "Here," he invited, "sign on the dotted line."

"INFERNAL CHEEK, I call it," declared Whitney. "Here I hire this

Parmelee fellow to come to New York and do a job for me, and he writes me to meet him at the station. He must think I'm a taxi driver."

Tony laughed. "Perhaps you expected him to crawl into your presence and kiss your hand."

"I didn't expect him to start ordering me around. I'm the employer, you know. Any orders that are given will come from me."

Tony nodded sagely. "I can see that you're going to get along well with him."

"He's taking my money, isn't he?"

"And giving you value received for it."

"That reminds me," said Whitney. "There's a point I want to discuss with you before we meet him. Really, don't you think we've agreed to pay him too much?"

Young Burnside had apparently given the matter considerable thought. Half the agreed sum; or even a quarter, or a tenth, had struck him, upon careful reflection, as being ample compensation for the proposed service. He mentioned as much to Parmelee when they met in the lunch room at Grand Central Station, and felt freer to mention it when he noted that Parmelee was of slight build and rather less than half his own weight. "When Mr. Claghorn recommended you to me," he explained, "I expected to find you a man of at least fifty, with a lifetime of experience behind him. Instead of that you're just a young fellow, not thirty—"

"Not twenty-five," corrected Bill genially.

Whitney accepted the correction. "Not twenty-five," he repeated. "I expected you to be a man of broad knowledge, not—if you will pardon me—just a hick." He smiled engagingly. "I hope you will pardon my frankness. I'm always outspoken. I say what I think—just like that."

"Go right ahead," Bill encouraged.

"To a man of mature years I would have paid a fee commensurate with his standing. Indeed, Mr. Claghorn and I tentatively spoke of an absurdly large sum. But to a young man like yourself, a young man with his future before him, the chance to work for me should be almost enough compensation in itself. Don't you think so?"

"I'm not doing any thinking. I'm just listening to you. Go on."

"If you handle this case successfully," pursued Whitney, "the advertising should be valuable. I will recommend you to my friends—in my clubs—" Whitney belonged only to the Himalaya, but Bill could hardly be expected to know that. "I'll do my best to put some business in your way. I'll even do better than that: the minute I'm satisfied that you've earned the money I'll hand you a couple of hundred dollars. It ought to go pretty far in the country." He beamed upon Parmelee. "Now, what do you say?"

Bill exploded into laughter. "Burnside," he remarked, "I had heard that you were a cheap skate, but I didn't think you were quite so cheap!"

"What do you mean?" sputtered Whitney.

"Don't I talk good English?" inquired Bill. "You're mean—you're petty—you're contemptible—you're small. You have a soul which would be too little for a dried-up bacillus and your ideas of honesty would make an ordinary self-respecting sneak thief blush. Aside from that I don't like your face, and I don't like the way you dress, and I don't like your manner of speaking. Now, if I've said anything you don't like, just put it in your pipe and smoke it."

Tony rose in alarm, expecting Whitney to leap at his friend's throat. But the young millionaire did nothing of the kind. Perhaps he had decided that Bill's slight frame was too well muscled. Perhaps he had made up his mind that a certain freedom of speech must be permitted to a farmer, a mere hick. Whatever the explanation he said nothing whatsoever in reply, while a sickly smile spread frozenly over his features.

Bill nodded his approval. "You've been doing a lot of talking. Now you'll do a little listening. You think I asked you to meet me at this station because I've just arrived on a train. You're wrong. I've been in New York forty-eight hours, looking over the ground. I visited the gambling house at which you played last night. I played red and black myself. I've made up my mind on the question of whether or not the game is crooked. And I've asked you to meet me at this station because I know all about you, because I know the kind of tinhorn sport you are, and because if you went back on your word—as you seem to want to—all I would have to do would be to jump on the next train home." He pulled out his watch and glanced at it. "You've got just seven minutes to make up your mind. Either you come through—live up to your agreement to the letter—or I drop out of this, here and now. To be perfectly candid, I don't care particularly what you do. I'm not hard up. I don't need your money. And I won enough at roulette last night to pay me for my trip a good many times over." He glanced at his watch again. "Six and a half minutes left. Well?"

Whitney smiled ingratiatingly. "My dear fellow," he said, "you don't imagine that I was serious in what I said before? I promised Mr. Claghorn to pay you a certain amount. You shall have every cent of it. Why, Mr. Claghorn doubtless has my check in his pocket this very minute!"

"Doubtless," assented Bill. He smiled grimly. "Burnside, if you mean business, if you want me to go further, you might give me an earnest of your good faith by telephoning your bank, and revoking the stop payment order you issued on that check the morning after you wrote it."

WHEN WHITNEY BURNSIDE, after a brief visit to the telephone, had departed, oozing cordiality and overflowing with what Bill described as "slimy politeness," Tony turned to his friend. "How on earth did you know that he had stopped payment on the check?" he demanded in utter amazement.

Bill laughed.

"I didn't know it myself," pursued Tony, "and I haven't the least idea how you could have found it out. Even if you knew on what bank he had drawn—which you didn't—you couldn't have walked in and asked questions about the private business of one of their depositors. They wouldn't have answered them for a stranger. How did you know?"

"I didn't know," admitted Bill, "but I knew the kind of man I was dealing with. Friend Whitney was running true to form—that was all." He put on his hat and led the way to the door. "Come; let's walk uptown. I have some business to attend to."

Much to Tony's bewilderment his friend turned into an obscure side street and piloted him into an establishment dealing in optical goods. "Finished?" he demanded of the proprietor.

"Not fifteen minutes ago."

He handed Bill a curious affair of leather and metal, which the latter promptly examined with care.

"What is it?" inquired Tony, with eager curiosity.

"Well, what do you think it is?"

"It looks like a pocket camera—but when you look at it more closely you see it isn't a camera; and it looks like a pair of binoculars—but it's quite plain that it isn't; and it has some resemblance to spectacles—though it can't be that."

Bill nodded vigorously. "You're right—and wrong—on every guess. It isn't any one of the three, though it's a little of all of them."

"What do you call it?"

"Considering that I didn't invent it until this morning, at precisely ten minutes of six, I haven't gotten around to naming it yet." He smiled at the aged proprietor of the establishment. "What would you call it?"

The man flung up his hands. "I made it according to your instructions, Mr. Parmelee, and I hope you like it, but I can't even guess what you're going to do with it. If it's an invention, why don't you patent it?"

"Now that's not a bad idea," assented Bill. "Maybe I will." He waved a solemn hand toward the curious instrument. "This," he announced, "is what I call a roulettoscope."

"A what?" inquired Tony.

"A roulettoscope."

"There's no such thing!"

Bill grinned as he patted his invention. "There is now."

To Tony's vexation he refused to answer innumerable questions during the remainder of the afternoon. "It may not work," he admitted frankly, "and if it doesn't work I'll be glad I didn't do any blowing in advance."

"But it may work."

"I expect it to work," said Bill, "and if that happens I promise you you'll have a chance to see it in action."

Tony snorted. "Do you know what I think? I think you're kidding me."

Bill nodded. "I may be kidding myself too," he confessed. "I wasn't brought up to be an inventor. This is my first attempt and it's quite possible that it won't be a good one. Now, let's change the subject: do you believe the Lord created Whitney Burnside, or is he just something that sprouted in a mushroom cellar?"

ONCE UPON A time, when the present generation was younger than it is to-day, a widely known and popular song celebrated the fame of "The Man Who Broke the Bank at Monte Carlo." But no song has ever been written to celebrate the innumerable banks which have broken men in nearly every city in the world. Such a song would not be popular. So rarely does the man break the bank that the event deserves headlines. So infallibly does the bank break the man that the episode is not worth notice.

Luck—the greenhorn's idol—whispers that he may be the fortunate person who is an exception to the rule; that he may be the rare individual who leaves the roulette table richer than when he sat down at it. Science—and to this the professional gambler bows—points out cold-bloodedly that in the long run approximately six cents out of every dollar hazarded in the game will find their way into the bank's coffers. It is the percentage in favor of the house: the dividend mathematically earned by the zero and the double zero. There is no escaping it; no getting away from it. For a time a player may win—not from the bank, but from other players—but sooner or later, as decreed by the immutable laws of chance, he will part with every dollar that he has. To the bank it makes not the least difference who wins and who loses: the percentage is there. Winner and loser, whatever their ups and downs, will pay it in the end. The bank, for the convenience of providing a wheel, a croupier, a dozen chairs, a floor underfoot and a roof overhead, will eventually take its toll.

When "Honest Jim" Floyd—any professional gambler who reaches the age of fifty without a trip to jail has a right to the sobriquet of "Honest"—first started in business, it was his intention to give his patrons a run for their money: to use a fair wheel and to be content with the percentage that it earned. The rewards were ample. Honest Jim had simple tastes: a peck or so of five-carat diamonds distributed over his person; a town house and a country house; a pair of prize-winning trotting horses—this was back in the 'nineties; and the game enabled him to gratify them. The patrons of his various establishments were supplied with unlimited champagne, with the choicest cigars, and when their turns came to part with their last dollars it was Honest Jim's boast that no gambling house, in any part of the world, sent them on their way in better style than his. His own carriage would take them to the station; transportation in the Palace cars of the period would be supplied gratis, and the departing victim of the laws of chance might reflect that even losing—if one lost to Jim Floyd—had its compensations.

But with the coming of the twentieth century there was a change. The percentage—six per cent—was no longer suffi-cient. More than that was demanded by corrupt officials for protection, and if it was not forthcoming, raids, with their destruction of furniture and with their damage to the following of the house were even more expensive. In desperation Honest Jim had moved from city to city, to find the same conditions prevailing everywhere; to find himself, for the first time in a long life, contending with a game which was even more unbeatable than his own. One by one his diamonds vanished; his town and country houses went under the hammer; his fast horses died off, and were not replaced. The times, reflected Honest Jim, were sadly out of joint—and getting out of jointer.

The year 1910 found him acting as a croupier in a Chicago establishment; 1915 saw him following the same pursuit in San Francisco; 1920 witnessed him amassing a small but sufficient capital, and the following year inaugurated his own little game, discreetly housed in the mazes of New York City itself. He had fallen into the depths, had risen again, and now, having deferred to changed conditions by investing in a wheel that was gifted in strange and mysterious ways, was rising very rapidly indeed. Instead of the conventional six per cent, Honest Jim's game now could be made to pay very nearly one hundred per cent. Diamonds were again sprouting in his ample shirt front. A sporty roadster had replaced the trotting horses of the previous century. Honest Jim was on his way to prosperity.

When Bill Parmelee and Tony Claghorn made their way to Floyd's establishment in the evening, Whitney Burnside was already there.

"You can come and watch, if you like," Bill had told him on parting, "but remember that you don't know me. It would make Floyd suspicious if you brought anybody along with you."

That Whitney had remembered his instructions was evident when he gazed into Bill's face with no sign of recognition. But the young millionaire had not been able to resist the lure of the game for the few minutes he had been compelled to wait. He was one of a group gathered about the roulette table and the pile of chips at his elbow showed that he had not been content to remain a spectator. He was not betting on the numbers: that he considered too risky. As always, he was playing red and black, hazarding small fortunes on each turn of the wheel.

Quietly Bill dropped into a vacant chair and pushed a ten-dollar bill into the square representing the black. He won. He waited a few minutes, and bet a second bill on the red. Again he won. A third time he bet, apparently at random, and won still again.

He rose from the table, and beckoned to Tony. "Looks easy, doesn't it?"

Tony gazed into Bill's innocent face, noted the twinkle in his blue eyes, and smiled. "Why are you stopping?"

"Oh, I'm here for business—not for pleasure."

Drawing his friend into an inconspicuous corner, Bill extracted the roulettoscope from a capacious pocket, leveled it at the gaming table, and gazed through it intently.

"Does it work?" whispered Tony.

"Like a dream!" chortled Bill.

"Let me see."

Bill handed over the instrument. "First you focus it," he explained, then you press this lever, and when you're ready, you press the little button."

Tony followed directions, to witness nothing more than a brief flash, during which, for a fraction of a second, roulette wheel, croupier, and players were visible.

"Get it?" whispered Bill.

"Get what?"

"Can't you see the wheel's crooked?"

"No."

Bill nudged him violently. "Well, act as if you did. Floyd's coming this way."

The proprietor of the establishment sauntered in their direction with the dignity befitting his years and prosperity. Tall, erect, with a clean-shaven face and kindly eyes, he bore little resemblance to the popular conception of what a professional gambler should look like. Diamonds he wore galore: but the heavily waxed black mustache, the paunchy abdomen, and the huge cigars generally associated with the role were conspicuous by their absence. Such an appearance, Honest Jim Floyd knew only too well, would more readily repel than attract patrons. It might be in order in a Western mining camp; but in the metropolis it would be far too striking. He found it more profitable to cultivate the outward aspect of an elderly clergyman— if one can imagine a clergyman lavishly adorned with jewelry.

"Something new, Mr. Grant?" inquired Floyd, addressing Bill.

"A little invention of my own," said Parmelee. For obvious reasons he had thought it well to adopt a nom de guerre.

"And what do you do with it?"

Bill lowered his voice. "You point it at the roulette wheel while it's revolving, and then—"

"Yes?"

"If you know what to look for, sometimes you find it. Is that correct, Mr. Claghorn?"

Tony, who had not understood a word, nodded with owllike solemnity. "Yes, indeed," he asserted. "Very remarkable invention."

Honest Jim Floyd stretched out a hand. "May I?" he asked.

"Of course," said Bill, and explained the operation of the instrument.

Being a professional gambler, Jim Floyd had cultivated a poker face, and not a muscle in it moved as he gazed through the roulettoscope for what seemed an eternity to Tony. Time and again he set the lever; time and again he pressed the little button. His hand did not tremble as finally he lowered the apparatus from his eyes. "Very wonderful, Mr. Grant; very wonderful. Am I correct in assuming that this little instrument is for sale?"

"Of course."

Floyd bowed and waved his hand with dignity. "If you will walk into my office I will be glad to discuss the price with you."

Whitney Burnside, watching out of the corner of his eye, had expected nothing less than a hand-to-hand combat. He was immensely surprised as he saw Floyd and Parmelee, arm in arm, conversing amiably, stroll out of the room together. He was still more surprised when Tony, fifteen minutes later, whispered into his ear, "It's all over. Parmelee says you're to meet him at my apartment to-morrow morning."

WHEN ONE HAS looked forward to a sensational exposé, a quiet evening, unmarked by any unusual feature, is likely to be disappointing. Whitney Burnside felt it so. Waiting for the bomb to explode, he had not hesitated to play even more recklessly than usual—in the brief space of half an hour he had separated himself from some thousands of dollars—and then the bomb had not exploded. He had expected a grand climax, having for its central feature a ceremony in which Floyd would return to him the sum total of his losings. Feeling this, he had not hesitated to lose still more. And then the climax had failed to put in an appearance.

Whitney Burnside Was distinctly vexed as he applied his brakes with a screech and leaped from his car at the entrance to Tony's apartment. But his hopes revived as the elevator whisked him skyward. Perhaps the lovely sight of Honest Jim Floyd in handcuffs, with a detective on either side, might greet him. Perhaps the table in Tony's living room might be covered an inch deep with the yellowbacks with which Whitney had so reluctantly parted. Tony had said, "It's all over." Whitney's spirits rose an inch or so.

But no tableau greeted him as he entered the apartment. Instead, Bill, nodding a curt greeting, led him directly to a huge object occupying most of the room, and whisked aside a cloth. "Recognize it?" Bill inquired.

"Of course," said Whitney coldly. "It's a roulette table."

"Not a roulette table," corrected Bill; "it's the roulette table; the table at which you played last night. Sit down and I'll demonstrate. You're betting on red, let us say. Now watch!" A dozen times Bill spun the wheel; a dozen times the ball dropped into a black compartment. "Get it?"

"How many more times will black show up?" inquired Whitney, fascinated.

"As often as you want it to. Twenty times; fifty times; a hundred times."

"Then all I have to do is bet on black."

Silently Bill twirled the wheel, and for the first time the ball came to rest in a red pocket. "Betting on black wouldn't help you."

"But I could shift," persisted the slow-witted young millionaire. "I could bet on red and black alternately."

"And the ball would drop black and red alternately. Watch." Again he turned the wheel, and the ball, as if charmed, obeyed his directions. "You asked me to prove that Floyd's game was crooked. Have I proved it?"

"How is it done?" countered Whitney.

"Very simply. A roulette wheel is supposed to be divided into equal compartments by copper bands."

"This is."

"Yes; but here there are two sets of bands. One set is connected to the hub; the other set, and that includes every alternate band, is connected to the rim. And underneath the wheel, if you lift it out, you will find a neat little mechanism, controlled by a push button, which will turn the rim on the hub a fraction of an inch."

"But what difference can that make?"

Bill smiled patiently. "Very little—but enough. If I don't touch the button I have a fair wheel: a wheel on which every compartment is of exactly the same size. But if I do touch the button, the rim rotates on the hub just the least little bit, and the black compartments become just too small to let the ball drop into them. That's what happened every now and then when you had bet on black."

"And if I bet on red?"

"Then I touch another button, and the rim moves the other way. You see?"

Under Whitney's staring eyes the red compartments abruptly narrowed as the black opened.

"You couldn't force the ball into a red compartment with anything less than a hammer!" explained Bill.

Whitney frowned. "They could never have gotten away with that."

"Why not?"

"In the first place, I would have seen the croupier press the buttons. I watched him."

Bill laughed. "Of course you watched him. But you couldn't watch the electric wire which ran to these buttons, and the man who operated them—just often enough not to make you suspicious—in the next room! For your convenience, I've hooked the buttons close up to the table. Floyd used them on the end of a twenty-foot connection."

Again Whitney frowned. "Even that would have been too raw. Look: I can tell with my naked eye that the black compartments are wider than the red."

"But you can't tell if the wheel is revolving rapidly at the moment! Floyd took no chances: whenever the wheel was motionless you could have measured it and found nothing wrong. The buttons were pressed only when it was rotating—when the eye couldn't follow—and everything was all right again long before it stopped. As a device for winning, and for winning fast, I have yet to find its equal."

Tony broke into the conversation. "Tell him about your invention, Bill."

Bill smiled shyly. "I had heard of wheels like this, and I suspected I was looking at one when I first visited Floyd's. But suspecting and knowing are two different things. I had to prove my case, and prove it up to the hilt. It would have been easy if I could have examined the wheel—but something whispered that Floyd would never allow that. For the moment I was stumped, and then, suddenly, it occurred to me how to solve the problem: a fast camera would show the wheel motionless! Take an exposure of a five-hundredth of a second—a thousandth of a second—and the wheel, revolving at top speed, would appear to be still. It was a lovely idea," commented Bill, "and I thought I had my answer until it struck me that I would need a flash light to make a picture possible: that no plate on earth would register anything at all at such a speed without better lighting than Floyd provided. Once again, something whispered that Floyd wouldn't take kindly to a flash light. He wouldn't know what I was about, but he might be depended upon to raise objections.

"Then, at ten minutes of six in the morning, the final solution came to me. The human eye is a better camera than the best camera made. Equip a pair of binoculars with a photographic shutter. Get a flash of the wheel—a flash lasting only a thousandth of a second—and your eye will tell you if there's anything wrong!

"That's all there is to the story," concluded Bill, "except that I let Floyd look through the instrument, and Floyd, being a good sport, presented me with his roulette table in exchange for it."

Without a word Whitney seized his hat and stick and dashed for the door.

"Where are you going?" demanded Tony.

"Downtown, to clean out Floyd's!" He tore open the door, and dashed down the stairs three at a time.

"Stop him!" shouted Tony. "That stick of his is made of steel! He'll do murder with it!"

"Not on Floyd," rejoined Bill calmly. "Floyd's an old man. He's had his ups and downs, but what he's taken from Burnside in the last two weeks will support him the rest of his life.

He told me last night that it was time for him to retire—he came to that decision right after he looked through the roulet-toscope—and if he stuck to his plans he left New York on an early train this morning."

Tony gazed at Bill and grinned. "Are you thinking what I'm thinking?"

Bill nodded. "When Burnside finds that Floyd has left town—"

"He'll make a trip to his bank!"

"And stop that check a second time!" laughed Bill. "Lucky we cashed it yesterday, isn't it?"

5

A CASE OF CONSCIENCE

WE MIGHT AS well admit at the beginning that it was none of Tony Claghorn's business. Neither Turner nor Folwell had asked him to interfere, and the governors of the august Windsor Club, had they known what he was about at the outset, would have suppressed him decisively. In the sacred precincts of the Windsor Club such things simply didn't happen—couldn't happen—and Tony's rashness in believing otherwise would have called for disciplinary action under normal circumstances. But then, having admitted so much, we might as well add that the circumstances were not normal—far from it. To say the very least, they were decidedly queer.

When an old man, known to be rich, and a young man, known to be poor, play cards evening after evening, and when the old man rises from the table a substantial loser ninety-nine evenings out of a hundred, spectators have the right to be suspicious. That right Tony exercised to its fullest extent.

It is only fair to add, however, that Tony had gradually acquired a deep-rooted distrust of humanity. A year ago he had been different. A year ago he had taken honesty for granted, and had blamed the laws of chance for his occasional misfortunes. Then, in rapid succession had come a number of startling experiences. Bill Parmelee had cast a surprising light upon a variety of subjects. There were such things as marked cards, and devices by means of which marks

103

might unostentatiously be placed upon cards during the progress of a game. There were such things as hold-outs, mechanisms invented for the sole purpose of keeping one or more cards in concealment until their possessor found an opportunity to use them in his hand. There were even such things as doctored roulette wheels, trained to obey their owners, and singularly unresponsive to the desires of players who believed that a given color or number must sooner or later be a winner.

Tony had learned of these things, and had reacted profoundly. In the beginning, he had been merely surprised. Odd, he had reflected, that a player should resort to dubious methods. Skill by itself was reasonably sure of a reward. Cheating devices, strictly speaking, were not necessary.

Then, as revelation had succeeded revelation, Tony's attitude had changed completely. It became the natural thing for him to examine the backs of the cards with which he was to play. Had they been marked, he would probably never have discovered it. But having become suspicious, it became second nature to him to scrutinize the pasteboards with painstaking care. He could not do it too openly, or his curious attitude would have called for comment; but having acquired that dangerous possession—a little knowledge—Tony promptly proceeded to make the most of it.

If, at one of his clubs, he heard that a friend had lost heavily at poker, or at faro, or at roulette, Tony would find himself wondering what dishonest device had brought about that result; and if he heard that the same friend had won, Tony would corrugate his brows and inwardly debate the question whether his friend was or was not a sharper.

Sometimes he discussed these important matters with his very clever wife, to be laughed at for his pains.

"Wild goose chase, Tony," she would assure him again and again. "Men are naturally honest."

"Then how do you account for Sutliffe, and Schwartz, and Floyd?" demanded her husband.

Mrs. Claghorn laughed. "The flies gather where the honey is thickest."

"Meaning?"

"Meaning that a young man who is well supplied with money, like yourself, or almost any one of your friends, attracts other men who are not so well supplied. Even at that, only one of the three was trying to fleece you. The other two were going quietly about their business when you took a hand in their affairs."

"Going quietly about their business!" snorted Tony. "Schwartz was robbing Ted Wayland, and Floyd was robbing any fool who walked into his gambling house. That makes three sharpers I've met in a year. Three is a good many."

"In New York City," Mrs. Claghorn pointed out, "it's less than one in a million."

Tony grunted. Now a grunt is an argument very difficult to answer, and Mrs. Claghorn held her peace. "If you keep your eyes open," resumed her lord and master at length, "you see lots of queer things."

"And sometimes you'd be better off if you didn't see them. Try closing your eyes for a while. If you go around looking for trouble, Tony, you're pretty sure to find it."

If Tony had paid a lawyer for this excellent advice, he might have followed it. But having received it gratis from his wife, he did not take it too seriously.

That, perhaps, may explain how he blundered into what the three or four persons who know its details now refer to as the Turner-Folwell affair.

"IN THE BEGINNING, the Lord created the Windsor Club." Thus old man Carver, chairman of the House Committee, son of a member, grandson of two members, and father of two more members, would have amended the Bible. Old man Carver could have told you the exact date, as he could have told you the exact date of every event in the history of the select organization, but he preferred to leave it shrouded in mystery. The Windsor Club, one inferred, came into existence in the days when Indians and not traffic policemen dominated Fifth Avenue, when pounds sterling were displacing wampum as lawful currency, when Canal Street was a canal, and when the corner of Broadway and Forty-second Street was vastly less dangerous than it is to-day.

In those remote, but not forgotten times, a dozen men met one evening, looked upon one another with approval, constituted themselves into the Windsor Club, and invented the Waiting List. From time to time they added to their membership individuals who, like themselves, traced their ancestry to the Mayflower, and had been rich so long that mere money meant nothing whatever to them; but it was not many months before aspirants were relegated to places at the tail end of an ever-lengthening line, and were elected, sometimes, after they had shuffled off their mortal coils.

"Most amusing, most amusing," old man Carver would relate. "In 1806—or was it in 1805?—Godfrey Pinckney was elected to membership, and by George, he'd been dead half a dozen years by then! I found it in the minutes."

"And what did they do then, sir?" inquired the youngest member respectfully.

"Well," chuckled old man Carver, "they couldn't bring him back to life, though I do believe that if they'd gone down to Trinity Churchyard and whispered the glad news at a certain tombstone, Godfrey Pinckney would have jumped right out of his grave, brushed up his beaver hat, and paid his initiation fee. The Membership Committee, however, took the case under advisement, and in view of the unusual circumstances, advanced Godfrey Pinckney, Junior, ten numbers on the waiting list, with the result that he was elected before the War of 1812."

Tony Claghorn was a member, having been put up at the ripe age of twenty-four hours by his proud father, and having been elected upon his thirty-first birthday, but Denton Thomas, who had made a fortune in steel, had been politely discouraged by the inflexible Mr. Carver.

"I'd propose you," declared the latter, "because you're a nice chap and desirable in nearly every way. But it wouldn't do any good. Even if the Membership Committee got around to you during your lifetime, which is unlikely, you might not be elected."

"And why not?" demanded the outraged Mr. Thomas. His newly acquired money had opened many doors to him. Surely this door too might be opened.

Mr. Carver shrugged his shoulders ever so lightly. "You're rich, aren't you?" he inquired.

"Immensely."

"Well, by and by you'll manage to forget that, and that will make you more desirable. You're a nice chap," he admitted, "but you—shall we say—you lack background. Now your son—"

"I'm a bachelor and I have no children," interrupted Mr. Thomas.

"Your son," pursued Mr. Carver, "would stand a reasonably good chance of election. If I were you, I think I'd get married."

Episodes such as these explained why the members valued their memberships. To be proposed was a compliment. To be elected was an honor so overwhelming that many never recovered from the shock. Of an evening a decorous company would move with hushed voices through the vast clubrooms, thoughtfully located on one of the most expensive Fifth Avenue corners. Friends would greet each other with proper solemnity, rejoicing in the fact that both had been chosen into this select body, and portraits of dead and gone Governors, looking down from the walls, invested the scene with impressive dignity.

In a quiet corner a pair of members might be seen indulging in a game of chess. In other corners one would find cribbage, bridge, and checkers. In still another corner, Phil Turner, whose grandfather had been enormously wealthy, whose father had been merely rich, and who, himself, was rather less than comfortable, would be discovered, four nights a week, playing casino with Ramsey Folwell, more than twice his age, and shareholder in so many corporations that a card index was necessary to refresh his memory.

Turner, like Claghorn, had been proposed for membership in the Club at his birth, and had been duly elected thirty-one years later. But in the interim the fortunes of his family had suffered a sad decline. The Turners were no longer millionaires. Turner's father, once in control of the family inheritance, had exhibited only a talent for diminishing it, and had exercised it to such good purpose that upon his death, which took place when Philip had been a member of the Club for two years, the estate consisted of a choice assortment of wildcats. A single parcel of land, which for some unknown reason his father had refrained from selling, brought Philip enough income to pay his dues at the Windsor. For the rest, he spent his days perched on a bookkeeper's chair, and earned barely sufficient to keep his wife and child.

He might have resigned from the Windsor: might have saved the amount which it cost him each year. But members valued membership too highly to think of resigning, and Philip was quite regular in his attendance. To him the Windsor represented the last shred of the one-time glory of his family. He clung to it savagely.

And then Tony Claghorn, chatting with a fellow member, heard the interesting news that Phil Turner's winnings at casino averaged not less than fifty dollars an evening, and Tony Claghorn began thinking....

NOW A TRAIN of thought is a dangerous train to board, for it may lead almost anywhere, and one has no assurance that its destination will meet with the passenger's approval. Yet Tony, having picked up a starting point, began more or less automatically to follow it towards its logical conclusion.

If a rich man and a poor man played cards together, and if the rich man lost, not most of the time but all of the time, skill might account for it, and then again, skill might not.

Old man Carver, who saw everything, heard everything, and knew everything, had learned months ago of the regularity of Folwell's losses, and had commented: "If Ramsey is a loser, he can afford it better than most men. Ramsey Folwell has ten millions if he has a cent. He wouldn't have to go to the poor-house if he lost ten times as much, no, nor a hundred times as much for that matter. Why, Ramsey's income must be close to ten thousand a week, and nothing that he's likely to do will make much of a dent in that."

Tony had heard, and had reflected that Phil Turner's income, barring his winnings from Folwell, was probably close to nothing a week, and that the sums which Folwell parted with periodically represented a larger revenue than Turner had ever been able to earn legitimately. If Turner had been content to win once in a while, Tony decided, there would have been no objection. But to win steadily, consistently, with never a Joss thrown in, was raw stuff.

Tony mulled the matter over, and came to the conclusion that Folwell, millionaire though he was, needed help. Magnanimously Tony elected himself a committee of rescue. Functioning in that capacity he pulled up a chair one evening, and invited himself to watch the game. "You don't mind if I look on?" he inquired after making himself comfortable at Folwell's side.

"Not at all," replied the aged millionaire. "In fact, I'm very glad to have you watch. I've never understood why the average man takes so great an interest in bridge or in poker, when casino, played as it should be played, is a far better game. Isn't that so, Philip?"

Being a steady winner at the game, Turner might well have been gracious. Yet he merely grunted "Umph!" and shuffled the cards carefully.

"I've seen you playing in this corner evening after evening," pursued Tony, undaunted by Turner's barely repressed hostility, "and I'm curious to see what there is to the game." He ventured a carefully calculated remark; "I take it that you break even most of the time?"

Folwell shook his head. "Mr. Turner is a very strong player. I'm improving, and in time to come I may be able to make it more interesting for him. But just now I'm learning the fine points."

"You've been playing many years."

"Playing at the game, perhaps, but not playing it," corrected Folwell, "but I think I'm getting better. Don't you think so, Philip?"

Without replying Turner laid down the ten of diamonds, the "big casino," as it is called, capturing a seven and a three on the table, and turning the last card face up to mark a sweep. "That makes three points," he announced.

"Two points for the big casino," explained Folwell, "and one point for the sweep. The game is thirty points."

Tony watched in silence as the game proceeded. When the deck had been exhausted Folwell glanced through the cards he had taken in and announced: "I have spades, little casino, and two aces. Four points. Mr. Turner has the rest: seven points."

"And two sweeps," corrected Turner.

"Nine points in all," amended Folwell. He turned genially to Tony. "Are you beginning to understand the game, Mr. Claghorn?"

Tony nodded as the players shifted chips from left to right to indicate the score. "And this keeps up until one of you has thirty points?"

"Until Mr. Turner has thirty points. You see, he leads twenty-eight to twelve already."

Turner annexed the two points he needed in less than that many minutes, and Tony fell to studying the two men while game followed game. The contrast could not have been more marked. Folwell, past his seventieth year, was a gentleman of the old school, dignified, courteous, genial, unobtrusive. The kindly outlines of his fine face were accentuated by a silvery beard and mustache; and near the corners of his eyes, close-gathered wrinkles testified to the existence of a sense of humor which had survived the passing of the years. There was something very lovable about the million-aire, and Tony felt himself warming to him.

To Turner, his reaction was diametrically opposite. Thirty-five or so, tall, powerful, and ungainly, his clean-shaven lips were set in a fixed scowl, and a mop of disordered black hair, surmounting craggy, eyebrows, deep-set eyes, and a hook of a nose, made him even more unprepossessing. There was character of a kind to his face; but Tony knew that he was right when he set it down mentally as the visage of a disappointed man. Life had been none too generous to Philip Turner; he had but rarely emerged the victor in his battles with it, and the sullenness written large upon his expression was a page of biography to any observer who could read.

Tony marveled as he studied the two men; noted how slowly and deliberately Folwell shuffled, how rapidly, yet carefully Turner manipulated the cards when it became his turn. On one side of the table an old-time aristocrat was meeting defeat with gracious sportsmanship; on the other side a man half his age was winning greedily—even rapaciously.

At ten o'clock to the minute Folwell pushed his chair away from the table, glanced at the score, and passed three twenty-dollar bills to his adversary. "Correct?"

"Yes," grunted Turner. He did not add a word of thanks.

Folwell bowed to Tony. "It's been so good of you to watch our little game. I hope we can make you a convert to it. And now, gentlemen, good night."

"How about a hand or two?" invited Tony after the old gentleman had departed.

"No," said Turner curtly, "I've got a long way to go home." He rose, buttoned his coat, nodded, and stalked out.

Tony smiled, and riffled through the cards which the adversaries had left behind them. "According to the laws of chance," he soliloquized, "certain things should have happened. I wonder why they didn't?"

Unfortunately for him Chet Moulton chose that moment to pass by and overheard Tony mumbling. "What did you say?" he queried.

Now Moulton had a reputation as a talebearer, and Tony knew it, yet with great unwisdom he repeated his observation.

"My God, Claghorn!" ejaculated Moulton, "you don't mean to accuse Phil Turner of cheating!"

"I don't know what I mean," confessed Tony unhappily.

"This is the Windsor Club!" declared Moulton. "Such things have never happened here."

"But that doesn't prove," persisted Tony, "that they couldn't happen."

"Under this roof?"

"Under any roof."

"Why, it's impossible!"

"In this world," declared Tony, "nothing—nothing at all—is impossible."

He gave himself up to wild speculations as Moulton retreated to another room, and he was still busy with them when a page summoned him to an interview with old man Carver, chairman of the House Committee.

Carver came straight to the point. "Mr. Claghorn, I understand you have made serious charges against one of the members of this club?"

"Er—yes," admitted Tony.

Old man Carver's lips set in a straight line. With the honor of the Windsor Club at stake, he knew no mercy. "Either you will substantiate those charges, Mr. Claghorn, or—"

"Or?"

"Or, as a friend, I should advise you to resign."

Mastering the icy feeling which suddenly manifested itself in the neighborhood of his heart Tony demanded "What chance have I to prove my case if Chet Moulton is going to talk?"

"Mr. Moulton will do no more talking than he has already done. I give you my word on that." Old man Carver rose slowly. "Let me know your decision within a week, Mr. Claghorn. That is all."

TONY WALKED HOME feeling thoroughly depressed. He had followed his train of thought, and it had led him straight into a large batch of Class A trouble. To elect himself Folwell's protector was one thing: to hazard his precious membership in the Windsor merely to save Folwell money which he did not need and would never miss was quite another matter. That the game which he had just witnessed had had several unusual features, Tony felt sure; but to prove that accusation to old man Carver's satisfaction might not be the easiest task in the world. Cold shivers ran down Tony's back as it occurred to him that

Turner, suddenly grown wary, might play strictly according to Hoyle upon the next occasion; that Chet Moulton, despite old man Carver's assurance, might do some fatal talking; that Folwell, being aged, might be taken sick—might even die—before another session. All of these events were among the possibilities, and from none of them could Tony extract the slightest comfort. It came to him abruptly that he had bitten off more than he could chew; that blinded by self-confidence, he had committed himself to a course from which there could be no retreat, and yet, upon which he might make little head-way.

He extracted his latchkey at the door of his apartment firmly resolved to throw himself upon the mercy of his wife, whose cautions he had disregarded, yet whose advice, even at this late stage, might perform miracles. Then, with his key actually in the lock, he stopped as if shot. From the interior of the apartment came the sounds of conversation.

"Thought I'd run down to the city for a day or two," declared a familiar voice, "the chicken show is on now, and I want to buy some breeding stock."

Tony plunged into the room without more ado. "Bill!" he shouted jubilantly. "Oh, Bill!"

William Parmelee, Esquire, farmer, dairyman, chicken raiser, and ex-gambler, rose to his feet and extended his hand. "I hoped I'd be welcome when I dropped in to visit you, Tony, but I didn't expect you to fall on my neck like a long-lost brother!"

"Bill," exulted Tony, "you're a sight for sore eyes! Why, you're the one man in all the world I want to see this very minute!"

Parmelee smiled happily. "Oh, you want me to explain something about farming, don't you?"

"I don't! I want you to pull me out of a hole, that's what I want!"

Pretty Mrs. Claghorn turned surprised eyes upon her husband. "Tony, have you gotten into another hole?" she inquired. "You promised—"

"I didn't break any promises," Tony assured her, "but I'm in a hole all right. It's different—from the last one—and the one before that. It's deeper—and wider—and more uncomfortable—"

Bill interrupted. "Stop rambling," he invited, "and come down to brass tacks. How have you been getting yourself into mischief again?" His face was serious, but his blue eyes twinkled.

Tony blushed. In the interests of truth this must be recorded. Then, assisted by an occasional question from his audience, he unburdened himself of his story. "You see, it all happened because I wanted to help Folwell," he wound up lamely.

Pretty Mrs. Claghorn threw back her head and laughed— laughed until the tears stood in her eyes.

"Millie!" Tony reproved sharply.

"I know—oh, I know it's anything but funny—your risking your membership in the Windsor," gasped Mrs. Claghorn, "but the idea of your helping anybody—"

"Why not?" bristled Tony.

"When you invariably get into trouble ten times worse yourself! You're the best-natured, best-hearted, most lovable man in the world, but I know that if you tried to help a blind man across the street, you'd have your pocket picked before you reached the other side, and if you ever attempted to save somebody from drowning, you'd have your leg bitten off by a shark!

Why, Tony, dear, don't you realize that you always need help more than the people you try to rescue?"

Bill laughed. "He realizes that after he's in so far that he can't back out."

"I don't want to back out," declared Tony, "I'm convinced that that game wasn't on the level."

Parmelee's face became suddenly serious. "Old man," he said, "I don't want to scare you too much at the outset, but has it ever occurred to you how immensely difficult it must be to cheat in a card game in which the entire pack is dealt out? In poker all of the cards aren't used, and if you put two or three in a hold-out, nobody will know the difference; but in casino you go straight through the deck, and just one card removed from it will make the deal come out wrong. Didn't that ever strike you?"

"If a man is clever enough to remove a card he's clever enough to put it back."

"Yes—if it happens to be his deal."

"And if it isn't his deal, he could stack the cards while he's cutting them."

Bill shook his head. "I was a professional gambler for six years, and I can do 'most anything with cards but make them talk; but I can't stack a deck on the other fellow's deal. If things break right, I can bring the card I want to the top, but it would come out on the very first hand in a game like casino, and I wouldn't dare take the chance more than once or twice in an evening."

"Once or twice would be enough."

"In poker—not in casino. In poker, you can make the other fellows bet high. In casino, you're playing a long-winded game and settling on the points. And don't forget: even if you could put any card you wanted in your own hand, it mightn't do any good—the wrong combination of cards might be exposed on the table."

"But suppose," persisted Tony, "on your deal, that you cheated at the right time."

"It's an even bet that it would be a waste of time. The other man plays first."

Tony made a rueful face. "I knew I was in trouble. All you're telling me is that it's worse than I thought."

Parmelee slapped his woebegone friend on the shoulder. "Cheer up!" he adjured, "you may come out on top. If a man wins a hundred times out of a hundred, and his opponent isn't an absolute dub, something's awfully funny. I think I'll let you take me to the Windsor the next time they play."

IF POSSIBLE, TURNER was less friendly than usual, while Folwell, as always, was his affable self. "I'm glad to see that our game is attracting so much interest," declared the old man. "If I had my way, casino would be the only card game played in this club. It's the only game that I've really enjoyed all my life. No matter how much you learn about it, there's always a little more that you can learn. Isn't that so, Philip?"

"I suppose so," grunted Turner.

Parmelee studied the suspect with interest. He was curiously dressed. His suit, of excellent quality, was spotless. But closer inspection revealed that it was far from new, and that it had been brushed within an inch of its life. His shoes, of fashionable cut, and polished so that they shone, were worn thin on the soles—so Bill's quick eye detected—and were probably as aged as the suit. His linen, faultlessly clean, and plainly expensive when new, was near the end of its wearing powers. Turner's gaunt collar bones, Bill predicted mentally, would break through what was left of his shirt after it had made another trip to the laundry.

Once the man had been prosperous—that everything about him proclaimed—but the last five or six years, by the same token, had witnessed painfully hard sledding. The income that the game provided meant more than a little to him, so Bill decided almost instantaneously.

Folwell turned graciously to the man from the country. "Do you play?" he inquired.

"I learnt casino when I was a boy," Bill admitted, "but it's been many years since I've taken part in a game. You see, I'm a farmer, and when night comes, I'm too tired to play cards."

"You would find a game an occasional relaxation."

"Relaxation?" laughed Bill. "When you know you'll have to be up at sunrise, there's nothing to beat bed! I may not know all there is to know about cards"—it was a carefully calculated confession—"but when it comes to sleeping, plain and fancy, short and long distance, cat-nap and marathon, I'm a champion of champions!"

Tony's expression was unconcerned, but inwardly he was far from easy. Turner was no simpleton. With a stranger at hand, he might play a scrupulously honest game. It would be so easy to bide his time and await a safer opportunity. Claghorn had watched, and had returned with a friend: the circumstance was suspicious. Turner could hardly fail to take cognizance of it.

"A beautiful game," Folwell proclaimed, never tired of his subject, "not bewildering—like bridge, and not just a gambling game—like poker; but a game with fine points all its own, a game that seems almost too simple—until you try it, and find that it's anything but simple." He offered the pack for the cut, and proceeded with his deal. "I don't know how many games I've played in the course of my life—it must be tens of thousands—but I'm always ready to play more."

Tony, riveting his glance on Turner, felt his sympathy surging hot for his opponent. Turner, silent, concentrating his energies upon the game, was winning quite as rapidly as usual, while his unsuspecting victim, a true sportsman, was losing with the best of good grace. It was all wrong, yet—and Tony's hair stood on end at the thought—it might not be all wrong. Turner might be benefiting by some unparalleled stroke of luck, some unheard of run of the cards.

He stole a covert glance at Bill, who was apparently immersed in the game; caught his eyes for the fraction of a second, and saw nothing reassuring in them. In an agony he felt, rather than saw, old man Carver watching from a corner across the room, and wondered if the Windsor Club was to know him no more. He had watched Turner's every movement; he was sure that not his slightest action had escaped him; yet if Tony had been compelled to go on the witness stand that instant, he would have been forced to swear that he had observed nothing contrary to the rules of any game.

He was silent as Folwell continued his incessant chatter; as Bill answered him from time to time; as Turner, sticking strictly to the business in hand, added momentarily to his winnings. He felt himself swelling with hatred for the impecunious young man who won so mysteriously, yet so consistently. Through some unexplained process Turner had held the biggest card in the game—the ten of diamonds—four out of the five times it had turned up in the evening, and had made it good by taking a trick with it each of those times. The laws of chance doubtless permitted such a run of cards; but precisely the same thing had taken place upon the only other evening that Tony had been present, and he debated hotly with himself whether any laws could account for so strange a series of happenings.

He glanced at his watch anxiously as nine o'clock passed and ten o'clock neared. The game would soon be over, and he would learn the worst.

Then, as the minute hand crept relentlessly over the quarter-hour mark, Bill rose, apologized, and led his friend across the room.

"Well?" gasped Tony.

"Well?"

"Is Turner honest?" he demanded.

"Honest as the day is long," said Bill.

Tony felt his heart leaping violently into his mouth. "Then I'm done for," he ejaculated.

Quite incomprehensibly, Bill shook his head.

IN THE PRIVACY of a committee room, old man Carver, fiercely belligerent under his impassive exterior, faced the conspirators and demanded: "Gentlemen, have you any proof to lay before me?"

Bill's twinkling blue eyes were serious. "We have proof: proof, that is to say, which is satisfactory to me, but which may be far from satisfactory to you." Silently old man Carver waited for him to continue. "If you will allow me to handle this in my own way"—Carver nodded—"I'll begin, if you don't mind, by asking Mr. Folwell to join us here."

"Why not Mr. Turner?"

"Mr. Folwell, as the loser, has the right to hear my conclusions first. It rests with him to decide what action, if any, is to be taken."

"It rests with me, Mr. Parmelee," corrected Carver incisively.

"Even so I should like to see Mr. Folwell first."

Without a word Carver touched a button. "Present my compliments to Mr. Folwell," he instructed the page who answered, "and ask him if he will be so kind as to join me in this room for a few minutes." He turned aggressively to Bill. "Let us understand each other at the outset, Mr. Parmelee. At your request, I shall permit you to handle this matter as you please; to present what proof you will, in your own way. But when you are through, I shall say what further steps shall be taken."

"That is more than satisfactory," Bill hastened to say.

Carver nodded. The matter touched the honor of the Windsor Club, and that lay very near to the old man's heart. No bereavement, no business reverse, no other calamity of any kind could have touched him on a tenderer spot.

He greeted Folwell when the aged millionaire appeared, and motioned him to a chair. "You have met Mr. Parmelee?"

"Why, of course."

Old man Carver turned to Bill. "Will you proceed, sir?" he invited.

Bill wasted no time in beating around the bush. "Mr. Folwell," he demanded, "what would you say if I told you that you have just been playing in a dishonest game?"

Tony, listening to every word, could not believe his ears. Barely five minutes ago Bill had vouched for Turner's honesty; yet he was now contradicting himself flatly.

Folwell's eyes had contracted ever so slightly. If the question came as a shock, he bore it with admirable self-control. "And do you say that I have been playing in a dishonest game?" he countered.

"I do."

"Then I answer, Mr. Parmelee, that you don't know what you're talking about."

Bill smiled. "To-night I kept count of the number of times that the ten of diamonds—counting two points—appeared in your opponent's hand."

"Phil Turner is the very soul of honor!" declared Folwell. "I'd trust him with—"

Calmly Bill interrupted. "A few nights ago my friend, Mr. Claghorn, kept count of the number of times the same thing happened."

"But I tell you that Phil Turner is above suspicion!"

"Even before that," Bill fabricated glibly, "other members of the club had noticed how often the ten of diamonds—the big casino—came to Turner, and how seldom it came to you."

"What of that?" stammered Folwell. His composure was beginning to be shaken.

"If it happened three out of five times, Mr. Folwell, I should say, 'Luck.' Even if it happened seven out of ten times, I should say, 'Luck.' But when it happens so often that it is the rule, and not the exception, I say—"

"What do you say?"

"I say that somebody, if he wants to, can shed some light on the subject."

Folwell glanced anxiously from one face to another. "I have told you that Phil Turner is the very soul of honor."

"I don't need that assurance, Mr. Folwell."

"No?"

"I watched the game closely. If Mr. Turner had made one questionable move, I would have seen it."

A tinge of incredulity crept into Folwell's voice. "You would have seen it?" he challenged.

"Before I became a farmer," Bill explained, "I made a tolerable living as a professional gambler. I am familiar with every cheating device known in the United States, and I am willing to take my oath that Mr. Turner used none of them."

Folwell was rapidly regaining his composure. "In that event," he suggested, "it is hardly necessary for us to go further. You admit that Mr. Turner played an honest game, and I, as the loser, have no complaint to make."

"Yet," persisted Bill, "yet the game was dishonest!"

Tony stared at him in surprise. His brain was whirling. Opposite him old man Carver, with an unlighted cigar in his hand, was as motionless as a statue.

Folwell laughed uneasily. "Perhaps you will explain how that is possible, Mr. Parmelee," he begged.

"Do you really want me to?" Bill's voice became very gentle. "Mr. Folwell, we are four men in this room, and believe me, we are all your friends. Whatever you choose to say will go no further—that I can pledge you—and the explanation, since it has to come, would come more gracefully from you than from me."

For a minute—two minutes—the aged millionaire pondered. Then, and it came to Tony as an overwhelming surprise, he inquired simply, "Mr. Parmelee, did you actually see me cheat?"

Bill shook his head. "I didn't see it. I inferred it."

OLD MAN CARVER was nearly as much astonished as was Tony. Indeed, he said of it afterwards: "If a regiment of purple angels, with wings, patent-leather shoes and horn-rimmed spectacles, had marched into the room to the tune of 'Hiawatha,' I wouldn't have been more flabbergasted!" Being discreet, and being as close-mouthed as the grave itself, old man Carver made this remark to his own image, as reflected in his shaving mirror, and to no other living soul.

But upon the occasion itself old man Carver looked at Folwell, dropped his cigar unheeded to the floor, and gasped, "Ramsey—you cheated?"

"Yes," admitted Folwell, "I cheated."

"And in spite of it, you lost."

Bill broke vigorously into the conversation. "You're wrong, Mr. Carver," he pointed out, "because of it he lost. Mr. Folwell wanted to lose. He couldn't lose fast enough by ordinarily poor play, so he managed to lose by extraordinarily sharp play."

Folwell nodded. "It's a long story, gentlemen," he prefaced, "but I hope I can make you understand. When a man does what I have done, there is a reason for it, and usually a very good reason. Mine—I think you will agree—was sufficient.

"Years ago—my old friend Carver probably knows this, but you young men weren't born then—Phil Turner's father and I were mixed up in business deals together. We owned properties in common. We put money into the same enterprises. We operated in a variety of ways for joint account. We lost sometimes, but far oftener we made, and we made a great deal.

"I shall not bore you gentlemen with details. I, myself, do not like to think back to the event which ended our partnership and cost me one of my best friends. Perhaps it will be enough if I say that I made a certain transaction for my own account solely, when fairness, justice, even decency would have given Turner half of an enormous profit. What I did was not illegal; it was not dishonest; it was not contrary to any written agreements in force between us at the time. But that does not alter the fact that it was not right, and that I knew it was not right.

"Gentlemen, explain it as you will—I know I have tried to explain it to myself many times—for the sake of a few paltry dollars which I did not need, and would never have missed, I treated my friend shabbily, and then he was my friend no longer."

Folwell paused. The silent men about him asked no question. Presently he continued.

"If my former partner had prospered as I did, I might have thought no more about it. But without my conservatism to check his rashness, he went from bad to worse. We had both been rich men. I doubled and tripled my fortune. He threw his away in unwise speculation. Sometimes I think that his experience with me broke his faith in human nature, and helped bring about his downfall. I do know that when he died, a few years ago, he left a pitifully small estate to his son, and I know also that while he lived, he never mentioned my name to him. When I met Phil at the club, I found that he had heard of me, but not through his father. Gentlemen, that hurt; that hurt bitterly!

"Then I found out all about Phil; found he was in straitened circumstances; found that he was having the greatest difficulty in making both ends meet, and I made up my mind to pay off my debt to the father by helping the son. A satisfying resolution, once I had made it, but how was I to carry it into effect? The boy was proud as Lucifer. If I had offered him money, he wouldn't have taken it. I did go so far as to put a thousand-dollar bill in an envelope, and send it to him through the mail. He opened a savings bank account as trustee—trustee, mind you—of the unknown owner of the money, and he hasn't touched a cent of it from that day to this!

"When I found he played casino, I gradually got him to increase the stakes, and I tried to lose to him. Gentlemen, it was difficult. I am a natural-born card player—my friend Carver will tell you of the games I used to sit in in my salad days—and Phil, poor boy, is the worst player I have ever met. I gave him opportunities. He simply didn't see them. Play as badly as I might, Phil was sure to play worse.

"And then, one evening, I remembered a feat of legerdemain I had mastered as a boy, and I palmed the big casino, the ten of diamonds, and gave it to Phil at a time when even he couldn't help making it. It worked so well that I repeated it—and got him to increase the stakes still more.

"Gentlemen, Phil isn't stupid, but he knows nothing about cards, and even after playing with me night after night he hasn't learnt enough to hold his own in an average game. He sits at the card table, and he thinks of his wife and child—thinks of the comforts which his winnings will buy for them—and doesn't realize that there is not another man in the world from whom he could win a cent at anything!

"You have watched him. Doubtless you think he is concentrated on the game. He is, in a way, a very peculiar way. He makes a sweep, and says to himself, 'Shoes for the baby,' takes in an ace, and notes that it will help to pay the doctor's bill, wins the big casino, and remembers his wife needs a new coat. It's funny, isn't it? Laughable? But somehow I find it infinitely pathetic. Phil always knows just how many points he's won—but that's about all he knows. Why, you may not believe it, but one evening I won the big casino by accident, slipped it out of my cards, and dealt it to Phil on the next hand, and he never noticed! To make the deck come out even I had to remove a king at the end. He never noticed that either!

"Gentlemen, this has been going on for some time. Phil has been costing me about two hundred dollars a week. I wish I had been able to make him increase the stakes still further, so that he would cost me more, but he's afraid: thinks luck may turn, so that he will lose some night. He doesn't want that to happen.

"You may ask where this is bound to lead; whether I expect to continue cheating myself forever. I would like nothing better, but there is always the danger that spectators—men like yourselves—may sympathize with the old gentleman who is being victimized by a card sharp, and I don't want to ruin Philip's reputation!"

He turned to Bill.

"It was easy for me to cheat while you watched, Mr. Parmelee. You, of course, were watching the winner. Nobody ever thinks of watching the loser."

"Quite so," assented Bill.

"So I practiced my legerdemain," gloated the aged millionaire, "quite unobserved! I am flattered to think that even an expert like yourself saw nothing out of the way!

"But to return to the subject: our little game of casino will not last much longer. Looking about for a good investment, I have acquired a controlling interest in the corporation which employs Phil, and 'round about Christmas he is going to be promoted. As assistant treasurer, with a salary which I shall fix myself, he will have a nice start, and if he makes good, as I know he will, there'll be no stopping him. I'll fire every man between him and the presidency, if necessary, until he reaches it, and when I die, Phil will find my controlling interest bequeathed to him.

"Gentlemen, that is my confession. I am a card cheat. What is your verdict?"

Old man Carver leaped to his feet. "Ramsey, you old scoundrel," he commanded, "I want you to do me the honor of shaking my hand!"

BILL AND TONY walked uptown together.

It was Tony who broke a protracted silence. "From now on," he declared, "I think I'll understand the real meaning of the word 'gentleman'!"

Bill nodded.

"Pretty fine, eh, what?" said Tony. "All wool and a yard wide—twenty-four carats—first water—the real thing and no imitation," he continued, mixing his metaphors happily. "I don't believe that what he did to Turner's father years ago was wrong—whatever it was!"

Again Bill nodded.

"But there's one thing that's puzzling me," pursued Tony, "he palmed a card and topped the deck with it, and you never caught him. He had to tell you how he did it."

"That's what he thinks," Bill agreed.

"Do you mean to say," Tony gasped, "that—"

Bill smiled. "Would it have made the old man any happier if I had told him that his work was amateurish? That I saw what he was doing the first time he tried it?

"Tony, old fellow, do you know that one of the biggest financiers alive is proud of his ability to bend his fingers back until they touch his wrist? Do you know that the president of a transcontinental railroad blows that he can walk a mile on a steel rail without falling off? There's a lot of the child in each one of us. Folwell and his legerdemain: why, he treasures that more than he does a million dollars!

"I'd take a million from him if I could do it," quoth Bill, "but before I'd take away his belief that he's the greatest little conjurer that ever topped a deck, I'd steal pennies from a baby!"

6

TONY SITS IN

THE WIND WHISTLED down the chimney, and the birch logs blazing in the old-fashioned fireplace sent up ruddy bursts of flame.

Bill Parmelee, one-time gambler, would-be farmer, and now, despite his will, corrector of destinies and terror of his former associates, gazed happily into the fire and murmured, "Tony, old man, this is the life!"

Chance, which had once flung Bill into the ranks of the sharpers, which had allowed him, for six long years, to lead a precarious life by ingeniously circumventing rules made for the guidance of others, had had its revenge by picking him up and dropping him upon another square of the human chessboard. Wherefore Bill, reformed, and possessing an encyclopedic knowledge of the devices by whose aid games of chance may be made less risky for the person employing them, had become a most formidable antagonist of the shifty gentlemen who persisted in supplementing their natural skill by unostentatious sleight of hand.

There had been the case of Sutliffe, who, by the use of a little instrument known as a poker ring, had separated Tony Claghorn from his income quite as rapidly as it rolled in; and there had been the case of one Schwartz, who had relied chiefly upon the machine known as the Kepplinger holdout, and there had been the case of Floyd, whose roulette wheel had possessed almost human intelligence; and besides these there had been many others. But Bill, equipped with an unparalleled knowledge of cheating devices, and himself an expert in the art of legerdemain, had come, like an avenging angel, to the aid of honesty in distress, and had exposed the sharpers with what had seemed ridiculous ease. His innocent expression, his twinkling blue eyes, his youthful features, his countrified air had deluded his victims into a sense of false security; his career, as the champion of fair play, had been a march from one success to another.

Yet Bill found little satisfaction in the role that had been forced upon him. Six years spent in the pursuit of fortune at cards, at roulette, at faro, at every gambling game to be found anywhere, had satisfied—more than satisfied—his every aspiration in that direction. Brought home by an accident, set upon a new track by another accident, he had turned to farming wholeheartedly—and had enjoyed it. In the beginning, doubtless, it was the novelty that had attracted him. But when the novelty had worn off he found himself engaged in an occupation which gave his intelligence almost unlimited scope. To make a blade of grass grow where none had grown before, to breed better cows and hogs, to contribute his share to the well-being of mankind: these were ambitions which were so intensely worth while that he was content to give himself up to them.

Even the winter evenings, when the windows were frosted over and the mercury shriveled up in the ball of the thermometer were filled with satisfaction for Bill. With his aged father smoking his pipe and looking dreamily into the fire, and Tony Claghorn, his best friend, whom months of persuasion had finally induced to try a winter week-end in the country, at his side, Bill found himself filled with contentment.

"This is the life!" he repeated.

Tony, sitting so close to the fire that his clothing was in danger of bursting into flame, cast a glance through the window at the thickly falling snow. "And they called Peary a hero!" he murmured.

"What did you say?" Bill inquired.

"Miles and miles through snow and ice," raved Tony, "but he didn't have to go to the north pole for it. He could have gone to West Woods, Connecticut. By George! I never knew how much snow there was in the world."

John Parmelee smiled. "You should have been here thirty-six years ago, in the winter of 'eighty-eight. We had real snow that year. This," and he waved his hand at the flakes falling densely over the whitened meadows, "this is what we call an open winter."

Tony refused to be comforted. "Never—never in all my life did I expect to find so much cold weather—all in one place. It wouldn't be so bad if it were sprinkled here and there; if it would stop snowing for an hour or so, once in a while. But that's just the trouble with your Connecticut weather: once it's begun, it doesn't know when to leave off. It was cold when I got here; and it's been getting colder ever since; and the end doesn't seem to be in sight."

"If you wait until May—" suggested Bill.

"I'll be frozen before then!" said Tony.

The crystalline tinkling of sleigh bells announced the belated arrival of the postman. Bill rose energetically. "Maybe the mail will cheer you up, Tony."

"More of the same kind?" inquired the New Yorker without turning his head.

"It looks like it."

With obvious disapproval Bill pawed over the half dozen letters, tore them open, and glanced impatiently at their contents.

"Well?" murmured Tony.

Bill made a wry face. "Tony, old man, you've been advertising me too much. Here's a letter from Philadelphia: they want me to have a look at a roulette wheel. Here's another from New York: somebody who forgets to sign his name wants to know if I can tell him where to buy a holdout. He doesn't want to use it to cheat, he says. He just wants to use it to make some experiments. Tony, do you get a mental picture of the experiments?"

Tony laughed. "What are the rest like?"

"A woman who uses violet-scented paper wonders if I could be induced to take part in a bridge game which she considers suspicious. She doesn't like to mention names, but she tells me in confidence that a prominent society woman is altogether too lucky with cards. She wouldn't accuse her of anything dishonest for the world—but what are my charges for investigating the case?"

"Go on," chuckled Tony.

Bill smoothed out a crumpled sheet.

"A young man—age eighteen, so he says—wants my expert opinion. Is it—or is it not—possible to cheat at checkers?"

Tony roared.

"Thanking me, and assuring me that he will be glad to reciprocate any time," concluded Bill, "he remains my very truly yours." Bill crumpled up the letter and flung it into the fire. "Now I ask you, how can you answer a question like that?"

"You've still got one left," said Tony, indicating an unopened letter.

"I'm not even going to read it," declared his harassed friend. "It goes into the fire."

"No! No!" exclaimed Tony.

"Why not?"

Tony snatched the letter, which Bill already had rolled up into a ball, and smoothed it tenderly on his knee. "Don't you see," he inquired, casting an eloquent glance at the falling snow, "that this letter comes from Florida?"

IT WAS SHORT and to the point.

> DEAR SIR: Do you know Pete Carney? Do you know his game? Will you come here and show it up? The other half of the enclosed will be waiting for you. Very truly,
>
> ALLAN GRAHAM.

The address was that of a famous east-coast hostelry; the enclosure, the half of a thousand-dollar note.

Tony whistled.

"Just look what I've saved from the fire! Why, this is real money."

"Not without the other half."

"No; but think how easy it would be to get it."

Bill raised his eyebrows. "What makes you think that?"

"You've done it a dozen times, haven't you? You can do it again."

"Maybe—and maybe not."

"Why not?"

"Well, for one thing," Bill pointed out, "men named 'Pete'— not 'Peter'—are generally experts at games of chance."

"Are you joking?"

"It is barely possible that this man Carney—Pete Carney— might be so good that I wouldn't be able to carry out my contract."

Tony, with memories of episode after episode in which Bill had shown his ability to match his brains against those of sharpers, gazed at him incredulously.

"You don't really mean that?"

Bill nodded seriously. "You think I'm good because you've never seen me up against the real thing."

"How about Schwartz? And Sutliffe?"

"Pikers! Pikers!" Bill declared; "a child could have tripped them up just as easily as I did."

"How about Floyd, and his electric roulette wheel?"

"That was a little more difficult," Bill admitted, "but I happen to know that this man Carney—Pete Carney—is in a class by himself."

"Because he's named 'Pete?'" scoffed Tony.

"No. Because I've played poker with him. You see, in the six years that I spent traveling around the country I met a good many professional gamblers; and Carney was one of them. I used to have a pretty good opinion of myself in those days. I changed it after I'd had a little session with Carney.

"We had just one rule: you could do whatever you pleased so long as the other fellow didn't find it out. You could use a holdout; ring in a cold deck; deal seconds; stop at nothing short of murder—if the other man didn't see it. But Carney did see it! When you played poker with Carney you played a square game. He'd catch you, every time if you didn't."

"And Carney?"

"When he played with me," declared Bill, "he played according to Hoyle, too. At least, I thought so. But that didn't prevent him from cleaning me out."

"No!" ejaculated Tony.

"Pete Carney is one of the very finest poker players I've ever met. When he bets a full house, you're sure he's bluffing; and when you make up your mind that his hand is unbeatable, and lay down your own, the chances are he has nothing better than a pair."

"There's nothing to stop you from calling!"

"Nothing except what it costs. And Pete used to have one awkward habit: whenever you did call, he'd have the cards. Then you'd think twice the next time, and you'd decide there was no sense in throwing good money after bad, and you'd drop. And Pete would rake in the pot, and shuffle his hand into the discard, and look at you with his head cocked on one side, for all the world like an intelligent cocker spaniel, and you couldn't get mad, even if you wanted to."

Bill smiled reminiscently. "That's one reason I'm not keen on running up against Pete Carney. He's good—really good."

"Are there other reasons?"

"Just a few. He doesn't have to cheat; he can win without cheating. And he can live without winning, because an aunt of his left him a fortune a few years ago, and he's been rolling in money ever since."

"He may have spent his money."

"Not Pete."

"He may be hard up. He may be doing just what this man Graham suspects he is."

"It's out of his line. Pete feels at home in a flannel shirt, riding breeches, and puttees. If he's stopping at a swell hotel in Florida, he's there on a vacation, and that means playing cards for fun—not for business. Pete wouldn't combine the two."

"But he must have done something to make Graham write that letter."

Bill gazed at his friend thoughtfully. "Do you know Graham?"

"Never met him face to face, but I've heard a lot about him."

"For instance?"

"He's in with all the best people."

"What else?"

"He plays a good game of polo."

"Any more?"

"Nothing, except that he's probably a very nice fellow."

"Probably." Bill nodded, and began to enclose the bisected thousand-dollar bill in an envelope.

"What the devil are you doing?" demanded Tony.

"I'm sending his money back to him."

"You're not going?"

"A thousand dollars for two weeks' time? No."

"But think of the sport, man! Why, it's better than hunting big game! And just think of somebody actually giving you money to go to Florida in winter!" Tony glanced at the windows and shuddered. "By George! I'd like to go there myself."

"Why don't you?"

"Do you mean it?"

Bill glanced at him keenly. "Why not?"

"You mean, introduce myself as Bill Parmelee?"

"Only to Graham. Remember, Carney knows me."

"And then?"

"Catch Carney cheating—that's all," Bill tantalized.

"You know I can't do it!"

"I don't know anything of the kind. You've learned a lot—and you'd bring a fresh mind to the problem. You know what they say about beginner's luck."

Tony hesitated—and was lost. "Suppose," he ventured, "suppose I watch and I don't find anything wrong?"

"You'll have a chance to try a bold bluff. Take Carney aside. Tell him you advise him to stay out of the game. I'll give even money that he follows your advice."

"He might," ruminated Tony; "he might at that! He might even confess!"

"He might," assented Bill.

The more Tony revolved the matter in his mind the more feasible it seemed. And buried somewhere deep in his soul was a craving to take the center of the stage himself; to emulate Bill's dramatic achievements.

He rose slowly, gathered his coat tightly about him, and nodded. "Bill," he said, "I'm going to sleep on it. I'll let you know what I decide to do in the morning."

Long after Tony had begun to snore the Parmelees, father and son, sat at their fireside and smiled at one another. John Parmelee had not contributed a word to the discussion, yet he had missed no detail of it.

"Well, Bill?" the father inquired at length.

"Well, dad?"

"You're very deep."

"Not too deep for you, dad."

"Not yet, anyhow." John Parmelee puffed his pipe thoughtfully. "You know, Bill, every time you show up a cheat you make up for one of the dark spots in your own career."

"I like to think that, dad."

"Otherwise I'd rather have you stick to farming."

"Same here."

For some minutes there was silence. Then John Parmelee spoke again.

"Your friend Claghorn will probably be starting in the morning."

"Probably."

John Parmelee smiled mysteriously. "And you, I take it, will be following on an afternoon train?"

Bill nodded.

TONY WAS IN high spirits as he boarded the train. In fact, he was so buoyant that it was with difficulty that he restrained himself from breaking out into a series of triumphant Indian war whoops.

His friend, whom in his idolatrous fashion he regarded as the world's greatest authority on his peculiar subject, had admitted him to a footing of full equality; had, indeed, sent him upon a mission which he frankly admitted would call for superlative skill. The inference was clear; the pupil had learned all that the master could teach him, and Tony, who had plunged into the joyous game of exposing sharpers with his characteristic abandon, felt that he had passed the critical period of his schooling with the highest honors.

"I'll wire you and let you know how I'm getting along," he assured Bill on parting.

"That will be kind of you."

"I may trip him up right off, you know."

"You may."

"But if I don't," announced Tony, as if the idea had struck him that instant, "I'm going to spring a bold bluff. I'm going to advise him to get out of the game. I'm going to act just as if I had the goods on him."

"Very ingenious," murmured Bill, "very ingenious. But Tony, if you don't mind my offering a suggestion—"

"Well?" said Tony kindly.

"I'd stick to the bluff if I were you. Even if you think you see something wrong while the game is going on, I wouldn't say a word about it in public. I'd tell Carney—Carney only. I'd take him aside and whisper in his ear. I wouldn't try to make any sensational announcement over the card table."

Tony nodded indulgently. "You mean that you would rather not have me humiliate him. Is that the idea?"

"Exactly."

"Well, I'll do that," said Tony.

"And remember," cautioned his friend, "Carney knows Bill Parmelee—Graham doesn't. There's no harm in calling yourself Parmelee when you introduce yourself to Graham, but see that he introduces you to Carney and his friends by some other name—Tony Claghorn, for instance."

Tony grinned. "That's a good one—masquerading under my own name! By George, that's a good one!" he repeated as the full force of the idea penetrated. "Tony Claghorn—disguised as Tony Claghorn. I'll do it!" he declared. Then a sudden thought assailed him. "But if I address telegrams to Bill Parmelee, and Graham learns of it, it will be a dead give-away!"

"Of course you won't do anything so foolish," murmured Bill.

"Of course not."

"You won't address telegrams to Bill Parmelee. You will

address them to John Parmelee, Bill's father. John Parmelee will naturally want to know how his son is getting along."

"Naturally. Naturally."

"And when an answer comes, signed by John Parmelee, you will know who the real sender is."

Tony nodded wisely. "Nothing could be simpler," he declared.

It was a particularly cold morning, and the ice caked upon the boards of the station platform crackled as the men marched back and forth upon it, but Tony, jubilating silently, was oblivious to such minor details as weather. He climbed into the train with great energy and waved his friend an exuberant farewell as his momentous trip commenced.

"I'm going to bring home the bacon!" he cried.

"Good boy!" Bill shouted.

Then the train slid around a curve and the sublimely ugly little station vanished.

Tony installed himself in a chair with great dignity, and frowned. Somehow a frown seemed to be in keeping with the role he had assumed. He glanced at an obese old gentleman seated across the aisle—and frowned. He observed two little girls giggling in a seat near by—and frowned. He gazed out of the window, noticed a herd of cows—and frowned. Yet somewhere, deep, deep down, Tony Claghorn was almost ridiculously happy. He was off on high adventure; off on a hunt for the biggest of all big game. The sensation was delicious.

He strolled into the club car, feeling as if every eye were upon him, lighted a cigarette, and threw it away. At Pawling he bought a morning paper, glanced at the headlines, and flung that away.

He returned to his chair, and noted that his valise, conspicuously lettered with his initials, would have to be exchanged for one not so lettered. But it occurred to him also that if he, Anthony P. Claghorn, were to masquerade as Anthony P. Claghorn, the initials would be quite appropriate. Then it struck him that the lettering was obviously old, and that it might be difficult to explain to Graham why it had not been newly painted.

The problem was one which would have been of no particular importance to any one other than Tony, but that earnest gentleman, resting his chin on the palm of his hand, gazed penetratingly out of the window and wrestled mentally with its intricate details.

He had made little headway by the time the train reached Brewster, and was nervously retracing his thoughts upon the subject for perhaps the twentieth time when White Plains appeared and disappeared. Once arrived, however, at the terminal, he marched resolutely to the telegraph office and dispatched a brief, soldierly message to one John Parmelee:

"Shall not change the initials on my suitcase period."

The reply, which reached him upon the Florida Limited that evening, consisted of a single word: "Good." And Tony exulted.

But in the interim Tony had passed several happy hours in New York. He had burst in upon his pretty wife in their comfortable apartment, and in brief, soldierly terms had explained that he was leaving for Florida.

Millie had crowed with joy. "I'll be ready in half an hour!" she declared.

In brief, soldierly terms Tony had broken the sad news to her. He was leaving on business—important business—and Millie would have to remain.

"Important business?" she had challenged. "Why, Tony dear, since when have you had any business at all?"

With impressive dignity Tony handed her Allan Graham's letter, brief and soldierly as one might desire.

She read it through and gasped.

"Why, Tony," she declared, "you're not going to try and handle this yourself!"

"That's just what I'm going to do."

"You have no chance."

"Bill doesn't think that. Bill told me to go—to introduce myself to Graham as Bill Parmelee."

"Oh!"

"If Bill says so, it's all right. Bill has confidence in me."

Now this story deals with several very deep persons. Two of them are named Parmelee; and one of them is named Mrs. Anthony P. Claghorn.

Millie corrugated her brows for a few seconds, smiled, and remarked, "Yes, dear."

Tony bustled about with great satisfaction. The brief, soldierly method had had its reward. "I'll be starting at once," he declared.

"We'll be starting."

"I will return in two weeks—or thereabouts."

"We will return."

Asserting his position as master of his own household, Tony explained lucidly just why it was impossible for him to invite Millie to accompany him. It was out of the question. Ridiculous. Preposterous. He forbade it.

Nevertheless when Tony boarded the Florida Limited he was preceded by a remarkably pretty young woman who remarked in the brief, soldierly manner that he so much admired, "Tony, dear, I'm going to have the time of my life!"

Tony thought it well to wire to John Parmelee:

"Am taking Millie along period."

The reply reached him at Richmond. It contained a single word:

"Good."

WHILE WINTER SEIZED the Connecticut hills in its grasp, while stormy winds howled, and thickly falling snowflakes covered the rolling fields, a group of men, thousands of miles away, sat in a luxuriously appointed room in the Hotel Palmetto, on the east coast of Florida, and hazarded large sums of money upon the verdict of the cards.

They wore the lightest of summer flannels and pongees, and they fanned themselves with Panama hats, for so far south cold never ventured. And being well-fed, prosperous individuals on vacations, they lived expensively, amused themselves expensively, and—gambled expensively.

Shearson, who presided over the destinies of a motor-car factory whose works covered miles, and whose employees were numbered far into the thousands, won and lost huge sums with utter indifference. The game entertained him. That was all that mattered. It never occurred to him to calculate whether, in the long run, he was a loser or a winner.

Manners, whose ancestors had bequeathed him acres of choice New York realty, admitted that his favorite game was bridge—at a tenth of a cent a point. But being agreeable, he consented to take part in daily sessions at poker, and systematically donated his profits—which were often considerable—to charity.

Haight and Marsden, who were financiers, played with nervous intensity, and frankly admitted that they enjoyed the betting because it was heavy. Unlike Manners, small stakes would never have given them a thrill. They reveled in the excitement of a game whose limit was always high, and they paid their losses with the good grace of men who have had their money's worth.

Graham and Carney completed the group. Graham, still in the early thirties, handsome, an excellent conversationalist, and an adept at a dozen different kinds of sport, played with careless expertness and generally managed to come out even. A natural-born player, Shearson had called him. Never carried away by the excitement of the moment, never deluding himself into the belief that five good cards in his hand precluded an even better hand somewhere else about the table, but never hesitating to back his judgment, he fared well on the whole.

Carney seemed to fit into the group least of all. Sixty, tall, heavy, bronzed, carelessly dressed and strangely taciturn, he sucked incessantly at an unlighted cigar and glanced seldom at his cards. Instead his deep-set eyes wandered incessantly from face to face, reading their expressions, interpreting them, while his own expression rarely changed. His hands were huge, showing the evidence of manual labor earlier in his life. Yet when it became his turn to deal they became strangely expert. Engulfing the entire pack in one of them, he would flip off the cards with amazing speed with the other. Like a rapidly moving shuttle his right hand would travel over the left. A blur—a mere blur—and the cards, in neat little piles, would be distributed about the table.

The first time Shearson, who was talkative, had watched in

utter amazement. "You've played cards quite a little," he had hazarded.

"Yes; quite a little," Carney had admitted.

There were many things he might have added. Indeed, as he paused, Shearson waited expectantly for him to continue. But Carney merely nodded, as if at some recollection which he did not propose to share, and went on impassively with the game.

During the few days that the play had progressed, five of the six men had come to know each other fairly well. Each, in turn, had contributed autobiographical reminiscences to the common fund. Shearson could neither lose nor win without being reminded of a story. Manners was interested in a variety of subjects, and managed to bring them into the conversation frequently. Haight and Marsden, being connected with Wall Street, had an unfailing supply of anecdotes on tap. And Graham, who despite his youth had seen much of the world, was a brilliant talker, enlivening every conversation in which he took part with an agreeable flow of observation and comment.

Only Carney held aloof. Occasionally—but rarely—a fleeting grin broke over his features; sometimes he would even contribute a monosyllable to the talk; but never a word about himself or about his past left his lips. He had engaged an expensive room, and he spent money freely, paying his bills not by check but from a huge roll of bank notes which he excavated from a capacious pocket. But even though Shearson, in an endeavor to learn something about him had deliberately touched on every subject in which Carney might have been expected to be interested, never a scrap of information resulted.

He played the game, uttering only the few words made necessary by the game itself, and he never exulted in his good fortune, though Graham, an acute observer, had noted from the very beginning that he had been a consistent winner.

"Either he's slick or he's simple," Shearson confided to Graham one evening. "There's no middle ground. Either he's got so much to say that he doesn't want to start, or he's got nothing to say at all. I can't make him out."

Graham had very definite conclusions of his own, but felt it best not to mention them. Instead, he kept his beliefs strictly to himself until an important young man whom he had never met before took up his residence in the hotel, and somewhat melodramatically introduced himself to Graham by presenting the half of a thousand-dollar bill.

Tony had expended much thought upon this detail. Its effect was as electric as he had hoped.

"So you're the man I've been expecting?" Graham exclaimed.

Tony bowed with dignity. "Yes," he murmured.

"Fine!" declared Graham. "Come up to my room and we'll have a chat."

Once in privacy, with the door bolted, Graham turned cordially to the traveler. "Light a cigar, Mr. Parmelee," he invited, "make yourself comfortable."

Tony, exulting in his role, lit one of his host's Havanas, crossed his long legs, folded his arms, and adopted a profoundly serious expression. "Proceed, Mr. Graham," he commanded.

"In the first place, you will notice I didn't call you 'Mr. Parmelee' in the lobby. You may not know it, but you have become an exceedingly well-known man."

"Quite so," murmured Tony.

"I would even suggest—if you approve—that you pass under some other name while you are here."

"I have registered as Anthony P. Claghorn—and wife," Tony mentioned.

"Clever—very clever."

"Even the initials on my suit case correspond."

"And the initials on your handkerchief," pointed out his observant host.

Tony bore the shock well. He glanced at the monogrammed corner of linen which protruded from his outside breast pocket, and nodded. "I believe in being thorough," he proclaimed. For the fraction of a second he thought of mentioning that his hose, his underwear, and his pajamas were embroidered with the same initials, but he thought better of it. "I do everything thoroughly," he repeated.

"So I see. I take it that you're acquainted with Claghorn?"

"Why do you ask?"

"Because it might be awkward if Claghorn showed up here. You see, Anthony P. Claghorn is a real person."

"Of course he's a real person!" declared Tony. "That's why I borrowed his name. And he won't show up here either. I saw him in New York before I left, and I arranged that with him."

"Excellent! Excellent! Now, to begin with, I keep my promises." From a wallet Graham extracted half of a thousand-dollar bill, fitted it to the half which Tony had brought as his introduction, and handed both halves to him. "I wrote that this would be yours when you arrived. Here you are. This is your retainer."

"Thank you," said Tony gravely. It was with a thrill which he hoped his exterior concealed that he pocketed the note.

"It is only a sample of what you will get if you are successful."

"I am always successful," Tony murmured modestly.

"So I have heard. That is why I sent for you. Now, as to this man Carney—"

"Pete Carney."

"You know him?"

"I know of him."

"What do you know?"

Magisterially Tony waved his hand. "Proceed!"

Graham nodded. "Very well, Mr. Parmelee. Handle this your own way. All I can tell you is that I think Carney cheats."

"You wrote that."

"Yes."

"What makes you think that?"

Graham, as previously mentioned, was an excellent conversationalist, and after one hour's uninterrupted speech he was still holding forth volubly.

Tony finally called a halt. "From what you have said, I gather that you think Carney cheats."

Graham gasped, but found the strength to reply, "Yes."

Gravely Tony helped himself to another of his host's excellent cigars.

"We shall see what we shall see," he declared.

NOW A GAME entered into for the sake of a little diversion, and a game entered into in the hope of catching one of the participants in the act of cheating, are two different things. Tony hoped that his calm exterior concealed the agitation of his feelings.

The six men, welcoming a seventh, had allowed him to buy a stack of chips, and had observed his play with visible interest. Tony, watching Carney with eagle eyes, hypnotized by the expertness which his victim-to-be displayed in his dealing, hardly did himself justice.

At his best he played a game which might have been described as passable; did not too often bet heavily on filling a straight open in the middle, and realized, more or less dimly, that a lone ace did not possess enough magnetism to attract three others to it on the draw. But in the company in which he found himself, Tony, it must be admitted regretfully, did not even shine faintly. It was disconcerting, for one thing, to find the players betting with consistent liberality; to discover that Shearson and Carney, between them, made it exceedingly expensive to draw cards. Tony, like most indifferent players, was addicted to calling. Shearson and Carney, having had more experience, backed their faith in their cards by raising, and allowed their opponents to call. Now it is an old adage that a good caller is a sure loser, and in less than an hour Tony found it necessary to invest in a second stack of chips.

Graham glanced at him keenly, but Tony shook his head ever so slightly. Had he spoken he would doubtless have remarked: "Don't worry. Everything is going according to plan." That may or may not have explained how the second stack went the way of the first in record-breaking time.

Tony had begun the session with an intense desire to catch Carney in an act of dishonesty. Halfway through this desire faded insensibly into the background and was replaced by an earnest wish not to allow himself to be utterly wiped out. He began to play more conservatively, and had the utterly miserable sensation that his opponents were reading his thoughts with the greatest ease. Shearson, who had raised with magnificent liberality earlier in the evening, gazed at Tony searchingly, and dropped more than once when Tony, holding big hands, was depending upon him to make the pot worth while. Carney, too, who had carried the art of bluff to incredible heights, seemed to sense the value of the cards which occasionally came to Tony, and contributed next to nothing. And Manners, Haight, and Marsden, taking their cue from Shearson and Carney, the sensational players, put on a soft pedal, and allowed Tony's streaks of luck to pass without serious damage to their pocketbooks.

In desperation, Tony began to bluff, and found himself once more in deep water. He resorted to the ruses which had worked so well at the Himalaya Club, in far-off New York; but his opponents, following the lead of Shearson and Carney, were never embarrassed by them. According to the best writers on the subject of poker, the other players should have laid down their hands, and permitted Tony to rake in a pot. Evidently they had not heard of the best writers, for they simply raised, and punctured Tony's bluffs in short order.

At eleven thirty the game broke up, Tony, to his chagrin having lost not only the thousand he had received from Graham, but some hundreds of his own funds as well.

His employer buttonholed him in a corridor. "Well?" he demanded.

Tony waved a hand. "I have made progress," he announced vaguely.

"I should say so!" assented Graham. "You've lost at the rate of sixty miles an hour! If you keep on progressing that way you'll—"

Tony interrupted with dignity. "I am handling this affair in my own way," he declared. "If I had won, Carney might have become suspicious. As it is—as it is—"

"As it is?"

"I have laid the groundwork for my future actions."

Graham gazed at him with an unfriendly eye. "You know," he commented, "that time you raised on a bobtail flush—"

Again Tony interrupted. "I had my reasons. Mr. Graham. Excellent reasons."

"Carney didn't even call you that time," persisted Graham; "he raised you back, and kept on raising. And at the finish, you called—not Carney. That may be advanced poker, but if it is, it is so advanced that I don't understand it. If you weren't an expert, Mr. Parmelee, I'd call it sheer lunacy. What did you expect to find in Carney's hand? Another bobtail flush? If that was it, you must have been disappointed when he laid down a full house, queens up."

Tony laid a forefinger at the side of his nose in an inscrutable gesture. "Ah, ha!" he exclaimed, and again, "Ah, ha!"

Then, with great dignity, he moved away.

Wandering through the dark corridors of the hotel, he gave himself up to painful thought. He had discovered absolutely nothing, with the exception of the fact that Carney, as Bill had warned him, was an extraordinarily fine player. He had entered the game with a light heart, buoyed up by too-great confidence in his own ability. He had left it separated from most of his available cash, and the progress which he had reported to Graham was wholly imaginary.

In his dilemma he woke up his sleeping wife and threw himself upon her mercy.

She listened attentively.

"If I understand you, Tony dear," she commented, "you haven't made much headway."

"None at all," Tony confessed with a groan.

"And you've lost a good deal of money."

"Too much."

"And you want to know what I would do next?"

"Yes."

Millie smiled. As previously remarked, Mrs. Anthony P. Claghorn was an exceedingly deep person. "Tony, dear," she advised, "I would do just what you think you ought to do. That's what Bill wants, isn't it?"

"Er—yes."

"Well, go ahead."

Tony gazed at the ceiling thoughtfully. "When I left Bill, I told him that even if I didn't catch Carney in the act I'd go ahead just as if I had the goods on him: I'd take him aside, and advise him to get out of the game."

"And what did Bill say?"

"He thought that was a good idea of mine. He approved of it."

"Then I approve of it also," murmured pretty Mrs. Claghorn, turned over, and soon was fast asleep.

For half an hour Tony wrestled silently with his thoughts. Then he made his way to the telegraph office and dispatched a wire:

"Am ready to proceed with second part of plan period."

The reply was handed to him at breakfast. It was one word: "Good."

ENTHUSIASM, PERHAPS, WAS Mr. Anthony P. Claghorn's most marked characteristic. It was not congenial to his volcanic nature to indulge in patience; to wait for a propitious moment; to underrate his own abilities. Tony had an incurable habit of going off at half cock, and while eating his breakfast he repented of it.

With his customary headstrong energy he had thoughtlessly committed himself to a course of action from which there was no retreat, had determined to beard the lion Carney in his den, and had made his decision irrevocable by telegraphing it to his friend. He had sent off the wire in moderately high spirits. Ten minutes later it had suddenly struck him that Carney, with a Western upbringing and with a lifetime spent in the company of men notoriously quick on the trigger, might not receive Tony's gentle hint to retire from the game in a truly Christian spirit. That, Tony foresaw, might be awkward.

During the night—for he had slept but little—he had mentally pictured the possibilities. He visioned himself walking up to Carney, speaking a single sentence—and he saw Carney, with a lightninglike movement, drawing a revolver and shooting him dead on the spot. That nightmare had wakened him all of three or four times in as many hours.

He had heard tales about the quaint habits said to be characteristic of old-time mining camps. It occurred to him that Carney, instead of shooting him, might insert an expert thumb into Tony's orbit and gouge out an eye. Tony shuddered, patted his optic thoughtfully, and admitted that it felt more at home in its socket.

Visions of bowie knives, of amputated ears and noses, even of captives burned at the stake, haunted his sleep. And his breakfast, which he always enjoyed, suddenly became unpalatable when Carney marched massively into the dining room, seated himself at a near-by table, and nodded. There was grimness in that nod, Tony decided, and his heart quaked.

Furtively he glanced at his pretty wife, busy with her grape-fruit, and reflected uncomfortably that she would look well in mourning—yet he was conscious of no desire to hasten the coming of that event.

With calculating eyes he appraised Carney's bulk—the powerful muscles—the heavy-boned frame. The enormous hands, each large enough to engulf a pack of cards, might, before the day was over, be fastened about Tony's throat. He recalled Carney's amazing dexterity in dealing, and wondered if, in true Western fashion, he fired from the hip with equal expertness.

Tony cleared his throat.

"Millie!"

"Yes, dear."

"You're fond of me, aren't you?"

"Yes, dear."

"Very?"

"Yes, dear."

"That's good," remarked Tony, and reflected that it was nice to know that he would be missed.

He finished his breakfast without another word, and on leaving the dining room came face to face with Graham. This latter drew him into a corner. "Mr. Parmelee," he whispered, "if you don't mind, I'd like to know something about your plans for today."

Tony was not in the best of humors. "I do mind," he retorted.

Graham was imperturbable. "In that event, Mr. Parmelee," he whispered, "I might as well tell you that I've been doing some thinking. Deliver the goods—deliver them any way you please—and you'll find me liberal—more than liberal. But if you take a hand in the game again, and if you lose again, please bear in mind that I am not staking you. I'd like that clearly understood, Mr. Parmelee."

Tony glared at him. "I am fully able to pay my own losses, Mr. Graham."

"I am glad to hear that," said Graham, and walked away.

Disconsolately Tony proceeded to the veranda and slumped into a chair. Much as he would have liked to appeal to Bill for help his pride prevented him from doing so. Then he turned his head and discovered that Carney, well fed and at peace with the world after an excellent breakfast, had installed himself in a chair not six inches distant from his own.

It was Tony's opportunity to remark manfully, "Mr. Carney, queer things were happening in that game last night. I don't want to accuse you of anything, but I do want to advise you to stay out of it."

He said nothing of the kind. Instead, he smiled in a friendly manner, though his heart was beating rapidly, and mumbled "G'morning."

"Good morning," Carney replied.

"Nice weather," Tony opined, and Carney agreed with that opinion. "Been here long?" Tony inquired, and Carney grunted.

"Umph."

Then, for ten minutes at least, neither spoke, while Carney sucked at an unlighted cigar and the young man at his side wondered whether he weighed over or under two hundred and thirty pounds.

Presently Carney, the silent, began to speak. "Nice, quiet game last night," he remarked in his deep, bass voice.

"Yes. Wasn't it?"

"Different from the games I used to sit in when I was your age, bub."

"How so?" inquired Tony.

"Quieter—much quieter," said Carney with a reminiscent smile. "In those days, when you sat down, you never knew if you'd get up again. You kept your shooting irons handy, bub."

Tony swallowed two or three times, and nodded. Here, again, he observed methodically, was an opportunity to warn Carney, in a firm, decisive manner that it would be well for him to retire from the game. But Tony let the opportunity pass.

During the day Carney seemed to dog his footsteps. Wherever Tony wandered, Carney was never far distant. He met him on a walk—and again on the veranda upon his return from it—and found him within easy speaking distance in the dining room at lunch. When he adjourned to a quiet corner for an after-dinner smoke the big Westerner was not far away.

"Upon my word," Tony whispered to his wife, "I believe he's following me around!"

"Have you spoken to him yet?" she whispered back.

"No."

"Why not?"

Now Tony was no coward. Being a reasonable man, he had estimated the prospective risks, and considering them great, had avoided them. But with his wife forcing his hand that course was no longer possible.

"I'm going to speak to him this minute!" he declared.

He rose, straightened his coat, and threw out his shoulders. If he were to die, a heroic death, with his wife on the spot to appreciate his heroism, would be most satisfactory.

He marched across the veranda, pulled up a chair next to Carney's, and plumped himself into it.

"Mr. Carney," he said, "I want to talk to you."

"Yes, bub?" The tone was incredibly mild.

Tony felt encouraged. "I was watching the game last night," he declared resolutely. "I took a hand just to watch."

"Yes, bub?"

Tony sensed that he was at the edge of the precipice. He leaped over with a rush. "If you know what's good for you, you'll get out of that game."

The die was cast. Tony waited with an oddly impersonal curiosity. Would Carney draw a knife or a revolver? Or would his thumb seek Tony's eyeball?

None of these things happened. Instead, the bronzed Westerner inclined his head ever so slightly, and murmured, "Yes, bub."

Tony gasped. "You heard what I said?" he demanded incredulously.

"Yes, bub."

"And you'll quit the game?"

"I sure will."

Like wine Carney's unexpected meekness went to Tony's head. "I said nothing last night," he declared, "because I didn't want to humiliate you before the others. But now we're alone and I can say what I think. If you know what's good for you, don't let me catch you in that game again!"

"I won't," Carney promised.

With dignity Tony rose. "That's all," he informed his victim, and stalked off. Victory was his, and he felt just a trifle delirious.

As he turned the corner of the veranda Graham came to him with outstretched hands. "Mr. Parmelee," declared that young man, "I apologize—I apologize most humbly. I overheard every word you said to Carney, and every word he said to you. You have done what I asked you to do, and I'm eternally obliged."

Tony waved a deprecating hand. "Don't mention it," he murmured.

Graham seized him by the arm. "I told you that you'd find me liberal, and I'm going to prove it. Come inside, Mr. Parmelee, and watch me cash a check."

IT WOULD BE pleasant to end this story at this point. It would be pleasant to relate that Tony marched into the telegraph office, reported the success of his mission, received the answer, "Good," and returned home covered with glory.

But in the interests of veracity, it is necessary to detail the events which took place after Tony, in brief, soldierly fashion, had indited that final telegram: "We have met the enemy and they are ours exclamation point."

Half an hour earlier the world had been overcast with gloom for Tony; a leaden gray pall had hung thick upon everything. But in the twinkling of an eye the mists had lifted and rosy tints had come in their stead. Success had come—overwhelming success—and Tony basked in its effulgence.

In company with his pretty wife he proceeded to the beach and enjoyed a swim. He felt entitled to relaxation after his labors. He splashed around merrily until a porpoiselike blowing warned him of the approach of some large animal. Then he turned, and to his boundless amazement discovered Carney, in a trim bathing suit, disporting himself near him.

Now according to all the rules of etiquette, Carney, being an exposed sharper, should have avoided the presence of his conqueror and should have fled from his sight like a thing accursed. But Carney, evidently, possessed no sense of shame, for he swam nearer, turned gayly on his back, and called out a greeting.

Tony replied—he could do no less—and when Carney offered to race him back did not see his way clear to refuse. Nor could he decline when Carney, having won the race hands down for all his sixty years, invited him to help sample the contents of a pinch bottle which the Westerner had thriftily buried near an abandoned hut.

During twenty-four hours Tony's opinion of Carney had fluctuated widely; and it fluctuated still more after a few swallows of an amber-colored liquid had gurgled down Tony's throat. Somehow Tony's vision began to clear. He feared he had overlooked Carney's good qualities, such as they were; and that fear became a certainty before the bottle was emptied.

"Good stuff," Tony remarked, smacking his lips critically.

"None better," Carney assented.

"But there's not much left in the bottle," Tony pointed out in alarm.

" 'Sall right, bub," said the Westerner, "there's more where this came from." He glanced around to make sure that he was not overheard. "How'd you like to meet me in my room to-night?"

"What for?"

"Well, if we're not going to play cards," grinned Carney, "time will be hanging heavy on our hands, and I've got a little valise— not too little—with several more bottles in it." He placed a hairy paw on Tony's knee as that worthy deliberated. "Bub, I've got a cocktail shaker, and we'll send down for some ice and a couple of limes, and I'll mix you something that you've never tasted in your life!"

When the next book on etiquette is written, the authority responsible for it will doubtless state the correct procedure for a young man confronted with a situation of this kind. Tony, somewhat mellowed by the excellent whisky he had drunk, reflected that Carney's invitation indicated a spirit of forgiveness as remarkable as it was praiseworthy.

He, Tony, had humiliated Carney as much as one man may humiliate another, had accused him of cheating, and had ordered him out of the game. Yet Carney, far from harboring the slightest ill will, had accepted his chastisement meekly, and was making unmistakable overtures of friendship to his former enemy.

Under the circumstances Tony could not very well show himself less magnanimous than his victim.

"I'm with you, daddy," he remarked with simple elegance, dressed, hastened through his supper, made a satisfactory excuse to his wife, and presently rejoined the convivial Westerner.

It became speedily apparent that Carney had not exaggerated in describing the little—not too little—valise. Tony had never seen another like it. The sides, fitted with nickel-plated racks, held a bewildering array of gayly colored bottles. Every ingredient of every known beverage was present in proper proportions.

Carney set the valise upright on a convenient table, removed his coat, and wrapped a towel around his waist.

"Bub," he confessed, "long, long before you were born, I used to tend bar. The drinks are on me. What will you have?"

Tony sighed blissfully. "A Martini," he murmured.

"Martini it is."

The hands which dealt so wonderfully were even more expert with a cocktail shaker. In an incredibly short space of time two glasses, filled to the brim with an ice-cold concoction, made their appearance. Tony quaffed his slowly and appreciatively.

"Daddy," he remarked, "you don't mind if I call you daddy?"

"Not at all."

"Very well, then. Daddy, you're a great man."

Carney bowed. "What will it be now?"

"Have you the makings of a Clover Club?"

"That—and anything else," Carney assured him.

The Clover Club was followed by a Manhattan—and a Bronx, which Tony encored enthusiastically—and an absinth frappe—and then Carney introduced his guest to the alcoholic mystery known as a stinger.

Now there are stingers and stingers, and their formulas vary widely, but Carney, so he modestly confessed, knew the formula of the one prehistoric, primeval, protoplasmic stinger from which all other stingers are descended. He demonstrated.

"Do you like it?" he inquired.

" 'Sgood," commented Tony blissfully, "lawfully good. 'Swonderful!"

Carney must have had a stomach of cast iron, for he matched his guest, glass for glass, and remained wholly unaffected. But Tony, being a younger man, and having had less experience, became mellower and mellower.

At ten he swore undying friendship with Carney. Carney had not asked him to do so, but Tony felt it was in order.

"There's so much bad in the worst of us, and so much good in the best of us," he misquoted happily, "that means you, daddy."

Carney bowed—both of him—Tony noticed. It struck Tony suddenly that here was an excellent opportunity to reform the old man, and he turned his forceful energies to it. He paused occasionally for refreshment, for his throat became dry at frequent intervals, but he noted with pleasure how respectfully Carney listened to what, by Tony's own confession immediately afterward, had been one of the most eloquent and moving sermons ever delivered.

Its effectiveness was demonstrable, for Carney professed his reform at two-minute intervals beginning at ten thirty. Tony was affected—almost to tears. And at eleven o'clock he prevailed upon Carney, who was himself beginning to show the influence of his potations, to accompany him downstairs to the card room, there to make public profession of his repentance.

"Come with me, brother—I mean daddy," urged Tony.

Navigating unsteadily, clinging to each other on the general principle that in union there is strength, the two made their way through the endless corridors, and pushed open the door beyond which the nightly session was in progress.

Around the circular table were seated Shearson, Manners, Haight, Marsden, and Graham. And Tony blinked in utter astonishment as in a sixth chair he discerned his good friend, Bill Parmelee.

"Bill," he gasped, "is that you?"

"You bet it is!" declared the apparition.

"Well, if it is," commented Tony, accepting the incredible fact with good grace, "I'm mighty glad to see you. Bill, I want to introduce my friend Mr. Carney. He may be a card cheat, but he's the right sort."

Bill laughed shortly, and rose from the table. "And I," he declared, "I want to introduce Mr. Allan Graham. He's a card cheat—the only one in this room—and he's the wrong sort."

Graham's face, pale with fear, distorted with fury, was a confession for anybody to read.

Tony pinched himself. "Graham? Not Carney?" he queried.

"Exactly."

Tony glanced around the room. In his befuddled condition he had not noticed the deathlike silence of the men who sat at the table. Shearson's features, usually so genial, had become set and stern. Manners, generally so dapper and smiling, was quiet—ominously quiet. And Haight and Marsden, with compressed lips, wore the expression of jurors about to convict a criminal upon a capital charge.

Though Tony did not sense it, he had burst into the room but an instant after Parmelee had unveiled the sharper.

He gazed incredulously from face to face. The unexpected revelation had nearly sobered him.

"Graham? Not Carney?" he repeated stupidly.

"Graham—not Carney," echoed Bill.

Impulsively Tony flung his arm about the big Westerner's shoulders. "If that's so," he declared, "I'm satisfied with life!"

IT WAS NOT until noon the next day that Bill made any attempt to answer the many questions that had been hurled at him. It was not until then that Tony was in a condition either to ask questions or to understand the replies, and Bill felt that his friend was entitled to a little enlightenment.

"I had my first suspicions," Bill explained, "the moment I saw Graham's letter, and read that he wanted me to come here and show up Pete Carney as a card cheat. That was suspicious—very suspicious—because I know Pete as I know myself, and I was willing to stake my life that he wasn't cheating."

Carney, who was listening, smiled broadly. "You were taking a big chance, weren't you, Bill?"

"Not even a little one!" Bill declared. "I knew you had turned over a new leaf, Pete, and I had faith in you. Aside from that," Bill added with a chuckle, "I knew that it wouldn't take you more than one or two sittings to clean up everything in sight; that is, if you really wanted to, and didn't care how you did it. It was a big game—a game which justifies a man in tearing a thousand-dollar bill in two, and mailing me one of the halves must be a big game—and if you were winning so slowly that Graham had the time to write me, and the further time to await my arrival from Connecticut, it was a fair inference that you were playing honest poker."

Shearson, another listener, nodded. "That sounds reasonable," he admitted.

"I began to ask myself questions," pursued Parmelee, turning to Tony, "the moment you placed that letter in my hands. Why did Graham want Carney convicted of cheating? To recover losses? No. If he had lost heavily he wouldn't have been able to spare a thousand-dollar bill. Did he have a grudge against Carney? Not likely. Nobody, in all the years I knew him, ever had a grudge against Pete.

"Then what other reason could there be? The solution came to me like a flash as I looked into the fire with the letter in my hand. This man Graham, for private objects of his own, wanted Carney removed from the game! It was the only possible, the only logical explanation.

"Perhaps Graham actually thought that Carney cheated; perhaps he thought me so clever that I would prove he cheated whether he cheated or not; perhaps he had found out something about Carney's past. Pete used to be a pretty well-known figure; there's no telling what Graham had heard.

"In any event, it was clear the moment I studied Graham's letter that he wanted to get rid of Carney, and wanted to get him out of the game because he cramped his style. He had learned enough about Carney to be sure that Pete would catch him like a shot if he, Graham, ever tried anything underhand.

"That was what I read between the lines of Graham's letter."

Tony whistled. "The letter was three or four lines long, and may have consisted of twenty-four words!"

Bill smiled. "It wasn't what he wrote—it was what he didn't write—that really mattered. I did some fast thinking during the next few minutes, Tony.

"What was I to do? My first impulse was to forget it; to return the torn money to Graham and burn the letter. Carney was amply able to look out for himself—that I knew.

"My second impulse was to mail the letter to Pete, and to tell him to punch Graham's head. That would have served him right.

"But then it struck me that if I refused to help Graham, he might think up some other devilish scheme, and I didn't like the idea of old Pete fighting an enemy who was as contemptible as that.

"I made up my mind to give Graham a fair chance—to remove Carney from the game and see what Graham would do then. In a big game cheating would be worth while. I decided to give Graham plenty of rope. Perhaps he'd hang himself with it. Perhaps he'd show that I had misjudged him. I was curious to know the answer.

"So I sent you ahead, Tony, to masquerade as Bill Parmelee—and I followed you just twelve hours later."

Tony gazed at his friend in amazement. "If you followed me, who answered my telegrams?"

"My father."

"How did he know what to answer?"

Bill grinned. "Before I left, I told him that no matter what you wired, he was to answer 'Good.' It may have been mean, Tony, old fellow, but I didn't dare let you into the secret. You're not a good actor. You might have given it away.

"I knew you wouldn't catch Carney cheating," pursued Bill. "There were two excellent reasons. In the first place, he wasn't cheating; and in the second place, if he had been, you would never have detected him at it. I'm fairly good with the cards myself, but Pete is a real artist. He can do anything with them, except make them talk. So when you suggested—it was your suggestion, Tony, and I give you credit for it," Bill fabricated generously, "that you spring a bold bluff on him, tell him to get out of the game as if you had actually caught him, I agreed with you right off—though I did write Pete a letter, telling him what was afoot, simply to make sure that he wouldn't wipe you off of the face of the earth as soon as he understood what you were driving at. Pete's an old friend, and I knew he'd follow instructions to the letter."

Carney grinned reminiscently. "It took him all morning to get up enough nerve to speak to me."

"But he did!"

"He did," Carney admitted, "he stood right up to me. Bub,

did you know that men have been shot for doing less than that?"

Tony was silent, but his wife spoke for him. "He knew it, and I knew it too," she asserted, "because the night before he could talk of nothing else in his sleep!"

Carney gasped. "And knowing that, ma'am, you let him walk up to me?"

Pretty Mrs. Claghorn smiled. "Mr. Parmelee approved—and I knew that if Mr. Parmelee approved, it would be all right."

It was Tony's turn to gasp. "Bill," he declared, "if she had the faith in me that she has in you."

"Go on, Mr. Parmelee," urged Shearson.

Bill nodded. "I lay low and waited—waited for the psychological moment. When Carney took Claghorn upstairs to sample his good liquor, I took Carney's place in the game. That was easy," he explained. "I struck up an acquaintance with Mr. Shearson and he invited me right in.

"I couldn't wait. I didn't dare wait. If Graham was planning anything, he would begin right away. As a matter of fact, the fireworks started within ten minutes."

"What did he do?" inquired Carney.

"He used a shading box, Pete," said Bill, producing an implement the size of a large button from his pocket. For the benefit of the others, he demonstrated. "A shading box holds a bit of colored paste—in here—and it comes out through this slot in the top. That's all there is to it, except that the man who uses one rubs his thumb over the slot now and then, and marks the backs of the cards with it. The boxes come in pairs, one red and one blue, so that he can match the color printed on the backs of any deck. The least little spot will tell him all he wants to know, and it's mighty hard for anybody else to detect unless, like me, you're looking for it. I waited until he won his first fat pot, and then I spoke right out in meeting."

Shearson laughed. "And then he tried to prove that you were the cheat!"

"It would have been awkward," Bill admitted, "if we hadn't found the shading boxes tightly sewed to the under side of Graham's vest."

Carney broke a long silence. "He knew better than to try that when I was in the game."

"That's why he wanted you out of it."

Carney smiled grimly. "He got his wish. Much good it did him!"

But pretty Mrs. Claghorn corrugated her brow. "Answer me one question, Mr. Parmelee."

"A dozen if you like, ma'am."

"What has Tony had to do with all this? What has Tony accomplished?"

"A great deal," Bill assured her.

"I wonder! You wanted Mr. Carney out of the game. A letter to him brought that about. You wanted to sit in the game yourself. You did, didn't you? Where does Tony figure?"

"He threw Graham off of the trail."

"That could have been done in a dozen other ways."

Bill grinned. "You're too clever for me, ma'am. Much too clever! You see, Tony was spending a week-end with me when Graham's letter arrived; and Tony couldn't talk about anything but the snow—and the ice—and the cold. And something told me—something told me—"

"That he might enjoy a Florida vacation?"

"Ma'am," said Bill with a bow, "I never could lie to a lady."

7

THE PILLAR OF FIRE

"BILL," **TONY INQUIRED** suddenly, "do you believe in mind reading?"

It was Bill's twenty-fifth birthday, and Tony, nobly resolving to help him celebrate it, had invited him—urged him—plagued him to spend a week with him enjoying the many attractions offered by one of Tony's clubs. Bill had held out manfully—some sixth sense had warned him that a week in the company of his restless friend would be anything but a vacation—but even granite will wear away under the drip of water, and after the forty-seventh invitation Bill had capitulated. "I want it understood, however," he bargained, "that if I go with you this time you won't ask me again for a whole year."

Tony stiffened. "Don't you expect to enjoy it?"

"Why, of course—"

"You know I'll do everything in the world to give you a good time—"

"I'm a farmer," Bill had explained hastily. "My idea of a good time is different from yours."

Tony had grunted, and Bill, reluctant to offend his friend, had hastily packed a suit case. But once installed in the privacy of a stateroom on the train, Tony had welcomed the opportunity to ask questions. Now an inquiring youngster of six can propound riddles which even a wise man cannot answer, and Tony, being five and one half times that age, was as many times as inquisitive—and even more persistent.

For six years Bill Parmelee had followed the hazardous calling of a professional card sharp. He had reformed; had done much to atone for his past by unmasking those of his former colleagues who still insisted upon preying on too-trustful acquaintances; and while the train speeded southward along the Atlantic coast he did even more by attempting valorously to answer the deluge of questions hurled at him by his insatiably curious friend.

For some deep, mysterious reason, unexplained and unexplainable, anything that has to do with the subject of dishonest gambling is fascinatingly interesting to the average man. Tony showed himself no exception. Methodically, proceeding in orderly fashion from year to year, from month to month, even from day to day, he pumped his informant dry of every detail having to do with his much-checkered career.

Bill had nothing to conceal and met him in a spirit of complete frankness. He told how he had run away from home at the age of eighteen; how he had been introduced to the methods employed to make games of chance less chancy; how he had gradually become so familiar with those methods that he had qualified as a master of them. He unlocked the door of his reminiscences, and dwelt upon its highlights—and its shadows; its triumphs—and its reverses; its brief periods of prosperity—and its long periods of adversity; and Tony Claghorn, like Oliver Twist, demanded more and more.

Time and again Bill leaped desperately for the end of his story, attempted to terminate his autobiography by explaining, in a few words, how and why he had finally turned a new leaf, become a farmer, and forsworn the devious ways of his youth. But Tony, enjoying himself hugely, would not permit this, and kept his friend busy describing and annotating the earlier episodes which he found so interesting.

Anything—even an autobiography—must come to an end, and at quarter past four in the afternoon Tony had asked and Bill had answered the final question. And then, while Bill, gazing out of the window, was mentally comparing a herd of Guernseys with his own sleek Jerseys, Tony opened a subject whose discussion might well prove interminable.

"Bill," he repeated, "do you believe in mind reading?"

Bill sighed. "Well, do you believe in it?" he countered wearily.

Tony settled himself in a judicial attitude. "Yes and no," he admitted.

"Meaning?"

"I'm a broad-minded man and I'm always open to conviction."

"And have you ever been convicted—I mean, convinced?" inquired Bill.

Tony nodded gravely. "Yes," he admitted.

Bill nodded with equal gravity. "Then there's nothing more to be said," he declared. The rhythmic click of the wheels was lulling him; he half closed his eyes.

But Tony had barely begun. "Bill," he commanded, "get your mind on this."

"I can talk just as well in my sleep."

"Not to me," declared Tony emphatically. "We were discussing mind reading," he recalled, somewhat superfluously, "and I was about to tell you that I had seen examples of it."

"Such as?"

"Well," said Tony reflectively, "there was a chap I met some years ago who could do a very wonderful trick with three cards.

He'd show you the faces before he started—one of them was a king—"

Bill interrupted. "And then he'd shuffle them clumsily, and bet you couldn't locate it."

"Yes."

"You'd win the first time, and the second time, but the third time, if the bet was big enough, you'd lose. You'd think that was impossible, because you'd noticed that the king was dog-eared. You knew the back of the card as well as you knew the face. Only when you put your money on it, you'd find that the dog-ear had gotten straightened out, and that another card—not the king—had become dog-eared at the same time. Is that correct?"

"Yes."

"And you called that mind reading? Tony, I'm ashamed of you!"

"He knew what was in my mind, didn't he?" persisted the clubman. "He knew I noticed the dog-ear. If that wasn't mind reading, what was it?"

"It was nothing but relying on an old, old maxim," retorted Bill.

"What maxim?" demanded Tony somewhat angrily.

Bill gazed innocently out of the window. "Tony, old fellow, it's a maxim to the effect that there's one born every minute."

"A sucker?"

"That word will do as well as any other."

Tony snorted. "Perhaps you'll say the same thing about the Marleys."

"Who are they?"

"Haven't you heard of them? The woman sits on the stage, blindfolded, and the man goes out into the audience—"

"And then the woman reads out what you've written on a piece of paper—"

"Yes."

"Or tells you the number engraved in your watch; or the initials on your ring; or the name of the maker of your hat—"

"Yes. Now that's mind reading, isn't it?"

Bill smiled wearily. "Tony, some time when we've got a few hours to spare I'll teach you how to do that with me. It might come in handy some time."

"You mean," gasped Tony, "that you know how it's done?"

Bill nodded. "I was taught by a tramp whom I met in a freight car. He had played the vaudeville houses with his partner. Then he took to drink, and got his signals mixed one night. That finished him. You see, when the sheriff's wife wrote on a bit of paper, 'Whom does my husband love?' something went wrong, and the blindfolded lady answered, 'A beautiful young woman with blue eyes and golden hair.'"

"What of that?" queried Tony.

"Not much," said Bill, "only the sheriff's wife was so far from beautiful that she had no delusions on the subject—and she wasn't young—and, barring streaks of gray in her hair, she was a decided brunette. And she'd been having her suspicions about that husband of hers for a long time! The show stopped right there and the mind reader hopped on the first train leaving that town. He knew that the sheriff would be after him if he lingered."

"If he had been a mind reader," commented Tony, "a real mind reader, he would have foreseen trouble."

Bill laughed. "He foresaw trouble without the least difficulty, and he wasn't a mind reader! It didn't take a mind reader to do that—it needed nothing but plain common sense." Again he closed his eyes. "And now for a snooze," he murmured.

"What happened to the mind reader?" insisted Tony.

"Oh, he stuck to his trade and became prosperous again. We landed in St. Louis together. We were broke, both of us. He fixed that in short order. He'd walk into a saloon. He'd start talking about cards. He'd start talking about mind reading. Then he'd get into an argument with the best-dressed man in the place, and he'd invite him to pick any card out of a deck, call me on the telephone, and hear me tell him what card he held in his hand."

"It can't be done!" ejaculated Tony.

"There were lots of fellows who thought that way. In fact, they'd bet real money that it couldn't be done. My partner never went near the telephone, mind you. He'd say, 'Call such and such a number, and ask for Mr. Parmelee.'"

"And you would name the card?"

"Every time."

"By George," admitted Tony, "that's wonderful!"

"Quite so," drawled Bill. "My partner visited eight or ten places a night. We started off with small bets: we had to, because we began with only five dollars between us. But we split up over a thousand when we decided that it was time for us to make tracks."

"There was no reason that you should not have stayed there indefinitely."

"Oh, yes, there was! You see, the men who lost their bets might have found out that—"

"What could they have found out?"

Bill grinned reminiscently. "They might have found out that

I had fifty-two different names! They'd call the same number every time—it was a public telephone in a cigar store—but once my partner would tell them to ask for 'Mr. Parmelee,' and once for 'Mr. Henderson,' and once for 'Mr. Bancroft,' and sometimes for 'Mr. Conroy' or 'Mr. Hanford.' Of course I'd be standing right next to the phone all the time."

Tony corrugated his brows. "What's the big idea?"

"Don't you see it yet?" laughed Bill. "Each name indicated a different card. 'Parmelee' was the jack of spades—that was my partner's idea of humor; 'Henderson' was the queen of hearts; 'Hanford' was the queen of spades. Nothing could have been simpler: the first letter of the name told me the denomination of the card; the first vowel told me the suit. We had memorized a code—that was all."

"Whew!" whistled Tony.

"We couldn't work it more than once on the same crowd. That was the only objection to the scheme," confessed Bill, "but in a good-sized town we wouldn't do badly—not at all."

He turned to his bewildered friend, who was gazing at him with open mouth. "Tony," he declared, "any time you hear of a mind-reading exhibition more wonderful than that, you let me know where it is—I want to see it."

"I'll remember that," Tony promised. And he was so impressed that he allowed Bill to go to sleep without a protest, not to be wakened until they reached their destination.

WHEN A MAN belongs to one club, he is likely to belong to another; and when he belongs to two, a third is nearly as inevitable as death and taxes. Tony belonged to the Windsor and to the Himalaya—had joined the first because it was the thing to do, and had joined the second in reaction against the oppressive respectability of the first.

The Windsor was rich, dignified, and exclusive; the Himalaya was rich, undignified, and the reverse of exclusive. By dividing his time between the two Tony convinced himself that he was neither too respectable nor too disreputable, neither a prig nor a sporting man, and ambled along on a middle course which impressed him as being just right. A spree at the Himalaya was atoned for by a staid evening at the Windsor; and after sojourning a while in the highly moral atmosphere of the latter organization, a visit to the former would bring Tony back to the less exalted plane upon which he felt that he belonged. Membership in the Windsor alone would have branded Tony a snob; membership in the Himalaya alone would have marked him out as a rounder; membership in both qualified him far more congenially as a man about town, a true democrat equally at home in every society.

Yet a third club was necessary to the complete happiness of Tony and of other young men similarly situated, with the result that a select group of them, taking into consideration the frequent vacations which a lifetime of doing nothing demanded, founded that justly celebrated organization, the Riggs Island Association.

There were rumors that the association had been formed because Huntley Thornton, who had owned Riggs Island, a scrubby patch of sand off the South Carolina coast, had been anxious to sell it, and being in the real-estate business had painted its attractions to his friends in such glowing colors that he had been enabled to get out at a profit. This, however, was mere hearsay, and was never substantiated. Certain it was that

Huntley Thornton had been a prime mover in bringing the Riggs Island Association into existence, and that his friends, oversupplied with money, and enraptured at the thought of an island paradise whither they might retreat to recuperate whenever so minded, had rallied loyally to his support.

To them it mattered nothing that the property consisted only of a few barren acres, a clump of discouraged scrub pines, and a billion gnats. The architect's drawings, prepared under Huntley Thornton's personal direction, featured a golf course, half a dozen tennis courts, a stone clubhouse, and a magnificent beach, and made no mention at all of the already existing features. Thornton's friends gazed upon the handsomely framed water colors, admired the details, commended the general plan, and dug deep into their pockets for the funds which presently transformed a dream into a reality. In the process the original subscribers nobly paid assessment after assessment, but, as Chet Moulton said, "After we've spent a fortune on the clubhouse we can't shy at the cost of a breakwater. Hang it all, if we do, the clubhouse will be washed into the Atlantic Ocean!" The breakwater had been merely one of the costly necessities which Huntley Thornton's architect had not thought it necessary to mention. There were others—many, many others.

When the clubhouse was finished, when the tennis courts had been rolled to a glasslike smoothness, and the golf course had been completed, Thornton's friends journeyed down in groups, strolled over the property, admired the perfection of its appointments, and decided that it would do. Tony Claghorn trod experimentally on the tennis courts, hazarded the opinion that they would be fast—and never played. Chet Moulton cast an appraising eye upon the golf links, opined that par on the first hole should be four and not five—and never teed up a ball. Steve Forrester inspected the billiard tables, cast a languid glance at the rows of gleaming cues—but did not remove his coat to click off a few caroms. By tacit agreement the older men—those over thirty—left all forms of exercise to their juniors.

But it was on the beach, a spotless white strip protected by the costly breakwater, that all members met. It was Chet Moulton who first donned a bathing suit, stuck an experimental toe into the water, and declared that the Atlantic Ocean, as sampled at Riggs Island, met with his approval. It was neither too cold nor too warm; there was neither too much nor too little current—this he discovered upon venturing in farther; and there was just enough tingle in the waves to make Chet— aged thirty-four—feel, as he himself expressed it, twenty years younger.

It was Steve Forrester, however, who discovered that the beach, gently sloping, firm, and warm to sit upon, was quite as suitable for games of chance as for more strenuous pursuits. "Think of it, boys," he exclaimed, "I'll go home tanned like a bronze statue, and if anybody asks me where I got it, I'll mention I got sunburned playing poker!"

The conception tickled Steve's risibilities mightily. To don a bathing suit immediately upon rising; to proceed to the beach after breakfast; to remain there, with occasional intermissions for meals, a stack of chips at one hand, and a long, cold drink at the other, from morning till night!—the program was most attractive. His fellow members voted for it enthusiastically, and the demand for lotions to be applied to smarting shoulders was heavy for a few days. But after that the participants in the game became well hardened, and at nearly any hour a group of young men, tanned to a chrome-leather hue, might have been discovered squatting on the sand, listening to the splash of the waves, and debating mentally whether to raise or to call.

The tennis courts were often deserted, the golf links neglected; but the beach was patronized so incessantly that one could not walk across it, Chet Moulton complained, without stubbing a toe on a poker chip. "What are the wild waves saying?" inquired Chet. "Are they saying 'Splash?' Not on your life. They're whispering 'Ante up!'"

In games, as everywhere else, there is the struggle for existence, and the survival of the fittest. At the Riggs Island Association, beach poker, as it was quickly called, drove everything else to the wall. They all played—all except Huntley Thornton, who made up for his nonparticipation in the games by acting as a lone spectator at them. Attired in immaculate flannels, jaunty in a Panama hat, with a cigarette, in a six-inch amber holder, decorating his smiling countenance all day long, Thornton wandered from group to group, congratulating the winners, sympathizing with the losers, and sooner or later squatting down to give his undivided attention to the play in the steepest game.

Repeatedly urged to take a hand, he had as often declined. "It may seem funny to you," he admitted, with a smile, "but I've never sat in a poker game in my life."

"No time to learn like the present."

"I promised my old mother," said Thornton, "that I would never gamble. I have yet to break that promise. I kept it in college. I kept it after college. I intend to keep it now."

Chet Moulton, who had just seen the most lucrative pot of the hour pass to an opponent, grinned ruefully. "Huntley," he declared, "I wish my mother had exacted a promise like that from me. It would have saved me a lot of money." Chet's sentiments were sincere. He had shown unlimited faith in a full hand, jacks up. He had backed it magnificently, only to see it lose dismally to a quartet of five-spots held by Don Felton. "If I had made a promise like that," mourned Chet, "and if I had kept it, I might have been a bloated capitalist today. Who knows?"

"And if I had made such a promise," said Felton, carefully stacking his winnings, "I wouldn't be taking in this pot now."

"Never too late to start," suggested Chet.

"You might give it back."

"I might—and then again I might not," murmured Felton. He glanced at his cards, grinned at the disconsolate Chet, and tossed a chip into the center of the little patch of sand about which they were sitting. "I'll open for the limit," he challenged.

It was into this atmosphere that Tony Claghorn brought his friend, Bill Parmelee, for a complete rest.

"YOUR COMING WILL be something of a sensation," predicted Tony, as he led the way to the launch which was to take them from the mainland to the island.

"How so?"

"You're a very well-known man, Bill. Everybody else knows it, even if you don't. I dare say that there's not a member of the club who hasn't heard of you."

"And you expect me to enjoy my vacation?"

"Why not?"

The ex-gambler shook his head. "I was never a great hand at advertising," he declared. "I'd prefer it—I'd prefer it greatly if not a soul knew me. Look here," he demanded suddenly, "have you told anybody I'm coming?"

"No," said Tony reluctantly, "I was saving that for a surprise."

"Well, suppose you save it a little longer."

"What do you mean?"

"Introduce me as your friend Brown—Bill Brown—that's a nice inoffensive name. Let me forget business—my peculiar kind of business—for a few days."

Tony's face fell. "I was rather set on introducing you to the boys. You see, I've told them so much about you."

Bill laughed. "Look here, old man," he inquired, "for whose pleasure did you get up this vacation? Theirs—or mine?"

"Yours, of course."

"Then remember my name is Bill Brown."

It hurt to do it, but it was under that name that Tony presented his friend to Huntley Thornton—and to Chet Moulton—and to Steve Forrester—and to the twenty or thirty other congenial spirits sojourning at the club. When, in conformity with established custom, the new arrivals donned bathing suits, and were promptly drafted into games of beach poker, Tony nearly burst in the effort to keep his secret buried in his bosom. Felton, indeed, had asked Bill if he played, and Tony, beginning indignantly, "Does he play!" had been reminded to keep silence by a violent dig in his unprotected ribs.

To his distress, his friend was separated from him. As a newcomer, Felton, who invariably played in the steepest game, invited Bill to sit in. Tony, being a regular, found himself seated some twenty feet away—and nearly broke his neck in an attempt to observe what was happening to Bill. From time to time voices reached his ear; from time to time he observed Huntley Thornton, the lone spectator, intently watching the game in which he never took part; from time to time the players in his own game invited him to pay a little attention to it. But it was not until darkness had put an end to the afternoon's play that Tony received any authentic news from the front.

He led his friend out of earshot of the others. "How much did you win?" he inquired eagerly.

"I lost," said Bill.

"W-what?" stammered Tony. "You—you lost?"

"I lost. I lost heavily."

To Tony it seemed impossible that such a thing should ever occur to his friend. Then an improbable explanation flashed into his mind. "I understand, Bill," he guessed, "you were afraid of making them suspicious. You lost on purpose."

Bill laughed. "Why should I lose on purpose?" he countered. "In any event, why should I let them get into me for more than five hundred dollars? And what on earth should they be suspicious of? No; I didn't lose on purpose. I'm not a philanthropist. I tried my darnedest to win. And I didn't win because another fellow played a better game than I did. That happens sometimes, you know."

Tony choked. "But—but it's impossible!" he sputtered.

"Thanks for the compliment," smiled Bill.

"It's impossible," Tony insisted, "and I know it's impossible because I've played with every man in this club. There's not one of them that's in a class with you."

"How about Felton?"

"Don Felton?"

"The big fellow with the sandy hair."

"Was he the big winner?" gasped Tony.

"The big winner and the only winner."

Tony swallowed hard. "I played with him in New York, at the Himalaya, only a month ago, and I cleaned him out."

It was Bill's turn to swallow. "You—you cleaned him out?" he stammered.

"Without the least difficulty," asseverated Tony. His brain was whirling. "Lord knows I'm no crack," he pursued, "I play a tolerable game—a good average game—and I've played with enough really good players to know just where I get off. I'm not an expert—"

"And Felton?"

Tony threw up his hands. "Felton's game is to mine as my game is to yours. A month ago he wasn't even near my class."

"Yet to-day he played better poker than I did. He outguessed me from beginning to end. If he called, his cards were just a shade better than mine. And every time I had a really good hand he didn't even raise. He'd drop."

"He must have improved," said Tony idiotically.

"I'll say so," declared Bill. "If the man I played with to-day wasn't in your class a month ago—"

"He must have improved lots."

The eyes of the two men met. Yet it was Tony who voiced the thought that both were probably thinking. "There are many cheating devices," he murmured, "but which of them could be used by a man sitting on a sandy beach, in blazing sunlight, dressed in a one-piece bathing suit?"

"None that I know of," said Bill.

TONY RETURNED TO the attack at the first opportunity and that meant immediately after supper. With great self-control he had refrained from alluding to the subject for ninety consecutive minutes.

"The cards might have been marked," he suggested.

"They weren't."

"Are you sure?"

"I gathered up three or four after our talk, Tony. I have them in my pocket this minute. They're not marked—and I've gone over them with a glass."

"Felton might have resorted to sleight of hand."

"Not with me watching," said the ex-gambler emphatically. "It's gotten to be unconscious with me, I suppose, but I always watch the deal carefully."

"Then how did he do it?"

Bill's blue eyes twinkled. "Maybe he studied some good book on poker."

"Be serious, Bill."

"All right, I'll be serious," Bill promised. "On my word of honor, old fellow, I don't know how he did it. But I mean to find out."

It was Tony's turn to smile. "Nice, pleasant way of spending a vacation, isn't it? This is how you get away from cards for a change."

Bill grinned. "If I learn something new I won't complain."

"And in the meantime the problem is how can a man cheat, without marked cards, without sleight-of-hand, and dressed in a bathing suit."

"That's all," assented Bill.

It is to be feared that Tony's night was far from peaceful. He tossed from side to side, a prey to weird speculations, racking his brains in an effort to discover some solution to the mystery. Dawn found him advanced not a step. In desperation he appealed to his friend.

"Bill, to-day when you play, let me watch."

"What for?"

"I might see something you don't."

Parmelee shook his head emphatically. "Tony, old fellow, you'd spoil it all. Felton's playing me for a sucker. It's an unusual part for me, and I'm enjoying it. But he'd stop like a shot if he thought I suspected. No, Tony, you can help me most by going about your own business and leaving me strictly alone."

Tony refused to be put off. "Look here," he insisted, "if you won't let me watch, you won't mind if I pass the word to Huntley Thornton?"

"What good would that do?"

"Huntley would keep his weather eye open. Huntley always looks on."

It spoke volumes for Bill's self-control that he replied civilly. "He knows nothing about cards. He told me so himself."

"Even so—"

"Tony, with what you know about me, are you really advising me to go to an amateur for assistance?"

"I don't know why not," ventured Tony.

"If you don't, then I do," said Bill decisively. "When I need a guardian, old man, I'll let you know. But for the time being I'll struggle on without help. And if you breathe a word to a soul I'll brain you!"

That threat kept Claghorn silent during the morning, but it

did not prevent him from sidling up to Bill at noon to inquire, "How did it go?"

"Great?"

"You won?"

"I lost six hundred more."

"And you call that great?" gasped Tony.

"I call that most satisfactory," Bill declared. "For the first time I'm beginning to get my bearings."

Despite Tony's urgent questions he declined to add another word and left his friend in a condition bordering on collapse. Not once, but a dozen times, had Tony been an eyewitness of Bill's expertness at the profession which had been forced upon him: the profession of unmasking sharpers. Yet the memory of his repeated triumphs was less potent than the realization that for once Bill was facing an extraordinary situation, and had, so far, met nothing but defeat.

Pride goeth before a fall; and Tony's pride in his idol departed on wings. Twenty-four hours earlier he would unhesitatingly have wagered his last cent that no problem connected with the devious arts of dishonest gambling was too difficult for the man who had solved so many. The events of the immediate past had shattered his faith to such an extent that he had seriously offered his own help. That declined, he had offered, with equal seriousness, to ask Huntley Thornton—whose ignorance of cards was well known—to take Bill—whose knowledge of the subject was profound—under his wing.

The utter insanity of his proposals never occurred to Tony. Uppermost in his mind was the thought that his friend was in trouble, and that any straw was necessarily a promising straw.

During the afternoon Tony played so carelessly that for the

first time in several sessions he found himself a winner. Had he stopped to analyze his own game he might have made the instructive discovery that it was undoubtedly at its best when his mind was not on it. But Tony was far too much concerned with graver matters to indulge in any such reflections. Being a winner, he retired from the game after an hour, and nonchalantly strolled toward the group which included Bill. At a distance of fifteen feet he was greeted with a look so fearful that he beat a hasty retreat.

Somewhat offended, he strode manfully into the water, and splashed around for an unconscionable period a prey to disturbing meditations. How, he asked himself repeatedly, could a man cheat—attired only in a baffling suit? The answer was perfectly clear: it could not be done, and Tony was reluctantly forced to the conclusion that his friend's formerly invincible game had deteriorated sadly.

This decision was confirmed when at the end of the afternoon's play he made his way to Bill's side and hissed, "Well?"

The ex-gambler smiled cryptically.

"Well?" repeated Tony.

"Very well," said Bill.

Tony might have pursued his investigations further had he not, at that moment, discerned Huntley Thornton, immaculate as always, stealthily endeavoring to attract his attention from the other end of the beach.

"CLAGHORN," BEGAN THORNTON, "you don't mind if I ask you a few questions?"

"Not at all."

"Not even if they're rather personal questions about a friend of yours?"

"Why, what do you mean?"

Thornton wasted no time in beating around the bush. "Claghorn, I want to find out something about your guest: Mr. William Brown. Who is he? What is he? What do you know about him?"

Utterly astounded, Tony sparred for time. "Why do you ask?"

"Because he's a card cheat," said Thornton flatly.

Tony gasped. "W-what did you say?" he sputtered.

"He's a card cheat," Thornton repeated dispassionately. "How he does it, what methods he uses, I don't know. But the fact remains, nevertheless. I don't pretend to be an authority on cards. Quite the contrary, I am rather less than a novice; so I can't say how it's possible for a man—dressed in a bathing suit—to cheat."

The familiar words echoed in Tony's ears. "Possible?" he interrupted. "Why, it isn't possible."

"That's what I would have said in advance; but after what he did to poor Don Felton—"

"What he did?" Tony interrupted again. "Why, he lost five hundred to him yesterday."

"Yes."

"He lost six hundred more this morning."

"Quite so."

"And this afternoon I suppose he lost seven hundred."

"Your supposition is incorrect, Claghorn," said Thornton coldly. "This afternoon he got Don to raise the stakes, and he picked him clean."

"What?" gasped Tony. "He won?"

"He began by winning back the eleven hundred he had lost," said Thornton. "Then he won as much more from Don. Then he suggested raising the limit—which Don did, very foolishly—and it took your friend Brown less than an hour more to separate Don from every last cent he had in all the world."

Something in Tony urged him to cheer; to execute a dance of triumph; to shout his satisfaction aloud. But, for once, soberer second thought was with him, and he only murmured, "Isn't that too bad?"

"It's much too bad, Claghorn; it's very much too bad!"

"Tst! Tst!" clucked Tony.

"Don isn't a rich man."

"No."

"The loss of the money means a lot to him."

"Of course it does."

"If he had lost it fairly and squarely, now—"

"What makes you think he didn't?" Tony interrupted.

"Impossible!" Thornton snapped. "This morning your friend Brown—so Felton said—played like a beginner. This afternoon he was infallible. Now, a man doesn't improve that much in an hour or two."

Familiar words! Familiar words! Inwardly Tony exulted, but he remarked shrewdly, "It was all right, you mean, so long as Brown played like a beginner, but it was all wrong the moment he began to play like an expert."

"That's not what I mean," said Thornton, "and you know it isn't."

"Well, what do you mean?"

"I mean this," and in the gathering darkness Tony could see his fists clench, "there's something wrong—something very wrong indeed—somewhere. I want to find out what it is."

Tony smiled happily. "Why do you come to me?" he asked innocently.

"Because, like everybody else, I've heard of this Parmelee friend of yours, this man who makes it a business to expose cheats. I've heard how he showed up Graham in Palm Beach; and I've heard how he showed up others in New York. Now, if you will be so kind, I'd like you to wire Parmelee, and ask him to come here at once, at my expense, to investigate this man Brown."

Describing the episode afterward, Tony said: "I don't know how I stopped myself from breaking out into laughter. The idea was rich: asking Bill Parmelee to investigate himself! I was thankful that it was dark and that Thornton couldn't see my face. Never in my life did I have a harder time keeping it straight!"

Thornton repeated his request: "I want you to wire for Parmelee. He's the man for the job. I want him to watch Brown play; to play with him himself if he wants to. And then I want him to expose him."

It was at this point that a familiar figure approached through the darkness, and Bill Parmelee—alias Brown—fully dressed, joined the speakers. "I couldn't help overhearing what you just said, Mr. Thornton," he declared. "I'm a great hand at coming right down to brass tacks. Let's have it out."

To say that Thornton was angry would be an understatement. He was furious; beside himself with rage; and he began to speak in a tone which trembled with passion. Tony, listening, wondered why Thornton should take Felton's troubles so greatly to heart; and he wondered still more why Parmelee, sitting near him in the darkness, allowed the vitriolic blast to continue unchecked. Thornton was nothing if not specific. He did not hesitate to call names; to couple them with unpleasant adjectives; to express his opinions in the most elaborately insulting language.

To the torrent of invective, Bill answered not a word. It was only when Thornton ran out of breath, and stopped temporarily that Bill asked calmly, "Mr. Thornton, have you a cigarette?"

Utterly taken aback Thornton offered his case. Bill reached for it in the darkness, and found it.

"Have you a match?" Bill asked.

Tony had never seen his friend smoke. To his boundless astonishment, Bill now lighted a cigarette, inhaled a breath or two, and turned to his enemy.

"Go ahead, Mr. Thornton," he invited.

What followed, according to Tony, beggared description. Thornton, curiously confused, launched again into his invective. That it did not disturb Bill greatly was evidenced by the intermittent glimmer from his cigarette in the darkness. And then, in the middle of a word, Thornton stopped—stopped dead.

For a minute—two minutes—while Tony marveled—there was absolute silence. Then, in a curiously different voice, Thornton said, "I understand, Mr. Parmelee."

"Mr. Parmelee!" Tony felt his hair rising on end. By what process had Thornton discovered his identity? But he was speaking again:

"I beg your pardon, Mr. Claghorn," faltered Thornton. "I'm sorry I made such a scene in your presence." He paused—paused for another unearthly wait while the cigarette twinkled. "In the morning, Mr. Parmelee; yes, I'll leave in the morning. Felton will go too. I will answer for him. We are grateful, both of us, for your forbearance." Again an unearthly pause, while

Tony clenched his fists and wondered what supernatural forces were at work. Then, in a broken voice, Thornton was speaking: "Do you insist, Mr. Parmelee?" Utterly crushed, he turned to Tony. "Mr. Claghorn, at Mr. Parmelee's request, I tell you that Felton cheated—and that I was his accomplice. Is that sufficient, Mr. Parmelee? Thank you. Good night."

Through the darkness came the sound of Thornton's retreating footsteps. Then, in a glowing arc, Bill's cigarette flew through the air, to fall with a gentle hiss into the ocean.

Again Tony felt his hair rising. He had been in the presence of something strangely mysterious, something so uncanny that it partook of the miraculous. He stretched out a trembling hand and seized his friend's knee. "Bill," he begged, "for Heaven's sake, what was it?"

Came the familiar laugh, and then, for the first time in many minutes, the sound of Bill's voice. "It was mind reading," he said.

IT WAS NOT until they were again seated in the train, nearly a week later, that Bill consented to answer Tony's innumerable questions. Prior to that time he had maintained a stony silence. Even when Huntley Thornton and Don Felton had suddenly decided to go fishing in southern Florida, and had departed, bag and baggage, before daybreak, Bill had had no comment to offer.

"Surely you could have told me then," Tony protested.

"Why? You would never have been satisfied until you had told it to every man in the club."

"And why not?"

"You would have shown them up."

"They should have been shown up."

"I wonder!" said Bill. "They were amateurs—nothing but amateurs—and it's so much easier to ruin reputations than to make them. If I had spoken I would have branded those two men for the rest of their lives. As it is, they've gone off together where they can think things over, and they may decide that honesty isn't such a bad policy after all."

"Humph!" snorted Tony.

"In the bottom of your heart, old fellow, you agree with me. I've shown up a good many men—but they've deserved it. These two were in a class by themselves. They'd made a mistake. I've given them a chance to let it be forgotten. If they go wrong again—well, it won't be on my conscience." He smiled. "Is that so, Tony?"

"I guess so," Tony admitted. "In fact, I'll agree with anything if you tell me just what happened. To me it's all as clear as mud."

Bill laughed. "It began in a funny way. When I lost to Felton on that first afternoon I had no suspicion that anything was wrong. He played as if he knew every card in my hand. Well, that's what I'd expect of a really fine player. I thought Felton was one.

"Then you told me what you knew about him: that he wasn't even in your class, and I tried to put two and two together. Generally two and two make four—but this time they didn't, and it wasn't until the next morning that I began to suspect what was going on. It was really the simplest thing in the world when I once put my mind on it. The cards weren't marked; Felton wasn't doing any legerdemain—he wasn't nearly clever enough for that—yet he played as if he knew just what I held.

There could be only one answer: he did actually know, and that meant that somebody was telling him.

"When you play indoors, your cards are dealt onto a table: you gather them together; you raise the pips just enough to read them, and you leave them right on the table. At any rate, that's what you do if you're a professional gambler—and I'm a professional. But playing on the sand you can't do that because it would take acrobatics. Instead, you take up your cards—and unless you hold them mighty close a man sitting behind you can read them.

"That's where Thornton came in. I'm not a stingy player, and the moment I started betting liberally Thornton plunked himself down where he could watch. Then he signaled my holdings to his partner."

"How did he do it?"

"It cost me six hundred dollars to find out. Naturally I couldn't face him. I watched him out of the corner of my eye: that was all I dared. Even then, it took me an hour to discover his system—it was so beautifully simple that you would never notice it if you weren't looking for it."

"Well? Well?" said Tony impatiently.

"Did you ever see Thornton without a cigarette in his mouth?" Bill inquired.

Tony could not control his vexation. "Bill," he pleaded, "I'm not a bit interested in Thornton's personal habits. And I'm very much interested in his method of signaling."

"You won't see a thing when it's right under your nose—or under his nose, I should say," laughed Bill. "That was how he did it. His cigarette, man! His cigarette!"

"What about it?"

"Well, it smoked, didn't it? It could produce short puffs, and it could produce long puffs—and it could produce any required alternation of them, couldn't it?"

"You mean—" gasped Tony.

"I mean Thornton's cigarette was sending perfectly good Morse. And I thanked my lucky stars that telegraphy was one of the things I picked up in my six years on the road. Of course Thornton abbreviated: he didn't have to spell out, 'He's holding two pairs, kings up,' when it took no particular genius to condense that into three letters, and he didn't have to telegraph, 'Mr. Brown has just filled a straight, jack high,' when he could say the same thing in two letters. In fact, he didn't have to use Morse—a prearranged code would have answered just as well—and it would have given me no more trouble."

"How on earth could you beat such a team?"

"By playing straight poker," said Bill. "In the afternoon, instead of sitting up, I lay down, held my cards so that I could barely see them myself, and played the great American game just as well as I knew how. One of the peculiarities of beach poker," commented Bill, "is that you can play it lying on your stomach. I did—and for twenty-four hours afterward I had a crick in the neck to show for it.

"I won back the eleven hundred I had lost in short order; and then Felton made the mistake of losing his temper. He had whipped me so easily that morning—and the day before—that he couldn't quite reconcile himself to the sudden change in the state of affairs. He got angry, and when I suggested raising the limit, he got angrier but he didn't decline." Bill sighed reminiscently. "It was quick work after that, and toward the end I had Thornton telegraphing, 'Stop! Stop! Stop!' That was all he could telegraph, and it only made his partner more furious than ever." He chuckled. "I enjoyed that game: 'pon my word, I did!"

"And then?" said Tony.

"What do you mean?"

"How do you explain what you did to Thornton? I never saw anything more wonderful in my life. He started in to abuse you—to call you every name he could think of—and you stopped him, you crushed him, you made him confess without saying a word. And then you insisted it was mind reading!"

Bill laughed. "Tony, old fellow, my artistic temperament is to blame. I hadn't thought of it until I walked back to the beach, but it suddenly struck me what a masterly touch it would be to pay Thornton out in his own coin—to tell him what I had to say with one of his own cigarettes!"

"You mean—you telegraphed?"

"I did."

"With puffs of smoke?"

"Not in the dark, old fellow. I remembered the good book: the 'pillar of cloud' and the 'pillar of fire;' I said what I had to say with the burning tip of my cigarette, and believe me, I didn't mince matters!"

He smiled as Tony gazed at him open-mouthed. "I am not ordinarily a profane man," said Bill, "but if you had been able to read what I said to Thornton, even you would have blushed. I'll bet he did."

He paused, to witness Tony shaking in the throes of Homeric laughter. "There's something about it," Tony gasped, between explosions, "something about—the idea—of swearing—profanely—with the end—of a cigarette—that strikes me—as being awfully—awfully—funny! Spark! Spark! 'You —— ——

——' Spark! Spark! 'How do you like what I'm handing you now, you dirty dog?'" For an instant he mastered himself. Then he was off again. "To think—to think—that he asked me to send for Bill Parmelee—to investigate Bill Parmelee!"

"It would have been awkward, wouldn't it?" Bill admitted. He grinned as his friend went into spasm after spasm of uncontrollable laughter.

But the final question came later. "Bill," asked Tony, long after, "did those fellows—Thornton and Felton—actually think you cheated?"

Bill chuckled. "They did, Tony, and that's the chief reason why I forgave them. I didn't cheat. Of course I didn't cheat. But they thought I did. They were sure I did. They were such awful dubs, such hopeless amateurs, that they didn't recognize really good play when they saw it.

"Tony, old man," Bill concluded, "in my long career I've had compliments—many compliments. But to be accused of cheating because my game is so good! I'll never ask for a finer one than that!"

8

THE ADVENTURE OF
THE FALLEN ANGELS

THE ATMOSPHERE IN the little room was electric. The explosion, one sensed rather than felt, would come soon.

From outside, far below in the street, came the occasional clatter of a belated taxicab. From above came the steady, unwinking glare of high-powered lights. The clock on the mantel—and the overflowing ash trays—indicated the hour of two in the morning. Yet the men seated about the bridge table in the Himalaya Club, cutting in and out at the end of each rubber, played with a concentration that was apparently regardless of everything else.

Straker, so he asserted afterward, had been on the verge of an apoplectic stroke since midnight. Billings clutched his cards in a nervous hand, and impatiently awaited the moment when the accusation would be made. Chisholm, who could watch the ticker spell out fluctuations which meant tens of thousands to him without turning a hair, bit the ends of his straggly mustache from time to time, and hoped that his exterior did not betray his excitement.

Like the others, Chisholm had absolute confidence in Anthony P. Claghorn—"Tony" Claghorn to his intimates—who, by his own admission, was an expert on everything having to do with games of chance; but as the minutes stretched into hours, and as Claghorn, with not a wrinkle in his lofty brow, confined himself to smoking the best cigars that the Himalaya Club—and his hosts—provided, and refrained from uttering a word, Chisholm's worries multiplied.

He could not assert that Tony had been an inattentive spectator. At nine, promptly, the game had begun. At nine, promptly, Tony had pulled up the most comfortable chair, and had anchored in it. At half-hourly intervals, or thereabouts, rubbers had ended, and the six players, cutting to determine the four to play next, had changed seats. At half-hourly intervals, or thereabouts, Tony, without moving, had called for a fresh cigar.

At ten Chisholm had glanced at Tony questioningly. Tony had replied with an innocent stare. At intervals from then on to midnight Straker, Billings, Hotchkiss, and Bell had glanced questioningly at the silent young man. He had given them glance for glance—but no satisfaction. Yet during the preceding afternoon Tony had discoursed eloquently upon the ease with which he would solve the mystery.

To be sure, it had been a mystery of Tony's own creating. Roy Terriss, the suspect, had not been looked upon as such until Tony, by a few well-chosen words, had called the attention of his clubmates to the fact that Roy was a remarkably consistent winner. Before that time it had been admitted that Roy was generally successful at bridge; that he enjoyed playing in an expensive game; and that the game was rarely, if ever, expensive for him. It was Tony who pointed out that Roy's gains, during a winter's play, probably mounted well up into five figures; and it was Tony who, without making direct accusations, had raised his eyebrows significantly at moments when that simple act was not altogether beneficial to Roy's reputation.

Having created the mystery, he had been invited to solve it. With becoming modesty, he had accepted the task, and after sitting solemnly through one five-hour session, had expressed a desire to sit through another. This wish granted, he had declared his intention of being present on yet a third occasion. The results had been painful to his friends, who, expecting they hardly knew what, had thrown caution to the winds, and had been divested of large sums by Terriss, who, knowing nothing at all of what was afoot, had played calmly—coldly—and with deadly precision.

Chisholm, indeed, had explained his own mistakes to Tony that very afternoon. "I'm a conservative player," he had asserted earnestly. "I follow the book. I know the rules and I don't try to improve on them. I don't overbid, and if the other fellow overbids I'm a sharp at doubling. But when I'm expecting the whole game to blow up any minute I can't put my mind on it and I don't play like myself."

"Even at twenty-five cents a point?"

"What does twenty-five cents a point matter when I'm waiting for you to start the fireworks? Take that hand last night: it was good for three odd. I bid up to five. That wasn't like me, was it? Then Terriss doubled—that's what any sane, levelheaded player would have done holding his cards—and instead of shutting up, and taking my medicine like a little man, what did I do but redouble! Claghorn, I put it to you: was that the act of a normal man? Was that the kind of play you'd look for from me? Then the finesses didn't hold, and I got set for eight hundred points."

Tony smiled reminiscently. "That was a most instructive hand," he commented. "Now, if you had doubled his four bid instead of going up yourself—"

Chisholm cut him short with a growl. "Look here," he pointed out succinctly, "we didn't get you into this to give us bridge lessons, you know. If we wanted lessons, we could get them for about a tenth of what this performance is costing us. You said there was something queer about the game. We're waiting to be shown—that's all."

At two o'clock, ten hours later, Chisholm was still waiting.

Billings, neat and dapper, a stickler for etiquette, had, upon this third evening, to his everlasting embarrassment, been detected in a revoke. He had paid the penalty promptly— graciously; had, indeed, insisted upon its being exacted. But the look which he had given Tony had explained more eloquently than could any number of words how he had come to be guilty. And Hotchkiss, fumbling his cards nervously, had failed to cover an honor with an honor—with results which bulked large when the score was added.

And at two o'clock, Billings and Hotchkiss, as well as Straker, Bell and Chisholm, were waiting—waiting.

THE GREAT MOMENT—THE long-anticipated moment—came when it was least expected. At two fifteen the men had adjourned hopelessly. Chisholm was balancing the score; his confederates had already opened their check books; Terriss, with folded arms, was waiting to learn the exact amount of his gains.

It was then that Tony flicked the ashes from the tip of his cigar, and spoke: "Mr. Terriss is again the only winner," he murmured, as if to himself. "I wonder what he would say if I mentioned that the cards with which he has been winning— are marked?"

In an instant Terriss was on his feet. "What did you say, Claghorn?" he thundered. "What did you say?"

Tony stood his ground stoutly. "I made the statement," he declared, "that you have been winning with marked cards." He took up the two decks that had been used in the bridge game, and balanced them in his hands. "I still make that statement."

"You—" shouted Terriss, and dashed at him.

Chisholm thrust his bulk between. "Take it easy, Terriss," he suggested, "we all know what's been going on. Mr. Claghorn has been looking into things for us."

Terriss gazed around the circle of faces. "What's this? A conspiracy?" he demanded.

Chisholm shook his head. "Terriss, you know us better than that. Bell—Hotchkiss—Straker—Billings—they've all got reputations to lose, not to mention me. We've asked Mr. Claghorn to investigate. That's all."

"And how is Mr. Claghorn qualified to pass upon such matters? What right has Mr. Claghorn to make accusations against me?"

A chorus answered him. Straker, it appeared, had been present upon a certain occasion when Tony had unmasked one Schwartz. Billings, who had been another witness of that feat, contributed details of the manner in which Tony had exposed a sharper at Palm Beach. Chisholm, a third witness, had half a dozen stories at his finger tips.

Tony Claghorn's career, it was evident from their testimony, had been one long succession of triumphs. His wake was dotted with discomfited cheats, prestidigitators, and impostors. Once put upon the scent, he had never failed to bring down his man.

With appropriate modesty Tony bowed his head while his

friends detailed his triumphs. To be sure, the credit for each victory was wholly due to one Bill Parmelee, an unassuming countryman whose acquaintance Tony had made one summer; and Tony, not once but a dozen times, had explained how his own contribution to the various episodes which had since become famous was of the slightest. But Tony's explanations must have lacked the convincing note, for his friends did not hesitate to trumpet his praises to the four corners of the earth. That they should forget the quiet young man who had played the leading role was not unnatural: Parmelee, farmer and reformed gambler, cared nothing for advertising, and chose to remain out of sight. Almost mechanically, his laurels descended upon Claghorn, who, despite his protestations, found the eminence thus forced upon him far from unpleasant.

When Terriss' monotonous success at bridge had come to Tony's attention he had attempted to interest Parmelee in the matter. He had failed. Parmelee, Cincinnatus of gamblers, cared more for his blooded cattle than for fresh laurels. And he had not agreed entirely with Claghorn's conclusions.

"Tony, because a man's a winner, it doesn't follow that he's a cheat," he had pointed out.

"No, but in this case—"

"In any case," Parmelee had interrupted, "you must remember that for every dollar won by dishonest gambling a thousand are probably won by honest play."

"You don't really believe that!"

"I don't know whether I do or not. But that's what I like to think."

Tony's enthusiasm had been damped but not extinguished. After revolving the subject in his mind overnight he had decided that he himself was entirely competent and that Bill's confidence in human nature was, to say the very least, exaggerated. Wherefore Tony had gallantly launched himself into the breach.

He smiled at Terriss across the table. Success was his, and its taste was sweet. "Marked cards, Mr. Terriss," he repeated, "marked cards."

Terriss glanced at the set faces about him, and his assurance decreased visibly. "I suppose," he faltered, "that it will be quite useless for me to say that I didn't know the cards were marked."

"Quite useless," said Tony.

"I won fairly and squarely. I played the game according to the rules."

"What's the good of arguing?" inquired Straker icily.

Terriss gazed about helplessly. "No; there's no good in arguing if you're all against me," he assented. "What do you expect me to do?"

"Make good."

"How?"

"Give back what you won."

Terriss snorted. "I'll be damned if I do!" he declared.

"If you don't," said Chisholm, "you will forfeit your membership in this club."

"And if I do," challenged Terriss, "will I hold on to it? Am I the kind of man whom you want to remain? What's the difference whether I give back my winnings or not—except to me? I've been caught cheating, haven't I? That makes me an undesirable member by itself, doesn't it? Of course I say that I played honestly: that's what you'd expect me to say. But even if I give back my winnings, you won't believe me."

"It's the correct thing to do, Terriss," said Straker quietly.

"What does the correct thing matter to a man who has been caught cheating? No; if I'm to be hanged, I'd rather be hanged as a wolf than as a lamb." He took up the score, and surveyed the totals. "Gentlemen, you owe me money. Write your checks."

"What?" gasped Chisholm.

"You've lost. Pay me."

"What about the marked cards?"

"Well, what about them? If there are marked cards, you may have profited by them yourself. Try and prove you didn't."

"I lost!" sputtered Chisholm, nearly speechless.

"What of that? If the cards hadn't been marked, you might have lost still more. And that applies to all of us." With supreme self-confidence, he beamed upon the players. "Pay me," he invited, "pay me, or I'll bring suit against every man jack of you. You see, I no longer have a reputation to lose, and it won't hurt me to go to court. But if you fellows think you will enjoy the publicity, if you look forward to seeing your names decorating the front pages of the newspapers, just try getting out of your debts."

Helplessly the conspirators turned to Tony. "What do you advise?" they asked as one man.

Tony shrugged his shoulders. "This is out of my department," he said modestly.

Straker glanced about keenly. "You know," he said brightly, "Terriss may be bluffing."

Terriss grinned. "If that's what you think, why don't you play your hand and call his bluff?"

There was a pause. Then Billings seized his pen and dashed off a check. "Here you are," he said ungraciously. "I have a wife and two daughters. I can't afford to get mixed up in a scandal."

"Quite so," said Terriss. "I thought you'd see the point after I'd explained it to you. Line forms this side."

One by one the men wrote checks, and passed them to the lone winner. He pocketed them carefully, rose, surveyed the conspirators. "Gentlemen," he murmured, "I am about to leave you, to return to my poor but honest domicile. And I have one last request to make of you: don't tell anybody what happened in this room to-night; don't breathe a word of it to your closest friends."

Straker laughed aloud. "Won't we?" he cackled. "Oh, won't we? I'll make it my business to see that every man in this club knows just what took place in twenty-four hours!"

Terriss smiled ominously. "In that event, Straker," he warned, "don't pretend you're surprised when I bring suit for criminal libel."

"What?"

"Against each and every one of you." At the threshold he paused. "I can't stop you from blackening my reputation among yourselves; you seem to have done that pretty thoroughly anyhow. But let me hear that any one of you has dared to say a word against me outside of this room, and I'll hit back! By George, I will! I'll hit back, and I'll hit back hard! Marked cards! Who brought them into the game? Who profited by them? Who didn't profit by them?" A mocking smile hovered upon his lips as he opened the door. "Gentlemen, think it over! Before you do anything, think it over—and then don't do it!"

The latch clicked behind him, and he was gone.

It was Billings who first broke an agonized silence. "Another such victory," he soliloquized, "and we'll all be broke. What do we do next, Claghorn?"

But that worthy, pausing only to light a fresh cigar, had prudently retreated to the threshold.

"What do we do next, Claghorn?" Hotchkiss echoed.

Tony shrugged his shoulders. "This is out of my department," he said modestly.

Long, long after he had left, gently closing the door behind him, the conspirators sat around the table, comparing notes, exchanging advice, and sympathizing with each other's misfortunes. But that, however interesting in itself, has nothing to do with this story.

THERE ARE ALWAYS several ways of looking at a matter. A disinterested judge, for example, might hesitate to characterize the episode which we have recounted as a triumph for Mr. Anthony P. Claghorn. But Claghorn himself spoke of it as a triumph without question. He had set out to expose a sharper; he had succeeded. That the operation had been monstrously costly to his friends was not so important as the fact that it had attained its object. Tony, indeed, did not use stronger terms than "triumph" only because stronger terms did not occur to him.

To his pretty wife he related his exploit with gusto. She understood nothing of cards, but Tony wanted admiration, and her admiration was better than none. But the approbation which mattered most was that of Bill Parmelee, and to that Tony looked forward eagerly. Half a dozen times Tony had been a mystified spectator while Bill, moving along curious lines, had laid the foundations of one of his many victories. It had been Tony's part to observe, to wonder, and to applaud at the conclusion of each carefully planned campaign.

Now, Tony felt modestly, the roles were reversed. Without help from his friend, acting entirely upon his own initiative, he, Tony, had brought his attack to a successful termination. It would be Bill's turn to wonder, Bill's turn to applaud, Bill's turn to listen while Tony condescended to explain. In the anticipation it was all very pleasant, and Tony lost no time in scurrying to the little Connecticut town in which Parmelee had immured himself.

"I was satisfied that something was wrong," Tony began magisterially, "oh, long ago—ever so long ago."

"In spite of what I said?" Bill, inquired.

"What did you say?" asked Tony tolerantly.

"I tried to convince you that a man can be a winner without being a cheat."

"Oh, yes; I remember that."

"I said that for every dollar won by dishonest gambling, a thousand are probably won by honest play."

"I remember that also," Tony admitted, and lighted a cigar, "but your faith in human nature is—shall we say—exaggerated? In this case the suspect—I'd rather not tell you his name—broke down and admitted everything."

"Well! Well!" said Bill. "Go on with your story."

"I investigated the case carefully. I used a process of elimination. The game was bridge. Certain methods of cheating were therefore useless."

"Quite correct."

"A holdout, for example, would be of no value," said Tony, and went on to explain the nature of a holdout to the man who had initiated him into its mysteries. "By a holdout," he volunteered graciously. "I mean a device which can be used for the purpose of keeping one or more cards in concealment until the player wants them in his own hand."

Not a vestige of a smile was visible on Bill's placid countenance. "I have heard there were such devices," he murmured.

"Quite so. But as I have explained to you, the suspect— whom I prefer not to call by name—could not possibly have used one. It would have meant introducing a fifty-third card into a complete deck, and that would have been detected at once. You see, if Ter—the suspect—had introduced a fifth ace into his hand, it would inevitably have duplicated an ace in some other hand. Whenever all the cards are dealt out, a holdout becomes worthless."

Bill stared at the carpet intently. "Not altogether worthless," he qualified.

"Altogether worthless," Tony insisted.

"A holdout might be used on the deal itself," murmured Bill, as if to himself. "The—ahem—suspect—might put all four aces and all four kings as well into a hold-out offer the deck to be cut without them, and pass them into his own hand on the deal."

"What?" gasped Tony.

Bill continued unemotionally. "Of course, that would be pretty raw. Nobody but a beginner would try to get away with anything like that. A really sharp player—playing bridge— would pass the top cards into his partner's hand. His partner, you see, wouldn't have to be a confederate; give him more than his share of aces and kings, and he'd go a no-trumper, wouldn't he? In all innocence he'd make the correct bid. It would be quite enough for the sharper—sitting across the table—to give him the cards warranting it."

"By George!" ejaculated Tony, "I never thought of that!"

"There are still other ways in which a holdout might be used without duplicating any one of the fifty-two cards in the deck, but it's not necessary to discuss them. Go on, Tony."

It was with a sensation that the wind had been taken out of his sails that the young man continued. "Rightly or wrongly I decided that the suspect was not using a holdout. You don't think he was, Bill?" he interjected anxiously.

"No."

"I continued with my process of elimination. There are many cheating devices. In bridge most of them are useless. But one cheating device is useful in every card game." He paused, to aim a long forefinger at his friend. "I refer, of course, to marked cards."

"Ah, ha!"

"I examined the cards carefully. They were not marked. But I risked everything on a bold bluff," chortled Tony, "and it worked. I made one heap of all my winnings," he misquoted, "and I risked it all on one pitch—on one pitch—I forget how it goes on."

"Cut out the poetry and tell me what happened."

"I picked the psychological instant. I've always been good at that—picking the psychological instant; and I boldly accused Ter—the suspect—of using marked cards. I knew well enough he wasn't using them. Here"—and Tony produced the cards themselves from capacious pockets—"here they are— unmarked. But I understand human nature, and I felt sure that if I accused a cheat of cheating, he would—ahem—collapse. Whether or not I happened to mention the exact method he was using did not matter: the accusation would be enough."

"Did it work?"

"To perfection. Ter—the suspect—was silent—and silence is confession."

Bill smiled. "Is it?" he queried. "If so, a sleeping man is guilty of anything."

"The suspect knew the game was up."

"Perhaps he felt you were carrying too many guns for him. What was the use of pleading innocence when you—and your friends—were convinced he was guilty?"

"I made it a point to treat—ahem!—the suspect—with scrupulous fairness."

"Why not call him by his name? Roy Terriss?"

"How did you know?" gasped Tony.

"That's neither here nor there. Go on."

But Tony was too astonished to continue. "How did you know?" he demanded. "How on earth did you know?"

Bill shook his head. "We'll skip that for the time being. Finish your story."

Tony gazed at his friend with some bewilderment. He had looked forward to this moment of triumph. In the realization it was not so satisfactory as in prospect. He passed a shaky hand over his brow. "Perhaps you can finish the story yourself, Bill."

"Perhaps I can. Terriss admitted nothing. Terriss denied nothing. He refused to give back the money he had won. That took nerve, and I admire him for it. He knew he had no chance of vindicating himself. He decided to wait for a better opportunity."

Tony nodded reluctantly. "Most of that's quite correct," he admitted grudgingly.

"You accused Terriss of playing with marked cards. He

replied that if the cards were marked he hadn't benefited by it. And he added what was, after all, a logical conclusion: that the marks might have been of value to your friends."

"Absurd on the face of it," commented Tony. "The cards aren't marked."

"Not so absurd as you think," qualified Bill, and his face set in stern lines. "The cards are marked."

SOMETIMES THE WORD "surprise" is too feeble fully to express a state of mind. Indeed, to picture Tony's reaction to his friend's simple announcement in reasonably accurate terms, it would be necessary to overhaul, refurnish, and expand the English dictionary.

Tony gazed at Bill with eyes that popped out of his head, opened his mouth two or three times, wet his lips, and sputtered, "Wh-what did you say?"

"I said," repeated Bill, "that these cards are marked."

"But they can't be!" exploded Tony. "Don't you see? That was the whole beauty of my bluff: that the cards were what they should be, and that I made him believe they were something else."

Bill smiled grimly. "Sometimes a bluff isn't a bluff. Sometimes a man shoots in the dark and hits the bull's-eye. Sometimes a well-meaning blunderer like you, Tony, tells the truth when he least suspects it."

"But it's impossible! I've examined those cards with a magnifying glass! I've gone over them not once but a dozen times! I haven't found a thing!"

"Tony, you didn't know what to look for." Bill spread half a dozen cards on a convenient table. "In the first place, the cards are of an uncommon pattern. You notice the two little angels in the center? They're what is known as 'Angel-Backs.'"

"They're the cards that the club supplies."

"I don't doubt that."

"For the last eight months no other cards have been used at the Himalaya."

"Then how about these?" Bill spread half a dozen cards from the second deck on the table.

Tony gave the cards, decorated with a conventional geometrical design, only a glance. "Oh, those? Those are poorer-grade cards which the club laid in when it began to run short of the better ones."

"The Angel-Backs being the better grade?"

"Of course. You can see that in a minute."

Bill half closed his eyes reminiscently. "When I made my living as a gambler—when I was just beginning to learn the ropes—Angel-Backs were fairly common. They were good cards. They were high priced, but they were worth it. They gradually dropped out of use; cheaper cards took their place. To-day people don't care about quality; it is price that matters. In fact, this deck of Angel-Backs is the first that I have seen in some years. I was under the impression that they were no longer being manufactured."

Tony could not restrain his impatience. "Come back to the subject, Bill," he begged. "You said the cards were marked. Which deck? And how are they marked?"

"The Angel-Backs, of course. Look at the angels closely."

"I see nothing."

Bill smiled. "This angel, for example, must have gone walking in the mud. His right foot is not as clean as it might be."

"What of that?"

"This other angel evidently put one hand into the mud. You'll notice it's dirty. This third angel knelt in it: there's some on one of his knees. And this fourth angel must have been doing somersaults: you'll notice his complexion has gotten darker."

"By George!" ejaculated Tony.

"Go through the deck," invited Bill, "and you'll find that there isn't an angel in it who wouldn't be the better for a bath. And you'll find—it's a pure coincidence, doubtless—that the kings have marks on their right shoulders, the queens marks on their left shoulders, the jacks marks at the waist line, and so on through the lot. The angels are small—and the marks are still smaller—but they're very evident when you're looking for them."

Without a word Tony whipped out a magnifying glass, and bent over the cards. "You're right!" he said excitedly, "you're right! And that proves my case beyond a doubt."

"What do you mean?"

"Terriss *was* using marked cards. My guess hit the nail on the head. Terriss marked the cards while the game was under way."

"Marked them as delicately as this? As accurately? Tony, don't you believe it."

"But cards can be marked during the progress of a game."

"Yes—with a prick—or with a spot of color. But to mark cards like this? To select a minute speck on the back of each, and dot it as neatly as these are dotted? That takes time, skill—and privacy. The man who marked those cards did it in his room."

"You mean Terriss brought the marked deck with him, and substituted it for one we were using?"

"Not likely."

"Why not? It could have been done."

"It's most improbable. You'll notice that every card in the deck is marked—not the high cards alone."

"What of that?"

"What would be the object—in bridge? Really fine players place the cards as far down as the sevens and eights. But whoever heard of taking a finesse against a three-spot? Or a four? Or a five? Why should any sane man take the trouble—and the risk—to mark them?"

Tony corrugated his brow. "Perhaps," he hazarded, "perhaps the man who marked the cards was keen on doing a thorough job. Having begun, he didn't know when to stop."

Bill shook his head decisively. "It won't do, Tony. It won't do at all. An amateur might have done that—you might have done that, at a first attempt—but the man we are looking for is a professional, or I know nothing about gambling and gamblers. Look at the beauty of the work! See how perfectly his shading matches the color of the backs! And remember if he marked the twos and threes there was a good reason."

Tony shrugged his shoulders. "Reason or no reason, I can't see that it's of any particular importance."

But Bill was already studying a timetable. "The next train for New York leaves in forty minutes," he mentioned. "I'm going to pack my bag."

Tony gazed at him with surprise. "Going to New York because the twos and threes are marked? Really, I think you're exaggerating their importance."

"It would be difficult to do that," said Bill. He rose and glanced keenly at his friend. "In the first place, they prove that Roy Terriss is innocent."

"How so?"

"I have been given to understand that he plays no other game than bridge."

"Yes; that's so."

"Well, the man who marked these cards didn't expect to play bridge at all. That's my second place, Tony. The man who marked these cards didn't neglect the little ones for the soundest reason in the world."

"And what's that?" asked Tony scornfully.

Bill opened his valise, and began to jam articles of clothing into it. He glanced at his friend, and smiled; opened his mouth to speak; closed it and smiled again. "Tony, hasn't it struck you yet?" he demanded at length. "The man who marked these cards expected to play poker!"

UPON EVERY OTHER occasion that Parmelee had accompanied him to New York, Tony had been filled with happy anticipation. It had meant, invariably, that the man hunt was on in earnest; that a pursuit which would end only with the exposure of the guilty individual was under way. In the past, Tony, a privileged spectator, knowing enough to whet his curiosity to the utmost, but never knowing quite as much as he wanted to, had enjoyed a long succession of happy thrills. Not once but half a dozen times had he observed Parmelee, picking up a scent like a well-trained bloodhound, disentangling it from others, follow it to a surprising conclusion. Tony had watched, wondered, admired: here was drama, hot off the griddle, served in the most appetizing fashion, and the clubman, whose chief entertainment, in earlier days, had been provided by the headlines of the sensational newspapers, had come to learn that a thrill, at first-hand, was worth a dozen relayed through print. It had all been most enjoyable—yet Tony, upon this particular occasion, was conscious of no pleasurable feelings.

He gazed gloomily out of the window, and gave himself up to unhappy reflections. The cards had been marked; Terriss was not the guilty man: both facts, Tony was compelled to admit, were crystal clear. It followed, as night follows day, that the criminal must be one of his own particular cronies: Chisholm, Billings, Hotchkiss, Bell or Straker. Tony reviewed the list to the accompaniment of the click of the wheels. Man hunting, he admitted, was a sport which eclipsed all other sports; but somehow it lost its zest when the prospective victim was one of his own friends.

After half an hour's gloomy meditation, he turned to the quiet countryman at his side. "Bill," he ventured tentatively, "I take it that when you reach New York you will want to go to the Himalaya Club."

"You take it correctly."

"It's not necessary, you know."

"Why not?"

"Well, really, I haven't asked you to investigate anything."

"That's all right, old fellow," Bill responded heartily, "I haven't waited to be asked."

Tony's voice carried a gentle tinge of reproof. "Don't you think," he inquired tactfully, "that you should wait until you are asked?"

Bill laughed. "Meaning, I suppose, that I'm butting in."

"I wouldn't say that."

"No; but it's what you're thinking." He glanced shrewdly at Claghorn. "Tony, old fellow, you shot in the dark, and you brought down the wrong man. You have branded Roy Terriss a crooked gambler—a cheat—a thief—a man unfit to be received in decent society. Do you want him to rest under that cloud?"

"No; no, indeed," began Tony vociferously, "that's not what I mean at all."

"Of course not," Bill chimed in. "You're too fair and square to tolerate anything like that. You want Terriss cleared—cleared triumphantly—only," and Bill smiled shrewdly, "only—you're rather scared that I'm going to fix the blame on one of your very best friends. Isn't that so?"

Tony nodded.

Bill grinned. "That's what might happen, no doubt. I'm not denying it. If I merely wanted to bag a man, and didn't care how I did it, I think I could convict any one of your friends— or you yourself, for that matter."

"Convict me?" gasped Tony.

"It could be done. How did you come by those marked cards?"

"Why—why—I took them from the table."

"How did they get there? How do I know you didn't mark them yourself? How do I know that you and your friends weren't banded together to rob Terriss."

It was Tony's turn to grin. "Well, we lost."

"To Terriss, perhaps. But the night before the same crowd won pretty heavily from somebody else—what?"

"How did you know that?"

"It doesn't matter," said Bill. "I know it—that's enough. I'm simply trying to show you how easy it would be to find a victim if I were after no more than that. You and your friends have touched pitch, Tony, and you can't touch pitch without being defiled."

Tony's brain whirled. "You mean, then," he sputtered, "you mean that the guilty man is Chisholm—or Billings—or Straker—or Bell—or Hotchkiss—or—or me?"

Bill laughed. "If it will comfort you—and I think it will—I'll let you into a secret, and tell you that I don't suspect any of them—of you, I mean," he corrected gravely.

Tony felt a crushing weight rising buoyantly—easily— happily. "Do you mean that?" he cried.

"We're looking for a professional cheat," said Bill. "Remember that. Hold fast to that. It's the only thing, Tony, between you, yourself and the deep sea. You've been worrying about your friends so much that you've completely overlooked what a suspicious character somebody else is."

"Who?" begged Tony.

"Tony Claghorn," said Bill. He smiled at his friend's consternation. "Tony Claghorn has been running around with me so much that he has acquired a firsthand knowledge of cheating devices. How do you know he hasn't used that knowledge? How do you know he hasn't tried to convert theory into practice? It would be profitable—very profitable—and he might get away with it. No, Tony," said Bill, "Roy Terriss is safe. It's Tony Claghorn we have to look after now. And if I'm going to New York it's because I think I see a chance to save his skin."

Tony was so completely dumfounded that he was silent for the rest of the trip.

IT WAS BETWEEN hours at the Himalaya Club when the two men walked in. The regulars, who ate their lunch in the raftered dining hall every day, had departed; and the even more regulars, who experimented with games of chance in its card rooms from late afternoon until early morning, had not yet arrived.

"We'd better go away, and come back later," said Tony.

"Why not wait here?" suggested Bill. He seated himself at a table. "Tony, how would you like to play some cold hands?"

Tony gazed at his friend with a suspicious eye. "What stake?" he inquired.

"Why any stake at all?" countered Bill. "We'll play for nothing—and the fun of it."

Tony assented doubtfully. Ordinarily filled with implicit trust in his friend, his adventure on the train had sadly shaken his equilibrium. He, Tony, was under suspicion. Any move of Bill's might therefore be dangerous to him. In some vague, incomprehensible manner, disaster threatened—with the most innocent exterior.

With noticeable lack of enthusiasm he seated himself at the table, and rang for cards.

Bill glanced at the box, and did not open it. "I don't care for these cards," he announced. "Can't we have some Angel-Backs?"

"I'll see, sir," said the man.

Tony's suspicions redoubled. "What's the matter with the cards?" he inquired.

"I like to play with cards of better quality," the countryman alleged. His eyes shone as the waiter returned with a deck of the required pattern.

He broke the seal, opened the box, and riffled the cards thoughtfully.

"Do you like these better?" Tony asked.

"Much better. Very much better." He dealt the cards, face

down, with amazing speed. "King of hearts. Two of diamonds. Eight of hearts. Ace of spades. Three of clubs. Seven of spades. Ten of hearts. Seven of clubs Five of hearts. Seven of hearts."

"What's this?" demanded Tony. "Legerdemain?"

Bill shrugged his shoulders. "Call it what you like. But if you will look at your cards you will find that you have a four flush in hearts. You will fill on the draw. The card on top of the deck is another heart."

"And you?" gasped Tony.

"Triplets; nothing but triplets," smiled Bill. "Three sevens."

"And they'll be four of a kind on the draw?"

"That would be too raw, old fellow. No: a full house will be enough. That will beat your flush."

Tony broke into a roar of laughter. "I see it!" he cried. "Of course I see it!"

"What do you see?"

"You stacked the cards!"

"That's pretty evident."

"And they weren't hard to stack because you substituted the marked deck—the deck I brought up to the country—for the new deck the waiter handed you!"

"Is that so?" challenged Bill.

"These cards are marked!"

"Admitted."

"They must be the same deck—unless—unless—"

"Well, say it."

"Unless," faltered Tony, with cold sweat breaking out suddenly on his brow, "unless every deck of Angel-Backs in the club is marked!"

Bill smiled. "That's what I'm trying to find out," he granted.

"They may all be—shall we say?—fallen angels."

Without a word Tony rang for the waiter. "We want another deck—two more decks—of Angel-Backs," he snapped.

The waiter shook his head. "Sorry, sir, I can't do it."

"Why not?"

"We're running very short of the Angel-Backs—and the members prefer them to the other cards. They're better quality. The steward instructed me not to give out more than one deck to a party."

Tony extracted a bank note from his pocket. "I want two decks of Angel-Backs," he repeated. "Do you understand?"

"I'll do what I can," said the waiter.

He was back in a few minutes with a single deck. "I couldn't get you two," he apologized, "there's not a gross left, sir. I'm breaking orders as it is, sir."

In silence Tony passed the unopened box to his friend. "Open it, Bill."

Parmelee put his hands behind his back. "Open it yourself. You might accuse me of substituting another deck."

Without a word Tony broke the seal, inverted the box, and allowed the cards to cascade upon the table.

"Well?" Bill inquired.

"Marked. Marked—every blame one of them!"

"Fallen angels!" murmured Parmelee. "Fallen angels! Tony, don't you think we might have a chat with the steward?"

Tony clenched his fists. "If he's the man who marked them I'll see that he's out of a job in ten minutes!"

"Why so excitable?" soothed Bill. "What would the steward have to gain by trickery? He isn't the man we want: you can depend upon that."

He listened quietly while his explosive friend summoned the steward, and explained the state of affairs to that worthy. The man examined the cards, paled, bit his lips. "Really, sir," he stammered, "this is most surprising—most surprising."

"I'll say so!" asseverated Tony.

"I wouldn't believe it if I didn't see it with my own eyes. It's monstrous—incredible."

"How do you explain it?"

"I—I don't."

"How do we know that you're not the guilty man?"

"Oh, sir, I've been in the employ of this club for twenty-eight years! It would be late in life for me to turn around and become a common cheat. Really, sir, you don't think that I could be capable of such a thing?"

Bill broke into the conversation. "How many more decks of Angel-Backs have you?"

"Less than a gross."

"Why didn't you order more?"

"I did. The jobber couldn't fill my orders."

"Oh!" Bill half closed his eyes. "When did you first buy Angel-Backs?"

"About a year ago, sir. Shall I tell you about it?"

"I wish you would."

"A sample deck was sent us by a mail-order house. The International Supply Company, they called themselves."

"What was their address?"

"A post-office box at Times Square Station, New York City, sir."

"Go on."

"Samples are sent to us frequently, but this sample was unusually good."

"Angel-Backs—I should think so!"

"Not only that, but the cards were remarkably cheap; so cheap, in fact, that the club could sell them at the same price as inferior cards and still make money."

"Didn't that circumstance make you suspicious?"

"The International Supply Company explained that the pattern was about to be discontinued, and that they had a large quantity on hand. If we would take them all, they would make us a special price, sir. I didn't make the purchase on my own responsibility. I referred the matter to the house committee. They told me to go ahead."

"What else?"

"That's all, sir. The members liked the cards, as I expected they would. We used nothing else for many months. Then the Angel-Backs began to run short. I tried to buy more."

"Your letters to the International Supply Company were returned unclaimed."

"Yes, sir. They had gone out of business."

Bill smiled. "The scent becomes more interesting as we follow it." He turned to his friend. "Tony, what's the next move?"

"To examine the rest of the cards, of course."

Bill's eyes twinkled, but he nodded soberly. "Suppose you do that, Tony. There are over a hundred decks left, so it will take time. But be thorough about it: go through every deck, and tabulate your results in writing."

AFTER HIS VOLCANIC friend had departed Bill motioned the steward to a chair at his side. "I have a good many questions to ask you," he began, "but Mr. Claghorn is safely out of the way for at least an hour. He will examine every deck of Angel-Backs in the storeroom, and he will find every card marked." The steward waited for him to continue. "In the first place, the membership of this club changes rapidly, doesn't it?"

"What do you mean, sir?."

"New members are elected—old members resign—or become inactive."

"More frequently than I like. Yes, sir."

"At a rough guess, how many members, very active a year ago, are inactive today?"

"Twenty, perhaps," said the steward.

"Write their names on a piece of paper." The man did so.

"Play for high stakes is common here?" pursued Bill.

"It is the rule, sir."

"But not all of the twenty played poker."

"No, sir."

"Scratch out the names of those who played other games. That leaves how many?"

"An even dozen, sir."

"Now let us take another angle: there have been big winners in the club during the past year?"

"Yes, sir. At least eight or ten."

"How many of them did their winning at poker?"

"Five or six."

"Write down their names. Compare the two lists. How many of the big winners—at poker—do you find among the inactive members?"

"Only one, sir."

"That's easy to explain, isn't it? A big winner doesn't become inactive. A big winner sticks to the game just as long as he continues winning."

"Naturally, sir."

"Yet one man who was a big winner—at poker—didn't wait for his luck to change. He stopped coming to the club."

The steward nodded. "That always puzzled me, sir. He played poker, and he had the reputation of being the strongest player that ever sat down to a table in these rooms. He played nearly every night for six months and then—"

"And then?"

"I never could understand it, sir, but he simply stopped coming."

Bill looked keenly at the other. "Was this man—by some curious coincidence—elected to membership just about a year ago?"

The steward nodded with dawning comprehension. "He was, sir. Mr. Ashley Kendrick was proposed one week after I had purchased the Angel-Backs. The membership committee has always been notoriously lax: it's easy to get into the Himalaya. Mr. Kendrick was elected five days after his name had been posted."

"He played poker."

"Yes, sir."

"With the Angel-Backs."

"Yes, sir."

"And he won."

"Invariably, sir."

"Then, six months later, when the cards began to run short, he stopped coming."

"Oh, no, sir."

"What do you mean?"

"He stopped coming: that part's correct, sir. But at that time we hadn't begun to run short of Angel-Backs."

Bill whistled. "This gets more interesting as we go along!"

"We were using nothing but Angel-Backs at that time; the supply was very plentiful. Mr. Kendrick simply failed to show up one evening—that was all."

"You had his address?"

"Yes, sir, but it was an address which won't help. His address was right here—in care of the Himalaya Club."

"No forwarding address, I suppose?"

"None, needed, sir. From the moment he joined until the last evening he spent here Mr. Kendrick never received a letter."

It was at this juncture that Tony Claghorn thrust his exuberant self into the picture. "Bill," he announced, "I've examined the Angel-Backs."

"All of them? So soon?"

"It wasn't necessary to look at more than a card or two from each deck. They're all marked."

He had expected his announcement to produce a sensation. He was disappointed.

"Yes; I expected to hear that," said Bill calmly. "In the meantime, I've been busy."

Tony swallowed his chagrin. "With what result?" he demanded.

"Tony, I've run up a blind alley. I've found out something, but it doesn't help—not a darn bit. I'm stumped. I found the trail getting hotter and hotter, and I followed it. I fetched up against a brick wall."

"If you had allowed me to help you," Tony declared, "that wouldn't have happened."

"Perhaps not. Perhaps not."

"It's not too late now," invited Tony.

Bill grinned ruefully. "All right, Tony. Show me how to lay my hands on a fellow named Ashley Kendrick."

"Ashley Kendrick? Ashley Kendrick? Why, he hasn't been here in months."

"I know that already."

"I can't tell you how to reach him, but I can put you in touch with his best friend."

"Also a member of this club?"

"He used to be," said Tony. "He's a chap by the name of Venner. A nice chap, but the unluckiest there ever was."

Bill glanced at the steward. "Is his name on your list of inactives?"

"Yes, sir."

"But not on the list of winners?"

"No, sir. As Mr. Claghorn says, Mr. Venner was—unfortunate."

Bill sucked in his breath sharply. "I wonder—I wonder—if by any chance his misfortunes began about the time that the Angel-Backs started to run short."

The steward started. "Come to think of it, they did, sir."

Bill lcapcd to his feet, and flung his arms above his head with excitement unusual for him. "What a fool I was! What a dunderhead! What a numskull! I should have seen it at once! I should have guessed it right off! Why, it's as plain as the nose on a man's face!"

Tony neither understood nor shared his enthusiasm. "I don't get what you're driving at."

"Don't you see? How Venner explains everything?"

Tony fixed a look of mild reproach upon him. "Bill," he cautioned, "don't let me hear you say a word against Venner!

He's as fine a fellow as there ever was—even if his luck turned—and I don't see how he explains anything."

By a superhuman effort Bill composed his face, and seated himself again. "Sorry, Tony. Perhaps I was too enthusiastic. But tell me about Venner; tell me all about him."

Tony stood on his dignity. "I don't see what Venner has to do with this case."

"All right, you don't see," said Bill, controlling his impatience with difficulty, "but tell me what I want to know anyhow."

Tony had acknowledged his friend's authority too long to shake it off easily. "If you insist—"

"I do."

"Then I'll tell you; though I warn you in advance that it won't help you at all." He bent a searching look on the steward. "This must go no farther," he warned. "This is to remain a secret among the three of us."

"I shan't say a word, sir. But if you'd prefer to have me go away—"

Magnanimously Tony shook his head. "Inasmuch as I suspected you, you have a right to listen." He turned to Parmelee. "Bill," he began, "Venner joined the club something less than a year ago—a fine fellow—a gentleman, every inch of him."

"Go on."

"He played poker—I played with him myself any number of times. He rarely played for high stakes, that is, in the beginning. He played a fair game—broke a little better than even. Then—to his misfortune—he met Kendrick.

"Of course I needn't tell you about Kendrick, one of the best poker players I ever saw; a man who could almost read your mind; who always played in the biggest game, and kicked because it wasn't bigger. Venner met Kendrick, and was fascinated by him. He gave up playing himself to watch Kendrick play; he said he had never seen anything so wonderful. And Kendrick used to like it; Kendrick always saved a chair near him for Venner.

"The two came to be close friends. You'd never see one without the other. Kendrick seemed to like teaching Venner; and Venner's eyes never left Kendrick. And when the game broke up, they'd go away together. Kendrick used to live here in the club. For a time, I believe, Venner shared Kendrick's rooms.

"Then, one night Kendrick didn't show up, and Venner acted as if he had lost the best friend he had in the world. He hovered around the table at which Kendrick used to play; he kept his eyes on the door as if Kendrick might come through it any minute; he asked every man he met if he had seen Kendrick.

"For a week Venner watched. He told more than one of us that he suspected Kendrick had met with foul play. Then he gave him up for lost."

Parmelee's eyes were fixed on vacancy. "It was then that Venner took Kendrick's place in the game—the big game."

"Yes. It was an asinine thing to do, but Venner thought he had learned enough from Kendrick to fill his boots. He did— for a night or so. He won—won heavily—and then his luck turned. He'd win one evening. He'd lose twice as much the next. He'd win a thousand—and lose three. He'd win two thousand—and lose five.

"I urged him to stop. I urged him any number of times, but he always explained that out of ordinary courtesy, he couldn't. He had won from the other fellows. He had to do the fair thing by giving them a chance for revenge."

Tony paused, and nodded gravely. "That's what Venner did: a chivalrous, gentlemanly, insane performance. Don't you think so?"

Bill turned to the steward. "What do you think?" he inquired.

"After twenty-eight years in the employ of this club I have learned that there are times when it is wisest not to think."

Bill nodded. "I can understand how you lasted twenty-eight years." He turned to Tony. "Finish your story."

Tony lowered his voice. "I'm coming to the part I want kept secret. Venner lost. Venner lost every cent he had. Venner had to stop coming to the club: he was posted for nonpayment of dues."

"Where is he now? And what is he doing?"

"Never tell a soul, will you? Venner's down and out. He's had to take a job as a waiter in a cheap restaurant; and I have to ruin my digestion by having a meal there every once in so often."

Parmelee grinned, and cast a grateful glance at his friend. "Tony, you've helped! You have no idea how you've helped!" He rose, and deliberately winked at the steward. "I presume you are good at reading riddles?"

"What's the riddle, sir?"

"This is a hard one. See if you can guess it." Gravely he propounded: "If a farmer, twenty-five years old, lives in Connecticut, goes to New York on the midday train, spends the afternoon at the Himalaya Club, and then, because he has a cast-iron digestion, has his dinner at a cheap restaurant, what—what is the waiter's name?"

"Venner, sir," said the steward promptly. "Go to the head of the class," said Bill.

WHILE PARMELEE AND his much mystified friend proceed to a frowsy, second-class eating place on lower Eighth Avenue, there to be served by one Venner, there to corral the said Venner in an untidy private dining room, there to tempt the said Venner with promises of immunity and gradually increasing amounts of currency until his silent tongue becomes exceedingly loquacious, let us turn back the pages of time two years to the very beginning of an exceedingly strange story.

The day was unbearably hot and sultry. Layers of heated air, writhing and twisting like heavy oil in their ascent, floated lazily upward from the broiling streets. The asphalt itself was soft and gummy; choking dust, the accumulation of a rainless week, lay in ambush to take suffering humanity by the throat; and in innumerable windows sickly geraniums drooped and wilted under the merciless rays of the sun.

A thermometer, hung at street level, would have indicated a temperature well into the nineties. The same thermometer, carried up five flights of stairs in any one of the near-by tenements, would gradually have registered higher and higher figures until under the metallic roof, assailed from above by the burning glare of the sun, and from below by the up-pour of scorching air, it would actually have indicated a temperature in excess of one hundred. Yet the man who bent over a little table in the inferno known as a hall bedroom in the topmost story of one of the most dilapidated buildings in the section was too intent upon his labors to notice such minor matters as the weather.

His single window was closed, its inside covered with soap, so that no observer across the street might peer through it. His door was locked—not merely locked, but barricaded by pieces of furniture which had been moved against it. And despite the heat, for not a breath of air traveled through the room, a kettle, placed on a portable oil stove, boiled briskly at the man's elbow.

On the table before which he sat paper cartons—dozens and scores of them—were stacked in orderly fashion until they reached the ceiling. At his right hand was a saucer containing a reddish liquid with an alcoholic odor. At his left hand was a second saucer containing a bluish liquid. Half a dozen minute camel's-hair brushes were carefully ranged before him. And as if the weather and the stove and the tightly closed openings had not made the room hot enough, a high-powered electric light was suspended from a cord, casting a blinding glare upon the man's hands, and upon the objects which were engrossing his attention.

He rose, removed a carton from the huge pile, and holding it dexterously, allowed the steam from the boiling kettle to hiss upon the paper seal. The carton flew open. With delicate care he set it upon the floor, and emptied it of its contents, an even gross of individually sealed small paper boxes. Each seal in turn was held for an instant in the jet of escaping steam; each gave way almost instantly.

The man placed the open boxes at one side, seated himself again, and wiping his hands carefully so that no moisture from them might make a mark, shook one of the boxes, and removed from it a new deck of playing cards. He spread them out on the table, took up one of his brushes, dipped it in the colored liquid, and with the expertness gained by long practice, placed a microscopic, but none-the-less telltale, dot on the back of each card.

Had an observer been present he would have noted that the

color applied matched the back of the card perfectly; stranger yet, he would have noted that after the minute spot of moisture had dried, the closest scrutiny would have been required to show that the card had been tampered with. While moist, the tiny speck of liquid was visible; when dry, it blended with the surrounding color so excellently that no person unacquainted with the secret would have been able to discover a mark.

During his manipulations the man had been careful not to disturb the order of the cards: factory-packed playing cards are always arranged in the same manner. He examined six or eight cards closely; satisfied himself that the marks which he had made were indistinguishable; leveled the deck, and returned it to its box. For a second time he held the seal in the jet of steam. Then he closed the flap, pressed the seal so that it adhered again, and laid the box to one side.

A dozen cartons under the table represented the labor of several weeks. Working at the greatest speed which he would permit himself, his output did not exceed ten decks an hour—and each carton contained a gross, one hundred and forty-four decks—and the huge pile before him numbered at least several hundred cartons. Had he paused to calculate, he might well have been terrified at the result; ten decks an hour; eighty to a hundred a day; at the very best, not more than five gross a week. And nearly a year would elapse before he might reach the completion of his gigantic task!

Presumably the man had made his calculations before commencing; had estimated the expenditure of time, and had decided that it was worth his while, for he paused not an instant upon finishing one deck before beginning on another. He worked rapidly yet carefully, with a concentration which might have been explained only had a slave driver, with a whip, been standing behind him. Practice had brought him surprising skill. There was no waste motion; no misdirected energy. Little by little the pile of unfinished work diminished; little by little the pile of finished work grew.

At seven o'clock, or thereabouts, he extinguished the oil stove, drew a clean white sheet over the mountain of cartons, washed, and made himself presentable, and went out, padlocking the door of his room behind him. Other tenants of the building, gathered at the entrance for a breath of air, nodded to him as he strode by them.

"Good evening, Mr. Kendrick," they chorused.

"Good evening," said Kendrick, and went on his way—to a lunch room around the corner.

"What's he do for a living?" inquired one of the neighbors.

"He's a littery man," said one better informed.

"A which?"

"A littery man. He writes novels and books and stories. Locks himself in his room from morning till night, and writes—just writes. He told me so himself. Keeps regular hours, just like a workingman, too."

"That ain't work—just writing," commented a listener, and broke off to inquire, "Have you ever read anything he's written?"

"Not yet. He says there'll be nothing of his published for a year. But he's going to let me know when something comes out."

Let us dive headlong for the end of that year. The pile of unfinished work had shrunk—finally vanished. The little room was filled with neatly stacked cartons, which one might have examined and sworn had never been opened. And the International Supply Company—alias Kendrick—having offered samples of superior-quality playing cards at ruinous prices to three clubs, equally notorious for the size of the games played under their roofs, and for the ease with which a stranger might secure membership, had arranged to sell the entire quantity to the Himalaya.

The following day a horse-drawn truck, specially hired for the occasion, and personally driven by the International Supply Company—alias Kendrick—delivered several hundred gross of marked cards to the Himalaya Club.

Within a week Mr. Ashley Kendrick was proposed for membership in that notorious organization.

He was elected five days later.

Within less than a month he was voted the best poker player who had ever' seated himself at one of the Himalaya's card tables. And his former neighbors, who had looked forward to reading his books, novels, and stories, waited a while—and then forgot him.

A GAMBLER'S PARADISE: a place where the play is continuous, where the stakes are high, where the players are liberal, and—where every card is marked! It was in such an unbelievably blissful spot that Kendrick now found himself. For a whole year he had worked and planned; for a whole year he had lived economically on his savings: if he was at length to be rewarded, he felt that he deserved it.

Yet he did not make the mistake of playing too well. An infallible player discourages his opponents; whereas an occasional loss is not expensive, and greatly heartens the victim.

Kendrick, who knew every card in the deck, who could read his opponents' hands as readily as if they had been exposed, who could tell every time whether or not it was worth while to draw, could have won far more than he actually permitted himself to. Hardly an evening went by without Kendrick sustaining at least one sensational loss; hardly a session without his going down to defeat on at least one well-advertised hand. But never did the gambler rise from his seat poorer than when he had settled himself into it; never did the end of a session make it necessary for Kendrick to produce his check book.

He limited himself strictly to a maximum winning, and his self-control was such that he never exceeded the fixed amount. Yet the maximum was a liberal maximum, for at the end of ten days he had recouped himself for the expenditures of the preceding year, and at the end of three months his bank account had begun to assume formidable proportions.

At the end of four months he increased his maximum liberally, and doubled his bank account, and at the end of five months he began to fling off all restraint. He began to play poker of a brand unheard of even at the Himalaya, where fine players abounded. He had put by a gigantic nest egg; the marked cards would not last forever; and it was his program to win as much as possible against the day when the Angel-Backs would begin to run short.

It was at this juncture that Venner, so he confessed to Parmelee, projected himself into the situation.

Venner, a shiftless ne'er-do-well of pleasing personality, had dissipated a modest inheritance, and was fast nearing the end of his slender resources. He played poker tolerably: upon occasion he had not hesitated to cheat, and in the hope of extending his dishonest operations enough to make a killing, he had purchased half a dozen decks of cards at the club, and had taken them home with him with the laudable intention of marking them. Once marked, he would find opportunities to substitute them for the club's cards.

He had marked two or three decks before he made the astounding discovery that the cards were already marked. He could not believe the evidence of his eyes. Feverishly he broke open the sealed boxes, to find that some pioneer in knavery had been before him. More cards, covertly examined at the Himalaya itself, confirmed the amazing truth.

Venner had intended to indulge in cheating on a small scale. His discovery of the existence of a swindle of such gigantic dimensions left him simply thunderstruck. For an instant he reflected that knowing the secret, he, too, could win as he pleased. But upon second thought it occurred to him that there would be quite as much gain, and far less risk, were he to make a cat's-paw out of the daring sharper who was doubtless at work this instant.

For months Kendrick had been a sensational winner. Within twenty-four hours after penetrating his secret Venner confronted him.

"You can't prove anything," Kendrick said.

"I know it," said Venner.

"I'm the most surprised man in the world to learn that the cards are marked," Kendrick alleged.

"Then you won't object if I pass the word on to the other members, and see that other cards are used?"

Kendrick's eyes narrowed. Venner was easy for him to see through. "What's the alternative?" he demanded.

"Divvy up with me," murmured Venner. "Pay me half of whatever you win, and I'll be as silent as the grave." He paused. "If you don't, I'll expose you. I'll say that you confessed every-thing—"

"Nobody will believe it."

"If that's what you think, turn down my offer."

Kendrick was in an unpleasant position, and was fully aware of it. The solution—the solution that flashed upon him at once was to pretend to accept Venner's terms, and to disap-pear forever from the scene. But the weak point was painfully obvious: Venner, out of spite, might set the authorities upon his trail. It would be better, Kendrick decided instantaneously, to wait until Venner too was thoroughly besmirched; to make Venner an accomplice who dared not open his mouth with-out imperiling his own freedom. And then, also, even if he had to divide his future winnings, a great deal of money might be amassed in a short time—say two or three weeks.

He shook Venner's hand heartily. "You're a man after my own heart," he said. "I accept your proposition."

Then began the short but interesting period during which Venner, according to Tony's description, sat at Kendrick's side and ostensibly studied his game, but during which Venner, according to his own confession, followed the play with an eagle eye to make sure that his partner in crime did not win more than he would admit, and thus defraud him of his share.

After a few days Venner invited himself to live in Kendrick's rooms; he could keep a closer watch on him in that manner; and for two brief but happy weeks Venner's income was exceed-ingly large. He treated himself to a new outfit of clothing, and began to sport small but costly scarfpins. He even looked at automobiles; his improved circumstances would warrant him in purchasing one.

Then, upon the evening of the day that Venner after convening himself in executive session, had voted that Kendrick should henceforth pay him three quarters and not merely half of his winnings, the astute gambler disappeared. Venner was worried; believed that his partner had met with foul play. At the end of a week a letter mailed en route to Mexico City told Venner the truth. Kendrick had disappeared for good. He had won enough to support him in comfort the rest of his life. He did not propose to share his winnings, even with so likable a chap as Venner. Nevertheless he gave Venner his blessing, and mentioned that he admired Venner's collection of scarfpins— which he had taken to Mexico with him.

At once Venner found himself in straitened circumstances. His income had vanished: his expenditure continued. But the Angel-Backs promised relief.

He took Kendrick's place in the big game, and won heavily for two nights. On the third night, to his unutterable horror, cards of a strange pattern were used, and Venner, compelled to play honest poker against men who qualified as experts, lost more than he had won in the two preceding sessions.

On the fourth night the Angel-Backs returned, and Venner did well. But on the fifth and sixth nights other cards were supplied, and the results were harrowing.

What followed partook of the nature of a nightmare. Venner had run into debt; willing or unwilling was compelled to play. And he was suddenly confronted with a situation far more dangerous than any that had ever faced Kendrick; the Angel-Backs were running short; other cards were being substituted;

and if Venner invariably won with the Angel-Backs and lost upon all other occasions, it would not be long before some astute observer called attention to the circumstance.

He used to lie awake at night, summoning up hideous pictures, visioning the possibilities. It occurred to him that he might purchase more Angel-Backs, mark them, and introduce them into the play. He found that cards of that pattern were not obtainable at any price. Even had they been obtainable, he could not bring them to the table without inviting suspicious comment. He thought of marking the cards which the club had substituted for the Angel-Backs; but he realized that the sleight of hand necessary to exchange them for the deck in use was far beyond him. In his petty cheating in the past he had occasionally indulged in the form of dishonesty known as ringing in a cold deck. That was possible, playing for moderate stakes, with no spectators. It was impossible, save for some sharper far more expert than he, in a big game closely watched by twenty or more men.

For a ghastly week Venner endured the tortures of the damned. Like Kendrick, he found it well to limit his winnings when the gods were good to him, and when chance brought a deck of marked cards to his table. But unlike Kendrick, he was compelled too often to play with strange cards—and he found it quite impossible to limit his losings.

For all of his sins in the past the cheat paid a thousand times over during that week. To put in an appearance each night, smiling and jovial, while his soul writhed in torment; to forgo pot after pot when the Angel-Backs offered it to him, because to win too much might have created suspicion; to lose upon other nights, and lose heavily—disastrously—because he dared not change his style of play; no wonder the man cracked under the strain.

He began to play wildly—recklessly. His opponents, shrewd students of psychology, sensed the change in the wind. In two consecutive sessions they stripped him.

Courtesy prohibits a man from taking another's last cigarette; but it does not prohibit a man from taking another's last dollar. His opponents showed him no mercy. When Venner left the Himalaya Club for the last time, he had borrowed as much as his friends would lend, he owned nothing, and his pockets were empty.

This, coming by driblets in the beginning, coming faster and faster as the man's emotions mastered him in the end, was the story that Parmelee and Claghorn heard from the lips of one Venner, a waiter in a frowsy, second-class eating place on lower Eighth Avenue.

IT WAS NOT until half an hour after they had left the restaurant, on their walk uptown, that Bill opened his mouth. Tony, completely floored, for once in his life, had marched at his side in silence.

"We started, didn't we," said Bill, "to find out whether or not Roy Terriss cheated at bridge? It's funny over what a long trail it has led us! Terriss—the Angel-Backs—the Himalaya—Kendrick—Venner—"

"Don't mention that man's name to me!" interrupted Tony.

"Why not?"

"When I think of what I've been doing to my digestion on his account: eating in that miserable restaurant at least once a week, because I sympathized with him! Ugh!"

"Venner is a whole lot worse off, isn't he? You have been a guest of the restaurant; he is a waiter in it."

"Serves him right!"

"Perhaps. Perhaps. Something—call it what you will—has a great way of getting even with the man who doesn't play fair. Venner is paying—Venner is paying heavily. If you're a real man, Tony, you might go on eating a meal in that restaurant once in a while."

"Why?"

"Some day you may be able to set Venner on the right path— and that would be your way of paying whatever you owe. How about it, Tony?"

"Er—I'll think about it."

Bill nodded his approval. "Pay! Pay! Pay! You can't get out of it!"

"No? How about Kendrick?"

"He'll be no exception. Think of the year's slavery he endured before he could bring off his coup! Think what he could have done—where he could have been today—had he applied the same energy to any honest pursuit!"

"He's living in luxury, in Mexico."

"Yes—for six months, perhaps."

"He won enough to support him the rest of his life."

"Lots of gamblers have done that, but somehow the money doesn't last. Money made that way never lasts. Like the angels—the fallen angels—it has wings! An honest man can call on the law to protect his property. Kendrick can't. The moment the others find that out—in Mexico—what chance will he have?" Bill shook his head vigorously. "No, of the two, I think Venner is the lucky one. He's alive, and I'll bet two to one this minute that Kendrick isn't. He worked too hard for his money to give it up living; and in Mexico life is cheap—very cheap."

"Maybe," said Tony, "maybe." He thought hard for a minute. Then he turned to his friend. "From the very beginning I've never understood why you've been so keenly interested in this affair. What was it? Love of adventure?"

"Not after six years of drifting about the country, old fellow."

"Then what was it?"

Bill permitted himself the luxury of a smile. "As I told you this morning—it seems so long ago, doesn't it?—it was nothing but a friendly desire to save your reputation."

"My reputation?" repeated Tony incredulously.

"That was all. You see, after you had exposed Terriss, it occurred to him that you were a pupil of mine, and he came straight to headquarters with his troubles."

"He went to you?" gasped Tony.

"That is the thought I am trying to convey," Bill assented. "Terriss was innocent. You know that now. He knew it then, and he convinced me like a shot. He wanted to be vindicated; but that wasn't all: he was dead sure that if the cards were marked, you had marked them yourself, and he wanted to see you—you and your friends—behind the bars! He is a clever man, a mighty quick-thinking man, and I'm pretty sure that if I hadn't taken the case, he'd have turned the tables on you before now!"

Tony's face became purple. "But I'm innocent! You know I'm innocent!"

"Sometimes it's very hard to prove, Tony. Terriss was innocent—but he couldn't make you see it."

Tony swallowed hard. "My friends and I owe Terriss a handsome apology."

"I'll say you do!"

"I shall see that it is forthcoming. And by the way, whatever fee you charge Terriss will be paid by me."

"Fair enough."

"Your expenses, too. Whatever they were, I will reimburse you."

Bill smiled. "Well, you heard me promise Venner a hundred dollars if he'd tell his story."

"I'll pay that."

"When you make out your check to Venner, make a mistake and slip in an extra nought before the decimal point."

"Why on earth should I do that?"

"No reason at all," said Bill, "except that I'm sentimental. For a hundred dollars—a contemptible hundred dollars—Venner turned his soul inside out. I'm going to improve his self-respect by convincing him that his soul is worth at least a thousand."

Tony nodded. "I get your point. The check will read a thousand. And now, your fee."

"That will come high."

"I expect that."

"Terriss expected it too, the quick-thinking devil! He insisted on your friends paying up because he wanted plenty of ready money on hand to satisfy me."

Tony smiled. His finances had taken a turn for the better since he had followed Parmelee's example, and had become merely a spectator, and not a participant in games of chance. His bank account had become plethoric, and the knowledge was pleasant. "Bill," he said, "you can't frighten me. Name what you want."

"It will come hard."

"If it does, it's worth it."

"All right, Tony, here goes." Bill stretched out his hand. "Pay me fifty-two Angel-Backs—fifty-two marked cards—fifty-two fallen angels. I'm going to nail them to the walls of my bedroom as a souvenir!"

AUTHOR'S NOTE

The central episode of this story, extraordinary as it is, is founded on facts related by the celebrated Robert-Houdin. Bianco, a Spanish sharper, marked an immense number of playing-cards, resealed them in their original boxes, and sold them to clubs in Havana at bargain-counter prices. Following his cards to Cuba, he won immense sums of money.

Everything went well until a second sharper, Laforcade, a Frenchman, wishing to mark cards for his own uses, took home a quantity, and to his astonishment discovered that they were already marked. Knowing of Bianco's sensational successes, Laforcade quickly satisfied himself that the Spaniard was the guilty man, and, instead of exposing him, invited him to halve his winnings.

To this proposal Bianco reluctantly acceded, but, tiring of it after some months, disappeared. Laforcade, left to shift for himself, lacked Bianco's expertness, was detected cheating, and was arrested. It was proved that Laforcade had not marked the cards and that he had not imported them; and it was quite impossible to prove that he was aware that the cards were marked. The prosecution broke down, and Laforcade was acquitted.

In his turn, Laforcade vanished, and neither he nor Bianco was ever heard of again.

P.W.

9

THE FIFTY-
THIRD CARD

TONY CLAGHORN WAS in an argumentative mood. Three deep lines, gracefully curving, corrugated his lofty brow; his lips were firmly set; his chin jutted out formidably; his mustache, waxed to fine points, quivered. His left hand poised a smoldering cigar, and his right hand aimed a long, well-manicured forefinger at the audience of one to which he was delivering his lecture.

Even Tony's clothes were argumentative. Knickers and coat of a screaming gray-and-green plaid, guaranteed to be the very latest thing in Scotland, golf stockings of an impression-istic pattern doubtless inspired by a close study of some rare and venomous reptile, shoes unlike any others that walked the earth, and a weirdly iridescent tie in whose folds gleamed a scarab, were the outstanding features of a costume as remark-able as it was appropriate to its wearer's disposition.

"I repeat," said Tony, "there are games in which cheating is impossible."

His friend, William Parmelee, ex-gambler, farmer, and unwilling corrector of destinies, shifted his gaze from the fertile fields through which the train was rolling to meet the determined eyes that interrogated his.

"I heard you the first time," he remarked.

"Nevertheless," said Tony, "I repeat it again: there are games in which cheating is impossible."

Parmelee fumbled with the lapel of his coat and gravely extracted a pin. Without a word he handed it to Claghorn.

"What's this for?" inquired that worthy.

"Have you a pencil, Tony? Preferably a large one, with a thick, heavy lead?"

Claghorn gazed at him suspiciously. "Yes," he admitted, after a pause.

"Well," murmured Bill, "suppose you take the pencil—the large pencil, with the thick, heavy lead—and jot down the names of the games in which cheating is impossible on the head of the pin."

Tony scowled. "Be serious."

"I'm perfectly serious."

"Of course, cheating is possible in most card games—"

"All of them."

"Most of them," Tony corrected firmly. "When an honest man and a rogue sit down together, the rogue will naturally try to get something for nothing."

"So will the honest man," commented Bill.

"What do you mean?"

" 'Something for nothing'—isn't that the greatest motive in life? What man is there who doesn't thrill at the thought of it? Gain something by the sweat of your brow—wealth, fame, position—and while you'll probably hold on to it longer than if you hadn't worked for it, will it give you the same excitement that you would have had if it had been something you acquired for nothing?"

"An honest man doesn't reason that way."

"I'm not talking about reason," said Bill. "I'm talking about feeling. You feel before you reason. You're a child before you're a man. And it's the child in you that thrills, that doesn't get tired and bored and disgusted, that makes every day of life worth living.

"Pay cash for a theater ticket, and you'll kick at the price. Get a pass for the same seat because you've presented the manager with a box of cigars costing ten times as much as the ticket, and you're pleased. Buy something for what it's worth—that's dull; it's business. Win it in a lottery, by buying up most of the chances, and you pat yourself on the back—even if it costs you more in the end. Get something for something—that's humdrum, tedious, an ordinary matter of buying and selling. Get something for nothing—that's adventure, that's romance, that's the cave man in your blood who was your ancestor a million years ago, and who painted himself purple and green and did a dance of triumph because a fish took his hook when there was nothing but a feather tied to it!"

Tony grinned. "I see your point," he admitted.

"Honesty!" ruminated Bill. "Honesty is sometimes hard to define. Tony, did you ever have an aunt—an aged, maiden aunt bound for heaven, if anybody ever was—who played solitaire?"

"No," said Tony. "Why do you ask?"

"Because I had an aunt like that. She sang in the choir; she spent her days doing charity. But she spent her evenings at a little card table. She would have thought it a deadly sin to gamble; she wouldn't touch euchre, which she considered the invention of the devil. But playing solitaire, with no opponent, with no stakes of any kind, she didn't hesitate to peek once or twice—or even oftener—or to give the cards a little shuffle, when it was strictly against the rules; or to take liberties of the kind that Hoyle prohibits. She was a moral woman, my aunt, and I have no doubt that if I live a blameless life I'll find her waiting for me at the pearly gates when I get there; but I have often wondered how she could do what she did and square it with her conscience. I decided that any human being as saintly as she was couldn't be called a cheat."

"Why not?" inquired Tony.

"It wasn't cheating," smiled Bill. "My aunt was just making up new rules as she went along. Hoyle cramped her style; she corrected him, just as she had corrected my school exercises."

Tony knocked the ashes from his cigar, adjusted his elegant self more comfortably on the leather cushions of the smoking compartment, and nodded energetically.

"Now we're getting back to the subject," he declared. "Sometimes you can't make up rules as you go along; the other fellow won't let you. Sometimes you have to play the game as it is meant to be played, because the man who invented it thought of cheats and made it impossible for them to have a chance. Sometimes you play fair because you have to play fair; because cheating is quite out of the question."

Bill gazed at his friend through half-closed eyes. "Are you referring to golf?" he asked innocently.

Tony laughed. "No," he said.

"I didn't think you were," Bill conceded. "You see, I've watched the play on the links down at the country club, and I made the discovery that the average man forgets how to count the moment he has a club in his hands. In plain, ordinary arithmetic four plus four equals eight. In golf—when there's nobody looking—four plus four equals four."

"Let's leave golf out of it," suggested Tony. "I've played it myself."

Bill reflected. "The one honest game. Do you mean tiddle-dywinks?"

"No, That's one game I never touched."

"Nor I," confessed Bill. He looked meditatively out of the window. "Perhaps you mean the game of matrimony," he hazarded.

"Heaven forbid!" said Tony. "There's more sharping at that than at any other game in the world! I've done well enough at it myself, but I know lots of fellows who thought they were drawing prizes only to find them blank."

Bill nodded. "Tony," he said, "I give up. Tell me the name of your cheat-proof game, so that I can pass the good news on to posterity. Tell me about the one game in which cheating is impossible. What do you call it?"

Tony lowered his voice, and prodded his friend in the neighborhood of the solar plexus with a lean forefinger. "I call it faro," he murmured.

TO PUT IT plainly, Tony was taking a mean, low advantage. To speak of faro as the one honest game, when he was fully aware that the mission upon which his friend was now engaged had to do with that particular subject, was tantamount to informing him that he had embarked on a wild-goose chase. All morning Tony had kept his opinions buried in his bosom; he had resolved to unburden himself of them now, better late than never.

Yet Tony had been present upon that occasion but a few hours past when the telephone in the little farmhouse had rung, when the operator had announced that New York was calling, and when a faint, barely audible voice at the other end of the wire had identified itself as that of the extraordinarily well-known Gilbert Cochrane.

If a young man inherits two or three millions, he ceases to be obscure—if he has ever been obscure. If he inherits ten millions, he becomes a figure of importance. If, however, he comes into an estate variously estimated between forty and seventy millions, he becomes a personage whose doings are front-page material for all the newspapers. Gilbert Cochrane belonged in this last category.

A shrewd father, who had thought no more of purchasing control of a railroad than another man would have thought of purchasing a packet of cigarettes, had vastly multiplied the by-no-means-inconsiderable fortune which had constituted his own inheritance. He had passed it on to Gilbert in flourishing condition, soundly invested, and so thoughtfully tied up that even Gilbert's wild extravagance could never impair the principal. Only the income, well into the millions itself, was under Gilbert's control; but that, the young man decided early in life, was sufficient for his simple needs. Useless and senseless, he resolved, to attempt to add other millions to the many which his forbears had provided; sufficient to the day was the income thereof. The young man devoted himself whole-heartedly to the task of spending it.

For a year or so the cost of additional residences actually kept his bank account stationary. There were already the family mansions in New York and in Newport; in rapid succession Gilbert acquired a camp in the Adirondacks, a villa at Southampton, and a shooting preserve in Georgia, each purchase being duly described and copiously illustrated in the newspapers. But Gilbert was too restless to be content in any of his numerous homes: for most of the year he flitted aimlessly from port to port on his seagoing yacht.

When twelve months had elapsed, and the young man was as affluent as ever, he electrified the newspapers by presenting the Adirondack camp, the Southampton villa, and the Georgia preserve to charitable institutions, by placing the yacht in dry dock, and by announcing that his interests would now be centered upon horse racing.

He embarked upon his new venture on a grand scale, building palatial stables, buying horses by the dozen, and entering mounts, at every track. Moreover, he backed his faith in his entries with large sums of money, and as the same perverse genius that had shielded him in the beginning continued to protect him, Gilbert won amounts so formidable that bookmakers were compelled for self-protection to decline his bets. This, however, did not embarrass Gilbert, who had begun to feel bored at his monotonous success. He disposed of the horses in which he had lost interest, and turned to fresh fields and pastures new.

Stock speculation did not attract him, for the very excellent reason that his far-seeing father had made it quite impossible under the terms of his will. Even the income would cease were Gilbert to carry his experimentation into Wall Street. Wherefore the young heir, craving excitement, and having already tired of all ordinary extravagances, commenced the study—at close range—of games of chance.

Bridge had not held his attention long. Something of his father's shrewd mind was in the son, who demonstrated an ability to win almost as he pleased. Poker could not fill the gap; consistently good luck, coupled with inherited skill, deprived the game of its thrills. Roulette had no charms for him; there was a mathematical streak in Gilbert's make-up, and he knew too well how to calculate that the odds were overwhelmingly against him. It was faro, one of the simplest, and surely one of the speediest of gambling games, that proved most congenial to his temperament; and it was at faro that for the first time his notorious luck failed to follow him.

Taken all in all, there are few methods of separating oneself from surplus wealth that are as clean-cut and agreeable as faro. The precautions taken to protect the players are numerous; the percentage in favor of the bank is far smaller than that in roulette; and action is swift—exceedingly swift. A deck of cards is shuffled, cut, and placed face upward in a metal container which allows only a single card—the uppermost card—to be drawn out at one time. The first card, being exposed, is dead; the two cards following, however, win alternately for the bank and for the players, who, disregarding suits, are at liberty to bet even money that any card—or any one of a number of cards— will either win or lose. The two cards constitute a turn, there being obviously twenty-five turns in a complete deck. The advantage to the bank lies in the fact that when the cards in a turn are of the same denomination—constituting a split— half of all sums hazarded upon them, either to win or to lose, is forfeited. A check upon the dealer is maintained by the case keeper, who records what cards have appeared upon a simple apparatus; a second check is maintained by the players, who keep a record of their own; a third check is provided by the mechanical dealing box; and there is still a fourth check in the fact that the bank is frequently bought and operated by one of the players.

It was at this simple, easily comprehensible game, hedged about with a series of devices expressly designed to protect the players, that Gilbert Cochrane parted with the respectable sum of a quarter of a million dollars in a little less than two weeks.

OVER THE LONG-DISTANCE telephone, despite the rapidly mounting charges, the young multimillionaire had been quite as leisurely as one might have expected him to be.

"I have heard of you, Mr, Parmelee," he explained in a gentle, unhurried voice; "in fact, there are few men in New York who haven't heard of you. You have built up quite an enviable reputation."

Bill, somewhat overcome by the honor of talking to one of the richest men in the world, swallowed. "Very kind of you to say so, Mr. Cochrane," he said into the telephone.

"Not kind at all," contradicted the invisible speaker; "it's nothing more than the truth. In your own field you have no competition—you're unique. And you deserve your reputation, I'm sure of that. Now, Mr. Parmelee, if it were made worth your while, would you run down to New York for a few days?"

"What for?"

"If you will, Mr. Parmelee, I'd like you to give me your expert opinion on a game in which I have been playing."

"What kind of game?"

"Faro."

Bill whistled.

"You are familiar with faro, aren't you?" inquired the unseen speaker.

"I've played," Bill admitted. He might have added much more. He might have mentioned that in some sections of the country which he had visited on his travels faro had quite eclipsed other games, and that he himself had spent several months manipulating the dealing box in a gambling house. But those months were part of a past which he was trying to forget. "I've played quite a little," he said.

"I thought as much."

"But I'm all through. I never want to see a faro layout again."

"I'm not asking you to play," said that voice over the wire. "I'm asking you to look on—nothing more. And then I want you to tell me whether or not the game is honest."

Not even the fact that he was talking to the possessor of the Cochrane millions could infuse Bill with enthusiasm. "If you don't think the game is honest, don't play in it," he advised. "I'm not keen about doing any more investigating. I'm a farmer. I'm not a detective. And I'm busy with the haying."

The voice over the wire was unruffled. "If your haying is worth more than ten thousand dollars," it suggested, "finish it, by all means. But if it's worth less than that, jump on the next train for New York."

"What?" gasped Bill.

"I'm willing to pay you ten thousand if you do no more than look around and tell me I'm playing in a fair-and-square game. I've lost a lot of money at it, you see, and I won't mind that at all if I know that it has been taken from me honestly. It's worth ten thousand to me simply to be sure of my ground."

"I see."

"Perhaps the game is what it should be. If so, I'll be very glad to learn that. But if there's something wrong, and you can point it out to me, and prove it to me, I shan't object in the least if your fee is considerably higher—say twenty or twenty-five thousand." The unseen speaker paused, while Parmelee hastily collected his thoughts. "I must know your answer at once, Mr. Parmelee. What is it?"

Bill ginned. "I'm not a millionaire, Mr. Cochrane," he confessed, "and twenty-five thousand is twenty-five thousand. When and where do I report?"

There had followed most explicit directions. Despite the fact that either of two later trains would have brought Parmelee to New York in ample time for the night's adventure, he was to pack his valise immediately, and to start at once. Upon his arrival in the metropolis he was in no event to communicate with Cochrane, but was to amuse himself as he pleased during the afternoon and evening.

At half past ten to the minute he was to wait in the street in front of an address in the lower Thirties; there Cochrane's secretary would meet him in an automobile. The voice over the wire described the car in detail; upon recognizing it, Parmelee was to enter it, and receive further instructions.

Perhaps unnecessarily Cochrane explained that his elaborate precautions were due to the fact that it would be well for him not to be seen in Parmelee's company; one breath of suspicion, and the trip would be in vain. It would be easy—so easy—for the hunted men—if once they thought they were being hunted—to eliminate all trickery from the game. That possibility must be averted.

Bill nodded his approval as he appreciated the shrewdness of Cochrane's plans. "They call that chap lucky," he remarked to Tony as he hung up the instrument, "but I don't—far from it. I say that he has luck because he deserves luck; because he looks so far ahead, and takes account of so many things, that he just naturally has to come out on top. Luck may be capricious, luck may strike where you least expect it; but my experience has taught me that it generally comes to the fellow who has planned to meet it halfway."

Tony's eyes gleamed. "How about your own luck?"

Bill shook his head. "Is it luck or isn't it? I thought I'd found my place in life as a farmer, and here's destiny knocking at my door and telling me—"

"That you can make more in a day by your knowledge of cards than you can in a year by your knowledge of crops."

"Exactly," said Bill. There was no exultation in his voice. Quite the contrary, an outsider would have come to the conclusion that bad news had suddenly reached him. "More in a day by my knowledge of cards than in a year by my knowledge of crops," he repeated. "That's wrong, Tony. That's dead wrong. The world shouldn't be built that way."

"Twenty-five thousand if you win—ten thousand if you lose, remember," tantalized Tony.

"Get thee behind me, Satan!"

Hastily Tony drew the conversation to another angle of the subject. It was dangerous, he sensed, to allow his friend to moralize. With centuries of New England forbears he might suddenly take it into his head to abandon the venture—and Tony yearned for the thrills to be extracted from it. Far better, decided Tony, to direct his restless mentality toward a neat little problem which had begun to occupy his own mind even while he listened to the telephonic conversation.

"Why, do you suppose," inquired Tony, "was Cochrane so keen on your leaving at once? He doesn't want you until half past ten to-night. Why wouldn't a later train have answered for his purposes quite as well?"

"If you want me to give a guess," said Bill—and the events which followed showed how surprisingly wrong his guess was—"it's because an early train is the one train which I would not be expected to take. Just put yourself in the place of the people whom Cochrane is fighting. They're gambling for big stakes. They've separated him from a lot of money already; they know there's more where it came from. If they are nearly as farsighted as he is, they'll have some man who knows me on duty at the station watching incoming trains. With the amount that they're putting into their pockets, they can well afford the expense of such a precaution. But Cochrane is reckoning on it, you see; the man will be watching the late trains—while I slip in on an early one."

Tony was a slow thinker, but sometimes he was an accurate one. "Possibly," he admitted, "but not probable. If you wanted to go to the city unnoticed, you'd get off at One Hundred and Twenty-fifth Street—instead of staying on the train until it reaches Grand Central Station."

Bill smiled, and guessed wrongly a second time. "That's what they might expect me to do if I thought I was being watched. But why under the sun should I think such a thing? No, Tony, you may depend upon it that Cochrane has foreseen all that a very, very clever man can foresee. I'm going to follow his instructions to the letter."

But Tony was still unwilling to relinquish the subject. Like a dog with a marrowy bone, he found great pleasure in turning it over and over, in attacking it here and there, in exploring its innermost recesses. "You know, Bill," he commented, "if I were a gambling-house proprietor, and I wanted to know what you were doing, I wouldn't have my man waiting in New York at all."

"What would you do?"

"I'd do something much simpler," said Tony. "I'd give him orders to camp out right here in West Woods, Connecticut. And I'd tell him to keep a very close eye on the little railroad station."

"Rot!" said Bill.

It was thus that William Parmelee, ex-gambler, farmer, and unwilling corrector of destinies, guessed wrongly three times in as many minutes.

OUT OF THE mouths of babes and little children, wisdom— sometimes. Tony was more nearly right than he suspected.

The morning train from New York had brought a curious passenger. Sleek, roly-poly, bland, innocent, good-natured, and attired, withal, in the vestments of a clergyman, he had disembarked at the West Woods station in a humor so cheerful that not even the misadventure which he promptly related to the agent could damp it.

Traveling from one parish to another, he had, by some incomprehensible error, boarded a northbound and not a southbound train. The conductor would doubtless have set him right immediately had not he, the clergyman, promptly dropped off to sleep. With well-meant consideration the official had refrained from waking him, and the mistake had not been discovered until, having slept his fill, he had tendered his ticket but a few minutes ago. There had been mutual consternation—and the clergyman had hastily descended from the train, to wait two hours, or thereabouts, for a southbound train which would carry him back over the way that he had come.

"I got on at Pawling," explained the clergyman. One might

have expected him to be vexed. On the contrary, he bubbled over with laughter. "I was going to White Plains. It's a trip I've made a hundred—no, a thousand—times! But my wits must have been woolgathering, I'm afraid. I was sleepy. I must have been thinking too hard about next Sunday's sermon. Perhaps that's what made me sleepy! Ha! Ha! My sermons have been known to have that effect on my congregation!" The rotund little man overflowed with merriment. "At any rate, I did a most incomprehensible thing. The northbound train comes in two minutes before the southbound one."

"I know that," assented the station agent.

"I know it quite as well as you do," chuckled the clergyman. "At least, I ought to know it. But in spite of knowing it, I managed to board the wrong train! And then, having started wrong, I dozed off—must have been that sermon again!—and the conductor had too much respect for the cloth to wake me!"

"Too bad," sympathized the station agent, "too bad." He might have been less sympathetic had he been able to compare notes with the conductor, now a dozen miles away. That worthy would have informed him that the clergyman, very wide awake and knowing exactly what he was doing, had boarded the train at New York City and not at Pawling. He would have added that the clerical gentleman had slept not at all, that his ticket, duly taken up, had read for West Woods, and that if he had alighted at that hamlet it had obviously been for the reason that it was his destination, and that he wished to go there.

Lacking an opportunity to compare notes with the conductor, a search of the clergyman's person might have been quite as surprising. Besides a small Bible, which he had read ostentatiously from time to time, it would have revealed a blackjack and a fully loaded revolver—surely an astonishing assortment. And the most casual examination of the clergyman's person, snugly hidden under his broadcloth, would have disclosed, most remarkably developed muscles—muscles strangely inconsistent with his peaceful avocation.

Yet upon a cursory inspection the man who claimed that his own sermons made him sleepy, looked the part. His round, unwrinkled face, which blinked up at the station agent like that of a suddenly awakened owl; his chubby hands, large but not strikingly so; his well-brushed clothes, across whose front glittered a thin gold watch chain—all were in harmony with each other.

The station agent looked him over, smiled, and made a mental note that such persons should not be allowed to travel unaccompanied by guardians. He refrained from expressing this opinion, however, and confined himself to stating that the down train was due in one hour and fifty-eight minutes.

"I know it already," said the smiling parson; "the conductor was kind enough to tell me so. And you"—once more he bubbled over with merriment—"you will be making it your business to see that I'm on it when it pulls out!"

The agent nodded. "I'll remind you, never fear. In the meantime, make yourself comfortable." He waved a hand at the long benches around the deserted waiting room. "I'll get you something to read if you like."

The man of the cloth was quick in his protest. "No reading, if you please," he begged. "I have overtaxed my eyes already, the doctor tells me. Perhaps that is why I felt so tired this morning. No; no reading, thank you. I'll manage to pass the time away without."

In recounting the episode several days afterward, Drummond, the station agent, admitted that he had been greatly relieved at this reply. His stock of reading matter consisted chiefly of the back numbers of periodicals devoted impartially to boxing, horse racing, and bathing girls; and had the reverend gentleman accepted his well-meant but thoughtless offer, Drummond would have found himself in an embarrassing situation.

He discovered quickly, however, upon what the clergyman depended for his entertainment. If his eyes were tired, his tongue and ears were most certainly not. Planting himself at the grilled ticket window, he drew the willing agent into a conversation which began with the antediluvian history of West Woods, and progressed by easy stages to a discussion of the leading men of the place.

Now in a hamlet whose inhabitants number fewer than six hundred, leading men are not likely to be plentiful, but despite that handicap Drummond did his subject full justice. He loved to talk—and the clergyman, it appeared, loved to listen; surely a happy combination! Wherefore the station agent, commencing with old man McGregor, who had become a notable by the simple process of living one hundred and two years, limned an admirably detailed biography of the individuals whose fame had shed luster on the little village.

Besides McGregor there was Pappagianopoulos, the shoemaker, worthy descendant of the Greeks who fought at Marathon. A bountiful providence had enshrined him among the immortals by bestowing six fingers on each of his hands, and—so it was rumored—a similar number of toes on each of his feet. Pappagianopoulos might be found in his shop under the

Motion Picture Palace any hour that the clergyman cared to inspect him.

There were others, too—men who had achieved renown in the hamlet because of circumstances that would have attracted no attention whatsoever in the great, busy world without, but which set them apart in a class by themselves in West Woods, Connecticut. The station agent, warming to his appreciative audience, dealt with them one by one in a series of brief but comprehensive thumb-nail sketches.

But there was one name which he did not mention at all, and the clergyman, after waiting in vain for him to bring it into the conversation, finally did so himself.

"Interesting, most interesting, and most entertaining," he commented. "The true study of mankind is man. Where else can one learn so much as from the thoughtful consideration of those individuals who have distinguished themselves from the great mass of humanity by some splendid, noteworthy accomplishment?"

If there was sarcasm beneath the remark, the station agent failed to detect it; and the bogus preacher, licking his lips over his rounded periods, congratulated himself on the function with which he was carrying off his part. To certain intimates, in the Tenderloin of New York, he was familiarly known as "Holy" Hutchins. Those intimates were aware that a protracted stay in a large, heavily barred building whose inmates paid no rent and who remained no longer than they were actually compelled to had given him both the opportunity of "getting religion" and of acquiring the sanctimonious manner which became him so perfectly. They would have applauded, he felt sure, had they been able to observe him impressing the station agent now.

But enough time had been wasted on preliminaries. Holy Hutchins half closed his eyes. "I have heard it said," he remarked blandly, "that one of your well-known men is named Parmelee—William Parmelee, I believe."

The station agent grinned, "Yes," he admitted.

"Why didn't you mention him?"

"To a minister?"

"Why not?"

"Well," said Drummond reluctantly, "he's a card expert, Bill is, and I had the idea that a clergyman wouldn't care to hear about him."

Holy Hutchins smiled his sweetest smile. "He is a man, isn't he? And I am interested in all kinds of men. Besides, if I have been informed correctly, he has given up the evil practices of his youth."

"Yes, that's true enough."

"He has adopted the remarkable profession of hunting down other—shall we say?—card experts."

"Card cheats, you mean."

"Card cheats, if you will." Holy Hutchins rubbed his hands benignantly. "Now it appears to me that Mr. Parmelee is doing something to make the world better—in his own way, of course, in his own way. It is a noble effort. I preach the Eighth Commandment, Mr. Parmelee does what he can to make the world practice it. We are colaborers, coworkers in the same field. Why should you not speak of him to me?"

Drummond laughed. "If that's the way you look at it, it makes all the difference in the world! If I had known you felt like that, Bill Parmelee would have been the first man I'd have told you about. We're mighty proud of him, here in West Woods. We think he's just about the greatest man that's ever lived in this little village! Why, there isn't a lad in miles ground who can't talk about him by the hour!"

The clerical gentleman nodded. "Suppose you tell me about him."

"What shall I tell you?"

"Everything."

Drummond smiled the smile of the man who is about to embark upon a most agreeable undertaking. As he had stated, there was not a child in the hamlet who could not relate tales about Parmelee; and in his admiration for the hero Drummond yielded to nobody.

He had heard stories—inaccurate—exaggerated—with gaps which Parmelee himself never could be persuaded to fill in. He accepted the inaccuracies and the exaggerations, and he bridged the gaps with highly colored episodes of his own invention. He traced Parmelee's beginnings, described his wanderings about the country, confided that he had a theory of his own to explain his return to his home town, and all but swamped the listening clergyman with the detailed history of a long series of more or less impossible exploits. Parmelee could see through a card cheat quite as easy as he could see through the back of a card—and that latter feat, the voluble station agent explained, was merely child's play for him.

When Holy Hutchins finally called a halt it lacked but five minutes of train time, and Drummond had been holding forth without interruption for nearly an hour.

The station agent locked the ticket office and escorted the passenger out of the station. "This time," he promised, "you'll take the southbound train. I'll see to that." Then an automobile came down the hill, rolled up to the platform, and stopped. "Speak of the devil!" whispered Drummond. "That's Parmelee himself!"

Holy Hutchins riveted his gaze upon the two men who emerged from the car. Upon the first, a blue-eyed, blond-haired young man, dressed in the simplest possible manner, he wasted no attention. Upon the second, a slightly older man whose mustache was waxed to fine points, whose knickers and coat were of an unearthly plaid, and whose shapely legs were encased in rattlesnake stockings, Hutchins focused his eyes as if he were endeavoring to make a permanent record in some mental camera.

"So that's Parmelee!" he murmured.

Then, with an inconspicuous motion he passed his hands over his hip pockets, and made sure that his weapons were readily accessible.

THEY HAD ENTERED the train with hardly a glance at the rotund little clergyman who boarded it with them; indeed, as the clergyman had selected a car one removed from that which they had chosen, they had not come within fifty feet of him. At Tony's suggestion, they had migrated to the smoking compartment, and once alone in it, Tony, almost bursting with the opinions buried in his bosom, had immediately launched into the debate whose beginnings we have already chronicled.

"I repeat," said Tony, crossing his shapely legs defiantly, "I repeat that faro is a cheat-proof game."

Bill smiled patiently. "Sometimes, Tony," he said, "sometimes you have too little faith in human nature—and sometimes you have too much."

"Faro is—" began Tony.

"Faro is a game like other games," Bill interrupted. "Where wits are matched against wits, somebody is going to try for an unfair advantage. The stakes are big. The rewards are worth while. And the man with a faro layout has a big head start even before he opens his doors."

"How so?"

Bill grinned. "Because the statement that faro is the fairest of all games has been made so often that it has almost become an adage. It's one of the most cherished beliefs of the public. What are the average man's convictions? That all heroes smoke pipes; that all villains smoke cigarettes; that all pretty girls are young; and that faro is fair! If he loses at roulette, he'll suspect the wheel—and there may be nothing the matter with it. Roulette has a bad name. But if he loses at faro, he feels that he's had a run for his money. Something about faro inspires confidence.

"It never occurs to him that the very devices which seem to protect him can be made to work against him. Unless he's a Cochrane he doesn't reason that nothing invented by human ingenuity can't be improved by human ingenuity."

He rose and smiled at his traveling companion. "Let that sink in, Tony," he adjured. "Remember that while the fellow who invents a newfangled sewing machine—or a phonograph—or an electric light—becomes famous, the chap who invents a new way to trim suckers at poker—or roulette—or faro—isn't looking for fame, and doesn't get the advertising he really deserves."

With this Parthian shot he made his way back to his seat in the car, to stare fixedly out of the window for an unconscionable length of time. There Tony joined him when his cigar had been entirely reduced to ashes, and offered the proverbial penny for his thoughts.

Bill shook his head. "They may not be worth it," he prefaced. "Yet—"

"Yet?" Tony prompted.

"Have you ever met Cochrane?"

"No; but I've heard a lot about him."

"So have I," admitted Bill. He turned his chair to face his friend squarely. "Tony, I may be dead wrong, but there's one little point that has been coming up in my mind again and again."

"What's that?"

"The telephone call—the long-distance call."

"What about it?"

"He must have talked for a quarter of an hour."

"He did."

"Well, the toll covers the first three minutes only. After that there's an extra charge for each minute."

Tony laughed. "Why should you care? You don't have to pay it."

"I care nevertheless."

"Cochrane can afford such little luxuries."

"That's just what's making me think so hard," confessed Bill. "Cochrane is an enormously rich man. He is an extravagant man. He is famous not only for the size of his bank account, but for his liberality in drawing on it."

"Well?" challenged Tony, considerably puzzled.

"There's this," Bill pointed out. "It has been my observation that millionaires—the few millionaires I've been privileged to know—may waste tens and hundreds of thousands on their pleasures, but they're extraordinarily economical when it comes to little expenses. Perhaps that's why they're millionaires. They don't object to paying a fortune for a particularly fine automobile—but they're mighty careful not to put two stamps on a letter when there is a chance that it will get by with one stamp. They'll lose any amount on the races without a pang—but they'll figure for half an hour to compress an eleven-word telegram into ten words, and save the few cents that the extra word would cost. They don't balk at spending more than the average man's yearly income on one night's amusement—but when they put in long-distance calls they speak with their watches in their hands to make sure that they don't use up one second more than three minutes! Now, that's just what Cochrane didn't do!"

"He couldn't have said all he wanted in three minutes."

"Yes, he could!" contradicted Bill. "He could have said it in one minute. Why didn't he? Why did he talk—and talk—and talk—when it cost money, and when he knew that I knew it cost money?"

"Maybe he wanted to impress you."

"Not Cochrane! It's the near-rich man who tries to make an impression. The millionaire doesn't care about it; there's no novelty in it for him; and something deep, deep down in him always tells him to save money on the small expenses. Why didn't he run true to form?"

It was Tony's turn to guess wrongly. "Because Cochrane is in a class by himself, that's why," he asserted.

"I have been trying to believe that," Bill admitted, "but somehow it doesn't ring true."

He turned to the window again, in so uncommunicative a

mood that Tony, after several attempts, gave up hope of engaging him in conversation, and retreated to the platform to smoke a solitary cigar.

The brakeman had left the doors open. Tony braced himself against a handrail, looked out, and breathed deep. To the rear swayed the three or four cars composing the body of the train; ahead, the engine, visible as it plunged into a curve, belched clouds of smoke. The air was filled with the clank and grind and clatter of chains and couplings and revolving wheels—but Tony found the din curiously soothing.

Along the sides-flitted a constantly changing panorama: green fields dotted with rivulets, marshes crowded with bulrushes, meadows in which grazed cows and sheep. The city man gazed—forgot where he was—thrilled with the joy of living.

Then, suddenly, some sixth sense began to speak to him; some deep-buried instinct handed down to him by warlike ancestors began to warn him; some eternally watchful self, looking out from the back of his head, began to scream: "Danger! Danger!"

Tony wheeled about like a flash, to come face to face with a convulscd, distorted countenance which glared into his. It topped a squat, rotund body garbed in the broadcloth of a clergyman.

For an instant there hissed through Tony's mind the frightful suspicion that had he not turned when he did, the man would have pitched him from the swaying train. His imagination reeled at the thought of what might have happened to him. Then, even while he told himself that his fear was insane and groundless, the clergyman inhaled spasmodically—once— twice—and unburdened himself of a thunderous sneeze.

The reaction was nearly as paralyzing as the icy horror that had preceded it. Tony gasped, and clutched at the handrail for support. Yet he mastered himself as the clergyman's countenance relaxed into smiling, placid lines; found his way to the door, though his legs trembled; murmured an habitual "God bless you!" and—bolted for safety.

SOME PERIODS OF time are so featureless that they do not linger long in the memory. Some are so eventful that they are never forgotten. Like familiar nightmares, they conjure themselves up in imagination for years and decades. When Tony reluctantly bade his friend farewell at the station, he little anticipated what happenings the next few hours had in store for him—nor did he foresee how utterly any man other than a native New Yorker would have been terrified by them.

He had urged Bill to spend the afternoon with him. Rather surprisingly Parmelee had pleaded private business, and had begged off. Not to be denied lightly Tony had suggested taking in a show, and when that had not produced the desired response, had mentioned that a two-handed game of poker in his comfortable apartment would logically be followed by a somewhat intimate investigation of a wine cellar which Tony admitted was excellently stocked.

Smiling, Bill had failed to rise to the bait.

"I'll meet you at supper," he promised, but refused to commit himself to anything for the hours between.

Chagrined and wondering, Tony watched him disappear into the subway. He would have given a great deal to be in possession of full details of the mysterious errand upon which Parmelee was bent; it was tantalizing to know so much, and yet to know so little—and Tony was an incurably inquisitive person. It was evident as the nose on a man's face that his friend had picked up a promising clew, and was determined to run it down; yet Tony, for all his familiarity with his methods, found himself quite in the dark.

Emphatically nettled because he had not been taken into the secret—and there was clearly a secret—Tony strode into Forty-second Street, and turned northward on Madison Avenue. A taxi would have taken him home more rapidly, but Tony wanted to think. The results of his thinking, he would probably have admitted had he been asked, would probably be of no particular importance. But that could not deter him from giving himself up quite whole-heartedly to it.

Engrossed in his speculations he crossed Forty-third and Forty-fourth Streets. Forty-fifth Street witnessed no progress, but midway to Forty-sixth Street a new and undeveloped angle suddenly occurred to him. Revolving it industriously in his mind, he reached the corner, stepped off—and then, for the second time in a single day, instinct came to his rescue.

Certain animals, authorities say, divine the presence of the hunter when neither sight nor scent nor sound reveal him. Born New Yorkers, other authorities will testify, anticipate the dangers with which their city besets them as naturally and as unconsciously as they set one foot before the other.

Tony stepped off the curb, plunged in thought. But hardly had he moved a yard before he leaped—leaped wildly and desperately—and as he did so, a careering motor car, sluing around the corner, whizzed through the space which he had just vacated.

A sight-seer from Chicago, observing the incident, felt his

hair rising on his head. "Gee, that was a narrow squeak!" he murmured. "It looked as if that driver was trying to run him down on purpose!"

Thus the man from Chicago; but Tony, typical New Yorker, had already caught his stride again, and proceeded unconcernedly on his way.

At Forty-seventh Street he halted in subconscious obedience to the traffic signal, while an endless stream of vehicles crossed the avenue. Parmelee, he told himself, had evidently considered the details connected with the long-distance telephone call of great importance; what inferences, if any, had he been able to draw from them?

At this juncture a heavily laden truck thundered by, and some person behind Tony chose that moment to bump him with great violence. Had Tony been a Westerner—or a Southerner—or a foreigner—he would doubtless have been precipitated under the ponderous wheels, and the name of Claghorn would have adorned the following morning's obituary column. Had one Bill Parmelee, of West Woods, Connecticut, been in Claghorn's boots, a unique and promising career would have come to an end in an instant. But Tony was Tony—and a native New Yorker.

With a powerful movement, none the less powerful because it was automatic, he drove his right elbow into the ribs of the jostler, extended his hand in a simultaneous motion, grasped the unknown firmly by the coat, and rectified his balance.

If the police officer in charge of traffic observed the occurrence, he took no notice of it. He blew his whistle; one traffic stream stopped, and another began to flow. With it flowed Tony, who had not paused either to exact or to offer apologies, who had not, in fact, looked behind him at all.

Had he done so, he might have observed a short, rotund clergyman, still doubled up from the impact of Tony's elbow, and gasping painfully for breath. But the New Yorker, busy with his thoughts, and not in the least disconcerted by what had taken place, paused not at all. In the streets of New York certain hazards were to be encountered. Sometimes they were more pronounced than at others; sometimes less. In either event, they were worthy of scant attention.

Tony continued his walk. At Forty-ninth Street the car that had deliberately attempted to run him down once before, made another attempt. Certain it is that Tony did not recognize it as the same automobile. He had hardly glanced at it the first time; busily engaged in bowing to a flapper acquaintance across the avenue, he hardly glanced at it the second.

Instead he merely sprang five feet or so in a detached, absent-minded manner—sprang, incidentally, the exact distance required to avoid the onrushing danger, and not an inch more—alighted gracefully, and finished the bow which he had begun. He had not dropped his cigar; he had not ruffled his hair; he had not even lost the current of his thoughts. "Sorry Bill isn't here," he ruminated; "there are several questions I would like to ask him."

He reached the corner of the street in which his apartment was located, paused, and gazed affectionately at the teeming avenue. "Little old New York!" he mused with the true devotion that the metropolis nurtures in the hearts of its sons. "No other town like it! No, not a one!"

His glance wandered into the distance, and fell like a benediction on the crowded streets and the overflowing sidewalks—while a hundred feet away a portly little clergyman, seeing Tony look back, dodged under a convenient awning and began to take the liveliest interest in a window display of sporting goods. Holy Hutchins had been much in evidence for some hours; his retiring instincts told him that it might now be well for him to merge unostentatiously with the background.

He ventured out as soon as he dared. The casual manner in which Tony had eluded his snares had vastly increased his respect for him. "Clever!" he murmured. "Clever as they make 'em! He's got eyes in the back of his head, that man Parmelee!"

As rapidly as possible he proceeded to the corner. Tony was nowhere in sight. One of the innumerable rabbit warrens in the city which he loved so much had swallowed him up in its elevators, and was whisking him up some hundreds of feet to his home on the fourteenth floor.

Holy Hutchins gazed east and west—likewise north and south—also up and down. His quarry had eluded him.

A motor car pulled up at the curb near him.

"He got away," remarked Holy Hutchins.

"You don't have to tell me that," remarked the driver sarcastically.

"Not my fault."

"Well, wasn't mine, neither."

The bogus clergyman opened the door of the car and stepped into it. "What does it matter whether he got away or not?" he commented philosophically. "A few hours more or less—who cares about that? We'll get him in the long run."

The driver let in his clutch with a jerk, and spun around the corner, narrowly missing three pedestrians and one Pomeranian dog. "We'll get him to-night," he said shortly.

It was at this precise moment that Tony, having deposited

his hat on the rack, having kissed his pretty wife, and having lighted the first of a brand-new box of his favorite cigars, made the sagacious comment: "There's just one thing wrong with this little old town."

"And what's that?" inquired Mrs. Claghorn.

Tony gazed out of the window. "New York's too slow," he declared.

IT IS INTERESTING to conjecture what dangers Tony unknowingly avoided by remaining at home, contentedly smoking one cigar after another, that afternoon. The bogus clergyman, despite his conviction that a few hours more or less mattered little, was apparently a tenacious individual, for he drove only as far as the nearest public telephone. A few minutes' earnest conversation was followed by the prompt arrival of reinforcements in the shape of two young men with cauliflower ears, excellently developed under jaws, and badly developed foreheads.

With their assistance, the street into which Tony had vanished was patrolled with a vigilance which would have done credit to professional detectives. It may be inferred, moreover, that life would have been made exceedingly full and interesting for any person answering the description which Holy Hutchins had given his aids. Parmelee, he had explained, wore a mustache waxed to fine points, and encased his lower extremities in rattlesnake-patterned golf stockings. Fortunately for the five million other inhabitants of the city, however, Tony was a stickler for buying wearables of exclusive designs, and while golf stockings of gray or tan passed once or twice during the afternoon, the vigil was unrewarded.

At seven Parmelee arrived for the evening meal. He had little to say during dinner, and that little was confined almost entirely to side-stepping his friend's questions. But immediately afterward he took Tony aside.

"Old fellow," he prefaced, "you know I'd like to take you along to-night."

"Of course you're going to take me along," said Tony. The thought that he might ever be omitted had never entered his head.

"It can't be done, Tony."

"And why not?"

"You know my instructions. I'm to go to an address in the Thirties. I'm to be there at ten thirty sharp. I'm to get into a car which will meet me there."

"There'll be room for two in the car," Tony pointed out.

"Doubtless—but Cochrane's orders are quite definite, and he didn't include you in them. Tony, I'm not going to take you."

"You can't do that!" Tony, pleaded earnestly. "Cochrane probably knows all about me. He probably knows that we've always hunted together."

Parmelee shook his head decisively. "Whether he knows it or not, Tony, you're going to stay home."

Tony rose, deeply offended. For over a year he had been Parmelee's companion on every adventure. "All right," he said, "if you haven't any use for me any more—"

Bill laid his hand on his arm. "It isn't that, old fellow," he soothed. "There's never a time that I haven't use for you; and when there's fun I like to have you along to enjoy it. But to-night, I'm afraid, things are going to be different."

"How different?" challenged Tony. His eyes sought those

of his friend shrewdly. "Bill, what's your real reason?" he demanded.

"I've told you."

"No, you haven't."

Bill shrugged his shoulders. "Well, if you must know, the real reason is that I'm running into danger."

Tony bounded across the room. "And that's why you don't want me to come along?"

"That's why."

Tony smiled happily. He laid claim to no more bravery than the average man; yet he could imagine no more joyful adventure than to face an unknown menace in company with his friend. "Bill," he declared, "if there's danger, I'm certainly going with you. Do you expect me to back out just because there's a chance of trouble?"

"There's more than a chance," Parmelee explained reluctantly; "there's a strong probability. I made a few inquiries this afternoon. I have friends in New York—fellows I used to know in the days when I made a living out of the cards. Some of them have settled down and turned honest. Some of them—haven't. Some of them are respectable business men. Some of them are crooks. Some of them are in the police department keeping some of the rest of them in order. Well, I went the rounds today, and I asked a few questions, and I found out where Cochrane is playing faro. Tony, he's playing at Seeley's."

"What's the point? I've heard of Seeley's. How is it different from any other gambling house?"

"The house isn't different—steel doors, and all that sort of thing, just as you'd expect. It's Seeley that's different." He half closed his eyes. "Tony, I've never met the man—never in my life. But it seems to me as if I've heard of him ever since I was a kid. He's dangerous. He was dangerous when I heard his name for the first time—and he's even more dangerous to-day."

"Dangerous in what way?" queried Tony.

"He doesn't care any more about a human life than he does about a white chip, that's all. He operated out West some time ago. He packed up and left in a great big hurry. They said that he had been mixed up in a shooting. He stopped a while in Chicago. He left there in a hurry, too. I don't know why, but I've heard rumors. He's been doing business in New York for two years now, and something tells me that if I break up his game to-night he may not take it kindly."

"What can he do?" scoffed Tony. "This isn't the West. This isn't Chicago. This is New York, the safest city in the world."

Bill laughed. "I've heard it called many things, but I've never heard it called that."

"In a Western mining camp he might shoot you," admitted Tony, "but here—"

"Here," interrupted Bill, "he might do exactly the same thing, with just one big difference: in a Western mining camp, if they ever caught him, he'd be lynched; here, they may never catch him, and if they do, he'll have a dozen eyewitnesses who'll be willing to swear through thick and thin that I took his revolver out of his pocket and shot myself with it."

"Nonsense," said Tony.

"It may be nonsense, but I take it so seriously that I'm not going to let you get mixed up in it. Tony, much as I hate to do it, to-night I play a lone hand."

Tony knew his friend too well to argue with him. Far

simpler, he noted mentally, to pretend to give in—and then to do exactly as he pleased. He merely inquired, "I suppose you are armed?"

"No," said Bill.

"I'll give you a revolver."

"I don't want it."

"Why not?"

Parmelee shook his head. "I'll be better off without it. My only chance is to manage things so that I won't need weapons at all—because if I do need them, I'll be so outnumbered that they'll be of no use. No, Tony; I'll do my fighting with my wits. I'll run less danger that way."

Tony thought an instant. "If Cochrane is as shrewd as you think he is, he will have taken steps to protect you against Seeley."

"I hope so," said Bill sincerely. He smiled. "It may sound unheroic, but I'm not a bit keen on taking unnecessary risks. Heroes do that only in books—and this is real life."

Tony nodded. Then a beatific expression spread over his countenance. "There's still another thing in your favor," he pointed out. "Perhaps you won't do anything to offend Seeley. Perhaps you won't find anything wrong. Faro," declared Tony Claghorn for the seventeenth time in less than that many hours, "is the one fair gambling game. Faro is a game in which it is impossible to cheat."

Bill grinned. "Oh, is it?" he murmured ironically.

CURIOSITY, THE ADAGE has it, once killed a cat. Curiosity came very, very near to killing Tony Claghorn. Let us qualify at once, however, by giving Tony credit for more than a modicum of devotion to his friend. Bill was running into danger; Tony did not propose to allow him to face it single-handed.

At ten o'clock Parmelee climbed into a taxi, told the driver to set him down at a corner in the lower Thirties, and departed.

Precisely thirty seconds later Claghorn climbed into a taxi, told the driver to trail the car which had just left at a discreet distance, and followed his friend.

Ten seconds after that an automobile which had been cruising through the neighborhood most of the afternoon and evening turned abruptly as Holy Hutchins recognized the man he was hunting, and joined unostentatiously in the procession.

Into Madison Avenue and down Madison Avenue turned Parmelee's taxi. A hundred yards in the rear Claghorn followed. And a hundred yards farther to the rear rolled Holy Hutchins and his driver.

The pseudo-clergyman had removed his coat, and had replaced it with a dark sweater. Somehow it had altered his appearance completely. The ministerial collar was still visible—but the sweater had accentuated certain unlovely features of its wearer's physiognomy. Hutchins was ready for business—and he looked the part. Gone was the oily blandness which he had assumed earlier in the day; come in its stead was an expression of unchangeable determination that boded ill for some one.

Parmelee's taxi came to a halt. He alighted, paid off his driver, and dismissed him. Quietly he walked into the side street in which he was to meet his employer's secretary.

Nearly a city block distant. Claghorn's taxi stopped. Tony disembarked.

"What do you want me to do now?" inquired his chauffeur.

"Stick around," said Tony. "Be where I can reach you when I want you."

Parmelee proceeded along the street. Once a fashionable neighborhood, it had long ago fallen from grace. On either side dingy, cheerless rooming houses lined it. Most of the first floors and basements had been given up to small tradesmen: tailors, milliners, shoemakers, and the like. Here and there table-d'hote dining rooms, which had been thronged earlier in the evening, flaunted their signs.

He paused for an instant in front of the address which had been given him over the telephone. It was a dingy rooming house, neither more nor less dingy than its neighbors. He glanced at his watch under one of the few street lamps that the dimly lighted block afforded; it was well before ten thirty. He put up his watch, and strolled toward the other corner.

Opposite him, and distant half the length of the street, Tony Claghorn moved stealthily from shadow to shadow. He had donned a dark hat and overcoat; even a few yards away he was quite indistinguishable against the background.

Parmelee reached the corner and turned. Claghorn retreated into an areaway and watched. Without pausing. Parmelee proceeded leisurely to the end of the street. He glanced at his watch again; it lacked but seven or eight minutes of the appointed time. He wheeled, and retraced his steps.

Once more he passed the address which had been given him, continued down the length of the street—and as he did so a long, gray touring car with the curtains closed swung around the corner which he had just left, rolled silently over the asphalt, and came to a halt at the rendezvous.

Tony, watching from across the street, felt his heart beating like a trip hammer—why, he hardly knew. The arrival of the automobile, tallying with the description that had been given of it, meant only that Cochrane's man was waiting for Parmelee. Yet something made Tony extraordinarily uneasy.

Blotted in the shadows, he flattered himself that he had not been observed; yet keen eyes, behind the curtains of the waiting car, had already picked him out. While his dark coat served admirably as protective coloration, it is greatly to be feared that his blond mustache, waxed and glistening in the dim light, made his discovery inevitable.

Holy Hutchins, sitting next to the driver, jerked his thumb in Tony's direction and whispered to the cauliflower-eared men in the back seat, "That's the fellow!"

They gazed with interest at Tony's glistening mustache. "How long do we wait for him?" they inquired.

"Wait for him nothing!" declared Holy Hutchins. "He's had a chance to come over. He isn't going to; he's got cold feet." He extracted his blackjack from his hip pocket. "Come on, boys," he murmured, and opened the door of the car. "No noise—but make sure you get him."

Tony, watching intently, saw Bill, having reached the corner again, turn and approach the gray touring car with quickened steps. But to Tony's utter amazement the three men who descended from the car paid no attention whatsoever to Parmelee. Instead they spread out fanwise and crossed the street, converging upon himself.

They approached, and Tony, utterly bewildered, racked his brains in vain for a solution of the problem. By no stretch of the imagination could their advance be called other than menacing. Their faces, dimly revealed in the gloom, were not prepossessing; their costumes were of a kind associated with a world with which Tony had not mingled, and their silent, simultaneous approach was distinctly threatening.

They neared. Tony, with his back against the wall of a house, saw that their hands were not empty—that they clutched short and ugly instruments known to the clubman by repute. As if by magic a pearl-mounted revolver leaped into his own hand.

They halted within a pace of him. "What do you want?" he challenged.

Holy Hutchins did not trouble to reply. He turned to his allies. "Let him have it, boys," he commanded.

It was then that things began to happen very quickly. Like one, the three men plunged upon their victim. Tony raised his revolver—and a vicious blow from a blackjack raised it still higher before he fired, the report echoing through the silent street like that of a cannon. He would have fired again had the weapon not dropped from a hand which had suddenly gone numb.

As best he could he fought against overwhelming odds: one good arm, and nothing but a fist at the end of it, against three desperate men armed with short leather clubs, heavily loaded with lead. He saw a slight figure rushing from across the street to his aid.

"Keep out of it!" he cried to him. He knew Parmelee had no weapons, and Tony, at bottom, was a very gallant gentleman.

If the advice was heard, it was unheeded. Like a wild cat the lithe figure of the ex-gambler bounded into the scrimmage, and the fight became general.

Had it been lighter, the outcome would not have been doubtful. Human flesh cannot withstand the crushing impact of blackjacks wielded by muscular arms. It would all have been over in a moment.

But darkness is always on the side of the lesser number—and Tony, resolved to sell his life dearly, had backed himself into a corner—and reinforcements had arrived—and the single revolver shot was presently followed by the swift patter of many feet running toward the spot from which it had rung out.

Holy Hutchins gritted his teeth as from the corner of his eye he observed the approaching multitude. "Beat it!" he commanded, and the three men ran for the waiting automobile. With muffler cut-out open, screaming its defiance of pursuit, it went roaring down the street.

The mob, headed by two police officers, engulfed the two men who remained. One of them, bleeding from half a dozen small cuts, was shakily on his feet; the other, quite unconscious, was stretched at full length on the pavement. And the mob, growing every second, filled the street and overflowed at the corners.

One of the police officers turned to the man who stood erect. "Are you hurt?" he inquired.

"No; not much."

The officer bent over the motionless shape at his feet. "They got this fellow, I'm afraid. He's a case for the ambulance." He opened his notebook methodically. "What's your name?" he inquired.

"Anthony P. Claghorn."

"New Yorker?"

"Yes."

"And this man?" He indicated the recumbent mass on the pavement.

The man who stood erect mopped his bleeding lip with a handkerchief. "His name is William Parmelee," he said.

"New Yorker?"

"No; he comes from a little out-of-the-way village in Connecticut."

"Let's get him to the hospital quick."

Somewhere within earshot in the crowd, and quite as safe there as if he were a thousand miles away, stood a portly little man whose heavy sweater nearly concealed the ministerial collar about his neck. He grinned.

IF SEELEY HAD indulged in only a little advertising, the brown-stone-front house in which games of chance were conducted every night for the benefit of men, young and old, who longed to get action for their money, would have been one of the notable landmarks of New York. But Seeley did not advertise. His clientele was as large as he desired it to be; and while it was his boast that his guests might indulge in any game they wished for any stake under the sun, he found it well, for many reasons, to shrink from the fierce light of publicity, and to conduct his business as quietly and unostentatiously as possible.

The ancient mansion in which Seeley operated differed in no external particular from those on either side of it in its highly respectable neighborhood. Its immaculate shades were drawn all day long, and at night no blaze of light came from its windows to distress the conservative landowners who resided in the vicinity. Quite the contrary, the select souls who had penetrated to the interior could have vouchsafed the information that behind the shades the windows were again guarded by massive steel shutters through whose crannies only tiny wisps of illumination might reach the outside world.

The steel-grilled outer door was like any other door; it was only when one had passed beyond it into the vestibule that a second, and very, very different door became visible. It was famous throughout the underworld, notorious with the gilded set which marched through it, and it was the pride of Seeley's heart. It had been manufactured to serve as the entrance to some exceedingly up-to-date safe-deposit vault. Three or four tons in weight, made from shell-proof armor, and fitted with a bewildering array of locks, bolts, and combinations, it swung easily on massive hinges to admit those whom Seeley decreed might enter. The others might work on its case-hardened exterior with acetylene torches, with hammers and sledges, with dynamite, with every destructive agency known to man, without doing more than marring the shining paint which covered its impregnable surface.

Within, two floors were given up to a series of luxuriously furnished, but moderate-sized rooms. Other proprietors of gambling houses might make much of some one great central space in which eight or ten different games might simultaneously be conducted. Not so Seeley. Long experience had taught him that it was human nature for a crowd to gather about some sensational winner or loser, and that such a crowd would find so much entertainment in merely looking on that its members would not dream of playing themselves. A second-hand thrill was nearly as good as one at firsthand; and it was even better if the stakes involved were larger than the spectator himself would dare to hazard. A second-hand thrill, moreover, was economical.

It was in order to combat this money-saving instinct that Seeley thoughtfully divided his crowd, gave up a separate room to each game, and made sure that no spectacular player would draw too great an audience from other tables. A newcomer might wander from room to room freely; might, at his leisure, make up his mind in what manner he would most willingly be divested of his surplus cash. But once having decided, his attention would not thereafter be distracted by events which, however interesting in themselves, had no direct bearing upon his fortunes.

This being the rule at Seeley's, no notice at all was taken of the young man who entered the gambling house barely half an hour after the occurrences which we have already related, and who circulated freely through the place. He had knocked at the grille the correct number of times. Having passed it, he had whispered the correct password to the guard on duty at the shell-proof inner door. Seeley had inspected him, had noticed that his lip showed a fresh cut and that his face was slightly battered. These, however, explained the young man, while exhaling an alcoholic fragrance in Seeley's direction, were the result of a recent tumble—a tale which the gambling-house proprietor did not doubt after a single sniff.

The young man's clothes were of good cut; the references which he volunteered were irreproachable; and while he had apparently imbibed enough to make sure that he would be a liberal player, he had not yet reached the stage at which he might be expected to be disorderly. He had a pocketful of money, he stated, without having been asked, and he had a system which he proposed to try out on Seeley.

Seeley smiled. Here, clearly, was an ideal patron. "What's

your system for?" he inquired genially. "Roulette—faro—twenty-one—poker?" naming a few of the games in progress at the moment.

The young man swallowed a hiccup. "It's good for all of them!" he declared. "It's as good for one as it is for the other. It's the greatest system there ever was."

Seeley bowed his satisfaction. "Walk right in," he invited. "Look around; find out what you want to play first. When you're ready the cashier will sell you chips."

"Much obliged," said the young man. He buttonholed the gambling-house proprietor for an instant. "You won't mind," he inquired, "if I win a lot of money? It's a good system, you know."

Seeley laughed. "Win as much as you like," he challenged. "The blue sky's the limit."

Thus encouraged, the young man proceeded within, and began to meander through the well-filled rooms. Had any one observed him closely, it would have been noted that, despite his intoxicating breath—a detail produced in the twinkling of an eye by the simple expedient of gargling a tablespoonful of raw alcohol—his glance was surprisingly alert. From table to table he passed unostentatiously, watched the play for a few minutes, and wandered on.

Seeley, who was everywhere, encountered him a number of times. He chuckled. His guest, like a fly, was buzzing around industriously before deciding on which sheet of fly paper to alight. That final freedom of choice Seeley begrudged no man; it mattered not at all to the gambler what manner of parting from his money his prospective victim selected.

He noticed that his new patron hovered about the faro table

after having studied the others. He was, apparently, deeply interested in the game.

"Going to try it?" inquired Seeley.

"I'm thinking about it," the young man admitted.

"Well, take plenty of time to make up your mind," said the proprietor genially. "Study it—and then try your system on it. It's the fairest game in the world."

"So I have heard."

Upon Seeley's next visit his guest was so profoundly engrossed with the play that he was keeping tabs on one of the score sheets provided by the house.

"Made up your mind yet?" inquired Seeley.

"Yes." He exhibited the score sheet. "I would have won—won heavily."

"The system?"

"Of course the system." His voice was apologetic. "If you don't mind, I'm going to watch one more deal, and then I'm going in."

"Suit yourself," boomed Seeley. "In this house you can do what you like."

The young man must have taken the permission literally, for he wandered out into one of the hallways shortly thereafter. Seeley, returning, noticed his absence, and was about to inquire about it when, suddenly, every one of the hundreds of electric lights in the place went out. Almost at once there echoed through the many rooms the sound of a terrific pounding on the armored door.

"A raid!" The words leaped from fifty mouths.

Matches were struck. In their dim light, Seeley appealed to his frightened patrons. There was no occasion for worry, he explained. The armored door had withstood many assaults; it would withstand one more. Seeley's men would dispose of all gambling paraphernalia—incriminating evidence—in hiding places prepared long in advance. Then, and not until then, the police would be admitted.

He finished his speech—a speech which he had delivered on many similar occasions. He turned with an engaging smile— and then the smile vanished as he observed that at least twenty of his listeners were in uniform, and that their familiar blue coats were decorated with equally familiar police badges.

The lieutenant in command answered his unspoken question. "Want to know how we got in, don't you? Well, we sawed through the steel-barred scuttle in your roof an hour ago. The hammering out in front is nothing but camouflage. We waited until we got our signal, and then we walked right in."

"Signal?" growled Seeley with an oath. "Who gave you a signal?"

The police lieutenant waved his hand at a young man with a strongly alcoholic breath who picked his way through the dark with the aid of police flash lights.

"I told the lieutenant I'd be ready when the lights went out," explained this latter individual, "and then I made sure the lights would go out by unscrewing a bulb, pushing a copper cent into the socket, turning on the current, and blowing out your fuses."

"You did, did you?" rumbled Seeley. "And who in thunder are you?"

"Haven't you met each other?" inquired the police lieutenant with surprise. "Mr. Seeley—Mr. Parmelee," he introduced.

SEELEY GAZED AT his unwelcome guest with eyes that almost popped out of his head. "Parmelee! Parmelee!" he sputtered. "I thought you were—" He broke off suddenly.

"Why not say it, Mr. Seeley? You thought I was in the hospital, didn't you? Well, that's precisely what I wanted you to think. That's why I said that the man whom your hired thugs had nearly killed was Parmelee and not Claghorn. I knew there would be somebody in the crowd who'd rush to the telephone and tell you the glad news. And that would give me a chance to catch you at your crookedness red-handed."

Suddenly the lights blazed on. The fuses had been replaced. Parmelee made his way to the seat lately occupied by the Faro dealer.

"Lieutenant," he suggested, "see if you can get everybody into this room. I'm going to deliver a little lecture."

The limited space became painfully crowded, but more than a hundred men had been jammed into it when Parmelee rose gravely, bowed, and announced as his text: "Faro—the fairest of all gambling games."

He looked from right to left, and smiled with an admirable platform manner. "First of all," he began, "let us consider how the bank cheats the players.

"Splits—like cards on a turn—are the dealer's life-savers. On each split the bank wins half of what has been staked on the cards, with no possibility of losing. If the dealer, when shuffling the cards, can manage to put up half a dozen splits, the game becomes unbeatable.

"Do you think it's difficult to put up splits?" He smiled. "I place the cards in two piles, just as they come from the dealing box. I have made up my mind what cards are to split on the next deal. I place them just a little to one side—do you see?—and then when I even up the piles the cards that are going to split find their way to the bottom of each pile. I stripped them out. You didn't see me do it, did you? But they are at the bottom nevertheless.

"Now I want to make the halves of the splits come together. I have a pile in each hand, and I tell you that each pile ends up with king, five, jack, two, and eight in the same order. I do what is called 'the faro-dealer's shuffle'—it's difficult, but you can learn it if you practice it long enough—and the cards come together alternately throughout the deck—like this. I cut a few times; that convinces you I'm fair. But notice what I'm really doing; I'm distributing the splits so that they won't come out in succession. Now I'm ready to take your money."

Bill faced the deck, and spread it out on the table. "Do you see, gentlemen? There are going to be seven splits on this deal. I put up five and two more just happened. What chance have you got against a game like that?"

A ripple of applause spread through the crowd. Bill bowed.

"Bear in mind," he warned, "bear in mind that in faro, the so-called fairest of all gambling games, the cards are taken from the box face up. They are placed in two piles face up. They are shuffled by the dealer. They are cut by the dealer. He has chance after chance to arrange them in an order that will be profitable for him and expensive for you. He has a big salary to earn. How do you think he earns it?"

He took up the deck and ran it rapidly through the dealing box.

"Of course," he resumed, "too many splits would be suspicious. I don't have to trust to them. I notice what the biggest plunger is doing—whether he is backing the high cards or the low cards—and in exactly the same way I put the deck so that his favorites lose. Really, it's no trouble at all." Expertly he demonstrated.

A bespectacled young man in evening clothes interrupted with a question. "Suppose, after I've backed the high cards for the first half of the deal, I change my system and back the low cards for the second half?"

"Then I used a 'two-card' dealing box—a box which lets me take out two cards at a time instead of one; I add a fifty-third card to the deck, and I change the run of the cards to beat you. It's a little more complicated," he explained. "I need a mechanical shuffling board—like this one." He trod on an unseen button under the carpet, and a dainty little lever flashed into sight with a card gripped in its teeth. He pointed to it with a flourish. "Gentlemen, the fifty-third card! In play, of course, you'd never see it. I'd keep it hidden with the deck. But once I have added the fifty-third card, I can change the run by drawing it out or letting it go by—or I can make the fifty-third card win or lose as I please."

The bespectacled young man was not entirely satisfied. "How do you know when the fifty-third card is coming? You have to know, don't you?"

"You bet I have to know," Parmelee declared. "With the players keeping tabs, they'd spot a fifth king like a shot!"

"Well, how do you find out?"

"You bring me naturally to the second part of my lecture. It is entitled 'How the players cheat the bank.' The fifth king and his duplicate—I never forget that duplicate for a second!—are what we call 'tell cards.' They are cut the least bit wider than the other cards in the deck—and when either one of them is coming—watch—do you see this bolt at the side of the box move? You'd hardly call it a motion, because it's so slight. But if you're watching for it, you'll catch it; That's how I know.

"Suppose, however, that some greenhorn has bought the bank. Do I bother with fifty-third cards? Hardly! They'd spoil the game. I simply hand the banker a deck of very special cards—a deck in which all the low cards are narrow, and all the high cards wide. The difference amounts to nothing. The greenhorn will never notice it.

"Then I take my seat at the table—I and my friends—and the bolt at the side of the box tells us what's coming next. We bet. We bet heavily. We lose once in a while, just to make the banker feel happy. But the bets we lose are little ones, while the bets we win are big ones!"

The bespectacled young man shook his head. "I can understand how such a box could be used to cheat me when I'm the banker, but if the bolt always moves, why don't I see it when I'm watching the box, and Seeley is the banker?"

Parmelee laughed. "You don't see it because you're not watching closely enough—and because you don't know what to watch. There's not a chance in a million of your catching on. Why, you've been playing this game right here—you've been losing your money to this box—and you saw nothing wrong with it until I pointed it out to you!

"But that isn't all! This box possesses almost human intelligence. Why should I take even a slight chance of detection when I have to take nope at all? I move the box about on the table like this—a triple combination, you notice—and in the words of the manufacturers, 'it locks up to a square box.' You can examine it now, and you won't find anything suspicious.

But another series of movements—so—unlocks it, and if I'm using a fifty-third card, I won't make any embarrassing errors."

Again the applause broke out—the applause of men who are being offered rare and valuable entertainment.

"This particular method of cheating," concluded Bill, "is a combination of what we call the 'two-card box' and the 'needle-tell.' There are other methods—many others. I hope you'll take my word for it." But the bespectacled young man had more questions to ask. "The box locks up with a triple combination?"

"Yes."

"That is to prevent strangers from finding out that it isn't a fair box?"

"Of course."

"Then how do you happen to know the combination?"

Bill actually blushed. "I used to be a professional faro dealer myself," he said. "The boxes we had weren't good for much, and this particular box—well, I hope you won't think I'm blowing, but I invented it!"

He bowed, gravely announced, "Here endeth the lesson," and was about to make his way toward the door, when his eye fell upon a curiously shrinking individual who had been found in the basement by the police, and who was making strenuous efforts to be intensely invisible. Over his dark sweater he now wore a coat, but the neck of the sweater did not entirely conceal a strangely incongruous element of his costume, a ministerial collar.

Through Bill's mind flashed memories: the ministerial collar which had boarded the train at West Woods; the ministerial collar which had alighted from the gray automobile; the ministerial collar which had figured prominently in the battle in which Tony had so recently succumbed.

"Grab that man!" commanded Bill. "Grab him! Grab him!"

THE BESPECTACLED YOUNG man insisted on driving Bill to the hospital in his own car, a luxuriously upholstered limousine. "We really ought to know each other, Mr. Parmelee," he declared. "My name is Cochrane."

The ex-gambler grasped the proffered hand with a grin. "I suspected as much," he said, "but, by George, haven't we had a deuce of a time getting together?"

In the few minutes following immediately upon the arrest of Holy Hutchins, much light had been thrown upon certain obscure subjects. The bogus clergyman, spurred on by promises of leniency, and thoroughly intimidated by Parmelee's obvious desire to throttle the life out of him, had owned up to his share in the day's thrilling episodes, and now Cochrane, supplying the few missing links, was in a position to clear up the entire situation.

Sitting next to Tony's cot in a private room at the hospital, the men compared notes in hushed voices. Tony was still unconscious. He had sustained a concussion of the brain, the surgeon in charge told them. They could only wait for him to come to—and in the meantime not all the noises in a boiler factory would make the slightest impression upon him.

"It's all my fault, I'm afraid," said Cochrane. "I had lost a lot of money at Seeley's. I became suspicious. Whenever I was banker, there was a group of young men—always the same group—which won with great regularity. I didn't know one of them—nor did my friends. Seeley had introduced them, and that was nothing in their favor.

"But that wasn't all. I didn't act as banker very often. I wanted action. As the banker, I could only accept bets. As a player, I could make them—and Seeley very obligingly raised his limit for my benefit."

"Benefit?" queried Bill, with a smile.

"Let's call it that," said Cochrane. "I wanted action. I got action. I got it in precisely the way that you described tonight. I'd back the high cards. I'd lose halfway through the deal. I'd switch to the low cards. I'd win a turn or two, and then I'd lost straight through to the finish."

"The fifty-third card."

"Exactly. I know it now. Sometimes I'd play with no particular system. I'd bet almost at random."

"Then there would be splits."

Cochrane nodded. "There would be a steady succession of splits. Not too many, of course—but enough to make it very painful for me. Whatever I did, whether I played with a system or without a system, whether I backed the high cards or whether I backed the low ones, I lost—not too steadily, but steadily enough anyhow."

"A good dealer would see to that," murmured Bill.

"I had heard of you, Mr. Parmelee. I had heard how successful you had been in similar cases. I made up my mind—just when I don't know—that I was going to ask you to drop in at Seeley's, and tell me whether the game was honest. I made the colossal mistake of confiding in one of my friends, because he promptly told another one, and the news must have gotten back to Seeley."

Bill nodded grimly. "That explains many things," he said. "Seeley didn't want me investigating his game. He decided to spike your guns. He telephoned me himself; he said that he was Gilbert Cochrane. He invited me to New York, and he hired thugs to make short work of me. Either they would kill me—Seeley wasn't particular—or they would beat me up so badly that I would go home and stay home."

"Exactly," said Cochrane.

"He sent one of his men to the little town where I lived to trail me onto the train. Tony Claghorn warned me that that might happen," he confessed with a grateful glance toward the unconscious figure on the cot, "but I didn't take it seriously. And then Hutchins—so he told us himself—mistook Tony for me, and the poor fellow had a mighty hard time of it."

A mighty hard time! A mighty hard time indeed! Never did Parmelee learn how near, how very near, death had stalked behind Tony on that momentous afternoon. Tony himself never told him, for Tony, native New Yorker, never knew. He was aware that the three men who had attacked him in the areaway had meant mischief; but he was blissfully ignorant of the fact that not once, but repeatedly, had they attempted to finish him. It was due to this that Hutchins and his accomplices were subsequently sentenced to terms much lighter than they had deserved.

"When Seeley telephoned me, and said that he was Gilbert Cochrane, I swallowed the bait—hook, line, and sinker. He offered me a very large fee—"

"How large, Mr. Parmelee?" interrupted Cochrane.

"Twenty-five thousand."

Cochrane, the multimillionaire, opened his bespectacled eyes wide. "That is a large fee," he admitted. "Go on, Mr. Parmelee."

"There was only one thing that made me suspicious—"

"And that?"

"The length of time the man who called himself Cochrane talked over the phone. Millionaires never waste money on long-distance tolls."

Cochrane grinned with delight. "You're dead right!" he exclaimed. "I would never have telephoned you. I would have written you a letter. In fact," and he opened his coat, "I've got the letter I was going to send in my breast pocket this minute."

"Why hadn't you mailed it?"

Cochrane grinned again. "I was true to my blood, Mr. Parmelee. I didn't mail it because I thought I'd find out what was wrong with the game by myself—and in that way I'd save the amount of your fee."

Parmelee nodded gravely. "I guessed wrong a number of times. I guessed right just once. That saved me; that—and Tony Claghorn.

"When I reached New York, I looked up some of my old friends. I found out where you had been playing. Incidentally I found out the password to the place, so that I could go there alone if I wanted to."

"And the raid?"

"I arranged that for my own protection. What would my life have been worth if I had dared to say what I did in Seeley's house without police to guard me? The raid was fixed up easily enough," Bill admitted with a grin. " 'Chick' Powers and I were both gamblers and good pals years ago. Now Chick is a police lieutenant, he took charge of the raid himself. You'll admit that he conducted it in great style."

Cochrane had listened soberly. Now, with reluctant fingers, he extracted his check book from his pocket. "Mr. Parmelee," he said, "if I had engaged you, I would have limited your fee to a suitable amount—five thousand dollars at the outside. I didn't engage you, but you have rendered me a very great service nevertheless. What do you expect me to pay?"

Bill waved a deprecatory hand. "Put up your check book," he commanded. "I don't want any pay at all. If Tony gets well I'll be entirely satisfied."

But Cochrane was already writing his signature. "Five thousand dollars is a fair amount," he said, "five thousand dollars—neither more nor less. But I haven't forgotten that Seeley, speaking in my name, offered you twenty-five. Seeley, I'm afraid, isn't going to make good on his promise, and I, Mr. Parmelee, I look upon an obligation incurred in my name as a debt of honor. I shall pay both fees. Mr. Parmelee, this check is good for thirty thousand dollars."

Bill gasped; but it was Cochrane's turn to wave his hand. "Don't hesitate to take it," he urged with a smile. "But for you, Seeley would have gotten it."

The figure on the cot had begun to stir. Now it opened its lips. "I repeat," Tony mumbled, "I repeat that faro is a cheat-proof game."

Cochrane turned to Parmelee with consternation written large upon his features. "Your friend is going insane!" he declared.

But Bill smiled happily. "No," he corrected, and subsequent events proved that he was right, "he's beginning to get well."

10

SLIPPERY ELM

WHEN THE MORAL adventures of William Parmelee, ex-card sharp and more or less unwilling corrector of destinies, are neatly collected into a volume dedicated to the speedy and permanent advancement of honesty among all those who tempt Fate in games of chance, this is one of the tales which will be omitted. At the very best, it will be relegated to a modest appendix where readers under twenty-one may skip it, and thus avoid its corrupting influence; but in the volume proper it can have no place, for, being veracious, it relates how Parmelee, upon a certain most remarkable occasion, allied himself with the forces of evil, and how the only honest man in the tale fared badly.

This, of course, is all wrong. Axiomatic it is that honesty should be rewarded, that dishonesty should suffer, that morality, in the end, should triumph. If this does not invariably happen in life, it should most emphatically happen on the printed page. Granted that in the vicissitudes of modern civilization the good man—even so good a man as J. Hampton Hoogestraten—occasionaly comes off second best, such episodes should be quietly hushed up, and not under any circumstances broadcast to undermine the virtue of the innocent rising generation.

But when the said William Parmelee, ex-card sharp and corrector of destinies stands face to face with the guardian or the pearly gates, the facts having to do with the downfall of that good man, J. Hampton Hoogestraten, will doubtless be investigated. Tony Claghorn will be interrogated, for Tony was a witness. Colonel Stafford, president of the Metropolitan Chess Club, will be examined mercilessly, for, despite his seventy years and his snow-white hair, Stafford was an accomplice. The rank and file of the members, from Aalders to Zysser, will be questioned remorselessly, for they, too, each and every one of them, took part in the dastardly plot.

Little Reynolds will not be excepted—he least of all; and the great Niemzo-Zborowski himself will be in for a grilling. And that last may result in utter calamity, for Niemzo-Zborowski may not be permitted to pass the gates, and without him there will be no chess in heaven—at any rate, no chess worth mentioning.

And while the many sinners concerned in the letting down of J. Hampton Hoogestraten plead and parley at the great portals, the shade of that good man himself, smoking one of his infamous cigars will stride into the blissful place unchallenged—maybe. And since that contingency is greatly to be feared, and since the facts in the case are more or less involved, it seems desirable to set them forth here and now, so that the matured opinion of mankind, rising upward like heated air, may reach the venerable guardian of the gate in good time, and in this manner prevent a miscarriage of justice.

Let the tale be passed from mouth to mouth; let there be an abundance of witnesses. Then, perhaps, the members of the Metropolitan Chess Club, with Colonel Stafford at their head, will march through the gates in battle formation, Aalders at one point of their phalanx and Zysser at the other. And somewhere in the midst, concealed by their numbers, will march little Reynolds—and the great Niemzo-Zborowski—and Bill Parmelee himself.

And as for that good man, J. Hampton Hoogestraten—Well, what about him?

HE BREEZED INTO the Metropolitan Chess Club for the first time on a stormy night in February. Hoogestraten had applied for membership in writing, and as the check for a year's dues which had accompanied his application had been promptly honored at the bank, he had been duly elected. Like other chess clubs, the Metropolitan was none too affluent; an ability to pay the exceedingly modest sum which it charged for the privilege of belonging to it was sufficient recommendation for any candidate. Wherefore the application of J. Hampton Hoogestraten was acted upon with all expedition, and the secretary duly dispatched him the card which certified that he was entitled to all of the rights, immunities, and benefits of the organization, including the right of paying on the spot for coffee, cigars and other refreshments as ordered.

J. Hampton Hoogestraten breezed in, poised his two hundred and twenty-eight pounds of oleaginous fat on the threshold, divested himself of a fedora hat and a heavy overcoat provided with a quilted lining and a near-seal collar, and surveyed the long, narrow room which was the home of the Metropolitan Chess Club.

The walls were adorned with the photographs of dead-and-gone masters—Morphy, Steinitz, Paulsen, Anderssen, Zukertort, Blackburne, Pillsbury, Staunton, Tchigorin. Between them, suitably framed or encased, were the trophies which the club's team had won in hard-fought battles.

A score of chess tables, ranged in a long line, and each provided with its complement of chessmen and a chess clock, more than accommodated perhaps a quarter of the club's total membership. Had the night not been stormy, a larger attendance might certainly have been expected, and the dozen reserve tables stowed in nooks and crannies would have come into use; the chess fan is true to his game, and spends four or five nights a week at it. But upon the momentous occasion that J. Hampton Hoogestraten first honored the club with his presence, thirty men, at the outside, were revealed to his appraising glance.

There was a curious family resemblance between the thirty. Their foreheads were of more than average height; their hirsute adornments were uncommonly plentiful, their clothing uniformly careless. Young or old, tall or short, lean or well fed, there was a strangely similar, patient look in the eyes of each. Above all else, chess demands single-minded concentration from its devotees; their expressions indicated it.

Nearly all of the players smoked; and those who did not smoke gulped down huge drafts of black coffee while they studied their games. From time to time one of them, after mature deliberation, would make a move; from time to time one of them would murmur "Kkkh!"—an odd monosyllable, which the initiated contender translates as "Check;" from time to time one of them, leaving an adversary to struggle with a knotty problem, would saunter to a near-by table to study another game.

For an instant—but only for an instant—the thirty looked up when the massive frame of J. Hampton Hoogestraten filled the doorway. Then they continued with their play.

Had they studied the new member closely, they would have observed a youngish, middle-aged man of moderate stature, well upholstered as to the paunch, and rather bare as to the scalp, whose entire get-up radiated success. Not that J. Hampton Hoogestraten was a captain of industry, or even on the way to become one—far from it. His occupation, that of a traveling salesman for a manufacturer of laundry soaps, provided him with a fair living and no more. But J. Hampton Hoogestraten believed to the innermost core of his being that success came inevitably to the man who looked the part.

His clothing, therefore, consisted of garments of cheap material cut in ambitious imitation of the lines of expensive ones. A white vest gleamed on either side of a brilliant tie; a huge pearl, guaranteed to defy any but expert inspection, topped a near-platinum scarf-pin; patent-leather shoes shone on his large feet; and his pudgy hands, well manicured, twinkled with their load of shoddy jewelry.

Half a dozen tiny diamonds, cunningly grouped in a cluster, may be made to produce the effect of a single large, costly stone. J. Hampton Hoogestraten had invested in a number of rings designed on this economical principle, and as he stood in the doorway and raised his cigar to his mouth, the flash that radiated from his fingers proclaimed affluence to the uninitiated.

HE GAZED ABOUT the room, saw the dignified figure of Colonel Stafford, president of the club, seated in solitary dignity at a table, and he committed his first mistake. J. Hampton Hoogestraten marched over, smote the colonel on the back in hearty he-man fashion, and extended a bejeweled paw.

"I'm the new member," he introduced himself. "My name is J. Hampton Hoogestraten. How about a little game?"

A blunder? Say rather a wild series of blunders. In the first place, the colonel, who had earned his title at the head of a regiment in war time, took himself seriously, and was a stickler for etiquette. The fashion in which J. Hampton had presented himself did not endear him to the old man's heart.

In the second place, the membership of the club, from time immemorial, had been neatly divided into fifteen classes, based on playing strength. For a newcomer, who automatically took his place at the foot of the fifteenth class, to hint at a game with a man who was ranked well up in the third class, before having himself fought his way within striking distance, was a presumptuous violation of the club's most sacred rule. A fine player does not relish a game with an inferior player. The overlords of the Metropolitan Chess Club had done what they could to make such unpleasantness impossible. Yet J. Hampton Hoogestraten, who had received a copy of the rules, began by flouting them.

In the third place, the tactful thing to do, as a new member, would have been to allow an old member to suggest a game. Indeed, once upon the scene, J. Hampton Hoogestraten could hardly have avoided playing. But to his ebullient soul this modest procedure had not commended itself. He had plunged in where angels feared to tread.

The colonel raised his leonine head, gazed at the newcomer, and reflected that, had it been war time, he would promptly have ordered J. Hampton Hoogestraten to a week's kitchen police for insubordination. But no war being on hand, the colonel bowed gracefully to the inevitable, and resolved to have his revenge by administering a merciless beating to the upstart.

"Sit down, sir," he commanded.

"Right you are!" boomed J. Hampton Hoogestraten, and overflowed into a chair. "I want to warn you in advance," he declared modestly, "I'm good. I'm very good."

"Indeed?" murmured the colonel, raising his eyebrows.

"Just that," said Hoogestraten.

The colonel's self-control was admirable. "Perhaps I will learn something from you," he said silkily.

J. Hampton Hoogestraten nodded vigorously. "I shouldn't be surprised," he admitted. If there was sarcasm beneath his opponent's remark, it had not touched him.

The colonel had taken a white pawn and a black pawn in his hands and had shaken them. He presented his closed fists to his antagonist. "Which will you have?" he inquired.

J. Hampton Hoogestraten indicated the colonel's right hand. It opened to disclose a white pawn.

"Lucky! Lucky right at the start!" declared the self-confessed good man. He arranged his pieces, and played his opening move. " 'Lead on Macduff!' " he invited.

That was precisely what the colonel intended. Boiling with rage, he would have defeated the new member in ten moves had that been possible. It was not possible, for J. Hampton Hoogestraten's play speedily disclosed that he was no novice. Indeed, before a dozen moves had been made, the colonel began to regret the careless assurance with which he had managed his opening. J. Hampton Hoogestraten had stated that he was good. He was; and the realization of that fact did little to soothe the irate colonel.

He realized that the task of winning would call for the best that was in him—and then a ghastly, pungent odor, strangely reminiscent of war time, broke upon his consciousness. He sniffed, raised his head, glared at the newcomer.

"I beg your pardon!"

"Yes?" invited Hoogestraten.

Colonel Stafford pointed a quivering finger at the cigar which smoldered in his opponent's mouth. Its aroma, which was now reaching him in huge, deadly blasts, was paralyzing, and even though years of chess had made the colonel immune to cigars of more than average frightfulness, he was compelled to place the object whose clouds billowed in his direction in a class wholly by itself.

"Mr. Hoogestraten," he demanded, "where did you get that gas bomb?"

As already indicated in this veracious chronicle, Mr. Hoogestraten's hide was so tough that ordinary forms of sarcasm could make no impression on it.

"You mean this?" He waved the malodorous cigar. "I'll write down the name of the place where I buy them when I finish this game. And that won't take long. You've left your knight en prise—see?" He captured it with a swoop.

THE COLONEL CHOKED. Overcome by the fumes with which his antagonist attacked him, he had committed the blunder of leaving a piece on a square where it could be taken without compensation to himself. It was contrary to his usual careful method of play, and it was irritating that it should occur with his present opponent.

Against any other player, the colonel would have resigned on the spot; the loss of a knight was enough to decide the issue. But a blind fury against J. Hampton Hoogestraten had seized him, and he played on, hoping against hope for a change for the better.

The change did not come. Instead, a bishop, neatly forked, went to follow the knight, and even the veriest tyro could see that a castle was soon to follow.

The colonel, outwardly calm, tipped over his king in token of surrender. He had been beaten by a fluke and by his own anger; and he had been beaten by a player who was certainly not his superior. He began to set up the pieces for a second game.

J. Hampton Hoogestraten surveyed him with a fishy eye. "What are you doing?"

"We're going to have another game, aren't we?"

"What for?"

"My revenge, of course."

J. Hampton Hoogestraten pushed back his chair and lighted a fresh cigar. "Brother," he remarked to the president of the club, "go home and study—study about six or seven years— and then, when you've learned something about the game, I'll give you the odds of a rook and beat you. Don't make me waste more time on you now."

The colonel flushed purple, but years of military discipline had schooled him to control his feelings.

"If we play a second game now, Mr. Hoogestraten, I think I will do better."

J. Hampton Hoogestraten rose ponderously and waved a jeweled hand. "Run along, run along, little boy," he suggested. At a near-by table, a dark, undersized individual with a luxuriant beard had just finished a game. His appearance promised well, and the new member hailed him. "Hey, you!" he called. "Want to play?"

It was thus that J. Hampton Hoogestraten began his career as a member of the Metropolitan Chess Club.

UNNECESSARY IT IS to detail the steps by which Mr. Hoogestraten made himself the most unpopular individual who had ever entered the clubrooms. Indeed, they were not steps at all; with more accuracy they might have been termed a succession of sharp, sudden shocks.

There was something about his face that inspired dislike even before he opened his mouth. Its self-satisfied, smug, complacent air paved the way for an impression which was but too well confirmed when, between puffs at his infamous cigars, he sang his own praises. He was good; he admitted it; he proclaimed it; he gloried in it. What was worse, he proved it by taking a place in the third dozen.

Under ordinary circumstances the club would have welcomed the advent of a strong player; in the case of J. Hampton Hoogestraten, however, the fact that the boaster could make good his boast was merely irritating. He had acquired skill. He had not acquired the modesty and the forbearance which should have gone with it. The few topnotchers could beat him and did beat him; but to be beaten by them was no disgrace; whereas the rank and file of the club, which thirsted for his gore and longed for an opportunity to humble him, had no chance whatever.

He made enemies as naturally as soap makes suds. Colonel Stafford, too much of a gentleman to prejudice the club against the new member, said not a word to his discredit. But the colonel's silence could not affect the result. With a talent amounting to genius, J. Hampton Hoogestraten proceeded gracefully from the frying pan to the fire.

There was the night, for instance, when Lindeberg and Strachan, players of but moderate strength, having concluded a particularly brilliant game, proudly replayed it for the benefit of the newcomer. J. Hampton Hoogestraten puffed at his overpowering cigar, blinked his little eyes, and, when requested to state his opinion, remarked simply:

"I think both of you were rotten."

Lindeberg, who had sacrificed a rook as the first move of what he considered a dazzling combination, recoiled as if struck by a whiplash.

"What do you mean?"

"What do you think I mean? Don't you understand plain English?"

J. Hampton Hoogestraten did not remove his cigar from his mouth as he set up the position.

"Here's where your combination started, isn't it? It took you fifteen moves more to lick him. Now, why didn't you do it this way?" To Lindeberg's consternation, he demonstrated a shorter and simpler combination, which won the game in one third the time. "See? That's the way I would have done it."

"I believe you said I playcd badly, too," Strachan remarked.

"I didn't," corrected J. Hampton Hoogestraten; "I said you were rotten."

Strachan controlled himself enough to inquire: "And how so?"

Once more the bejeweled fingers of the good man flew over the chessboard.

"Look at that combination of his! Just look at it!"

"I couldn't find any flaw in it," returned Strachan.

"No? Well, at this point you took his bishop—"

"It was a forced move."

"Forced nothing! If you hadn't taken it, you could have played this"—his pudgy fingers manipulated the pieces—"he would have played this—or this—or this, and either way you could have announced mate in three more moves."

THE WORST OF it was that he was right, and Lindeberg and Strachan were compelled to admit it. Had he stated his views more tactfully, he might have made worshipers of both men. As it was, he added two more to the considerable roll of those who hated him.

His tactics, when he discovered that chess might be made moderately lucrative, were what might have been expected of him. A stake of twenty-five cents a game was customary. By playing exclusively with weaker players, he might earn as much as three dollars in an evening.

Under the club rules, he was compelled to concede a handicap to them; but since the whole theory of handicapping is based upon the intention of bringing about a fairly level contest in which the advantage, if any, will go to the scratch man, he did well. Under scientific handicapping—and the Metropolitan Chess Club was nothing if not scientific—the weak contender will win only if he performs unusually well, which is unlikely, whereas the strong contender will win if he runs true to form, which is highly probable.

It did not take J. Hampton Hoogestraten long to find out that he could concede odds, and still win pretty much as he pleased. Once sure of that, he no longer played with the men in his own class, but confined himself strictly to more remunerative chess. Little Reynolds, for instance, had for years occupied an undisputed place at the foot of class fifteen—the lowest class. He loved chess; he studied it; and the more he studied it, the worse he played. His only chance of winning, even his many friends admitted, was to seize a handful of pawns and ram them down an adversary's throat.

His games were invariably lost so quickly that the disparity in material mattered not at all. Had he been able to survive twenty moves, his handicap might have decided the battle; as a rule, however, he would perpetrate some ghastly blunder before reaching that point, and would resign gracefully.

It was upon him, therefore, that J. Hampton Hoogestraten concentrated—at twenty-five cents a game. Playing him, Hoogestraten could run through a whole series of games in the time that one hard-fought, level game with a man of his own strength would have required. And it was more profitable, too.

During the day, little Reynolds filled quite a place in the sun as the chief official of a huge trust company, at a salary which would have made J. Hampton Hoogestraten's eyes stick out. He cared nothing at all about the few dollars that the soap salesman relieved him of nearly every evening, but his fellow members, among whom he was popular, and to whom an imposition was no less an imposition because it was practiced upon a man who could afford to lose, resented Hoogestraten's tactics bitterly.

We must not, however, discuss the advent of the good man without paying particular attention to the alleged cigars with which he was always well supplied. They were large, blunt, and liver colored. They were ornamented with huge red-and-gold bands, and as Strachan, who was the club wit, pointed out, they would not have smelled so badly had their owner merely smoked the bands and not touched off the cigars.

There was something about their aroma which was indescribably devastating. It was heavy, penetrating, overpowering, and its effective range was great. Colonel Stafford, with memories of war time, mentioned that it reminded him of an enemy offensive, and recommended the use of gas masks. Zysser, who ran a wholesale grocery establishment, murmured incoherently that it recalled thoughts of a Camembert cheese that had once gone very wrong. O'Neill, who was a mining engineer, swore that it was a variety of choke damp; and Beers, who was a physician, stated that, in his professional opinion, it was twin brother to a fumigating agent sometimes used to combat the plague. Thereupon Strachan had voiced the general sentiment by declaring for the lesser of the two evils—the plague—and the club had emphatically endorsed him.

That it was a factor in Hoogestraten's success was undeniable. Strachan contended—and there was some truth in his contention—that the soap salesman, minus his cigars, would rank fifty numbers lower. The cigars themselves, he declared, were entitled to a place in the first class. The place which Hoogestraten occupied represented the average of his talents and his tobacco.

That it was difficult to play at anything approaching top form while inhaling whiffs of Hoogestraten's smoke was only too apparent to his clubmates. Brilliant combinations perished in the making; inspirations gasped and expired; ideas which might have won games died a-borning; and while his adversaries contended with his cigars, the soap salesman, hardened to them as a serpent to its venom, mowed down opponents who should have defeated him. It was unfair. It was unheard of. And, coupled with his blatant personality, it was monstrously irritating.

IT IS HARD to say how the movement began—movements which are the expression of a mass soul simply leap into existence; they do not properly start—but suddenly every one of J. Hampton Hoogestraten's fellow members found himself overflowing with a consuming desire to see J. Hampton Hoogestraten soundly and properly punished.

"Of course, there are fellows in the club who can lick him," said Strachan. "Macpherson can do it, and Golding can do it, and so can any of our first-string men. But to be licked by them isn't punishment; it's a compliment to have them play with you, and if you can make them work a little, you're satisfied. You don't expect to win."

"Quite so," said Colonel Stafford.

"What I'd like to see is something very much different," pursued Strachan. "I'd like to see Hoogie play a match with one of our tenth-raters—"

"Reynolds, for instance."

"Reynolds would be ideal. And I'd like to see little Reynolds play him even, and knock the everlasting stuffings out of him."

"That," remarked Zysser, "would be my idea of heffen on eart'!"

"I'd like to see Reynolds stand him on his head," said Strachan savagely. "I'd like to see Reynolds turn him inside out and upside down! I'd like to see Reynolds make such a laughing-stock out of him that he'll never dare to show his face in this club again. I'd like to see—I'd like to see Reynolds kerflummox him!"

"Rave on," said O'Neill, who was listening.

"It's a pipe dream," commented Beers. "Too good to be true," sighed Lindeberg.

Strachan lowered his voice. "Boys," he said, "I don't know if it can be done."

"Neither do I," said O'Neill.

"Nor I," assented Lindeberg.

"You can search me," declared Beers.

Strachan hypnotized them with a long, lean forefinger. "Perhaps it can't be done at all. But if it's possible, if it's possible by hook or crook, I've heard of the one man in the whole world who can show us how to do it."

Colonel Stafford tugged hopefully at his mustache.

"What is he? A magician?"

But Strachan, fixing his eyes ecstatically upon the ceiling, did not appear to hear him.

"Boys," he inquired, "how many of you will join me in a petition to Bill Parmelee?"

TAKEN ALL IN all, it was one of the strangest of the many strange communications that Parmelee ever received. It arrived while he was enjoying a leisurely breakfast in his friend Claghorn's apartment, and its arrival was timed to a second with his remark that here, at least, he felt safe from the regiment of his pursuers.

Much against his own inclinations, circumstances and his peculiar talents had forced Parmelee into a unique role; that of an expert on everything having to do with the devious and little-understood art of cheating. For the space of six years— nearly a quarter of his life—he had wandered about the country, subsisting by his wits and by his dexterity in giving himself more than the usual chance at every gambling game indulged in by his compatriots. Poker—roulette—faro—to mention but a few; he had had profound experience with them all. He had become familiar with cheating devices because he had either used them himself or had seen them used; and, being of a creative turn of mind, he had added devices of his own invention to the many already in existence.

He had played fair—when he had to—and at other times had taken every advantage that he could; and, in spite of his acknowledged expertness, the six years of his vagabondage had but vindicated the truth of the Biblical injunction: "In the sweat of thy face shalt thou eat bread." He had won large sums upon many occasions. He had parted from them as rapidly as he had amassed them. His periods of prosperity had been short and hectic; his periods of adversity had been long, many, and painful. Fortunes had been in his grasp—and had passed out of it.

In six years he had endured vicissitudes which would have crushed an ordinary man; he had survived dangers which, more than once, had threatened to put an end to his existence; and then, brought home by chance, the blood of his forefathers— Puritans, all of them—had asserted itself in no uncertain terms. As naturally as he had fallen into one rut, so he had fallen into another and a better one. He had turned a new leaf. He had put the ways of his past behind him. He had devoted himself to the industrious life of a farmer with an energy comparable only to that which he had expended upon his earlier and less-creditable adventures. And then Fate, in a sardonic mood, had tapped him on the shoulder, and had called upon him to use his hard-earned knowledge of gambling and gamblers' tricks in a manner which he had never foreseen.

It had begun naturally enough when, out of the goodness of

his heart, he had come to the rescue of a chance acquaintance, the same Anthony P. Claghorn with whom he was now breakfasting. Claghorn, spending the summer at a hotel near Parmelee's home, had been the victim of a sharper who had separated him from his income as regularly as it arrived. Parmelee had heard of the circumstances, and out of sympathy for Claghorn's pretty wife had taken a hand in a game which promptly assumed a remarkably different character.

He had succeeded beyond his hopes. Not only had he exposed the cheat, but, by meeting him with an improvement on his own tactics, he had recovered more than Claghorn's losses.

Parmelee had accomplished a good deed. He had made use of his unusual knowledge in a worthy manner. He had atoned for one of the blots upon his own career. It had not occurred to him that he had embarked upon a series of adventures leading inevitably from one to another, encroaching more and more seriously upon his time, and destined, in the end, to bring him prominently into the public eye.

HE HAD RETURNED to his farming—and Claghorn, electing himself a disciple, had idiotically attempted to apply Parmelee's methods to a problem of his own. The result—a result which Claghorn could have foreseen had he been possessed of less assurance—was utter disaster, and Parmelee, appealed to for help, could not very well refuse his aid. A second time he had made use of his unique talents, and had, a second time, been able to snatch victory from the jaws of defeat. And then, thick and fast, had followed adventure after adventure.

Parmelee had not deliberately adopted a profession so

unusual that no name existed for it. Quite the contrary, he had made heroic efforts to escape when the trend of events had become evident. But Claghorn, singing the praises of his idol to his innumerable acquaintances in his many clubs, had discovered a surprisingly great demand for Parmelee's services, and as the demand had been accompanied by a willingness to pay fees running high into the thousands of dollars, Parmelee, who was by no means a wealthy man, could not see his way clear to decline.

Apparently scores of men, dabbling with games of chance, doubted the honesty of their opponents. Parmelee, possessing a past master's knowledge not only of the tricks of legerdemain but of the amazingly ingenious mechanical devices used to fleece unsuspecting victims, was in a position to help mightily. He did so, uncovering villainy where it was least expected and exposing one sharper after another—and, with each adventure, his fame spread.

Knowledge, alone, could not have accounted for his success. With it was coupled intelligence of no mean order, resourcefulness, and a shrewd understanding of humanity. He possessed the rare ability to adapt himself to circumstances, to meet an emergency with emergency measures, to think quickly when quick thinking was necessary. Moreover, his appearance—youthful, unsophisticated, countrified—was an invaluable asset. An older man might have created suspicion where Parmelee passed unquestioned. An older man might have put his quarry on his guard; Parmelee's frank, blue eyes, his innocent expression, his ingenuous manner, led more than one incautious observer to label him a victim—to his undoing.

His fame had spread. The rural free delivery to his home in a little Connecticut village rarely deposited fewer than five or six appeals for assistance in his tin mail box; even worse, would-be clients themselves, too often cranks, made the pilgrimage to his abode in such numbers that in order to have a moment's peace he had been obliged to invest in a pair of large and vicious dogs. He had not courted glory. It had come, and its unpleasant features were well to the front. In his friend's apartment, however, he felt safe. Here callers would not come. Here annoying letters need not be expected. He remarked as much, and then Tony, smiling broadly, handed him the petition of the Metropolitan Chess Club, addressed to Parmelee in his care.

Bill gazed at the superscription and looked inquiringly at his friend.

"Have you been saving this for me?"

Tony laughed. "It came with the morning's mail."

"Why didn't you destroy it?"

"Criminal offense, old man," exulted Tony. "You wouldn't ask me to commit a crime."

"No," said Parmelee, "I'll destroy it myself. Give me the letter." He turned it over and over, weighed it in his hand, held it to his ear and shook it. "There's not the least hope that this is nothing but a bill?"

"Not the least." Tony smiled. "By the way," he added brightly, "I want you to go the round of my clubs with me some time."

"What for?"

"Well," said Tony, relishing the situation, "there's mail for you at every one of them."

Parmelee groaned.

"You don't realize," Claghorn chortled, "what an institution you've become. In the old days when a chap thought that he was being rooked in a game, he'd simply get out of it. In these days, under the same circumstances, he doesn't even think of backing water. He just sends for Bill Parmelee. Bill Parmelee can set things right if anybody can. Bill Parmelee can set things right even if nobody else can. Where there's Bill Parmelee, there's hope. Our motto: 'See Us First!' That's what a little judicious advertising has done for you!"

"Tony, I ought to kill you for it!"

"Instead, you'll probably be incorporating a company to handle your growing business. Think of the possibilities, just think: two or three magicians-in-ordinary, a pair of expert prestidigitators, a flying squad of sleight-of-hand artists, and a platoon or so of assorted card sharps, guaranteed reformed. A small, highly trained organization—"

"With you at the head of it." Parmelee grinned.

"Where could you find a better man?" demanded Tony unblushingly. "You've offered me the presidency; very well, I'll accept it. We won't go out after business—not we. It just comes to us; it swamps us; one client sends us half a dozen more. We sit in a magnificently furnished office, watching our underlings endorse checks. We can't do that ourselves; there'd be too many of them. We smoke good cigars and put our feet on our desks. We discuss the weather—politics—the latest automobiles—my wife's new hats—whatever it is that the big financiers discuss. Every now and then we go into conference. We raise salaries—not forgetting our own. We declare dividends. We decide to move into roomier quarters—"

"And just about that time all of the crooks stop being crooked. They go out of business—and so do we."

"Bill," said Tony earnestly, "I hope we live that long."

Parmelee put a period to the discussion with a shake of his head. "I'm a farmer, not a detective!" he insisted. "You're forgetting that."

"And you're forgetting to open your letter."

With a sigh Parmelee slit in open, revealing three closely written sheets of foolscap and a check. Tony's eyes glittered as he spied the latter.

"Ah-ha!" he exclaimed, rubbing his hands. "A client who pays in advance! A client who helps to build the Parmelee fortune! How much is it this time? A thousand? Five thousand? Ten thousand?"

Without a word Parmelee handed him the check.

Tony took it with a smile, glanced at it—examined it more closely with incredulous disbelief. "It's for—it's for—" he sputtered.

"The sum of twenty-nine dollars and forty-five cents!" Bill chuckled.

IT TOOK TONY a few seconds to recover his breath. "Is that—is that by any chance a fee?" he demanded, horror-stricken.

"It seems to be," said Parmelee, who had glanced through the three sheets of foolscap.

"Twenty-nine dollars and forty-five cents?"

"That's the amount that's mentioned in the letter."

"Are you joking?"

"Never more serious," replied Parmelee.

"Who on earth would insult you by offering you so little? Why, it's an outrage! Let me see that letter!"

Parmelee raised his hand. "Wait! I'm not through yet—and I'm enjoying reading it." He bent over it with more interest than he had displayed in hundreds of similar communications. "Aalders—Aalders," he said aloud; "did you ever hear of vegetables known as Aalders?"

"No," Said Claghorn impatiently.

"Neither have I," Parmelee admitted. "Strange as it seems, Aalders must be a man's name." He scrutinized another signature. "Z-y—Zysser, that's it! What under the sun is a Zysser?"

"Well, what is it?"

"I'd give a guess that it's another man's name. Yes, that's what it must be. Poor chap! I sympathize with him, going through life labeled like that." He proceeded to the end of the communication, grinned happily, and handed the sheets to his friend. "Tony, read this. It's unique. It's in a class by itself. It deserves a medal."

Tony cast his eye over the closely written pages. Strachan, who had drawn up the petition, had been commendably brief. Being a life-insurance agent, he had understood how to present his case with a minimum of words.

In not more than a dozen sentences he had touched upon the coming of J. Hampton Hoogestraten, the personality of the man, his appearance, his manners, his egotism—his cigars. He had epitomized his story as a member of the Metropolitan Chess Club, his victories, his unpopularity. He had explained the object of the conspirators; he had expressed his conviction that Mr. Parmelee could help them to achieve that object if anybody could; he had hoped they would not be disappointed.

The devoted members of the club had taken up a collection, he added. They did not expect Mr. Parmelee to take their case without remuneration. He enclosed his personal check for the total, and mentioned the telephone number at which he could be reached.

The few words that Strachan had written occupied the upper half of the first sheet. The lower half—and two more sheets—were filled with the signatures of the subscribers. Strachan had led off munificently with three dollars. Reynolds, being a banker, and Colonel Stafford, being the president of the club and solicitous for its welfare, had contributed like amounts. Beers had added two dollars, and O'Neill and Lindeberg had donated one dollar each. A few members had taxed themselves seventy-five cents; more had contributed a half dollar; the rank and file had given twenty-five cents each, and a few poverty-stricken individuals, meaning well, but lacking funds, had scraped up ten cents apiece.

Tony read over the pages with growing indignation. "Twenty-nine dollars and forty-five cents! It seems incredible," he said at length.

Bill laughed at his serious friend. "Add it up, Tony," he recommended; "perhaps Strachan has held out a nickel."

Tony crumpled up the sheets impatiently. "Let me answer them," he begged. "Let me tell them."

"What would you say?"

"I'll tell them that your last fee was far above the puny amount they are offering. I'll tell them that their letter is impudent, impertinent, and insulting. I'll tell them that you're not a mountebank, to sell your services so cheaply."

Parmelee shook his head gently. "What a mercenary soul you are!" he exclaimed. "Tony, if I were to write the Metropolitan Chess Club, I'd say that their letter has more human interest in it than any other letter of the kind that I've ever read—and Lord knows I've received plenty! I'd say that I understood their feelings perfectly, because there have been times when I felt like that myself—only more so. And I'd thank them most sincerely because, instead of asking me to expose somebody else's cheating, they're asking me to do some cheating myself. By George, what a relief! To be asked to cheat in a good cause!"

"Surely you're not going to take the case!" ejaculated Tony, aghast.

"Most surely I am."

"For twenty-nine dollars and forty-five cents?"

"For the sheer fun of it! For the pleasure of helping regular fellows like Aalders and Zysser and Strachan and the rest of the men who had the blessed innocence to take up a collection for me! Twenty-nine dollars and forty-five cents? I'll take it like a shot, and I'll be thankful. With it, I'll get the eternal gratitude of the men who subscribed it. That's a whole lot better than pocketing some fat check and have the millionaire who signed it dismiss you from his mind because he knows that he had paid you in full."

"I think you're insane," said Tony candidly, "but if you want to do charity, I won't stop you." He handed back the letter. "I take it that you know a good deal about chess?"

Parmelee's eyes twinkled. "Tony, how much do you know about it?"

Tony scratched his head. "Well, I know that the game is played on a checkerboard; and I know that there are kings and queens; and I know some of the pieces when I see them. I know the pawns, because they're little; and I know the knights, because they have horses' heads. And I guess that's about all I know."

Bill chuckled. "You know more about chess than I do!"

"You don't mean it!"

"I've tackled checkers—when I was a boy, I used to play across the counter in the grocery store back home—but I've never touched a chessman in my life." He glanced at his horrified friend with a smile. "Tony, you said there were kings and queens in the game?"

"Yes."

"If that's so, it ought to come easy to me."

"Perhaps it won't be as easy as you think."

"All the better, then," said Parmelee sincerely. "I've had an advantage in every affair I've tackled in the past; I've known more about poker—or faro—or roulette—or gambling in general than the fellows whom I was fighting. If I nosed them out, it's because I had a head start; because they've had to concede me handicaps. This affair is different. I'm a greenhorn, and the advantage is with the other chap. He gets the handicap; I start from scratch. He knows the game; I don't. I've got nothing to rely on but my wits. Tony," cried Bill, and threw up his arms in exultation, "for the first time I'm fighting against real odds, and I'm a good enough sport to relish it!" His enthusiasm did not visibly move his unemotional friend. Tony glanced through the letter again.

"As I understand it, the members of the Metropolitan Chess Club want their very worst player to take on this man Hoogestraten on even terms, and they want you to work out some way for him to lick him."

"Exactly."

"You know nothing whatever about chess. Yet you are undertaking to teach a dub how to beat an expert." Tony raised his eyebrows. "May I ask how you are going to do it?"

Parmelee grinned cheerfully. "I'll be damned if I know," he admitted.

IN RESPONSE TO a telephone request, Strachan, who did not hesitate to sacrifice his ordinary business for the far-more-interesting business now on hand, came running to the apartment. He found Parmelee, divested of his coat and with a wet towel bound around his head, reading up chess in the pages of Hoyle.

"You're going to help us?" Strachan demanded eagerly.

"If you can be helped."

"Fine! I know you'll turn the trick."

Parmelee smiled. "I wish I were as sure of it as you are." He dog-eared a page in Hoyle carefully and closed the book. "Now," he demanded, "just how good is Hoogestraten?"

"He's in our third class."

"What does that mean?"

"It means that there are less than twenty-five men in the club—and that means in New York City—who are better."

"How much better are they?"

"Well, a man in our second class would win not less than three out of five games from him."

"And one of your first-class men?"

"Four out of five—or five out of five."

"The first-class man wouldn't win every game?"

"He might—but I wouldn't bet on it. When you come to our topnotchers, Mr. Parmelee, our first three classes, you find that all of the men in them are good."

"So I see," assented Parmelee ruefully. "Now, the man whom you want to beat Hoogestraten—"

"Reynolds."

"Reynolds. How good is he?"

Strachan smiled. "It would be more like it to ask how bad

he is. Mr. Parmelee, Hoogestraten can give him a rook and a knight and knock the tar out of him."

"A rook and a knight? What does that mean?"

Strachan gasped. "Mr. Parmelee, don't you understand chess?"

"Not a bit," said Bill cheerfully. "Now explain what you said."

Strachan was visibly shaken, but he composed himself manfully. "In terms of tennis," he translated, "it would mean that Hoogestraten could give him forty on each game and beat him a love set. In terms of golf, Hoogestraten could give him two strokes a hole and come to the turn nine up. In terms of poker—"

"Now you're talking," said Bill.

"In terms of poker, Hoogestraten could present him with a pair of aces on every deal and still wipe him out in an hour. In terms of billiards—"

"You needn't go beyond poker," Bill interrupted. "You've said enough to make it plain that Reynolds hasn't a chance in a million of winning on even terms—"

"No."

"And when you asked me to think up some way in which he could do it, you handed me a man-size job."

"If we could have worked out the answer ourselves, we wouldn't have gone to you," returned Strachan, with a smile.

"That occurred to me long ago," Parmelee admitted. "Let's get back to your first-class players, however. Nobody in the world, I take it, can beat them."

"Oh, no!" said Strachan surprisingly. "You're forgetting the masters."

"I'll bite," said Bill. "What are masters?"

Strachan explained. There were players; there were good

players; there were very good players; there were exceptionally good players—such as those in the first class at the Metropolitan. But far, far above them, inhabiting the heights, living, breathing, dreaming chess, were the few world geniuses who were to the ordinary expert what the siege gun is to the sporting rifle. They played serious games only with one another—for nobody else could extend them; they saved their efforts for international tournaments, where a dozen of their kind would gather and battle titanically; they took on ordinary first-class players eight or ten at a time, simultaneously, and thought nothing of making a clean sweep of such a series.

Parmelee listened attentively. "What chance would Hoogestraten stand against one of these super-experts?"

"None," replied Strachan flatly.

"He wouldn't win one out of five?"

"Not one out of twenty-five," answered Strachan. "Not one out of fifty! Once in a while he might get a draw game—but I'd give odds against that."

Parmelee rubbed his hands with satisfaction.

"Our next step is pretty clear. Let's get one of these masters here in the flesh, and then let's ask him some questions."

Strachan frowned. "I know what you're thinking of, but it's no use," he said. "You want a master to coach Reynolds for the game. Well, it won't work. The more you try to teach Reynolds, the worse he plays."

"We'll talk to the master, anyhow," Bill insisted. "Whom can we get?"

"There's Lasker," said Strachan.

"Send for him."

"He's in Germany."

"Who else is there?"

"Capablanca."

"Where's he?"

"In Cuba."

"Isn't there some master, guaranteed to be the real thing, right here in New York?"

"I'm afraid not," said Strachan. He interrupted himself. "No! Wait a minute! There's a chap who came here just a few days ago from Russia, He's negotiating with the club now; he wants us to engage him for an exhibition."

"Is he a real master?"

"He's one of the three or four greatest in the world," enthused Strachan. "He took first at Budapest; he came in second at Petrograd; he took another second at Christiania—"

"Can you reach him on the telephone?" Parmelee interrupted.

"Yes," said Strachan. "Of course, he talks no English, but he'll find an interpreter."

Parmelee handed him the instrument, "Tell him to bring the interpreter with him when he comes here."

He listened to Strachan's brief colloquy with interest.

"What did you call him?" he inquired, as his caller hung up the telephone with the remark that the master was on his way.

"Niemzo-Zborowski."

"Say it again."

"Niem-zo-Zbo-row-ski."

Parmelee chuckled. "If I had a name like that, I'd be able to play chess myself! I hope he lives up to it."

"You won't be disappointed."

HE WAS NOT—LEAST of all in the master's person. An amazingly round little man, two fifths grin and three fifths hair, stood presently in the doorway, and smiled—and smiled—and smiled. A magnificent beard, luxuriant whiskers, an abundant mustache, and bushy eyebrows struggled for the domination of his countenance. But through them, like a light in a dense forest, the magic of his smile broke through.

Strachan introduced him. "Well, will he do?" he demanded. "You can say anything you like before him; he doesn't understand a word of English."

Parmelee nodded gravely. "I like that grin. Once I saw a grin like that on a wrestler's face just before he broke his opponent's leg with a toe hold. I know what it means."

Zysser—the one and only Zysser of the Metropolitan Chess Club, who had accompanied the great man as interpreter—translated Parmelee's remark into explosive Russian.

The grin became still wider as Niemzo-Zborowski beamed his delight. A horizontal groove manifested itself along the front of the frock coat in which the chess master had encased his butter ball of a body, and he bowed.

Parmelee turned to the interpreter. "Ask him if he won't sit down."

Again Zysser imitated the sound of a string of exploding firecrackers, and Niemzo-Zborowski, bending at another unsuspected groove, eased himself into a chair.

Parmelee opened Hoyle to the page he had marked.

"I am going to ask you to translate a passage from this book into Russian," he said to Zysser. He read aloud: " 'The various moves which take place in the course of a game are recorded by a system of chess notation, the number of the move being given first, and then the pieces moved and the direction of their movement.'"

He waited while Zysser translated. Again Niemzo-Zborowski bowed.

"Ask him now," directed Parmelee, "if he is familiar with that system of chess notation."

Strachan interrupted. "That's an unnecessary question, Mr. Parmelee," he pointed out. "Every beginner is familiar with that system; he learns it, in fact, before he learns to play chess. As for Mr. Niemzo-Zborowski, he has played as many as forty games at a time blindfold—that is, without sight of the boards or the men. It would have been impossible for him to have done that if he hadn't been familiar with the system of chess notation."

Parmelee nodded. "I stand corrected," he admitted, but he could not hide his satisfaction. "Now I have some other questions to ask."

The four men were deep in conference when Tony Claghorn, who had beaten a prompt retreat when his friend had begun on Hoyle, returned to the apartment. Through the crack of the door, he heard explosive bits of Russian, and, peering within, he saw four heads close together.

One head, however, seemed to dominate the others. Perhaps it was because its supply of hair easily surpassed the combined contributions of the remaining three; perhaps it was because a perpetual smile flickered over its features. The owner of the head was a foot shorter than his companions, but he took the center of the stage as inevitably as if spotlights had been focused upon him.

Tony did not lack an abundant share of curiosity, but the

mysteries of chess, he realized, were far beyond him. Noiselessly he closed the door and shook his head.

THE SEQUENCE OF events at the Metropolitan Chess Club followed along lines distinctly military in character. Colonel Stafford, as president of the club and as one greatly concerned with its welfare, consulted with Parmelee. As a result of that consultation, the colonel took command and organized a campaign.

Its first gun, and that surely a big one, was fired when Reynolds informed J. Hampton Hoogestraten, to whose support he had been contributing nightly for many weeks, that he had decided to abandon their customary games for a while.

"What's the big idea?" inquired the soap salesman. There were many other men whom he could beat in the club; but there were none who would continue losing to him at twenty-five cents a game as rapidly and as graciously as Reynolds.

"I have decided to spend at least a week studying by myself," said Reynolds. "I'm going to go home and lock myself up in my study. I'm going to take an armful of chess books with me, and I'm going to perfect my game."

In view of little Reynolds' great importance in the business world, and in further view of the monstrous salary which a week's devotion to anything but the affairs of his trust company would sacrifice, the statement was fishy on the face of it. But J. Hampton Hoogestraten could think only of the two or three dollars a night which the absence of his victim would cost him.

"You needn't go home to study," he said easily; "I'm teaching you by playing with you."

"Very kind of you, I'm sure, Mr. Hoogestraten."

"You have improved since I began," said the soap salesman magnificently. "Keep on, and you'll be a strong player one of these days. Why, the first thing you know you'll be beating me."

Little Reynolds actually blushed. "Now, Mr. Hoogestraten, don't make sport of me," he begged.

"In any event, you can go on playing with me while you're studying."

Reynolds shook his head decisively. "No, Mr. Hoogestraten. I have made up my mind. I can't do both. I'm going to retire from the field, and when I come back I hope you will find an improvement in my game."

Nothing that Hoogestraten could say could budge him from his determination, and the fat man, after exhausting his powers of persuasion and cajolery, ended up by losing his temper. It was perfectly apparent to him that Reynolds had tired of their arrangement, that Reynolds would lose to him no longer, that Reynolds, in all probability, would never play him again. There was, accordingly no reason why he should not insult Reynolds as grossly as he pleased.

"What's the good of your studying?" Hoogestraten asked, giving full vent to the endearing qualities that had made him so beloved by his clubmates. "You've played twenty years, and you're rotten now. Study, and you'll only learn how to be rotten in more ways."

Reynolds kept his self-control admirably. "In that event, the variety—when I come back—will make me a more interesting opponent," he said placidly.

"Huh!" sneered J. Hampton Hoogestraten, considerably beyond his depth. "Huh!"

"If I can't get worse," said Reynolds craftily, "I may get better.

Who knows? I've always been a great believer in study, Mr. Hoogestraten. A week of concentrated application may accomplish wonders."

Hoogestraten opened his eyes wide. It was only too evident that Reynolds was taking himself seriously.

Now, the soap salesman was well aware that improvement in any game rested to a certain extent upon the mastery of its principles, but to an even greater extent upon natural aptitude. This last Reynolds lacked; and, lacking it, was condemned for all eternity to remain a duffer—a bungler—a member of the awkward squad. He had reached his zenith, such as it was, already. Nothing that either he or anybody else could do could cause him to rise any higher.

This observation, perhaps, explains why J. Hampton Hoogestraten fell so readily into the trap which his clubmates had laid for him.

"I suppose you'll be such a great player when you come back," he snorted disdainfully, "that you'll be taking smaller odds from me."

"Of course, Mr. Hoogestraten."

"At the present odds, you'll beat me?"

"I hope to."

"Why don't you come out with the color? You hope to beat me at smaller odds?"

"That, too."

The eyes of the soap salesman narrowed. If he could tempt Reynolds, who had plenty of money, into betting—

"Perhaps," he ventured, "perhaps you are hoping to beat me on even terms?"

Reynolds smiled diffidently. "I didn't like to say so before," he admitted. "It might have sounded like conceit. But since you ask me point-blank, I might as well say that that is my ambition. You can beat me to-night, Mr. Hoogestraten. You can beat me badly. But a week from to-night, after I have devoted myself to the books for seven consecutive days, who can tell what will happen? You can be beaten, you know. I might be the man to do it."

"You wouldn't, by any chance, like to back that up with a little small change, Mr. Reynolds?"

"Why not? It would make the game more interesting."

"Just one game?" The soap salesman was plainly disappointed.

"That should be enough."

"Then how about a side bet?" He paused, wondering how large an amount he might name.

"A dollar," said Reynolds.

"Two," said Hoogestraten.

"Five."

"Ten."

"Fifteen."

"Twenty."

"Twenty dollars," said Reynolds, following his instructions to the letter, "that will do nicely. And now I bid you good night, Mr. Hoogestraten."

THE HEART OF the soap salesman leaped with joy as his prospective victim made his way out of the room. In a moment of idiocy, he felt, Reynolds had done an amazingly foolish thing, and he would benefit. That he himself had been cowardly and unfair occasioned him no concern. It was far more congenial to reflect that Reynolds would inevitably lose, that he might study his head off without benefiting.

Nevertheless, Hoogestraten listened eagerly to reports on little Reynolds' progress as relayed to him nightly. This, the second part of Colonel Stafford's program, was referred to by the old gentleman as "breaking down the morale," and it began its insidious attack when Howells, twenty-four hours after the match had been arranged, burst into the club with the startling news that he had spent the afternoon with Reynolds, and that Reynolds had beaten him in three consecutive games. Howells ranged two classes higher than Reynolds, and had never before, so he declared, lost to him.

Hoogestraten, puffing his rank cigar, bore the shock well. "You're not much better than Reynolds," he said ungraciously. "I can give you a rook any time and lick you."

"Yes, you can," admitted Howells, "but the point I'm making is different. I'm telling you that Reynolds, after a day's hard study, has improved so much that I can't beat him any more— and I used to. I'm wondering how good he'll be after he's studied a week."

Hoogestraten jingled his change pocket. "Are you wondering a dollar's worth?" he inquired.

"Yes," said Howells.

"I'll bet a dollar on Reynolds myself," Beers chimed in.

"Same here," said Aalders.

"I'll take five of that," said Strachan.

Hoogestraten had no desire to escape bets. He accepted twenty dollars' worth in a few minutes.

Yates, who topped the eleventh class, was selected to lead the assault the following night.

"Boys," he declared, "a most remarkable thing has happened. Reynolds phoned me to come to his house at five o'clock. I went. He played three games with me, and he made a clean sweep."

Hoogestraten managed to exhibit a placid exterior, though inwardly he was far from calm. In two days, according to reports, Reynolds had made progress which would have been sufficiently remarkable in two years. It was disturbing—very disturbing.

The soap salesman accepted a dozen more bets, and reflected that he was hazarding over fifty dollars. He began to be decidedly uneasy.

On the third day, O'Neill succumbed. He ranked in the eighth class.

"Study—concentrated study, that's how he does it," he explained. "He's sitting in his library with the shades pulled down, and soft green lights scattered around the room. He has a pot of black coffee on his desk, and a package of yeast tablets in his pocket. He has all the books that have ever been written on chess, and he's soaking up what's in them just as if he were a human blotter. He doesn't even leave the room for his meals; they're brought to his desk—and they consist of nothing but vitamins."

Had Hoogestraten possessed a sense of humor—which he did not—he would have seen through the conspiracy on the instant. Instead he inquired nervously: "Where can you get vitamins?"

"Imported from Scotland," answered O'Neill gravely. "They're small animals like squirrels—only furrier."

Hoogestraten accepted a few more bets that night, though he

trembled in his boots. Common sense—such common sense as he possessed—told him that the whole affair was incredible, that no human being on earth could improve so rapidly and so consistently as Reynolds seemed to be improving. But the succession of assaults began to have its effect. What was unthinkable on the first day was merely improbable on the second day. Quickly it became not only possible but reasonable.

Strachan, according to his own account, was bowled over like tenpins by the invincible Reynolds on the fourth day, and when he suggested increasing his wager with Hoogestraten, the soap salesman, for the first time, demurred. The thought of the large amount at stake no longer comforted him; it distressed him, and when Harbord, of the fourth class, and Forsythe, a really strong player, accustomed to battle Hoogestraten on even terms, were sunk without a trace on succeeding days, the fat man's agitation became very noticeable.

"Did he really beat you?" he asked Forsythe, in the privacy of the cloakroom.

Forsythe, filled with old-fashioned scruples, would not tell a lie. "I didn't take a single game from him," he said quite truthfully.

It was then that Hoogestraten strolled casually into the clubroom and made a determined, but unsuccessful, effort to hedge his bets. He failed to relieve himself of a dollar of them. His fellow members, in unanimous agreement, declared that he, too, would fall before Reynolds. He believed it himself, and it did not need the knock-out blow, deftly administered by Macpherson, to bring him to the depths of misery.

Macpherson, the finest player in the club, and a highly imaginative individual, put in an appearance twenty-four hours before the time scheduled for the great match, and his expression spoke volumes.

"Did he beat you?" chorused his audience.

Macpherson nodded sadly. Unlike Forsythe, he had no scruples against a lie—if in a good cause.

"Boys, he knocked the tar out of me. He told me to sit down at the chessboard, and he never looked at it. I called off my moves to him, and he called off his moves to me. Boys, there was never a minute that I had the advantage. He got the jump on me from the start, and he blew me off of the map."

"He beat you blindfold?"

"Ruined me," said Macpherson.

From a near-by corner came a heavy thud. J. Hampton Hoogestraten had collapsed.

THE LENGTHS TO which high-principled men will go to avoid downright cheating are great. Colonel Stafford's elaborate campaign of demoralization had been undertaken in the hope that more decisive steps would not be necessary. If the soap salesman could be sufficiently terrified, calculated the colonel, he would find some pretext to avoid the match. Despite the betting, no actual stakes had been posted. Hoogestraten would save his money—and would never dare show his face in the club again.

Until a few hours before the great game, the colonel's scheme was entirely successful. Unfortunately for him, however, it was altogether too successful. Hoogestraten, after a sleepless night, and in a state of panic, made a hurried trip to his physician. To him he confided his woes, and mentioned the amazing results of Reynolds' diet of vitamins. He had tried to purchase some himself, he admitted under seal of secrecy, but his butcher had been unable to supply them.

"The butcher?" repeated the physician in amazement. "Don't you know what vitamins are? You find them in fruits fresh vegetables—salads—"

"Then they're not imported from Scotland? Small animals like squirrels—only furrier?"

"No, indeed!"

Hoogestraten slapped on his hat and walked into the street, feeling decidedly better. The fact that his tormentors had departed from the truth once made it highly probable that they had done so more than once. He did not understand exactly what had happened; but he grasped enough to realize that he had been the victim of a conspiracy.

With that realization, the colonel's campaign of demoralization ended in defeat. Indeed, he had barely remarked to the crowd that had gathered for the match, "Gentlemen, I do not think that Mr. Hoogestraten will put in an appearance," when the door opened, and the soap salesman, thoroughly and complete angry, marched into the room.

He singled out O'Neill, author of the vitamin tale.

"I've been eating vitamins, too," he hissed. "Imported from Scotland—small animals like squirrels—only furrier; and I'm ready to play the game of my life!"

He discerned Reynolds, waiting at a table in the center of the room. Somehow, the sight of the little man in the flesh was less disconcerting than the tales about him that had been related to him during the week.

He waddled over, plumped himself into a chair, and lighted one of his notorious cigars. "Come on," he sneered.

Twenty feet away Colonel Stafford, observing developments, threw up his hands and turned to Bill Parmelee. "I resign," he whispered. "Now it's up to you."

Now, a game of chess, except to an expert, does not hold the visible thrills of football—of tennis—of golf—of polo. There are no forward passes; no cannonball services; no holes under par; no breath-taking charges down the length of the field. Yet the huge audience—a hundred and fifty at least—gathered around the contenders, took seats, or stood, occupying every spot from which the chessboard was visible, testifying to its interest by the sudden hush which fell upon the room.

J. Hampton Hoogestraten opened his well-filled cigar case, lighted one of his liver-colored cigars, moved, and the game was on.

Before replying, Reynolds, in his turn, produced a paper box, opened it, and popped a tablet into his mouth.

"What's that?" inquired Hoogestraten suspiciously.

"Nothing but slippery elm," said Reynolds. "I'm hoping to neutralize the effect of your tobacco."

The fat man grinned and puffed more vigorously. If any antidote for his infamous cigars existed, he was anxious to put it to the test.

And in the background, understanding nothing of what was going on, Tony Claghorn turned to Parmelee and whispered excitedly: "They're off!"

"Hush!" said Bill. In silence he watched the first half dozen moves, accompanied on the one side by furious blasts of smoke, and on the other by a rapid consumption of slippery-elm tablets.

Lindeberg was at his side.

"How's the game going?" inquired Bill.

"Not well."

"What do you mean?"

"Reynolds has managed the opening badly—very badly," said Lindeberg mournfully.

With ill-concealed consternation, Parmelee waited the ten minutes required to complete three additional moves. "Well?" he asked.

Lindeberg shook his head. "Worse and worse," he said. "Reynolds is playing like a novice, and Hoogie—well, Hoogie is playing chess. Reynolds is going to lose a bishop in a move or two." Even as he spoke, Hoogestraten, puffing like an engine, moved triumphantly. "Of course, Hoogie sees his chance," Lindeberg pointed out. "If Reynolds doesn't brace up pretty soon, he'll be done for."

Parmelee, gazing helplessly at the game which was beyond his comprehension, saw his deep-laid plans crashing down to defeat. And then a thought, sharp and blinding as a flash of lightning, burst suddenly upon him. "Good Lord!" he exclaimed. "I know just what's happened! What a fool I was not to have thought of it!" He turned and dashed from the room.

It was Tony's turn to nudge Lindeberg. "How's it going?" he asked.

"Still badly." A groan came from the audience. "As I predicted," Lindeberg pointed out, "Reynolds has lost a bishop."

It was then, while Hoogestraten was gloating over the victory almost in his grasp, that an abrupt change came over the game. Reynolds moved, it seemed, with new assurance, and Lindeberg, for the first time, found himself beyond his depth.

"What's the matter?" demanded Tony anxiously. "Did he make a mistake?"

Lindeberg shook his head emphatically. "It's not a mistake; that's all I can tell you. It's either good—or it's extraordinarily good."

Hoogestraten seemed to share Lindeberg's opinion, for he gazed at his antagonist incredulously, and pondered his own next move well.

HE MOVED. REYNOLDS moved—again a surprising move which worried the fat man; and then, while the audience held its breath, it became apparent that Hoogestraten was meeting his match. No longer was the spectacle one of a strong player toying with an inferior; quite the contrary, the strong player, for all his strength, was as an infant in the mighty grip which his opponent was fastening upon him. He struggled; he called upon every weapon in his armory, but all to no avail. Relentlessly, mercilessly, brushing aside his resistance, the black pieces converged upon his weakest spot in a tremendous attack.

"What's happening?" gasped Tony. The very air was electric; the excitement in it was overpowering him.

But Lindeberg was in no condition to answer coherently. "Wonderful!" he whispered. "Wonderful! Marvelous! Amazing! Superb!"

Tony nudged his informant viciously. "Who's wonderful?" he demanded. "Which one?"

"Reynolds, of course!" crowed Lindeberg. "Of course, Reynolds!"

But for the uninterrupted crunch of Reynolds' strong white teeth on slippery-elm tablets, the room was still as death. Great beads of sweat began to roll from Hoogestraten's brow. His bejeweled hands trembled. He began to think of the tales of Reynolds' progress which had come to him during the last week, and, vitamins or no vitamins, he found himself believing.

His cigar, unnoticed, smoldered out, its vicious fumes first tapering off to a thin blue line, and then ceasing altogether; but Reynolds never suspended his continuous crunch. The only sound in the all-embracing silence, Hoogestraten found it curiously disconcerting.

He saw the attack, marvelously conceived and miraculously executed, pressing home. He realized its menace, and found himself helpless before it. He had won a bishop. In half a dozen moves he found himself compelled to give it back, and saw the black forces marching on irresistibly toward victory.

He cursed himself for his stupid greed. Even on an apparently sure thing, he had had no right to wager so heavily. To pay his bets would cripple him for weeks. And then an icy hand seemed to clutch his heart, as looking ahead, he saw the end. First this, then this, then this and this—four moves, simple, beautiful, masterly, and their climax his own checkmate. In an agony, he verified his calculations. There could be no doubt; four moves more, and then defeat.

His cigar case had fallen to the floor. Unthinkingly he ground his heel into the contents. And then, through the silence, came Reynolds' voice.

"Mr. Hoogestraten," it was saying, "if it's agreeable to you, I'll call this game a draw."

Agreeable to him! He leaped from his chair so vehemently that he upset it. "You're on!" he shouted. "You're on! It's a draw!" Then, to the audience, he tried to explain that in four more moves he would have been mated. Strangely enough, he found none to listen. After Colonel Stafford's brief declaration that all bets were off, interest in Hoogestraten had suddenly lapsed.

Only Strachan made his way to the fat man from the other end of the room.

"Mr. Hoogestraten," said Strachan, "our year book goes to press to-morrow."

"What of that?"

"In it our members are listed according to their classified playing strength. You will be listed at the foot of class fifteen— our lowest class."

Hoogestraten suddenly exploded. "Reynolds didn't beat me!" he expostulated.

Strachan corrected him pointedly. "You mean, you didn't beat Reynolds." He smiled happily. "It's a bit complicated, but I'll try to make it clear. If Reynolds had challenged you, and had beaten you, he would have taken a place above you in class three."

"Well?"

"That didn't happen. What did happen was that you challenged Reynolds and didn't win. You take a place below him in class fifteen. You needn't argue about it," he added encouragingly; "the directors of the club have ruled on it already."

Hoogestraten grew pale. He had bragged about his chess to his friends, and to be listed publicly as the club's worst player was punishment more than he could bear. He would be the victim of numberless gibes—and he did not relish the thought.

"Mr. Strachan," he faltered, "isn't there some way in which my name can be kept out of the year book altogether?"

"Only one way, Mr. Hoogestraten," said Strachan mercilessly. "Perhaps it will occur to you on your way home."

It did occur to Hoogestraten. In the morning he called up Strachan and resigned.

IT WAS A jovial foursome that gathered around a table in a convenient restaurant half an hour after the match. In it were Parmelee and Claghorn, and Strachan and Niemzo-Zborowski. Zysser, the chess master's interpreter, had been lost in the confusion, wherefore Niemzo-Zborowski was silent. This, however, did not prevent his radiant grin, now more radiant than ever, from lighting up his face like a lamp.

"Why," demanded Tony, "didn't Reynolds go on and lick that cad?"

Strachan looked at him reproachfully. "Mr. Claghorn, that would have been cheating. You forget that there was a great deal of money staked on the game. We didn't want to lose it; and we didn't want to win it unfairly. A draw was the one happy solution."

Tony glanced at him shrewdly. "Then the game, I take it, was not quite what it seemed?"

Parmelee laughed. "As you say, not quite."

"How so?"

"Well, Reynolds couldn't beat Hoogestraten—not in a million years."

"But I saw him—"

"You don't know what you saw. You saw Reynolds sitting opposite Hoogestraten at the chessboard. You saw Reynolds handling the pieces and making the moves."

"What more was there to see?"

The conspirators exchanged delighted glances.

"Tony, old man, if you had gotten past the sentries, you might have seen Mr. Niemzo-Zborowski, sitting in a little room to one side and playing that game for Reynolds! I got the idea out of Hoyle the day that the letter from the Metropolitan Chess Club arrived."

"Niemzo-Zborowski p-playing the game?" sputtered Tony.

"Why not?" asked Strachan. "Chess matches are sometimes played by mail—by telephone—by telegraph—by cable—by radio."

"There is a system of chess notation." Parmelee explained. "There's a kind of shorthand by which you can describe every move. When Hoogestraten moved, his move was reported to Niemzo-Zborowski. Niemzo-Zborowski worked out the answer on a second chessboard, and his move was telegraphed back to Reynolds."

"How telegraphed? It couldn't have been whispered. Hoogestraten would have overheard a whisper."

"It wasn't whispered."

"It couldn't have been signaled. Hoogestraten would have seen a signal."

"It wasn't signaled."

"Well, how was it done? Let me into the secret."

Again the conspirators exchanged delighted glances. Then, from his vest pocket, Parmelee drew a small, flat lozenge.

"This is how!" He chuckled. "Hoogestraten's move was reported to Niemzo-Zborowski by word of mouth. One of the fellows near the door saw it, and passed it on. Niemzo-Zborowski's move was written down—in chess nota-tion—on a slippery-elm tablet, and went from hand to hand until it reached Reynolds. Reynolds would glance at it—would make the move—and then he'd pop the tablet into his mouth and eat it! I'm no chess player, Tony; I don't even know the moves. But that was my idea, every bit of it!"

Niemzo-Zborowski understood no English, but the sight of the slippery-elm tablet, with a move scrawled upon its surface, explained the nature of the conversation. His grin became even wider, and emerging from the thicket of beard and whiskers about his mouth came a high-pitched, triumphant cackle.

But Tony was not yet completely satisfied. "If that's what you were doing, you low, unprincipled ruffians," he demanded, "how was it that the game started off so badly?"

Parmelee's smile vanished. "It started off so badly," he admitted, "that we might have lost it."

Strachan made a correction. "Any other man than Niemzo-Zborowski would have lost it," he said.

Parmelee nodded. "That's what they tell me. Well, I saw the pieces being moved, and I saw the slippery-elm tablets reaching Reynolds in plenty of time, and I knew something was wrong, but for the longest time I couldn't think what it was. Then, all of a sudden, the answer flashed on me, and I corrected things like a shot. I had found the mistake."

"What was it?"

Parmalee grinned nearly as widely at the chess master. "Different languages have different chess notations," he explained. "Mr. Niemzo-Zborowski was writing his moves in Russian!"

Tony's final observation did not come until the two friends were alone.

"An adventure in charity," he summed up. "We've had an

entertaining evening, and you're ahead twenty-nine dollars and forty-five cents. Not so bad."

Parmelee laughed. "I'm ahead nothing," he corrected. "Mr. Niemzo-Zborowski is a professional; he had to be paid to give his performance. I offered him twenty-five dollars. He asked fifty. I went up to twenty-six. He came down to forty-five. I went to twenty-seven. He said forty. We finally compromised—"

"At how much?"

"Twenty-nine fifty."

Claghorn went into a spasm of laughter. "So the net result, now that it's all over, is that you've lost a nickel."

"Lost fifteen cents," corrected Parmelee gravely.

"How so?"

"I stood treat for a box of slippery-elm tablets," said Parmelee, with a twinkle in his eye. "That cost a dime."

SOONER OR LATER there will come a time when William Parmelee, ex-card sharp and more-or-less-unwilling corrector of destinies, stands face to face with the guardian of the pearly gates, and when that time comes, the facts having to do with the downfall of that good man, J. Hampton Hoogestraten, will doubtless be investigated. Tony Claghorn will be interrogated, for Tony was a witness. Colonel Stafford will be examined mercilessly, for, despite his seventy years and snow-white hair, Stafford was an accomplice. The rank and file of the Metropolitan Chess Club, from Aalders to Zysser, will be questioned remorselessly, for they, too, each and every one of them, took part in the dastardly plot. Little Reynolds will not be excepted—he least of all—and the great Niemzo-Zborowski himself will be in for a grilling.

And while the many sinners concerned in the letting down of J. Hampton Hoogestraten plead and parley at the great portals, the shade of that good man himself, smoking one of his infamous cigars, will stride into the blissful place unchallenged—maybe. And since that contingency is greatly to be feared, and since the facts in the case are more or less involved, it has seemed desirable to set them down here and now, so that the matured opinion of mankind, rising upward like heated air, may reach the venerable guardian of the gate in good time, and thus prevent a miscarriage of justice.

Let the tale be passed from mouth to mouth; let there be an abundance of witnesses. Then, perhaps, the members of the Metropolitan Chess Club, with Colonel Stafford at their head, will march through the gates in battle formation, Aalders at one point of their phalanx, and Zysser at the other. And somewhere in the midst, concealed by their numbers, will march little Reynolds—and the great Niemzo-Zborowski—and Bill Parmelee himself.

And as for that good man, J. Hampton Hoogestraten—well, what about him?

PERCIVAL WILDE

MYSTERY AUTHOR, PLAYWRIGHT, short story writer, and novelist, has always been original and unconventional. As a boy he was expelled from one school after the next; yet he got a BS from Columbia University in 1906, at the age of nineteen. He sold his first story in 1912, and following its publication he was besieged with requests for dramatic rights.

Taking his cue from this reception, Wilde turned to show business and for several years wrote and directed one-act plays for vaudeville, then in its prime. Vaudeville taught Wilde many things, but he felt its limitations and desired a broader field. He published a series of plays in 1915 which were pounced on avidly by the then-new Little Theatre movement. "Finger of God," his greatest hit, has played more than 10,000 performances, and the "Confessional" is a close second. His gauges, including Mahrathi, Afrikaans, and Serbian, besides the more obvious ones. After World War I he collaborated in Hollywood.

Wilde is married and has two sons, and is still unconventional. He works at night, his usual starting time being after midnight. His afternoons are devoted to sports and social life. Sleep is sandwiched in in the mornings. His pet hobby is photography. His mystery novels—all unusual—include *Inquest, Tinsley's Bones, Mystery Weekend,* and *Design for Murder.*

www.ingramcontent.com/pod-product-compliance
Lightning Source LLC
Chambersburg PA
CBHW020637030726
47498CB00002B/251